GENESIS

By

Kaitlyn O'Connor

Futuristic Romance

New Concepts   Georgia

Be sure to check out our website for the very best in fiction at fantastic prices!

When you visit our webpage, you can:
* Read excerpts of currently available books
* View cover art of upcoming books and current releases
* Find out more about the talented artists who capture the magic of the writer's imagination on the covers
* Order books from our backlist
* Find out the latest NCP and author news--including any upcoming book signings by your favorite NCP author
* Read author bios and reviews of our books
* Get NCP submission guidelines
* And so much more!

We offer a 20% discount on all new Trade Paperback releases ordered from our website!

Be sure to visit our webpage to find the best deals in e-books and paperbacks! To find out about our new releases as soon as they are available, please be sure to sign up for our newsletter (http://www.newconceptspublishing.com/newsletter.htm) or join our reader group (http://groups.yahoo.com/group/new_concepts_pub/join)!

The newsletter is available by double opt in only and our customer information is *never* shared!

Visit our webpage at:
www.newconceptspublishing.com

Genesis is an original publication of NCP. This work has never before appeared in book form. This work is a novel. Any similarity to actual persons or events is purely coincidental.

New Concepts Publishing, Inc.
5202 Humphreys Rd.
Lake Park, GA 31636

ISBN 978-1-58608-892-7
© 2006 Kaitlyn O'Connor
Cover art (c) copyright 2007 Jenny Dixon

NCP books are available at special quantity discounts for bulk purchases for sales promotions, premiums, fund raising, or educational use. For details, write, email, or phone New Concepts Publishing, Inc., 5202 Humphreys Rd., Lake Park, GA 31636; Ph. 229-257-0367, Fax 229-219-1097; orders@newconceptspublishing.com.

First NCP Trade Paperback Printing: February 2007

Chapter One

Noticing her fingers had begun to cramp and her hands to sweat, Sabrina consciously relaxed her grip on the steering wheel, trying not to think about the poor decisions she'd made that had led up to her current situation. Outside the car it was as black as the inside of a cave despite the fact that it was a clear night. For that matter, it was as black as pitch inside the car, too.

She glanced down at the clock again--12:05--two minutes later than it had been the last time she'd checked.

Realizing her foot was getting heavier and heavier on the gas pedal the more anxious she became, she eased off on the gas, glancing in her rearview mirror, her side mirrors, flicking a quick look at the darkened woods that crowded close to the narrow highway.

With the exception of the greenish glow of her clock and dash lights there wasn't a sign of any light in sight that said 'civilization'. Even if there were any houses nearby, it seemed that everybody had gone to bed and she was the only person in the world still awake.

"Stupid," she muttered, irrationally comforted by the sound of her own voice.

She should've stayed on the main highway, she chastised herself for the dozenth time. But she'd been stopping periodically since before dark trying to get a room, and everything was full. Of course, it hadn't been until it was getting around nine o'clock that she'd decided to lower her standards and try anything that looked even reasonably respectable. By that time, though, even the cheapest, meanest looking places were full.

She hadn't realized the middle of the country was still almost a no man's land for travelers. She hadn't fully comprehended the massive destruction and long aftereffects of hurricane Katrina. It hadn't occurred to her that two years after it had hit every hotel for several states were still full to overflowing with the homeless and the construction workers that had piled into the area to rebuild.

When she'd stopped for a fill up around ten, she'd finally decided to try looking for something off the main highway.

She was scared shitless, and her eyes were still so tired from driving so long that every time she blinked it felt as if the inside of her eyelids were sandpaper.

She was almost tempted to speed in the hope that a state patrol would pull her over.

Almost.

The thought of being pulled over on such a deserted road by a cop was almost scarier than being alone.

Stories she'd heard of serial killers posing as cops immediately began to fill her mind. And then, of course, any position of power always attracted the unscrupulous. A *real* cop might be tempted to take advantage of a stupid woman, alone, on such a deserted stretch of back road.

Taking one hand off the steering wheel, she felt around blindly and finally managed to turn on the radio. The blare of static almost made her jump out of her skin. Feeling around again, she found the search button. Country music filled the car.

She *hated* country music!

After listening to the twang as long as she could stand it, she started punching the search button again. A road sign appeared in her headlights just about the time the search settled on an oldies station.

"Fuck!" she exclaimed in fear inspired agitation. "Shit! Shit! Shit! Hell! Damn it!"

She'd only caught a glimpse of the sign. It might have been indicating a town up ahead--or not. It could've just been a county line or the state line. She slowed down, wrestling with the temptation to find a place to turn around so she could see what the sign had indicated.

The music faded out, became an ear splitting static. At almost the same instant, the engine died.

It took Bri several seconds to assimilate the fact that the engine had flat lined. Panic swept through her, annihilating anything approaching common sense. Almost a full minute passed before she realized she didn't have to come to a full stop to try to start the engine again because she was wrestling with the terrifying thought of stopping on the deserted road. The car had already dropped a good bit of speed before it occurred to her to slip it into neutral and try to re-start the engine.

Relief touched her, but only briefly. She was shaking like a leaf by the time she managed to shift to neutral and grabbed the key.

Nothing happened. Absolutely nothing. She didn't even hear the whir of the engine trying to turn over.

The car coasted slower and slower.

She checked the door locks a little frantically, not terribly reassured when she heard the locks click all around.

Abruptly, light surrounded her.

Stunned, she simply stared at the blinding light for a time, blinking, trying to figure out where the light was coming from. Helicopter, her mind finally deduced as the car rolled to a halt. With an effort, she guided the car off onto the shoulder of the road, praying there wasn't a deep ditch or a swamp. The alternative of sitting in a stalled car in the middle of the road wasn't acceptable, however. She hadn't seen a car in at least an hour, but that didn't mean a semi wouldn't come barreling out of nowhere and flatten her.

The light grew brighter. Her heart rate spiked as the thought flitted through her mind that the helicopter was going to land right on top of her.

There was no sound, she realized abruptly just about the time she began to feel woozy and heavy. The sensation of falling swept over her just before she slid into unconsciousness.

A sound rather like a clap of thunder jolted her back into awareness. Disoriented, sluggish, Bri struggled with that thought and finally decided it hadn't really sounded like thunder. It had been more like the crash of something heavy and metallic against metal--like heavy doors closing. It took an effort to lift her head and open her eyes.

The disorientation deepened as she did. She was surrounded by a strange light, an eerie bluish-green glow that didn't seem to have any obvious source. Blinking, trying to adjust her vision to the dim light, she stared uncomprehendingly at the cavernous room that surrounded her car, supported by curved arches of metal that looked more like the steel columns and beams of a building than anything else she could think of, and yet not the same at all beyond the fact that she knew it must be some sort of support for a structure.

Before she could even begin to sort through her chaotic thoughts to figure out where she was and how she'd gotten there, movement caught her gaze. A wave of shock rolled through her.

A--thing was moving toward her car. Her mind was entirely unable to supply her with an explanation of what it was beyond the vague sense that it was bug like in that it had many legs. It was as big as the car and moved stiffly, mechanically.

Sucking in a sharp cry, Bri clawed a little frantically at her door handle and finally turned to locate it. As she did, she saw another one of the things was almost at her door. Screaming, she fought with her seatbelt and finally managed to unfasten it. The car rocked as she struggled to climb over the seat into the back. But she saw two more behind the car.

The crunch of metal and shattering glass filled her ears as she screamed again. Even as she sucked in another breath to scream, though, a fine mist filled the car around her. A sensation of cold washed over her, dizziness. Her body began to feel heavy, too heavy to hold her up. She oozed into a limp puddle in the floor, floating in an odd state of awareness, staring up at the things that surrounded her car and methodically shredded it. When the roof of the car vanished, one of the things reached for her. A pincher like hand moved over her, closed around one ankle, and lifted her from the wreckage.

She dangled head down for a moment, wondering why she felt no pain, wondering if the thing was about to dismember her the same way it had taken the car apart. She was too divorced from her senses to feel more than a vague relief when, after apparently studying her for a moment, the thing slowly lowered her to a hard, icy cold surface.

She should try to escape, she thought vaguely. She found she couldn't put any other thoughts together, however, nor could she manage more than a twitch of any body part. She lay still for a time, feeling the coldness beneath her back slowly seeping into her. After a while, she felt the sensation of movement and realized the robot--it had been a robot of some sort, not a living thing--had placed her on something like a gurney, or maybe more like a conveyer belt. She passed from the dark, cavernous room into blackness and then after a time into a smaller room with the same strange lighting of the first room, except that it was brighter.

Uneasiness flickered through her when she saw that this room was occupied by what at first appeared to be people, but she still felt divorced from her body and her surroundings. After staring at her for a time, they moved toward her, and she saw they weren't people at all.
* * * *

Bri's first vaguely clear thought when she woke was that she felt hung-over. She was still grappling with that and the fact that she seemed to have fallen asleep on the floor when she finally managed to lift one eyelid enough to see. A brightly colored blurry image came into view. After staring at it for several moments, blinking, she finally realized she couldn't focus on it because it was too close, and she gathered herself, pushing away from it.

The image resolved itself into some sort of floral print.

She stared blankly at the bright comforter and finally rolled onto her side, scanning the room she found herself in.

It looked like a hotel room.

The problem was, jog her brain though she would, she couldn't recall checking into a hotel, much less making her way into the room and lying down on what was surely to god the hardest frigging bed she'd ever lain on in her life. Shifting until she was sitting up, she drew her knees up and dropped her face into her hands. Nothing became the least bit clearer. Bits and pieces of memories surfaced, but she thought they must be from a nightmare, because she could hardly make sense of the little she could recall.

Little by little, she became more alert, but she was none the wiser for it. She still couldn't remember checking into a hotel.

Hang-over--hotel--no memories.

A flash of fear went through her, and she lifted her head with a jerk.

She was still fully clothed, she saw with relief.

Ok, so she could ditch the idea that she'd stopped somewhere for a drink, been drugged, and raped.

"This is just so weird!" she murmured, slipping from the bed and looking around the room as if that might jog her memory. When it didn't, she headed toward the door she knew must lead to the bathroom.

The fixtures looked a bit old fashioned, but she was relieved to see they looked clean. She could remember thinking she would stop anywhere she could find a vacancy just to get off the road.

That wayward thought brought an avalanche of memories along with it, and relief. She'd been driving home, she remembered, from her business trip and hadn't been able to find a place to stay.

Obviously, she *had* found a place, but it bothered her that she couldn't seem to jog her memories past a specific point--that point being her car dying on the road. How could she *not* remember past that point? She must have gotten the car started again and made it to this hotel, or motel--it reminded her of one of the old motor courts that had been popular years earlier.

When she'd relieved herself, she automatically reached for the flush handle and pulled it. The toilet made an ungodly noise, and she nearly tripped over her pants around her ankles as she leapt away from it. A nervous chuckle escaped her as she righted herself and jerked her pants up, turning to look at the toilet. The half laugh died in her throat, though, as she stared at the toilet.

There was no water the bowl, and she could see that there was some sort of trap at the bottom, sort of like the toilets in an airplane or bus.

Feeling perfectly blank, she stared at it for several moments and finally moved to the lavatory. The lavatory didn't work at all. After turning both knobs around and around and getting nothing, she finally gave up and looked at the shower rather doubtfully.

"Surely to god the shower works, at least," she muttered, not believing it for a moment.

It occurred to her just then, though, that she didn't remember seeing her suitcase in the room. "God! I was out of it last night," she said under her breath, heading out of the bathroom toward the outer door. Turning the lock, she gave a tug at the door. It didn't so much as budge an inch. She frowned, turned the lock the other way, and tugged again. Nothing happened.

Planting her hands on her hips, she looked around for a phone. She'd scanned the room twice before her gaze lit on the black, clunky, ancient looking thing on the table by the bed. "Geez! I must have touched down in the twilight zone!" she murmured. The telephone looked like an antique!

It didn't work either, damn it! There was no dial tone. "Well, goddamn it to hell!" she cried, slamming the receiver back down. "Does nothing in this god forsaken hotel work?"

Stewing over the fact that she couldn't get out to retrieve her suitcase, or even call the front desk for help, she flopped down on the edge of the bed. It didn't give one iota, and a jolt traveled all the way up her spine and into her skull. "Fuck!" she shouted, leaping off the bed and grabbing the coverlet and tossing it back.

Her jaw slid to half mast when she saw what was beneath the cover. There was no mattress, rock hard or otherwise. There was nothing beneath the comforter but a box. "What the hell?"

After staring at the thing blankly for several moments, she leaned down and rapped on the thing with her knuckles. The sound that echoed back told her that, whatever it was, it was hollow, but she couldn't even determine what it was made out of. Oddly enough, it felt like some sort of metal--except it wasn't cold like metal. The temperature and texture was more like plastic-- cool but not cold, and smooth, but almost porous.

She studied it for several moments more and finally moved across the room to the easy chair. It was as well she'd begun to feel deeply suspicious of everything in the room because, although the thing looked like an overstuffed easy chair, it was just as hard and unyielding as the 'bed'.

She settled on it anyway, looking around the room while it slowly sank into her mind that where ever she was at, she was *not* in a hotel room.

Fear began to creep into her, try though she might to hold it at bay. Flashes of memory from her 'nightmares' went through her mind, but she couldn't seem to fully grasp anything. She remembered being afraid. She remembered that she hadn't been able to run, or scream, but whereas before remembering that had reassured her that the images had been part of some sort of strange dream, it failed to comfort her.

She'd felt drugged when she woke up. If she had been, then that would also account for the gaps in her memory, and not being able to move or speak.

Trying to discount the fear clawing at her, Bri got up and moved around the room, checking everything. The TV, like the bed and the chair, was merely a hollow box, formed in the shape of what it was supposed to be. The 'chest' the TV was resting on wasn't a chest either. The drawers didn't open.

The light switch didn't work.

The curtains didn't cover a window, either. When she shoved the curtains back, she found that the source of the light wasn't the sun at all. It was a glowing box.

Struggling with the urge to give into hysteria, she moved to the furthest corner from the door, slid down to the floor, and curled into a tight ball against the wall, staring at the door that should have been the exit to the room and wasn't.

Time passed. She had no way of marking it beyond the slow cramping of muscles from being held tensely for a long time, the cold seeping up through the floor and into her until she began to shake. When she couldn't stand the chill any longer, she got up and moved to the platform that posed as a bed and dragged the coverlet around her.

Like everything else in the room, it wasn't actually what it appeared to be. It wasn't nice, fluffy, insulating cotton or polyester fibers sandwiched between woven fabric panels. She'd been too disoriented earlier to notice, but the moment she gathered it around her for warmth she realized the thing was made of some material unknown to her but rather closer to plastic than fabric. She clutched it around her anyway, trying to hold her own warmth close, still tense with fear.

In time, the fear lessened because she became too tired to hang on to it and there'd been no overt threat. She knew the danger was as real now as it had been before she'd become aware of it, and since she'd first become aware of it, but high emotion was exhausting. She'd actually begun to doze when a scraping sound brought her to full alert again. Jerking upright, she looked around the room with wide, terror filled eyes. When she didn't see anything she could identify as a threat, she calmed slightly and looked more closely.

There was a plate of food and a cup sitting on the table near the fake window. She stared at it, but she knew it hadn't been there before. After looking all around it to see if she could figure out where it had come from and coming up empty, she settled against the hard 'bed' again, pulled the cover tightly around her, and lay staring at the wall with her back to the 'offering'.

It would have been harder to ignore it if not for two circumstances.

She couldn't smell it.

And nothing in the room, so far, had been 'real' in the sense that it actually was what it was made to represent. In all likelihood, the food was made out of the same stuff that everything else had been molded from and completely inedible, however appealing it looked.

She'd replayed her scattered memories over and over in her mind until she had begun to have a horrendous picture in her mind that she could not dismiss and still had trouble accepting.

She hadn't gotten out of her car. She knew that now. She'd blacked out for some unknown period of time and woken inside something vaguely like a hanger. And the strange, horrible, many legged creatures had come out of the dark and disassembled her car.

There'd been blinding light before she lost consciousness. She could remember thinking a helicopter must be above her with one of those blindingly bright spot lights they used.

And after she'd been taken from the car, she'd been in a room filled with men wearing strange looking suits--except they weren't men at all. They'd been humanoid, but they hadn't looked human when they'd placed her on something like an examination table and studied her.

She'd finally narrowed everything down to two possibilities.

Either her mind had snapped and she had woken up in a mental institute.

Or she'd been taken.

Chapter Two

Bri discovered she'd been wrong about having no way to mark the time. Hunger came, gnawed at her, and dissipated. Her bladder filled, and she was forced to go back into the bathroom and use the toilet, which she found was an unnerving experience and hard to grow accustomed to. The light in the fake window dimmed and brightened as if marking the cycle of the sun.

She was in a habitat, she realized, not a mental institution, a habitat designed specifically for the human animal by a species not human and therefore unfamiliar with the objects they had so carefully placed inside her cage to make her feel 'at home'.

The room had dimmed when she heard a hiss that startled her from a state near sleep to complete wakefulness.

She registered a strange smell a split second before she felt the effects of the gas they'd filled the room with. In spite of all she could do, she felt herself falling under the effects of it, growing heavy, weak, and very quickly unable to move at all.

She would almost have welcomed complete unconsciousness, but she supposed they were afraid that might kill her.

She hung on to the thought that they wanted her alive.

She was placed on something that moved like before, a gurney she supposed, and taken to another room, the same room, she thought, that she'd dreamed before that had looked like an examination room in a hospital or perhaps a surgery room.

This time her clothing was removed. She wasn't certain how. One moment, she was clothed, the next she was naked.

There as a strong similarity to the things they did to experiences she'd had over the course of her life with doctors. The instruments they used looked strange and unrecognizable, but then so, too, did most medical instruments, and her mind was too foggy for her to trust her perceptions. It could have been exactly the same things used by doctors on Earth, but she didn't think so anymore than she believed the men around her were just ordinary human beings distorted by drugs into seeming like monsters.

Her perceptions *were* distorted, however. She knew that. Mostly, she was only aware of pressure here and there, occasionally almost to the point of pain, but she was only mildly discomforted.

The main reason she knew her perceptions were distorted, however, was because she knew she would have been terrified if she had not been drugged.

She still felt a vague sense of relief when they returned her to the habitat.

Assuming the light was an indication of Earth days passing, by her reckoning three days passed before she woke to discover a change in her circumstances that was more disturbing than anything before.

She'd been afraid to eat or drink. The hunger, after the first day of fasting, wasn't as hard to deal with as she'd thought it would be because she wasn't hungry all the time. The hunger was painful, but it would pass. The steady declining of her strength didn't, and she knew she was becoming dehydrated very quickly.

The second time they came for her after her arrival, one of them spoke for the first time. He had leaned down until she could see his face clearly through the helmet he wore. "You must eat--drink what provided, or we must feed with tube."

The words were clearly enunciated, and in English, and it had still taken her several moments to translate because it had sounded like those peculiar messages pieced together digitally from a recording of someone pronouncing a random collection of words. Without emotional inflection, with her mind clouded by the drugs in her system, she still had not fully grasped the implied threat until she'd been returned to the room where they kept her.

It comforted her in a way. Not only did they at least seem to believe they were providing her with sustenance to keep her alive, the threat that they would feed her if she didn't feed herself assured her that they meant to keep her alive.

It was almost as unnerving, though. She'd finally accepted that she had been taken, but she had fallen back on those wild reports and claims that she had never believed before. Everyone who'd claimed to have been abducted by aliens had said they were studied and returned.

The implication that they might not have the intention of returning her seriously undermined her determination to keep her fear at bay.

When she woke the third day and discovered that her clothing had not been returned as before--that she was wearing nothing but a loose, shapeless shift like a hospital gown--she felt an instant stab of uneasiness that became more pronounced when she discovered she had been fitted with a thick collar such as one might place on an animal. As she sat up abruptly to tug at the thing, she saw that the door was open.

Her heart leapt immediately at that discovery and stilled in the very next second as the realization sank in that they would not have simply left the door ajar for her to escape. Dismissing her consternation over the collar for the moment, she stared at the sliver of light revealed in the opening, wondering if this was some new test they'd devised.

It was hard to escape the sense that she'd become a lab rat.

Had they decided, now that they'd thoroughly examined every inch of her body and run every lab test they could conceive, to run her through a series of tests to judge her intelligence? Like a rat in a maze? Or had they decided that she needed the exercise just as she needed the virtually tasteless food they provided?

She supposed tasteless was better than what it might have been, but the fact that, no matter what they made the food appear like, it still had the taste and consistency of mush hadn't encouraged her to eat more than what she absolutely had to to keep them from shoving it down her throat with a tube.

The water was more bearable, and she'd never liked to drink water.

Ignoring the opened door for the moment, she got off the platform and went into the bathroom to use the facilities. The lavatory still didn't work like a normal lavatory, but they had obviously been observing her from the moment she arrived because when she'd begun trying to bathe herself with the little cups of water, they'd provided her with a grudging supply for hygiene. Grudging, because the taps in the bathroom worked rather like the pretend faucets in a child's playset. She could pump little spurts of water into her palm and mop off with it.

She supposed it was rationed, and for a good reason. But for someone who was accustomed to bathing at least once a day, preferably twice, and brushing her teeth three times a day, and washing her face and hands in between, it was miserable.

She hated being confined.

She hated having nothing to do with her time but worry about what they intended to do with her.

She hated having nothing but water to drink.

She hated being fed food that might as well have been saw dust for all the taste it had.

But most of all she hated having to struggle just to feel a modicum of cleanliness.

Ok, so maybe she was borderline OCD about bathing, especially her face and hands, but she couldn't help it, and she began to think if anything was going to break her down into a blithering moron, not being able to bathe like she wanted to might do it.

When she'd bathed the best she could, she studied the collar in her reflection in the mirror-like thing they'd hung in the bathroom. It wasn't an actual mirror, either because they were afraid to put glass where she could get to it, or because they hadn't actually grasped what the point of the mirror was. But it did reflect a wavy image. Unfortunately, it was so distorted that she couldn't really tell much more about the thing around her neck than she'd already been able to determine by touch.

It seemed to be made out of the same material they used for pretty much everything. She could not find a fastening on it. She looked for that first.

It wasn't tight, but she wasn't used to having anything so close around her throat, and it bothered her as badly as getting a ring stuck on her finger, or her hand or foot wedged into a crevice, in a claustrophobic sense.

She didn't think it was *just* a collar. There was a reason they'd placed it there, and she feared it had to do with control, which meant there was no telling what the thing could do to her.

She wanted it *off*! After wrenching at it until she'd managed to rub the skin around her neck raw she finally accepted defeat, for the moment, and desisted.

The purpose of it was still prominent in her mind, however, as she left the bathroom.

A tray of food had appeared, and she moved to it and dutifully drank the water and nibbled half-heartedly at the food because she knew they were watching to see if she ate it, and she didn't want to find out what they could do to her if she didn't.

She studied the door while she ate, wondering if the collar was part of this 'test' and how. Would it shock her if she tried to go out? Or shock her if she retreated from the door and into the corner?

It might be to control her, but the underlying purpose might be to teach her the futility of trying to escape.

She knew that already, though, had realized it from the moment she finally accepted that she was in the hands of aliens because she very much doubted that they'd built this elaborate prison on terra firma. They weren't on Earth anymore. She was convinced of that, and if that was the case then it wouldn't do her any good at all to get out of the room because she still couldn't escape them.

She had fought back hysteria for two reasons. One, it wouldn't accomplish a damned thing except, possibly, to convince them she was crazy and therefore useless. And two, in the back of her mind, she hoped that they'd let her go when they were done 'playing' with her.

Deciding about the time she'd finished eating that they had left the door open because they meant for her to go out, she moved slowly toward the door, glancing around the room futilely to see if she could spot the camera they used to watch her. She hesitated when she reached the door and then placed her hand slowly on the knob, expecting any moment to feel a jolt shoot through her.

When nothing happened, she tightened her hold on the knob, pulled the door open slowly, and leaned around the edge to peer out.

Her heart nearly failed her when she did, and the urge to collapse on the floor and weep nearly overwhelmed her.

She'd been right. She'd been *so* right she felt like screaming and never stopping.

There was no end to her habitat. Beyond the fake hotel room lay an entire fake world that went on for as far as she could see into the distance.

Bri had already begun unconsciously backing away from the view beyond her room when a painful jolt went through her that stopped her in her tracks. She uttered a muffled cry as fiery pain slithered along her nerve endings. By the time it subsided she was no longer in any doubt at all that she was meant to go out or what they'd do to her if she didn't comply.

Panting with fear as the pain finally began to subside, she moved toward the door, hovered there for a moment, and then stepped outside when another, milder jolt, urged her on.

The first thing she noticed, because she was already struggling for breath because of her fear and pain, was that the air seemed thick, and it was a struggle to breathe. It was also hot. Within a matter of seconds she could feel moisture begin to pop from her pores.

As accustomed as she was to high humidity given that she'd grown up in the semi-tropical region of the U.S., she was still uncomfortable within moments and she hadn't even exerted herself.

Just above the 'horizon', a fake sun hovered in a strangely colored sky studded with stranger colored clouds. Beneath her now bare feet was black soil that still looked somehow different from Earth's dark soil, possibly because of the texture, and a smattering of strange, low growing vegetation. A few trees and shrubs dotted the landscape between the almost dome-like habitats that surrounded the 'green', but none of the vegetation looked familiar.

Why, she wondered, would they go to so much effort to reproduce a landscape and not make it Earth-like?

Because she was the only occupant from Earth, she wondered, feeling faint at the thought? Because this looked familiar to the majority? Just as her 'room' looked like something she was at least vaguely familiar with, or that they had reason to believe would be familiar to her.

When she'd fully emerged, the door closed behind her. She heard a distinct click that indicated it was sealed and she would not be allowed to go back inside.

Her heart kicked up several notches in beat, but when she turned and surveyed the landscape again, she began to have serious palpitations.

Emerging from the other habitats were--beings. Even from a distance, she could see that they were alien, not human, although they were humanoid in appearance and their proportions appeared to be very similar to humans. Their flesh tones, though, were not like any race she was familiar with even if she wasn't close enough to tell much about their features. It was golden, but distinctly more yellow than brown. Most seemed to have dark hair, brown or black, pulled back from their faces to the crown of their heads and worn in a 'pony tail' that reached to their waists. The light from the false sun brought out greenish-gold glints, but she wasn't certain if it was just a trick of the light or if their hair actually had that color of highlights.

They all seemed to be male, every one that she could see from where she stood--either that or their women did not have breasts, because they were bare chested, covered only below the waist by some sort of breeches and either leggings or boots that came up to their knees.

As they moved further from their habitats and closer to her, she began to see their features somewhat better, but it was no relief to see that their faces were as human looking as their bodies. They still seemed alien. They looked fierce, somehow almost barbaric, although she had no idea what gave her that impression except, maybe, plain old fashioned fear. That didn't mean they were, and she certainly couldn't judge them by their clothing considering what she'd been given to wear, but that was still the impression she got. Maybe because, besides looking fierce and dangerous, they appeared to be tattooed--either that or they had really strangely patterned skin--not necessarily a sign of being primitive since everybody and his brother seemed to be getting them these days--and they were built like a people accustomed to hard physical labor. Also not necessarily indicative of primitives since there were plenty of body builders and professional sportsmen that were bulked up similarly on Earth.

They reminded her strongly of the hulk, except they were yellow not green.

She was relieved to see that although they appeared to have noticed her and seemed curious, they didn't seem inclined to approach too closely, for they stopped before they'd covered more than half the distance that separated her from them.

She refused to actually look in their direction at first, fearful that doing so might encourage them to move closer. After a few cautious glances, however, she noticed something odd.

They'd formed almost a straight line--a line which she noticed several paced along as if there was some invisible barrier preventing them from moving closer, but they were considering attempting to breech it.

Frowning, she transferred her attention from the aliens to the landscape again. She noticed the demarcation then. Stones had been set at regular intervals in perpendicular lines to separate each exercise yard.

Like dogs, they'd been fitted with control collars to keep them within their separate boundaries.

The aliens obviously already knew this, so even if they were primitive, they didn't lack intelligence.

Curiosity surfaced, but she decided she didn't want to test to see if they could cross the barrier.

* * * *

Frustration was not an emotion Kole had been intimately acquainted with before the Sheloni had raided his village and captured them--taken everyone they hadn't killed outright. He'd become far too familiar with it since that time, though, and it irked him no end to be forced to behave as if he'd been cowed by their superiority, to sit idly by as docile as a grazing *nyak* and do nothing more than wait and watch for the opportunity to strike. His people looked to him to lead them, however. If he could not contain his impatience to strike back, they would not, and more would die uselessly.

They'd lost almost a third of the female warriors since they'd been taken. The knowledge made him sick with the rage he had to hold inside, but he was almost as angry with the women as the Sheloni. It was one thing to give one's life in battle. Even ritual suicide was honorable in the face of defeat, but to throw their lives away only because they'd been impregnated just to destroy the lives they'd created?

He could not fathom why they had done that. There was no honor in it even though many had claimed it was to prevent the Sheloni from using them as leverage against the men, to prevent the unborn from being born to slavery, because they had known that they would not be able to fight if they were heavy with child.

None of those reasons were acceptable for aborting their seedlings, he thought with thinly repressed fury. The Hirachi race was being systematically wiped out and *they* had contributed to that directly … and many of them had died forcing their bodies to abort.

At best it was insubordination, completely contrary to his orders, and it had weakened their force for the time when they *could* strike back.

At worst … it had demoralized the men … demoralized *him*, because their young were their hope for the future--an unexpected gift--something above themselves worth fighting for. They would have fought harder knowing it was to protect their unborn.

Now it wasn't nearly as hard for the men to behave as if they were cowed--they were--not by the Sheloni and their machines and torture devices, but by their women. Many wondered if there was even any point in trying to throw off the yolk of the Sheloni. What future did they have anyway? With many of their women dead already and the lives of the others hanging on the decision of the Sheloni, and their young dead, all they had left to inspire them to fight was the need for revenge--and that was an emotion that made wise men into careless fools who would throw away their own lives without regard for the consequences to their brothers in arms.

He was so deep in his morose thoughts he didn't at first notice the timid creature that emerged from the hut almost directly across from his own--or rather he did. The movement caught his attention at once. He simply didn't consciously acknowledge what his gaze rested upon at first.

It moved cautiously. He imagined he could almost smell the fear emanating from it. The pale coloring of the creature threw him off, brought his mind to focus on it as he realized it walked on two legs. It was wearing one of the gowns the Sheloni dressed the female slaves in, which indicated that it was a creature of intelligence, not merely a beast –and female.

Curious despite himself, he moved to the perimeter of his yard to get a better look.

The creature halted, staring at him and the other men who, as curious as he was, had moved closer for a better look. After hesitating for several moments, she moved to a scrubby *mushmi* that grew in her yard and looked it over, then began to walk around it, studying it.

He more than half expected her to either mark it or begin to graze upon the leaves of the stunted tree.

What was it? It appeared to be much like the Hirachi in form. He could tell little about the features of her face from the distance, but she assuredly had two eyes, one nose, and one mouth--two arms, two legs and hands and feet. This was no Hirachi, though....

Unless it was a child, he thought, realizing abruptly that it wasn't merely distance that made it appear small to his eyes.

He had not seen a child since he had *been* a child. Fully half that spawning had been snatched away by the Sheloni, and the females had refused to return to the spawning grounds thereafter.

It wasn't a child, he decided. It looked … mature if the round globes pushing against the top of her gown, bouncing and swaying with her movements, was any indication … and his cock said it was. Mindless marvel that *that* was, controlled purely by instinct, it roused in interest. It was a … miniature … something … not Hirachi, similar, yes, but not the same. The skin was such a *strange* color, almost pink, but more white … like the freakish things occasionally born without color at all! The hair, as well, not dark but a mixture of red and brown and even gold.

If he hadn't been bored out of his mind, he might not have found the strange female so fascinating.

Then again, he thought wryly, he had been known to lie to himself on occasion.

It occurred to him, though, that the Sheloni never did anything without reason. They were not impulsive creatures. They'd brought the female for a reason.

He wondered, if he had not been in season, if he would have been more than mildly interested, but it was a mute question. He *was* in season, just like everyone else, and his reasoning mind took a back seat to his needs when that was upon him. His mind might be telling him--alien--small, weak, and strangely colored, but his body had no interest in anything beyond the fact that it was female.

I must learn what I can about this creature and the purpose the Sheloni have in mind for her, he told himself--strategically it could be of importance.

Torment, the primitive side of his mind told him. They have brought females too spindly and weak to mount and breed just to drive us mad. They *know* we have to fight the urge to spawn, and they are bent upon using our weakness against us!

* * * *

Unnerved by the watchful gazes of the aliens, and, if the truth were acknowledged, the tension she sensed in them, Bri moved to the closest plant-like shrub and examined it, thinking it must be as fake as everything else. On closer examination, however, she decided that, as strange as it looked, it was a real, living--something.

As she moved around the alien plant, trying to focus on studying it and ignoring the aliens that watched her so intently, movement caught her attention, and she looked up to see a tiny, dark skinned woman emerge from a habitat across from hers. After blinking several times in disbelief, a surge of excitement went through her. A smile curled her lips, and she hurried toward the woman.

Looking as disoriented and frightened as she probably had when she'd first been thrust from the security of her habitat, the woman looked up and met her gaze. Relief seemed to flicker over her features. She hurried forward to meet Bri.

She didn't know about the boundary, Bri realized when she saw the woman rushing upon the line. "No!" she shouted, breaking into a trot to try to stop the woman. "Don't …!"

The jolt that went through the other woman made her body jerk and seize. When it stopped, the woman wilted to the ground. Bri stopped abruptly in her tracks, too stunned to react at first. Her throat closed. Tears clogged her nose and filled her eyes. "No!" she cried, rushing forward again. "No! Oh god!"

One of the nightmarish robots appeared--Bri had no idea where it had come from. She'd been focused on the woman lying in the dirt. She stopped again as the thing gripped the woman's body and began to drag her back across the line. "You bastards!" she screamed, lifting her head and looking around as if she could see the aliens that had orchestrated the nightmare she'd found herself in. "You killed her! You slimy sons-of-bitches!"

Seeing that the robot had stopped dragging the woman when she turned in that direction again, Bri rushed to the edge of her compound, dashing the blinding tears from her eyes to study the woman hopefully.

She was breathing!

Bri wilted to the ground, watching, waiting, hoping the woman would regain consciousness.

Human! She'd never realized how happy it could make her just to see another human being! She'd wrapped her arms around herself and was rocking agitatedly when the woman let out a gasp and her eyelids fluttered.

"Hey!" she called, straining forward as far as she dared. "Are you alright?"

With obvious effort, the woman lifted her head. Finally, she struggled upright.

Opening her mouth finally, she uttered a string of … Spanish.

Bri stared at the woman blankly for several moments and then uttered a hysterical giggle. She couldn't seem to stop once she started. She laughed and laughed until her sides hurt. The woman was giving her a look that spoke volumes, foreigner or not, about her doubts about Bri's sanity. "It's just so fucking typical! One Earth woman on this whole god damned ship, or whatever the hell it is, and you can't even speak fucking English! And I can't speak Spanish! Isn't that fucking wonderful?"

"Si!"

Bri gasped for air and started laughing again. "I don't care! It's so fantastic to see somebody from Earth I'd kiss you if I could cross this line without being laid out!"

The woman gave her a strange look. "No habla Espanol?"

Bri mopped her eyes and face and wiped her nose. "Not a damned word! Nacho!" she exclaimed, chuckling again. "Taco! Oh god!" she added, chasing the laugh with a sob.

"Anglais?"

Bri nodded, recognizing the word. "At least--Gringo, or maybe that's gringa? That's supposed to be insulting, though--not that I am because I don't know what the fuck it means. American."

"El Savatore," the woman responded.

Bri blinked at the woman, finally subduing the hysteria as she struggled with her geography. South America? Central? "We're neighbors then!" she exclaimed, feeling a kinship--a closeness--

she would never have felt before. The woman frowned, and she turned and pointed to the habitat she occupied and then pointed out that it was adjacent to the one the Hispanic woman had come from. "Neighbors." She placed her hand against her chest. "I'm Bri … Sabrina MacIntyre, but most people just call me Bri."

The woman stared for a moment before that sank in. She smiled wanly and placed her hand against her own chest. "Consuelo."

"Kole."

Both Bri and Consuelo jumped at the deep, resonant voice. Turning, Bri saw that the alien nearest them had come as close to the line as he could. He'd knelt down so that he was nearly on a level with them.

Not quite. Up close, she saw that he was … massive.

Bri stared at him uneasily for several moments before she turned and looked at Consuelo questioningly. They exchanged a speaking glance and turned to look at the alien again.

He placed his hand over his chest as they had. "Kole."

He couldn't cross the line--she was fairly certain, for she could see he wore a collar as they did, and Bri still felt uncomfortable, fearful. She might have felt that way if it had been any strange man that was so big and looked so fierce, but that went double because he was also alien.

She couldn't seem to refrain from staring, though, studying him. Except for a few notable differences, he looked so human it was as if he was--just some race she'd never encountered before. The differences were striking, though. The strange flesh tones and even his hair. His eyes were different, too, not just a different color--a yellowish-brown, but the irises weren't the same. His ears, exposed by the way he had his hair drawn back and tied, were pointed--sort of like the Vulcans from the Science Fiction TV show that had once been so popular.

The moment that thought popped into her head, she realized that his features rather reminded her of that character, too, for his face was all harsh plains and angles--not handsome by any means, but memorable--interesting.

Somehow she doubted he was the logical, emotionless sort of alien portrayed in the TV show, though.

He was tattooed, she saw now that he was crouched within a few yards of her. His nipples were pierced, too.

She dragged her gaze from his hairless, tattooed chest to the knotted ridge of flesh that ran along his arms from his wrists, across his shoulders, and along the sides of his neck, wondering if, like the tattoos and piercings, if it was something he'd done to his flesh to 'adorn' it or if it was a genetic trait. There was extra skin on his forearms, a loose flap of skin, a thin, almost transparent membrane that she didn't notice initially. She couldn't imagine what purpose it might serve, either.

He must be every bit of six and a half feet tall, maybe taller, she decided. Not that there weren't humans that tall, but when combined with the sheer mass of muscles that bulged all over him it made him seem like a veritable giant, because he was no bean pole. He was large boned and fully loaded with hard, bulging muscles. She suspected he could play 'make a wish' and snap her in two without straining himself.

His palms were roughly the size of her face, his fingers--five she noted, almost surprised--were about as long and thick as an average human dick--then she wished she hadn't thought about dicks at all. If his was proportionate to his size, it was a behemoth--scary thought!

She didn't want to talk him. He was scary. Being deliberately rude wasn't something she felt comfortable with, though.

Besides, she didn't want to get on his bad side.

She managed a tremulous smile. "Bri."

He frowned faintly and said something to her in a language that was as alien to her ears as he was to her eyes. She exchanged another look with Consuelo. Consuelo shrugged.

A look of frustration crossed his features. Finally, he lifted his head and pointed to the sun above them, making a sweeping motion as if following the path from horizon to horizon.

Bri frowned in confusion, but it occurred to her after a moment that he must be asking how long she'd been there. She shrugged and held up three fingers. "I think," she added.

Consuelo apparently understood, as well. She held up five fingers.

Abruptly, the spurt of happiness Bri had been feeling from even a modicum of human contact deserted her. She needed to talk, desperately. She'd lived alone for years. She'd thought she was used to not having anyone to talk to, but she wasn't. She'd always been surrounded by the sound of voices when she went anywhere, voices on her TV, her radio--not being able to hear any familiar sounds, not even being able to share work related conversations with her co-workers was worse than everything else.

She would've welcomed listening to Consuelo babble in her own language, even if she couldn't understand a word of it, because it was at least somewhat familiar.

Resisting the urge to yield to another emotional outburst, she struggled to communicate with hand motions and finally began to draw in the dirt.

The alien, Kole, lingered, studying both her and Consuelo, but she couldn't help but notice most of his focus was on her. Every time she glanced in his direction she met his gaze.

She couldn't tell how much he understood of anything that she was doing, but there was a look of intelligence in his eyes that encouraged her to think he wasn't as primitive as she'd first thought.

What possible difference that could make, she had no idea.

Apparently, the aliens didn't particularly care for her efforts to communicate, however. They had not been together more than fifteen minutes when a shrill noise erupted around them. It brought her head up instantly.

Kole met her gaze and lifted his hand, pointing toward her habitat. Bri merely stared at him blankly until he rose to his feet and made the motion again.

Surging to her feet, she glanced around and discovered that everyone else had already turned toward their quarters. As reluctantly as she'd left it a short time before, Bri nodded her understanding, waved unhappily at Consuelo, and headed back.

Chapter Three

Bri found her safe corner and huddled when she had returned to the room, dropping her head across her arms and weeping for the first time since she'd been captured. When she'd finally exhausted herself, she moved listlessly to the bed and sprawled across the hard surface, trying to figure out why she felt like crying when she'd actually had the best day since she'd been there.

She realized after a while that it was a sense of hopelessness. She allowed herself to think of her despondency as disappointment for a while, that she'd finally gotten the chance to interact with a fellow human only to discover there was as much of a language barrier between them as between her and the aliens.

She *was* disappointed, vastly. She was also disappointed that she hadn't been able to make physical contact. She'd yearned to just be able to touch, hug, hold hands--anything to feel the reassuring warmth and closeness of being around another human being after having been kept in a sterile tank for days.

After a time, though, she acknowledged that it was a sense of hopelessness that had brought on the bout of tears. She forced herself to face the fact that the root of that was a growing certainty that the aliens who'd captured her meant to keep her, not simply study her and put her back.

If she understood why, maybe it wouldn't be so bad--maybe it would be worse. She tried to comfort herself with the belief that they meant to keep her alive for some reason. As awful as it was to think she might never go home again, she didn't want to die. She especially didn't want to die horribly.

She didn't want to consider why there were so many male aliens, but she couldn't avoid it.

However intelligent or technologically advanced the yellow aliens might or might not be, it seemed unavoidable that they had been chosen for their powerful physiques. She'd only seen the one who called himself Kole close up, but she'd noticed all of them at least appeared to be as big and strong as oxen--and that seemed to indicate the aliens that had taken them all needed or wanted them for something physical. She had only a vague idea of what the other aliens had been like, but she had had the impression that they were physically frail, taller than her, but thin and weak--robots seemed to do most of the physical labor for them.

The collars they had all been fitted with, she realized, might signify more than simply a means of controlling their 'lab animals'. There was a very real possibility that they might all have been enslaved and just didn't know it yet.

The thought boggled her mind, but as enlightened as the human race was, slavery still existed all over the world. It might be illegal everywhere, frowned upon, despised, but it was still going on-- mostly sex slavery.

An image of Kole rose in her mind at that thought, and she shuddered.

She pushed the half formed thought aside. If the slaver aliens had taken her for a sex slave, it wouldn't be to toss her to their other slaves--she didn't think.

What purpose could she serve for them, though?

She'd never thought of herself as particularly weak, frail, or dainty, but beside this yellow race she certainly was, so she couldn't delude herself into thinking they had taken her for physical labor or because she was an excellent physical specimen. They didn't seem to have a great deal of respect for other intelligent beings, so she couldn't imagine they'd wanted her for her mind either.

Maybe she was just scaring herself? Maybe she really was just a part of some bizarre experiment and they would take her back when they were done studying her?

She wanted to believe that, but, deep down, she didn't, not anymore. The fact that they did not come for her that night seemed to support instead of refute that fear.

The door was ajar when she woke the following morning as it had been the day before. She studied it distrustfully, but instead of dawdling as she had the day before, she rushed through her morning ritual, ate, and moved to the door.

In her rush to see Consuelo, she almost fell over the thing lying on the ground just outside the door.

Horror filled her even as she jolted to a halt and stared down at it.

She thought at first that it was dead, but as she cringed, clamping a hand over her mouth to stifle a scream, she saw it's eyes flicker.

Shocked, revolted, she glanced around, half expecting someone or something to appear and scoop the thing up--as if they'd dropped it or inadvertently left it. Slowly, it sank into her mind that the appearance could not possibly be accidental. It had been placed there for a reason. She just didn't know why.

What was she to do with it? What?

Calm was slow in returning, and her revulsion didn't abate. Pity began to seep into her, however, as she studied it's emaciated body. After several minutes had passed, she knelt down to study it more closely.

It was male infant, she saw, for it was naked, lying naked on the cold dirt as if it was no more than a discarded piece of garbage. Unlike the hulking brutes she'd seen the day before, the infant looked frail, starved, near death. It lay completely motionless, merely staring at her blankly, unblinkingly, as if appealing to her for help.

Releasing a shaky breath, she reached to touch it. The infant's eyes followed the movement of her hand, but otherwise there was little reaction until she touched it lightly with her fingers. Its face crumpled then, and she expected it to set up a wail of fear. Instead, it merely jerked and twitched uneasily as she stroked her hand over it soothingly and finally captured one tiny hand in her fingers. Slowly, its hand curled over her finger.

A knot of emotion welled in her throat, partly because it clutched at her, partly because, despite the heat, she could feel that it was cold.

A wave of panic followed the empathy. She didn't know anything about babies, not even human babies! Was she supposed to take care of it? Or had they simply placed it there to see how she would react?

She had no clue, but she found she couldn't ignore it. Clumsily, she scooped a hand behind his head and bottom and lifted the infant, cradling it against her chest. It wiggled, but it didn't put up a fuss, didn't cry.

It bothered her that it didn't cry. Was it too weak to cry?

When she lifted her head, she saw the yellow aliens had come out again. The one called Kole stood at the very edge of his yard, staring straight at her. She held his look for a long moment and, finally realizing the door hadn't closed and locked behind her, took the infant inside.

She needed to warm him, she decided. She could at least do that.

Easier said than done. She had nothing but the shift they'd given her to wear.

Remembering the towels in the bathroom, she laid the infant on the bed and headed into the bathroom to grab a towel. It wasn't soft, fluffy, or warm, but she thought if the baby was wrapped in it it would at least hold the infant's own warmth to it.

There were no diapers to cover its bottom, but, search the room though she might, she couldn't find an acceptable substitute. She finally simply wrapped it in the towel and cuddled it close to her chest.

It made a weak sound then. She loosened her hold, fearful she'd squeezed it too tightly and checked the wrapping. It didn't seem too tight. The baby had closed his eyes, but he seemed to be breathing alright.

Deciding may it was a sound of gladness to be warm, she wrapped it snugly again, cradled it against her chest and finally went outside.

Kole was still standing watchfully. After a moment's hesitation, she headed directly toward him. Halting when she reached the perimeter, she lifted the baby away from her chest and showed him what she held. "What do I do with him? I don't know anything about babies. Nothing! There's something wrong with him," she added, unwrapping his frail body to show the alien. "He looks like he's starving, and he's so … listless."

Kole stared almost dispassionately at the infant for many moments and finally lifted his gaze to her face to study her and said something that, needless to say, she couldn't understand at all. There was something about the inflection of his words, though, that she didn't like.

He held out his hands as if demanding she place the baby in his arms.

It wasn't her baby. It was a yellow alien child.

But it didn't belong to him.

The other aliens had given it to her for a reason.

Instead of handing the baby to him, she pulled it tightly, protectively against her chest again and stepped back. Spying Consuelo near the line holding a bundle similar to the one she held, Bri hurried toward the other woman.

Even before she reached the woman Consuelo began to babble a stream of Spanish, gesturing to the infant she held. When she unwrapped the baby, which Bri saw she'd wrapped in a towel as she had, Bri saw that it, too, was pathetically thin and listless. It was also another male child.

After staring at the other baby for several moments, Bri settled on the ground, folded her legs and rested the infant in her lap, staring down at him, trying to make order of her chaotic thoughts.

Where were the women who'd borne the infants? Had they

died? Was that why she and Consuelo had been taken? To adopt the infants?

As *if* one only had to be a woman to know how to tend to a baby, damn it!

Why would the slavers care anyway? If they could snatch beings from anywhere they pleased and enslave them, why would they give a damn whether the babies lived or died?

She couldn't wrap her mind around it, but she found herself stroking the baby's cheek gently. A half sob, half laugh escaped her as she studied his little 'old man' face. "Poor, ugly little thing!"

A frown flickered briefly across the baby's face, and she felt shame wash over her. He couldn't help being ugly anymore than she could help thinking he was. And maybe he wouldn't be ugly if he wasn't so scrawny and underfed? After a moment, she lifted him up and brushed a light kiss of apology along his cheek. "I was just teasing, sweety. I didn't really mean it. You're not ugly. You're a handsome little man!"

He reacted--either to her voice or her touch, a thread of emotion flickering across his tiny face, and she felt a peculiar sense of triumph wash through her, a strange warmth of pleasure. Maybe, like her, he needed to hear the sound of a voice? Needed to feel the contact of another being?

Maybe, but he also needed food.

She might not know much of anything about babies, but she'd observed enough to know they seemed to eat all the time--and need changing. She had no idea how old the infant was. He didn't look very old at all to her, but she wouldn't have been much of a judge of a human infant, and she certainly had no clue of the development of an alien child. She could tell, though, that he couldn't really hold his own head up. He certainly couldn't lift and support it.

His head seemed disproportionately large to her, but she thought maybe it was because he was so skinny and not a sign of some birth defect. She couldn't help but feel like the fact that he kept watching her so hard must be a sign of intelligence.

Where was his mother? Had she died when it was borne?

The thought made her glance at Kole. She saw that he'd knelt as he had the day before. His gaze was keen, unwavering, and focused on her hands as she moved them soothingly over the baby, patting his back as she'd seen mothers pat their babies. As if he sensed her gaze, his own lifted to meet hers.

Frowning, she looked away again.

Consuelo might be a mother--she looked old enough, Bri thought, that she could have had children. Unfortunately, even if the woman had vast maternal experience, Bri couldn't ask her a damned thing.

The realization scared the hell out of her. She held the baby's life in her hands, and she was pretty sure she was going to fail him.

"I need help," she said plaintively, knowing Consuelo couldn't understand her.

She seemed to grasp the desperation in Bri's voice. She began to act out tending a baby.

Or maybe she was trying to tell Bri she wasn't holding him right?

Tamping her fear of inadequacy, she watched the woman carefully, mimicking the way she held the baby.

Her frustration surfaced in anger, though, when she'd returned to the room.

"I don't know how to do this!" she screamed at the ceiling. "I've never had a baby! I've never even tended to a baby! And you didn't give me anything for him either, damn it! How am I supposed to feed him?"

There was no answer, but she hadn't really expected one. She discovered, though, when her noon tray of food appeared, that they had decided to feed the baby, too. A bottle appeared and wraps, which she decided must be to use for blanket and diapers.
* * * *

Trying to figure out how to take care of the baby was as frustrating as it was rewarding when she seemed to get something right. He consumed her time, but she welcomed it, preferring to worry over him and work to keep him fed, warm, dry, and clean than to think about her situation.

Each day she was herded out into the 'exercise' yard as she thought of it, although they didn't seem to care if she did nothing more than sit face to face with Consuelo, rocking, or feeding the baby, each of them talking just to hear themselves, because she still didn't speak Spanish and Consuelo still didn't speak English.

She'd decided after a few days that he needed a name besides baby. After giving it some thought, she'd settled on Corbitt, her mother's maiden name, and then found herself shortening it to Cory.

He never cried.

She would've liked to think that that was because she was so good at taking care of him, but she couldn't convince herself of that because she knew she wasn't. She had no idea how often she should feed him but because he didn't eat much and he was so skinny, she fed him every couple of hours at first until he began to take more of whatever it was in the bottle.

It looked disgusting and smelled worse, but he seemed to like it. He didn't make faces when she fed it to him and after a week he seemed to be filling out some.

"What do you think, Consuelo?" she asked the other woman, pointing out his rounding belly and arms and legs. "Does he look better to you?"

Consuelo dutifully watched and seemed to catch the drift after a moment. She nodded vigorously and displayed her baby, whom she was now calling Manuel. She said something about *gordo* and then puffed out her cheeks.

Bri chuckled, but she felt a flicker of irritation, too, because it seemed to her that Manuel *was* getting fat and all she could say about poor little Cory was that he wasn't as skinny as he had been. "Cory's getting fat, too," she said somewhat defensively. "And, watch this," she added, smiling down at him and cooing at him.

His lips curled tentatively, and Bri looked up at Consuelo triumphantly.

"See! He smiled at me!"

Consuelo looked suitably impressed, and Bri felt a little less defensive. It occurred to her, though, to wonder if she failed at mothering the infant if the slaver aliens would decide she was worthless.

A flicker of fear went through her at the realization that her own life might depend on keeping Cory alive, helping him to thrive. She'd taken to him because she needed him as much as he needed her, needed something warm, and alive, and responsive. And also because she simply couldn't ignore his needs. And because she was going slowly insane with nothing to do but twiddle her thumbs and wait for the ax to fall.

She hadn't done it because she'd considered she was making herself useful to the cold blooded aliens who'd taken her and that her survival might depend on her usefulness.

Lifting Cory protectively against her, she glanced toward Kole. He hadn't attempted to communicate since he'd tried to get her to give the baby to him, but he was generally hovering nearby, watching her, when she was outside.

She didn't know what thoughts were running through his mind. She wasn't certain she wanted to know.

She'd caught a look on his face a few times that made her distinctly uneasy.

She'd had men look at her with interest.

She'd had men give her flirty or seductive glances.

He was the first male that had looked ... hungry, and it startled a thrill of both fear and excitement in her when ever she encountered that heated look.

The fear she could understand. The guy was the next thing to a giant. He looked like a head bashing barbarian.

The excitement was something she didn't especially want to analyze.

She *must* have lost her mind! The guy was probably a fucking caveman.

Her gaze flickered over him speculatively. The clothing was a long way from anything a caveman could manage, but then the slaver aliens might have given him the breeches and boots.

"Niño die."

Bri's jaw slid to half mast in stunned amazement when Kole spoke. She was so surprised that he'd managed to pick up enough English and Spanish to put a 'sort of' sentence together that it was several moments before she registered exactly what he'd said. When she did, fear and fury surged through her.

She'd known, instinctively, that he couldn't be trusted with the baby!

"You bastard! That's a hell of a thing to say. He's ... he's whatever you are! One of your kind. How could you even *think* such a horrible thing!"

Anger contorted his own features, but although it seemed he'd grasped the general trend of her tirade, he couldn't come up with a suitable response. Instead, he grasped the collar around his neck, tugged at it, and burst into a flood of words in his own tongue. "Better," he ground out finally.

It dawned on her that he was suggesting Cory would be better off dead than a slave. She had the frightening feeling that he knew what he was talking about, that there was more to his fury than anger at being caged within the alien space ship.

She clutched the baby a little more tightly, squeezing him hard enough he began to whimper and struggle in her hold. Relaxing her frantic hold with a conscious effort, she put her back to the alien and soothed him. "Don't pay that hateful thing any attention, darlin'. I won't let that bad old alien anywhere near you," she murmured to the baby, sending Kole a drop dead look.

His lips tightened. "Earth woman!"

He ground the words out like a curse.

Bri set her jaw. "I don't think he approves of us, Consuelo," she murmured, pointedly ignoring him.

"No like."

Bri nodded in agreement, although she wasn't sure if Consuelo was saying she didn't like the alien, or agreeing that, no, he didn't seem to like them much.

That was why she and Consuelo had been given the babies, she realized, because the yellow aliens *were* barbaric! They'd rather kill their young than allow them to be enslaved!

Dead wasn't better, regardless of what he thought--what any of them apparently believed! It was certainly not pleasant being held against her will, but as long as she had breath she had a chance of escaping, maybe not home, but somewhere. They couldn't stay in space forever. Sooner or later they were going to set this thing down somewhere.

She had to believe there was some hope. She had to believe that she wasn't coaxing life into a child that would suffer endlessly because of a misplaced act of kindness.

They must be a very war-like race, she decided, if they could be so callous about their own young.

She discovered that she'd undoubtedly guessed close to the mark a week later when she went out to walk the baby as usual and got her first look at the females of Kole's tribe.

The noise caught her attention immediately, and would have even if she hadn't noticed that the voices speaking were higher in pitch than male voices. She couldn't see where the noise was coming from at first, though. She'd nearly reached the back of her yard, where Consuelo stood, clutching Manuel and staring into the distance, when she finally caught a glimpse of a mob of yellow skinned aliens several sections over from her own.

They were still too close for comfort in Bri's book.

A half dozen or so were lying on the ground twitching from trying to jump the line--or from being pushed over it. Bri wasn't certain which, but even as she struggled to understand why they'd been grouped together, she realized that there was a distinct difference between this group and the males.

They weren't as tall as the males, but they didn't miss it by a hell of a lot. They weren't as muscular, but they didn't miss that by much either. Like the males, they wore nothing over their upper bodies, which was why she deduced fairly quickly that it was females of the same species. Many of them had breasts as big as her head--hard to miss.

They, too, appeared to have long, dark hair, but unlike the males, it appeared that they shaved all but the hair in the back and instead of wearing it lose, the hair was braided and coiled tightly against the crown of their heads.

She didn't have to wonder if they were fierce. They were fighting among themselves--and it wasn't a cat fight. They were slugging it out like prize fighters. Like Consuelo, she tensed, staring at the melee in frozen dread.

The awful moment of truth that she'd hardly acknowledged came when one of the women happened to glance in their direction. The moment she did, she went rigid, like a pointer that had spotted a covey of quail. One by one, the other women stopped and stared. Even those who'd been moments before trying to pound the life out of each other stopped.

Fear washed over Bri, leaching the strength from her limbs. She clutched the baby a little more tightly, grabbing the blanket and covering his head.

It was too late.

The women knew she and Consuelo had their babies.

Rage contorted their features as they moved almost as one toward the edge of their yard.

"Oh my god!" Bri whispered in a suffocated voice, looking wildly around for help, protection, a weapon of any description, an avenue of escape.

Chapter Four

One of the women screamed something that sounded like a challenge or a battle cry. Bri wasn't certain which, but she doubted there was much of a distinction anyway.

Kole, she saw when she glanced around, was staring at her grimly, condemningly, she thought.

Consuelo, looking as pale as she felt, was gazing wide eyed at the savage horde.

Bri retreated closer to Consuelo, who was smaller even than she was and probably no more capable of fighting anything like these creatures than she was. It was the best she could come up with by way of 'safety in numbers', though. "They're wearing the chokers. They can't cross the line," she muttered more to herself than to Consuelo, trying to convince herself they couldn't. She wasn't as certain as she wanted to be, though, and after she and Consuelo exchanged a look, they both whirled and fled toward the door of their habitats.

The door was locked. Bri beat on it with her fist when she discovered she couldn't open it, demanding to be let in, cursing the aliens with every curse word she'd ever heard and resorted to name calling when she couldn't think of any more swear words. When she finally wore herself out enough that the mindless panic began to recede and her hand was numb and bruised from beating on the panel, she turned to cast a terrified look over her shoulder.

There was no sign of the savage alien women.

The collars, she decided, must have held.

The fear had seized her that the aliens might not use them to control the women, that they might be bent on entertaining themselves watching the alien women rip the two puny Earth women to shreds.

Too weak with relief to stand, Bri wilted to the ground and promptly burst into tears of profound relief. Her reaction startled the baby or frightened him. Bri wasn't certain which, but after uttering several noises that sounded like coughs, he set up a wail to match hers.

Surprised, Bri choked back her own tears, wiped her eyes, and looked down at the squalling infant. Sympathy and remorse filled her. She'd scared him. He hadn't let out a peep until she'd lost control. Sniffing, she began to rock him, patting his back, stroking him. He subsided after a few minutes, looking up at her with an expression that was almost accusing.

Feeling more shame for scaring him than for running like a rabbit, Bri chuckled a little huskily at his expression.

It was the first time, she realized abruptly, since she'd had him that Cory had cried. Was it reaction to fear he'd sensed in her, she wondered? Or was he just mimicking her?

Rage seemed to be an emotion the yellow tribe was familiar with, but she doubted they were more than passingly familiar with fear. Maybe the babies were taught not to cry? Or was it just that he'd been too weak before?

She frowned. It seemed important. Crying was the only way a baby could communicate fear or hunger or hurt, but he hadn't before.

A vague memory surfaced after a few moments. She remembered something she'd heard on TV about infants in an orphanage that didn't cry because nobody came.

She felt nauseous at the thought.

She'd been right, she decided. Cory had needed her. He'd needed loving care as much as he'd needed food. He hadn't been so weak and listless because the aliens hadn't tried to feed him. He'd been dying by inches because no one cared.

She cared, she realized, feeling warmth fill her chest, feeling it tighten with emotion. She loved him, as strange as it seemed even to her that she could come to love a child not even her own, a child, moreover, that wasn't even of her kind. The determination to protect him filled her, as well, but how could she do that? She couldn't defend herself against those creatures, or the aliens that had captured her.

She was as helpless as he was.

She shook that thought off. She'd never thought of herself as being helpless. She'd thought of herself as being self-sufficient. She'd been taking care of herself forever, it seemed. Her mother's health had always been bad, and it had deteriorated more and more as she'd grown up until by the time she'd graduated from high school, she'd been supporting her mother instead of the other way around.

She'd taken the skills she'd learned keeping house as a youngster and turned it into a lucrative business--homemaking for the working woman.

She'd tried not to think about her business falling apart since she'd been taken, tried not to think about the time and money she'd invested in the trip to expand into new markets. It didn't really matter if MacIntyre Prepared Home Cooking survived if she didn't. She had a half dozen employees, but they could find other jobs.

If she lived, if she managed to go home, she could start over.

As daunting as that prospect was, it beat the alternative.

And there was no point at all in thinking about it when she couldn't do anything to change the situation.

The worst thing was that she was not prepared to protect herself. She hadn't even had 'in home' training squabbling with siblings to give her a clue in self-defense. She'd always had 'authority' to run to for protection. Then she'd had money to provide protection, and common sense--like staying away from dangerous situations.

None of that was going to do her any good now.

She would've liked to think she could fall back on her intelligence, but she was certainly no 'brain' and she was up against some serious heavy weights from what she could tell of the slaver aliens.

The yellow race--maybe, maybe not. She still hadn't quite decided whether they were on an intellectual par with humans or not, but Kole seemed to be picking up both English and Spanish faster than either her or Consuelo were picking up each other's language.

That didn't say much for either her or Consuelo.

Maybe he was exceptionally bright for his race, and maybe not. He didn't strike her as being the nerd of the pack. If anything she was more inclined to think he might be a leader. He had a way about him.

In fact, now that she thought about it, he'd stalked over to the side closest to the women and bellowed something at them just as she'd whirled to run for her life.

Dismissing that for the moment, she focused on the physical threat the women represented.

Physically, as pathetic as she was, Consuelo was hopeless. The woman probably didn't weigh ninety pounds soaking wet, and she was barely five feet tall, if that. Short of biting one of those amazons in the groin, Consuelo might as well throw in the towel. Any one of those women could probably snap her in two like a dry twig.

Her own situation was only marginally better--not enough to

give her any confidence that she could hold her own.

If she could bench press a couple of hundred pounds, maybe.

Brains, that was all she had.

She was screwed.

* * * *

Kole's fury and frustration nearly got the best of him when he saw the females who referred to themselves as Earth women had two of the Hirachi infants. He'd thought all of them had died. He'd been too stunned, at first, to accept that the babies really were alive and to grasp that it could only be some of their own-- perhaps even his, though his instincts told him that neither was of his blood line--the babies were too young, he thought, to have been born *before* they left Ach, and, in any case, the Sheloni had never been known to take infants.

They would die without their mothers--without either parent-- slowly from the look of them.

Were the women too stupid to realize they were only prolonging the inevitable, torturing the innocent by making their death a lingering one? Or was it simply that it didn't matter to them because the babies were not of their own kind?

He was tempted to reach across the barrier and throttle the pink one when she refused to give over the baby, enraged as much by her defiance as he was by the way she looked at him--as if he meant the baby harm! As if *he* was in the wrong!

The woman's defiance had nearly overwhelmed his good sense. Coldness washed through him when he realized how closely he'd come to yielding to the impulse to reach across and grab her.

And he wasn't completely convinced that impulse was pure anger toward her.

Truthfully, he'd been itching to get hold of her from the moment she'd finally come close enough for him to see her really well … and throttling her had been the furthest thing from his mind.

His reaction to her revolted him and thoroughly confused him. The instinct to spawn was supposed to be an urge to propagate his species and line. He wouldn't have considered accepting an invitation from a Hirachi woman that was inferior in any way, physically or intellectually. He wanted to produce strong, intelligent, young.

Almost worse, she'd very clearly turned her nose up at *him*, not issued an invitation. There was nothing wrong with him! He'd proven he was the best of the best or he wouldn't have been chosen to lead.

Damn her!

Was that it what it was? A challenge to his ego?

Maybe, he thought, that was part of the reason--an urge to prove himself--but that didn't explain why he got hard all over every time she strolled past him. That was lust, and he, frankly, didn't think the spawning faze had anything to do with it. Spawning was the last thing on his mind, in fact. He just wanted to fuck her blind and bow legged, and to hell with the consequences.

He spent half his time trying to reason with his lust, reminding himself that children were forever and once spawned, one was stuck with them, however they turned out--even if weakened in mind, body, and spirit by mating with a female that was obviously all those things.

Except she had spirit--or she was stupid--or brave because she thought he couldn't get to her. He couldn't decide which, but the doubts didn't turn his mind from the images that had been tormenting the hell out of him of shoving those pale thighs apart and burying himself so deeply inside of her he lost his mind in the ecstasy of having her hot, tight flesh wrapped around his cock.

When she'd looked at the women threatening to tear her limb from limb if she didn't hand over the baby she'd stolen, he'd felt like all his doubts about her were confirmed. Then again, they had been threatening to dismember her and use the bloody stumps to pulverize her--and it had been all of them, not just one. It would have been more stupid if she'd been willing to take on the mob.

He'd told himself he'd ordered the women to stop because they were threatening to ruin his plan of surprise attack--and they certainly had risked it with their undisciplined fury--it infuriated him that they'd degenerated into an undisciplined mob that scarcely deserved the honor of being considered trained warriors.

But he knew if any of them had attacked, he would've protected her from them, and the realization that he was willing to side with her over his own people wasn't a pleasant thing to discover about himself.

The imprisonment, the sheer boredom, the frustrations were beginning to weaken his mind as well as his body.

* * * *

Bri did not want to go out again. She realized the moment the thought entered her mind, though, that she had unwittingly given the slaver aliens something else to use to control her--Cory. She'd been afraid to go the first time until they'd shown her the extent of pain they could cause her with the push of a button. As debilitating as that had been, as reluctant as she was to experience it even once more, she realized that balking would not only result in another lesson, she might well drop the baby and hurt him if they zapped her with that nerve paralyzing jolt again. Worse, if they hit her hard enough to knock her out, Cory would be completely helpless until she regained consciousness.

She didn't regret adopting Cory. If she had it all to do again, she would have done the same, but she very much feared that the slavers were well aware of the added leverage the baby gave them.

A quick survey of her surroundings assured her there was nothing in the room she could use as a weapon. Frustration filled her but not surprise.

She hadn't consciously looked for anything like that before, but she realized that, unconsciously, she had, because even as the thought occurred to her, her mind produced a mental inventory of the contents of the habitat and instantly registered a negative.

It wasn't just that she was too civilized to consider it, or that she was too afraid, or too unaccustomed to trying to protect herself. Nothing but a gas mask would have protected her from the slaver aliens because they used the gas to render her helpless, and nothing short of a bazooka, she was sure, would take down one of their robots.

As far as that went, she doubted much short of a bazooka would take down one of the six foot amazons that wanted her blood. A club might have made her feel better, but she wouldn't have had enough strength to wield it as a dangerous weapon even if she had one. More likely, if she did have a close encounter with one of them, they'd simply wrest the club from her and use it on her.

She didn't trust the slaver aliens, at all, but she saw no alternative to going out and wondered even as she gathered the baby and cautiously left the room if there was any way she could climb the tree in her yard if push came to shove.

Not in a rush, and not with Cory in her arms.

She didn't think there would've been any possibility of climbing with him even from the first when he'd been so thin. He was growing so rapidly now that she was having a hard time adjusting to his increasing size and weight. One would think, lifting him so many times a day, her strength would keep pace, but that wasn't the case. It was harder and harder to lift him, harder to hold and carry him for any length of time. He was getting stronger much faster than she was. He no longer lay still and passive. He lifted and held up his own head, wiggled and rolled over when she put him down, and tried to move as if he knew he could escape if only he could figure out how to use the arms and legs he could only flail ineffectually now.

He looked like a bobble head when he held up his head because he wasn't quite strong enough to hold it steady. And when he tried to move, he looked like he was imitating a swimmer, but he was getting so strong so fast she thought it wouldn't be long at all before he was sitting up by himself, and then racing around all over the place under his own steam.

Unfortunately, that could create even more problems for her, make it that much harder to protect him.

And none of that made any difference at all at this point.

On impulse, she snatched one of the curtains off the fake window as she started out the door with Cory. She'd seen women carrying babies around in a sort of sling. She doubted she could figure out how to form one with the curtain, but it was worth a try, because if she could she would have her arms free and at least stand a chance of climbing out of harm's way.

Instead of crossing the yard to 'visit' with Consuelo as she usually did, after looking around cautiously, she examined the trees growing in her yard and headed for the one with the lowest growing branches.

Spreading the curtain on the ground, she settled Cory on it and planted her hands on her hips, studying the tree. She'd never climbed a tree before in her life. Her mother had hardly even let her out of the house--when she was really young because her mother was afraid she'd get hurt, or pick up germs. Later, her mother had kept her close because she just wasn't physically able to chase her around the yard and as she grew older, because she was afraid a psycho would snatch her.

How hard could it be? Children climbed trees.

The first time she fell on her ass, Cory's eyes widened for a split second and then he laughed.

Momentarily distracted by the sound, Bri turned to stare at him blankly for a split second before pleasure suffused her. Grinning like an idiot, she rolled over and crawled to him, pushing her face close to his and rubbing nose to nose. "Are you laughing at me, you bad old boy?" she demanded teasingly.

He stared back at her wide eyed for a moment and finally grinned up at her, boxing her face with his fists and then grabbing two fistfuls of hair and trying to bite her nose.

She disentangled his fingers from her hair, got up, dusted herself off, and surveyed the tree again. Grasping the branch firmly with one hand, she found a hold along the bark of the trunk with the other and tried to lift herself with her arms as she placed a foot against the trunk to push up. That time she almost managed to lift herself high enough to get a more secure hold before she slipped and fell.

Cory laughed as she pin-wheeled her arms trying to catch her balance, lost the battle, and sat backwards on the ground hard enough to jar every tooth in her head. She looked at him ruefully, but his giggle was infectious, and she couldn't help but chuckle. "I'm glad you think this is so funny, Mr. Man."

Getting to her feet once more, she studied the tree again and finally walked all the way around it looking for a better place to try. The third time, she tried grabbing the limb with both hands and walking up the trunk while she supported herself with her arms. It worked after a fashion, but she discovered she was too close to the trunk to throw her legs over.

Deciding she needed just a little more distance from the trunk, she lowered herself carefully to the ground, backed up a step, and grabbed the limb again. This time, she managed to get one leg over the branch. She hung like that for several moments, trying to gather the strength to pull herself up.

It was at that moment that she realized two things.

Kole was standing at the very edge of his yard staring straight at her with a look of intense concentration on his face.

And her gown, which was all in the world she had between her and decency, was rucked up almost to her waist and billowed beneath her.

If she'd set out to fan her coochie in his face, she couldn't have done a better job of it. She was in such a rush to get down, she damned near fell. She *did* succeed in raking the hide off her thigh with the rough bark. Putting her back to Kole, she lifted her gown once she was on her feet again and examined the scrape on her thigh.

Cory, she saw when she glanced at him again, was looking doubtful, as if trying to decide whether he should laugh or cry at her latest antic. She forced a smile, albeit a wry one. "Ok, that's enough for today," she told him, bending to gather him up.

Her hands were almost as scraped up and sore as her leg. Her palms burned as she caught him to her and looked for Consuelo, studiously ignoring Kole. Seeing that Consuelo was sitting next to the line, she realized the other women must not have been allowed outside, and she trudged across the yard to settle across from the woman.

"Why?" Consuelo asked, pointing toward the tree as soon as she'd settled Cory on the ground beside her and lifted her palms to examine them.

Bri rolled her eyes, thought it over for a moment, and finally merely pointed toward the habitat that housed the other women.

Consuelo nodded then frowned. "No climb."

"I noticed that," Bri said dryly. "I thought I could. I wonder if I could climb the habitat any better?" she asked idly, twisting around to study it. One look assured her she had even less chance of that, though. The thing was virtually smooth and seamless on the outside, as if it had been shaped in a one piece form. "Maybe I could drag a chair out of the habitat?" she added speculatively as she picked up the curtain she'd filched and examined it thoughtfully.

"Climb?" Consuelo asked.

Bri lowered the curtain panel and stared at Consuelo blankly. Seeing she was pointing at the panel she decided Consuelo was asking if she intended to use the material to form a rope. She hadn't thought of it. After studying the panel and then turning to study the tree, though, she finally shook her head. "No. If I can't climb without it I don't think it would help to have a rope. The problem isn't that I can't reach. The problem is, I'm not strong enough to pull myself up. I don't think even pure terror would lend me enough strength to drag my ass up that damned tree. I brought this for the baby.",

Consuelo stared at her uncomprehendingly. "*Ropa para niño?*"

Bri's jaw dropped to half mast. "Why would I want a rope for the baby?" she demanded indignantly.

It was Consuelo's turn to look dumbfounded. After studying it over for several moments she started laughing. "No rope. *Ropa.*" She cast around for a moment and finally plucked at her gown.

Bri frowned. "Oh! Ropa means … like a gown?" She shook her head, then took the panel and looped it around her shoulders. "To hold him," she explained, trying to get her point across with hand and arm motions.

Consuelo looked at her doubtfully, but she wasn't certain whether that meant she hadn't exactly understood or she doubted Bri could do it. Shrugging, she focused on trying to figure out a way to knot the thing to form a sling that would hold the baby securely while leaving her arms free--not that that was going to help her if she couldn't figure out how to climb the damned tree.

She'd envisioned it as a defensive position where a club might actually do her some good. If she could climb, they probably could, too, but she thought if she could get high enough the thin branches might not support their weight and then, if she had a club, and they could only come at her one at the time, she could use the club to beat them loose.

It wasn't a wonderful thought, but she sure as hell didn't have a chance of defending herself against them any other way that she could see.

"*Ropa*," she repeated, trying to roll her 'r' the way Consuelo had. "Gown-*ropa*, gown-*ropa*. It sounded like robe so she decided she must have the translation right. "Woman," she said to Consuelo while she worked, then lifted her head and pointed to Consuelo. "Woman."

"*Madre*," Consuelo came back.

Bri looked at her doubtfully. "Woman is *madre* in Spanish?"

Consuelo nodded vigorously, but Bri still felt doubtful. She pointed at Kole without looking at him. "Man--woman--woman. Man--*madre*--*madre*?"

Consuelo looked surprised and then chuckled. "No, no." She formed a cradle with her arms. "*Madre*."

"Oh god!" Bri exclaimed covering her face. "At this rate I'm going to fucking *die* of old age before I ever manage a decent conversation! And a hell of a conversation its going to be at that if half the words I learn mean something completely different from what I'd trying to say, damn it!"

A commiserating expression flickered across Consuelo's face, but she didn't look particularly distressed about the fact that they were the only damned humans on the fucking ship and couldn't even talk to each other. *Why* hadn't she learned Spanish in school?

Because it hadn't occurred to her that she might ever *need* it!

If Consuelo had known even a little English, or she a little Spanish, they would've at least known when they were on the right track! As it was, they were only guessing they understood each other.

"Shit!"

"*Mierda*!"

Bri's head snapped up from what she was doing, and she burst out laughing.

Consuelo looked a little disconcerted and embarrassed, but she chuckled, too.

The expression on Consuelo's face was enough to set her off again just when she thought she'd mastered the urge to laugh. "I suppose it says something about the human race that there are probably more people that can curse in a half dozen different languages than there are who can carry on a conversation in those same languages," she said wryly. "I'm not sure what--That we like being able to express our displeasure?"

Shaking her head, she went back to the lessons, pointing to first one thing and then another and saying the word for it, and then listening and carefully repeating the translation. She wasn't sure how helpful it was, besides passing the time and allowing her and Consuelo to stab at communication, but at least it made her feel as if she was making progress and there was less room for error in learning the words for nouns they could both look at and verify.

When she'd finished knotting the length of material into something that looked useable, she settled it over one shoulder and under her other arm, tugged at it to make certain the knots would hold, and then picked Cory up and carefully arranged him in the sling she'd made.

The minute she settled him, he flung both arms and legs out and went rigid, as if he felt like he was falling.

Whether it would work or not was immaterial if Cory didn't feel secure in it. She gathered him in her arms to soothe him when he let out a panicked wail.

"Bri!"

Frowning, Bri responded to Kole's call before she could stop herself, her head swiveling toward the sound of his voice.

Chapter Five

Kole held out his hands. "Give de ting."

Bri glared at him distrustfully and held Cory tighter. "Hell no!"

His lips tightened. "No *niño. Ting--ropa.*"

Bri gaped at him in outrage. "My gown?" she demanded indignantly. "I don't think so!"

She could almost hear him grinding his teeth. Using his hands, he motioned from shoulder to waist and then looped his arms as Consuelo had. It dawned on Bri fairly quickly that he wanted the sling she'd made. She glanced down at it and then at him, debating, but finally shrugged inwardly. Cory hated it. Sighing, she settled Cory on the ground again and pulled the sling off. "The sling?" she asked, holding it up.

He nodded. "Sling, yes, si."

Mildly annoyed that he was obviously learning her language a lot faster than she was learning Spanish, she tossed it to him.

When he'd caught it, he untied the knots she'd made, smoothed it, studied it, and then began to rip strips off.

The play of muscles in his arms, chest, and shoulders as he shredded the thing mesmerized her, sending her into a sort of trance of fascination that she didn't emerge from until she discovered that he was staring back at her, grinning.

Blood flooded her cheeks. Wrenching her gaze from him, she glared at Consuelo, who was giving her a knowing look.

"Bri?"

She sent him a narrow eyed glare. "What?"

He made a motion with his hand over his face and neck. "What this?"

"You are so funny!" she snapped, feeling the blush that had begun to recede wash back into her cheeks.

He chuckled. "That. Change color. Can do this all over?"

His chuckle brought her head around again with a jolt. He was actually sort of handsome when he smiled, she realized vaguely. Maybe a little more than sort of. As it dawned on her what he'd asked, though, her eyes narrowed suspiciously. Was he teasing? Or making fun of her?

It was strange to think of an alien teasing. For that matter, it was strange to think he might be making fun of her. Weren't those exclusively human traits?

How conceited!

It still seemed peculiar, and she couldn't entirely credit it. Maybe she was attributing human traits to him only because it was what she was used to?

Not that she was *used* to being teased, but she'd observed that sort of exchange between other people. "No, I can't," she said finally.

"Just face?"

This time the blush wasn't as pronounced. She hoped. She gave him a look and then pointedly ignored him.

"What mean this?"

He sounded curious this time, but she refused to look directly at him, merely glancing at him out of the corner of her eye.

Ignoring her refusal to acknowledge him, he gestured toward the tree. "Climb tree." He made a falling motion with his hand. "Face color. Look at Kole, face color. Look at woman, no color," he ended, jabbing a finger in the direction of the Amazon enclosure.

Bri couldn't stand it anymore. She turned to glare at him. "You *are* observant!" she said testily.

He looked confused.

She pointed to her eyes and then made a sweeping gesture. "You see everything."

He nodded. "Observant," he said seriously and then a slow grin dawned. "See *tup* when Bri climb tree," he agreed good humouredly, staring pointedly at her crotch. "Eyes good."

Bri didn't have any trouble at all understanding what he was getting at. Her jaw dropped with indignation. "You *looked?*" she demanded angrily, knowing he had because she'd seen him looking at her.

His eyes still gleamed with amusement, but his expression changed subtly, became almost predatory and rife with carnal hunger. "Like look Bri."

Liked looking at *her*? Or her--*tup*?

His expression said both.

A distinctly sensual warmth washed over her, but so, too, did uneasiness. She looked away from him. Consuelo, she saw, was dividing a knowing look between them. Irritation flooded her. She could see Consuelo thought she was flirting with the big, dumb brute.

As *if!*

She frowned. Was he flirting with her, she wondered, sending a sideways glance in his direction? Remembering what had started the conversation, she wondered about that, too. He seemed … fascinated with the way her color changed with her emotions. Did they not blush? Or turn pale with fear? She didn't remember noticing his color fluctuating, now that she thought about it. Even when he seemed angry, she didn't remember his skin darkening.

Lucky them!

It dawned on her that, despite the broken English and the Spanish words he'd thrown in and even some words from his own language--at least one--she hadn't had any real trouble following what he was saying.

Assuming she actually *had* and hadn't misinterpreted anything, but she didn't think she had.

She realized she couldn't delude herself anymore with the comforting thought that she was better 'armed' intellectually than the yellow race, at least. Kole wasn't dumb. He might be a big brute, but he wasn't a big, *dumb* brute--even if he did have that 'Me Tarzan, you Jane' sort of lingo going on. At least he could communicate his meaning, and some fairly complex meanings, at that. She and Consuelo were still struggling with one and two word sentences, damn it all!

That sucked a big hairy one! She didn't *want* to talk to Kole, didn't want to encourage him in any way. He still scared the shit out of her--not as much as he had, but that was only because she'd grown used to his size, a little, and she knew he couldn't reach her. As long as she was careful to stay out of range, he couldn't grab her and snatch her across the boundary.

The thought that he seemed to want to pretty badly was unnerving to say the very least. She didn't think she'd misinterpreted *that*! She didn't want anything *that* big trying to hump her! For all she knew, he could be hiding *anything* in those breeches! She'd been very careful not to look in that direction for fear she might give him the idea that she was interested in finding out.

She was afraid, though, that there was a real possibility that that wasn't something that weighed heavily upon him--whether or not she was willing, eager, or completely opposed to the idea.

It seemed inescapable that he hailed from an intelligent species, a tribe at least as smart, and maybe smarter than her own, or at least her, but it seemed equally indisputable, given what she'd seen of the behavior of their women, that they were, indeed, violent, war-like, barbaric compared to her own kind--be humans ever so prone to violence themselves.

A shiver skated down her spine. "I think I'll go back," she muttered to no one in particular. "It must be about time anyway."

The material landed in her lap even as she made to rise. She aborted the movement and picked it up to examine it, flicking a glance at Kole as she did so. She saw when she returned her attention to the piece that he'd fashioned something far more likely to work than the sling she'd tried. A rectangular piece formed a pocket of sorts with two holes at the bottom that she realized were for Cory's legs. He'd torn the remainder into narrow strips and tied them to form straps. After studying it for several moments, she got to her knees and slipped the baby into the pouch and then sat back on her knees with him clutched against her chest, trying to adjust the straps.

It took some trial and error, but Cory seemed to feel safe and comfortable when she'd finished, and most of his weight was supported by her shoulders and back. It would take some adjusting, she decided, before she could actually carry him that way leaving her arms free, but it was close.

Reluctantly, she lifted her gaze to meet Kole's. "Thank you," she said uncomfortably, looking away almost at once. She hesitated, trying to think of something else to say and finally turned away with a sense of relief when the buzzer sounded, hurrying back to her habitat.

She paused at the door, though, and turned to look back.

Kole was still standing at the edge of his yard, watching her.

* * * *

The women, Bri decided, must have been housed in that one habitat the entire time she'd been on the alien ship. There was no sense of movement in the ship, like there would've been in a car, plane, or train, so she wasn't certain if they were still where they had been when they had taken her or not, but it seemed reasonable that they would've had all the people of the yellow tribe when they'd come for her. She didn't know how old Cory was, but it seemed to her that it must be several months, at least, which suggested as much--maybe he'd even been conceived after they'd taken the yellow tribesmen?

So why had they decided to let the women out that day when they had been keeping them confined when everyone else was out? And since they hadn't done it before, nor any time in the week since, did that mean they'd decided it wasn't a good idea?

Did that mean she was safe from them?

Or were they all bound for the same place?

They wouldn't have collected so many, she didn't think, just for study. They must have plans for them, a destination in mind, and that meant she was probably going to find herself face to face with those women--and the men--at some point.

She liked the idea that, maybe, they had something else in mind for her and Consuelo, or at least better than the idea that they were all going to be dumped off together, but she couldn't convince herself of it.

It *had* occurred to her that the women might have been furious because she and Consuelo had their babies. She would've empathized more with a mother's fury, though, if not for the condition of the babies when she and Consuelo had gotten them--which might be the fault of the aliens, not the women, except for the suggestion that Kole had made that it would be better off dead than a slave.

Broken English or not, she knew she'd understood that much.

There was always a chance that she'd been wrong to believe he meant the baby harm, that he'd merely been trying to tell her that what the aliens had in mind would be far worse, but she wasn't about to chance it.

She couldn't hand Cory over to them, not if there was any chance at all that they believed strongly enough in 'death before slavery' to take it upon themselves to end it for him.

How could she protect him, she worried? How?

She was no match for even one of those women let alone the men! And she had a bad feeling that she wouldn't get the chance of one-on-one even if that hadn't been the case. They had *all* seemed pretty stirred up, and there was no doubt in her mind at the time that, if they could've breached the barrier, they would all have come after her.

Fear might have lent her enough speed to outrun them on her own--which she doubted--but she certainly couldn't if she was carrying the baby.

It would be unthinkable to abandon him, even if they were his people when she didn't trust them not to harm him, and even so, she doubted it would satisfy them. They'd seemed pretty intent on having her blood.

Strength training seemed like a woefully inadequate defense, but Bri decided it couldn't hurt even if she was fairly certain the possibility of developing enough strength to actually hold her own against any of the yellow tribe members was zilch. She'd had no idea just how weak she was because she'd never needed to concern herself about it before. Except for the short period before her mother's death when she had grown too weak to get around without help, her natural born strength had been enough to do the things she needed to do--and she had *not* wanted to look like the women body builders she'd seen in magazines.

She knew though, that although everyone was not created equal, anyone who worked at it could increase their strength. She'd read that, and as she was, she was too weak even to have a chance to flee or to climb out of harm's way.

She might be able to outwit them and she might not. She couldn't do anything about that, though, unless it was utilizing her time to try to formulate a plan that she could put into motion without having to think at the moment of truth--like the idea about the tree.

Try though she might to come up with anything better, she couldn't. If she couldn't hope to outrun them, or to overpower them, she would need an advantage like that, something that would not only make it impossible for them to gang up on her but would also give her the advantage of superior position. However strong they might be, and well trained in fighting, she didn't think they'd be able to withstand being beat on the head.

It occurred to her that she might be able to move faster--at least for short spurts, like dodging. Her height, or lack thereof, could give her some advantage over them if she used it to evade them. For that matter, her smaller size would make it possible for her to get into a space too small for them.

That could be a disadvantage, too, though, as in she could be trapped.

And a tree could be cut down, or pushed down, or they could just shake her loose.

None of those thoughts comforted her. They did, in point of fact, undermine her morale until it was difficult even to consider possibilities.

The only alternative to figuring out a way to take care of herself that occurred to her, though, was the possibility of picking the biggest, baddest mother fucker of the lot and convincing him to beat the others off of her.

She wasn't at all certain she could do that first off because she hadn't even had that much experience with men of her own kind, and none of her handful of experiences had led to a guy falling madly in love with her. Or, in fact, becoming fond enough of her to let go of their freedom, or even much of their hard earned cash for her pleasure or entertainment--certainly not enough for them to consider protecting her at risk to themselves.

She thought Kole wouldn't mind fucking her senseless if he could get hold of her, but that didn't mean he'd be willing to fight his own kind to protect her. The only thing that *might* convince him to try to do that would be an emotional attachment to her, and she not only didn't know how to go about getting him to develop an attachment, she wasn't sure he was capable of it.

Maybe she didn't understand the yellow tribe as well as she thought she did--there was a hell of a lot of room for error since all she could really do was watch them--but she had the distinct feeling that they weren't really all that emotionally attached to each other, and that didn't bode well for theoretical attachments to beings that were different.

Beyond that, she couldn't even try without being way more intimate with one than she wanted to be. Even if she'd been a natural borne flirt, even if she'd had enough experience with Earth men to know how to dangle the carrot to get them to dance without actually *giving* them the carrot, she had a feeling it wouldn't work with one of them. If she waved coochie in their face to use as an enticement, she thought it probable they'd just throw her down and fuck her to death.

It wasn't something she wanted to try. She knew that.

She would have to try to keep her distance from Kole, she decided--not talk to him--not encourage him at all. She had a feeling he wasn't struggling to communicate with her just because he was bored and needed human contact--or the contact of another being--as badly as she did. She was certainly of no use to him beyond a female body he could expend himself on.

It seemed to follow, then, that he was trying to 'gentle' her, trying to convince her he wasn't dangerous so she'd let her guard down and he could get hold of her.

Once she'd decided on a course of action, Bri felt better in spite of the nagging doubts that continued to plague her. It was comforting to at least feel like she was doing something that might make a difference.

She couldn't move the chair. She finally decided that it must be bolted down. After surveying the room, she tried the 'TV', but it, too, was immovable. Either the slaver aliens had done it to keep her from moving anything or, possibly, to keep everything from flying around when they hit turbulence--which would mean the ship *did* take off and land on land since she didn't think there was any sort of turbulence in space.

Irritated as she was, she tried to brush it off. It wasn't like she was likely to get the chance to find something to help her in an emergency situation. She'd have to be able to climb without help.

Over the next week, instead of going to sit to try to make conversation, she walked, round and round until she was huffing for breath, paused long enough for her breathing to even out and walked some more. It gave her an excuse to avoid Kole without seeming to, and by the end of the week she had progressed to the point that she didn't have to stop to rest as often. The carrier for the baby was not only awkward, though, Cory pressed so heavily against her chest that he made it harder for her to breathe when she was struggling for breath.

He didn't like it when she shifted the carrier to her back, at least not when he was facing outward. She'd thought he would like that since he could look around, but apparently it made him feel like he was going to fall. When she turned him to face her back, though, he nearly pulled her bald besides choking on her hair, which he stuffed in his mouth.

She tore off a strip of material long enough to tie her hair up high on her head and twisted it into a ball, securing it with another strip and then adjusted the carrier to hold him high enough on her back so that he could peer over her shoulder.

The first week she carried him like that was pure agony. It felt as if her spine was going to buckle, but it didn't hurt as much the second week. Encouraged, she set herself a goal of being able to circumnavigate the entire yard twice before stopping to rest and then building up to a jog, and then a run.

Consuelo looked so abandoned and dispirited when she stopped going to sit with her that after a week she couldn't ignore it anymore. As she passed near Consuelo, her back to Kole, she caught the other woman's eye and motioned for her to follow. Perking up at once, Consuelo glanced toward Kole as she got to her feet and then turned to keep pace with Bri as she followed the line to the far corner. "You need to walk," she told Consuelo in a low voice, using her fingers to imitate a walking motion.

Consuelo seemed to grasp the walking part, but Bri could see she didn't know why Bri was so determined to walk.

God! It was so frustrating not being able to just talk to explain things! Especially when she needed to try to get across a warning that was complex, fears, speculation. She lifted her arms, flexing them like a body builder showing off their muscles.

Consuelo snickered at the puny muscles in Bri's arms. Her smile faded as Bri made a motion toward the aliens, though, and she lifted her hand high above her head to point out how much bigger they were. She used her fingers on both hands to act out a little skit, two people running, the one in front screaming 'eke'. A smile flickered over Consuelo's face but quickly died, a look of fear widening her eyes.

She was pretty sure Consuelo had gotten the general idea when she cut loose with a string of Spanish that sounded like a dozen questions colliding. Unfortunately, she didn't know what the questions were and couldn't have answered them anyway. She had to fall back on the 'Tarzan/Jane' language of grunting, motioning, and acting out.

"I think we're in serious trouble," she said finally in a low, frightened voice, hoping Consuelo could understand at least some of the words, or the urgency behind them. "I think the ones who took us mean to put us out together--with those huge aliens, and they don't seem to like us much. If they don't protect us from them, we're going to have to run for our lives."

She was almost sorry she'd even tried to warn Consuelo because the woman looked absolutely terrified--which meant she'd gotten the general idea.

Maybe she shouldn't have tried to warn her? What if she'd scared the poor thing half out of her wits and she was wrong?

She shook the thought off. Better to prepare for the worst than just to hope for the best. She might not have much experience of the 'street wise' kind, but she hadn't exactly had a cushy life. In her experience, anything that could go horribly wrong usually did.

For all her diminutive size, Consuelo was a lot stronger than she looked and in better shape, Bri thought wryly, than she was. As soon as the woman grasped the situation, she took to walking, as well--except she was jogging.

Dismayed to discover even Consuelo was better equipped than she was, Bri ignored the doubts clamoring in her mind and pushed herself harder.

Unfortunately, despite the great effort Bri had gone to to make sure Kole could neither hear her conversation, nor see the hand motions she'd added to try to get her point across, it seemed to her that he caught on really quickly to what she and Consuelo were doing.

He'd watched them thoughtfully at first, even looking vaguely amused at their antics, but his expression had turned speculative fairly quickly.

As unnerving as the thought was that he seemed to have figured out the game plan, that wasn't the worst of it.

The slavers figured it out, too.

Chapter Six

Strength, speed, agility--Bri was surprised to discover that she had more of all three naturally than she'd thought she possessed--a hell of a lot less than she needed, but she decided she wasn't hopeless. She still deeply regretted that she hadn't spent more of her life previously in being in the best shape she could be. She'd watched her weight, but she hadn't worried about anything but keeping a neat figure and good grooming and trying to stay healthy because she didn't want to be sickly like her mother--because she couldn't *afford* it, financially or otherwise. Unlike her mother, who'd had *her*, she had no one to take care of her.

After the first couple of weeks, she'd gone back to trying to climb the tree again, but this time she'd focused on just trying to pull herself up over and over, trying to build up her upper body strength. Her legs were strong, but she couldn't very well push herself up the damned tree. She needed strength in her hands, her arms, and her back and chest.

Mindful of the view she'd inadvertently given Kole before and his interest in that direction, she'd knotted the back and front of the gown together between her legs before she tried to climb up again. Unfortunately, it wasn't really enough to preserve her modesty very well, and the knot in the sensitive crotch area was downright painful when she finally managed to sling her leg over that first branch and haul her heavy ass up on top.

It brought tears to her eyes. Trying to rub the sting away, she glanced down at Cory, whom she'd left lying of the ground beneath the tree, and discovered he'd turned over and was trying to wiggle off the 'blanket' she'd spread out for him. She was going to have to master this soon, and with him on her back, she realized, or he would be able to wander off while she was climbing.

She didn't even want to *think* about what might happen to him if he managed to cross the boundary before she could catch him.

She hadn't meant to do more than get over the first hurdle, but that thought encouraged her to push herself further.

She had her back to the trunk. After trying to solve her dilemma for several moments, she finally concluded that she was going to have to 'mount' the limb differently if she wanted to climb higher. Sighing, she got down again, dragged Cory back to the middle of the blanket, and faced the challenge again, sifting scenarios in her mind.

Reversing directions, she gripped the limb close to the trunk, but she quickly discovered that she wasn't strong enough to just lift her lower body and grip the limb with her legs.

Dropping to the ground again, she blew on her burning palms until they stopped throbbing and went up the same way she had the first time, hung beneath the limb for several moments and then struggled up on top of it, trying to ignore the knot digging into her sensitive cleft when she sat on it.

There was another limb, she knew, a few feet above her head. Vertigo hit her when she tried to look up, though. When the dizziness had passed and she'd managed to stay on the limb, she pushed back until her back was against the trunk and felt around blindly until she managed to catch a hold on the limb above her. Feeling a little more secure, she released her death grip on the limb beneath her and caught another hold above her head and then brought her legs up one by one and used them to push her upward.

She was shaking so badly she almost fell twice executing the maneuver, but she managed to turn as she went up and the move from the second limb to the third was a little easier.

She was weak with exertion and fear by the time she managed to get to the top, but triumphant--until she looked around.

One of the dreaded many legged bots had appeared, and it was heading straight for her. Uttering a sharp squeak of fear, Bri reversed directions with more haste than caution and scrambled down the tree as quickly as she could. The fear and probably her weakness cost her. She slipped about half of the distance down, scraping the hide off her hands, arms, elbows, and knees as she clawed to catch herself, and lost her grip altogether before she could drop from the last limb. She hit the ground so hard it gave her whiplash, knocked the breath out of her, and jarred every tooth in her head. Ordinarily, that would have been the end of it, but fear was driving her, and she scrambled in a crab walk toward Cory before she had even managed to catch her breath or gather her wits.

Grabbing him up, she looked around frantically for the bot, saw it was nearly upon her and fled, hoping against hope that they'd call it off when they saw she'd come down from the tree. They didn't. The next time she looked back it was virtually on her heels and reaching for her.

Uttering a scream, she ducked, reversed directions, and ran between the thing's legs. It halted abruptly, seemed to hesitate, and then turned. The 'confusion' she'd managed didn't give her much in the way of leeway, though. She gained a little distance, enough to dodge it, but the thing was between her and the habitat, even if she could get inside.

Defeat settled in her. She wasn't going to be able to evade the damned thing. She couldn't because she was hemmed in by the boundaries. Without consciously making a decision, she locked her arms around the baby, whirled, and dashed straight toward Kole.

The jolt that went through her when she broke the barrier snatched the breath from her lungs. Darkness followed like a light switch had been flipped. She caught a split second image of Kole's face, fought the darkness and paralyzing muscle spasms to hold onto Cory, and then nothingness.

Cory's panicked wails of distress ripped through her mind before awareness of anything else. Her arms tightened instinctively, and she realized with relief that she'd managed to hold on to him in spite of everything.

The sensation of movement layered over the wailing, and then pain. It took her several moments to pinpoint the pain because it was slamming into her from so many directions at once.

She was being dragged, she realized even as she managed to open her eyes. Part of the pain was friction from being dragged, part from the metal clamped around her ankles, and part from the fall down the tree.

Dimly, she recalled that she'd led the damned robot to Kole. She didn't know why she'd done that. If she'd been able to think at all she would've realized he was no more capable of fighting the thing than she was. He had no weapon. The robot couldn't feel pain.

Remorse settled in a knot in her stomach, and she struggled to twist around enough to try to look to see if Kole had been hurt. She couldn't manage more than a glimpse, but it was enough to see he *had* been hurt, whether from trying to protect her, or just fend the thing off, or because he'd just felt like trying to take it down, she had no idea, but she saw him crumpled on the ground and bleeding near the wall of his habitat, as if he'd been flung there.

He wasn't moving that she could see. She couldn't tell if he was dead or just unconscious, but a wave of nausea washed over her as it flickered through her mind that he might be dead.

Trying not to think about the possibility that she'd gotten him killed, she focused on trying to sooth Cory. She'd didn't know if he was hurt or just scared, but he responded to her attempts to quiet him--or he had just exhausted himself--she hoped it was the former.

When the bot had dragged her to her room it more or less scooped her up and shoved her in.

It was too big to get inside, she noted absently, more focused on trying to catch herself without dropping the baby or falling on him.

When the door had closed and locked behind her, she stood shakily for a moment more and finally wilted to the floor. Settling Cory on the floor in front of her, because she was too weak with reaction to continue holding him, she examined him carefully for injury. She found a couple of scratches and a pretty nasty looking bruise on one cheek, but he seemed to be relatively unscathed.

She wished she could say the same for herself. Her entire body hurt. She wanted nothing more at the moment than the chance to doctor her wounds, but Cory had been through a traumatic experience, and he needed more soothing. Finally, she managed to get him to sleep, settled him carefully in the center of the platform bed, and then went into the bathroom to try to clean her scrapes and scratches.

As poor as the reflecting surface of the 'mirror' was, she could see she looked like hell. Her hair had been torn from the strip she'd used to tie it up and was a tangled mess filled with dirt and everything else small enough to catch in it. Her face was bruised and scratched. Her gown had been torn half off of her--probably, she realized, when the bot had tried to catch her and managed only to grasp the material--or maybe from being dragged across the yard, or when she'd slipped climbing down from the tree. Otherwise, she had scrapes and cuts and bruises all over the parts of her body she could see, and probably the parts she couldn't see if the pain was any indication.

She bathed off the dirt and blood, washed her hair and untangled it. She couldn't do anything about the gown, so she simply discarded it. Still weak from her ordeal, she returned to the main room, lay down beside Cory, and tried to ignore both the pain and the anxious thoughts running through her mind, and eventually managed to sleep.

She was confined for almost a week, not allowed to go out at all.

As punishments went, she thought that wasn't too bad. She was in no shape to try to exercise the first few days anyway. In fact, she discovered when she woke up that she could barely move and not at all without a great deal of pain. It was probably just as well that she *had* to move because Cory needed to be tended. Otherwise, she might have been tempted to do nothing but lay around. As it was, she thought she managed to work the soreness from her muscles more quickly than she would have otherwise.

By the third day, she was chafing at not being able to go out. Since there was nothing she could do about it, and she had no idea how long she might be confined, she got on the floor and did all of the exercises she could remember over and over until she was exhausted, rested until she felt like she could do more, and repeated them.

She was stronger than she had been. She might still be weak compared to the Amazon Hirachi, but she'd managed to climb the tree. She'd managed to outmaneuver the bot, at least briefly. As terrifying, and painful, as the experience had been, she felt heartened that she had made progress and might stand a chance of surviving.

They came for her on the fifth night for the first time in over a month. There would've been no way to prevent it even if she'd been expecting it, but she was taken completely by surprise.

The hissing sound of the gas wakened her. Instinctively, she gathered Cory closer, fighting the effects of the gas to try to hold on to him. She succeeded after a fashion, but once she reached the room they simply took him from her.

She struggled inwardly anyway, trying to focus her mind to *make* her body cooperate.

* * * *

Kole made no attempt to resist when the *Sheloni* sent their droid to fetch him. He had expected it since he had pitted himself against the thing and received far more damage to himself than he had been able to inflict. His ribs still hurt, and he suspected he had cracked at least one when the thing had flung him away.

His apathy had little to do with the injury, however. He had not attempted to pit himself against one of their machines since the *Sheloni* had first captured him, and he had discovered that the newer droids were far more powerful than the ones they had brought to his world before. Those earlier droids had been difficult to disable, but not impossible. These seemed virtually indestructible, and he had contained his fury and frustration when he'd failed to destroy the thing that had captured him. If his strength was not enough to destroy or at least disable it, he had no intention of allowing his anger to drive him to pound against it in mindless, useless fury. He would have to find another way to destroy the things, study it, find a weakness.

There had to be one. There always was, because the *Sheloni* were arrogant bastards, certain of their superiority in the scheme of things.

And, aside from their physical frailty, their arrogance was probably their only weakness … unless it was their greed.

It was that greed that prompted them to ensure their slaves arrived at their destination in excellent condition--not any sense of right or wrong, not sympathy for any creature they believed inferior to them.

They would send a droid to fetch him to be examined to make certain he hadn't been permanently damaged.

And fortunately he hadn't been. Anyone who became too ill, or who was injured in any way not easily fixed, was destroyed.

He wasn't particularly afraid of dying. In some ways it would almost be more welcome than living as their slave, toiling for them on whatever godforsaken cosmic ball of dirt they found that contained the mineral so precious to them. He wanted, with every fiber of his being, however, to destroy the *Sheloni*, and as hopeless as that task seemed whenever he allowed himself to dwell on it, he wasn't ready to simply give up.

They'd been enslaving his people for generations. The first *Sheloni* had arrived on his world as 'friends'. In exchange for helping the *Hirachi* advance their technology, the *Sheloni* had asked for help in mining their precious mineral. He supposed it could be said that it was their own greed that had resulted in the downfall of his people, the *Hirachi*, the destruction of the world as they'd known it, the breakdown of their society that had thrown them backwards much further than the technology they had so anxiously sought had taken them forward.

The *Sheloni* were cold blooded bastards, but they were clever manipulators. It was disgusting how easily they'd turned the *Hirachi* kingdoms against one another, favoring one above another until they had them fighting among themselves and then handing them the technology to cripple themselves with. Once they'd killed off half their population, destroyed their cities, and lost the technology that supported their civilization, they'd had no recourse except to fall back on their instincts for survival. In three generations they'd gone from a civilized people to barbarians using sticks, and rocks, and clubs to defend themselves and their territory, to exist.

With no way to throw off the yoke they'd allowed the *Sheloni* to place around their necks, they'd become grimly determined to thwart the *Sheloni* in any way they were able and those ways were pathetically few--in fact there was only one thing they had managed that had had any effect at all.

They'd refused to procreate. If they couldn't prevent the *Sheloni* from enslaving them, from stealing their young to be reared as slaves, they could at least refuse to bring more slaves into the world for the bastards to use.

That only worked while they still had the freedom to choose, though. Once the *Sheloni* captured them, the women no longer had control of their own bodies, or access to the herbs they used to prevent or abort a pregnancy.

Many had chosen ritual suicide to keep from bringing a child into the world, and, when even that option was denied them, they had killed their newborns.

And then the *Sheloni* had begun taking the infants.

The females they destroyed themselves. They had tried to cultivate the males since those were the most useful to them. They had not been able to make the infants thrive, however. Without their mothers, the infants had grown weaker and weaker despite everything the *Sheloni* could do and died a slow death instead of the quick death the others had had.

Deep down, Kole had known from the moment he first saw the alien females that the *Sheloni* had decided on a new tactic.

And he had still been inexplicably drawn despite his certainty that the *Sheloni* would use them against the *Hirachi*, despite the strange coloring of their skin and hair, drawn particularly to the pink one with the strange reddish brown hair.

It still fascinated him that these tiny beings looked so much like the *Hirachi*.

It said a lot for the ruthless determination of the *Sheloni* that they'd searched the cosmos until they found a world that had beings so similar to the *Hirachi*.

When had they found them? And were they, even now, systematically destroying their world as the *Sheloni* had destroyed *Ach*?

There was no chance that they would be left in peace, replaced by this weaker race of people, he decided. If the females were any indication, and he was certain they were, then it was doubtful the males would be as big and strong even as *Hirachi* females.

They would not be as useful to them, therefore they were safe from the machinations of the *Sheloni*.

Why take the females then?

In spite of their strangeness, they were pretty creatures in a way-- in the way that a flower was pretty--and just as fragile he was certain and virtually useless as slaves.

The *Sheloni* could not think they could breed the *Hirachi* with these weak creatures, surely? Even if they did, the offspring could not help but be less.

But any offspring, if it survived, would still likely be stronger than the female's race.

What would make the *Sheloni* think that the *Hirachi* males, who had grimly denied their manhood and shunned their own beautiful women to prevent bearing offspring, would not be able to resist these females?

Maybe it was their arrogance? Maybe they thought the *Hirachi* were too stupid to realize that they would not introduce the females unless it was possible to breed with them? Maybe they thought the *Hirachi* males, having been denied access to any female at all for so long, couldn't control their needs if a female was dangled in front of them? Especially if the female was not *Hirachi* and therefore could not breed more *Hirachi* for slaves?

Unfortunately, once he had allowed those thoughts into his mind, he could not shake them. Partly, he knew, it was because denying his physical need for a woman was sheer torture anyway. The *Hirachi* accepted that as a testament to their strength of mind, body, and will. To refuse to yield to something so basic to their nature was to have power over their destiny--not much, granted, but at least something. Abstinence ceased to be nearly as much torture over time, but the need never completely went away.

Partly it was because he allowed himself to think that, even if he did breed a child on one of these females, it truly would not be *Hirachi*. He would not be giving one of his own kind into the hands of the *Sheloni*.

Partly, though, it was because his interest in the female had turned to fascination and the fascination had turned into obsession. If he had not watched her day after day strolling back and forth just beyond his reach, he might not have come to such a pass.

Then again, he might have anyway, he acknowledged wryly.

Her strangeness, especially her frailty, should have put him off, revolted him or at least not appealed. Instead, those things had instantly riveted his attention, fascinated him.

Her fear should have disgusted him. Any weaknesses he detected within himself did--and he had certainly not looked for such a thing in a woman in the days before, when he had been a free man. He had wanted a woman of strength and intelligence to bear his young when he had considered the possibility of being able to do such a thing--when he had been naïve enough to believe there was a chance of destroying the threat of the *Sheloni* and building a life.

Not only had it not, her fear had aroused something inside of him that he hadn't even been aware was there--a fierce desire to protect. It had made him feel stronger, more capable, more determined--and stupid.

It had given him a false sense of his manhood and his abilities as a fighter.

Which was why he'd been so stupid as to throw himself between her and the damned droid, even knowing he couldn't stop the thing, and gotten cracked ribs for his stupidity.

He'd been enraged when she'd taken the infant. It was *Hirachi*. It deserved freedom or a quick death to prevent its suffering.

It wasn't her kind. She looked at him most of the time as if he was a monster, and he'd thought she would surely ignore it. Instead, she had picked it up and coddled it, coaxing it from the brink of release--teaching it the weakness of dependence.

And in the process, even though he had tried his utmost to distance himself from the infant, tried hard to feel nothing for it so that he could focus on what was best for it, he had lost his ability to shield himself from his emotions. Her determination to protect and nurture the infant when she was even less able to protect the child than their own women were had begun his fall from interest to an obsession to have her.

To begin with the fact that the alien females seemed perfectly content to accept slavery made him doubt their species was particularly intelligent, especially since they didn't even appear to have the capability of communicating with each other except with some sort of bizarre hand language. They had the capability of speech--both females tended to babble excitedly when they were together, but obviously it wasn't much more than babble because he could see they weren't actually communicating by the puzzled looks they exchanged.

When it had finally dawned on him that they weren't

communicating because they were each speaking two totally different languages, he'd thought maybe they were from two different worlds. But it seemed farfetched that the *Sheloni* had found two species so similar on two different worlds, especially when both were so similar to the *Hirachi*. True, there was a notable difference in their skin and hair color, and the brown one was even smaller than the pink one, but he decided they had to be from the same world if for no other reason than the astronomical odds of finding three different worlds that was home to three such similar beings.

Besides, they had both appeared in the hold of the *Sheloni* ship within days of each other … and both referred to Earth, which he'd come to realize was their name for their home world.

Unless they were from related tribes but two different worlds in the same solar system?

That seemed plausible, though it didn't explain the subtle difference in their appearances and the difference in their languages.

He would have liked to have mastered their language so that he would know how closely he had guessed the situation, begin to understand the miniature aliens better, and perhaps from that figure out just what the *Sheloni* had in mind. Unfortunately, he was far too interested in the one who called herself Bri to be able to focus his thoughts on learning her tongue. No matter how hard he tried to concentrate, he found his mind wandering to the expressions that flickered across her face, the movements of her lips and her hands, the subtle fragrance that clung to her, the smoothness of her skin, the rise and fall of her breasts beneath the thing she wore--but mostly to the darker pink lips of her *tup,* which he'd caught just enough of a glimpse of, that the desire to thoroughly investigate it was driving him slowly insane.

He could tell himself that it was because he had not been able to pinpoint enough reference words to understand their sentence structure all he wanted--and that *was* true--but it was because he had not paid close enough attention to what Bri was saying. There were some words she used often enough he should have been able to grasp their meaning--if he could've prevented his mind from wandering.

His obsession with Bri, Kole discovered when the *Sheloni* sent their droid to fetch him, was going to be his downfall.

Chapter Seven

Kole's first clue that this was no mere examination to assess his injuries and repair damage if necessary came when he saw that the examination room had two tables and that both were configured for a purpose other than a simple examination.

The second was when he discovered that the Sheloni had 'inadvertently' left on a monitor that was focused on Bri's sleeping form.

And the third clue came when, instead of escorting him back as soon as they had mended his cracked ribs, they moved 'the device' over his groin.

He hadn't experienced this particular form of torture before, but he had heard about it from those who had.

Sweat instantly began to form on his pores and fury to roil within his veins.

He should have realized something was up when they didn't gas him. There was only one reason, after all, that it would be more important to them to have him lucid than docile from the drugs.

He wasn't capable of an erection much less release if he was drugged.

He gritted his teeth, feeling a sense of triumph threading through his anger.

If they thought staring at Bri on the screen was going to be enough to push him over the edge, they were going to find that they were mistaken.

"Your cooperation will be appreciated in extracting a specimen," one of the Sheloni told him as he was hooked up to the 'milking' machine and felt it close snugly around his flaccid member, using the mechanical voice they communicated with the *Hirachi* with since they were incapable of forming the words of his language.

"Appreciate it all you like," he snarled. "You won't get it."

They couldn't form facial expressions like the Hirachi either since the muscles in their faces didn't allow for it, but he saw the perpetual grimace the creatures wore relax in what was their closest approximation to an expression of amusement.

"Perhaps," the creature responded.

The response made Kole long to wrap his fingers around the

thing's neck and squeeze until its eyes popped from the sockets, but they'd restrained him as soon as he'd entered the examination room, and, in any case, he knew one of the droids in the room would frustrate any attempt on his part to harm the Sheloni. They moved slowly, but they processed at lightening speed and fired with uncanny accuracy. No matter how fast he could move, the droids were far faster, and he would be hit with a debilitating ray before he could even launch himself at the Sheloni.

Instead, he nursed his seething anger, focused his gaze on the wall, instead of the monitor, and his thoughts on the bloody battle he and his tribesmen had fought, and lost, when they were taken. It was unlikely they would have won anyway, but the fact that a good half of the fighters had been elders in his village--including his parents--hadn't helped.

They'd been rebels and dreamers--the elders--believing they could escape the Sheloni by moving deep into the wilderness--far from the ruins of their ancient cities where everyone else lived, or rather struggled to live. All they'd succeeded in doing, though, was breeding a new crop of slaves for the Sheloni. His entire youth--all of them--had been trained almost from birth to fight and where had it gotten them?

A faint whisper of sound distracted him from his dark thoughts, but it was Bri who completely captured his attention and ruined his focus.

Clearly, she'd been drugged. She struggled to hold onto the child anyway, for all the good it did.

He looked away after a moment, frowning, trying to regain his focus, but even his anger had been redirected away from his personal tragedy toward their treatment of Bri and the infant, which was crying now that they'd taken it from her.

It was a mistake to look toward her again. By that time they'd stripped her naked and strapped her to the table, and he saw what the odd looking supports were for.

They'd hooked her knees over them and spread her thighs.

Blood engorged his cock the instant his gaze connected with her *tup*, which they'd turned up to him. Dimly, he realized that it was completely calculated, that they'd guessed it would have that effect on him, and he was still helpless to fight the reaction.

The sweat that had leapt from his pores before was nothing compared to the rivers that formed and slickened his skin as he fought to regain the ground he'd lost. He couldn't drag his mind from it. Looking away did no good. Closing his eyes didn't help.

The image was printed indelibly on his mind.

And once his flesh responded to her, he was facing a loosing battle. The machine kneaded his sensitized flesh mercilessly until containing the expulsion of his seed became sheer torture.

Nothing he could think of to do served to distract his mind--mostly because his mind was in as much torment as his body and chaos reigned, making it nigh impossible to put two thoughts together. "It will do you no good," he growled finally. "The women will find a way to expel the seed, even if you succeed in planting it."

The Sheloni that had spoken before favored him with another look of amusement. "Not this creature. These beings are docile, far easier to manipulate because they are very emotional and weaker than your kind, as you see."

He'd been afraid of that. He tried to look contemptuous. "Then I should not concern myself," he gritted out. "Even to attempt to bear a Hirachi babe would kill such a creature. She is too small, too frail."

The Sheloni almost seemed to shrug. "We have plenty now for our purposes. They are very nurturing, willing to rear a babe not their own. You have seen this for yourself. Even if she can not survive the birthing, it will not matter. We have some for breeding, some for nurturing."

The rage that went through Kole at that cold assessment almost succeeded in diverting him enough to regain control.

Almost.

Unfortunately, it produced more than rage. It produced fear--for her. It clouded his mind with thoughts of her, focused his entire being on Bri. She wasn't replaceable. He wasn't going to be able to bear watching her swell with his child, knowing it would probably tear her apart when it made its way into the world. Nausea swept through him, and he felt a lessening of the clamoring of his body for release. "Better a Hirachi than a halfling," he bit out, nauseated that he could be bartering the life of one of his own women, one of his tribesmen whom he'd grown up with, for this alien female, but helpless to fight the urge to try.

"Perhaps it will not be as fine a specimen, but it is bound to be stronger than the weaker parent, and more docile than the Hirachi," the Sheloni said complacently. "In any case, we have disposed of the Hirachi females. They were far more trouble than they were worth."

That comment went through Kole's chest like an arrow.

Abruptly, his member went flaccid and he very nearly *did* throw up.
* * * *

Bri would have liked to believe that she was dreaming the strange things that she remembered when she woke, but after the third incident she couldn't comfort herself with that lie anymore-- not when she'd awakened with drying semen on her thighs.

The examination table, and the positioning of her body on it, had been reminiscent enough of pelvic examinations she'd had that she thought at first that she was confusing the actuality with her memories. She'd also thought she had imagined Kole being in the room.

One plus one equaled two, though. Spread thighs, plus Kole, plus semen equaled an attempt to impregnate her.

Plus her IUD was gone. She hadn't even thought to check it after earlier examinations. The moment it occurred to her what they might be trying to do, though, she'd checked.

She should have realized they weren't stupid enough to miss something like that.

She'd been too stunned at first even to feel anything but stunned. She still couldn't feel much besides stunned until the nightly visits stopped and the fear gripped her that they'd stopped because they'd succeeded, not because they'd given up.

How was she going to protect Cory if she was pregnant? She'd felt as if she stood some chance of protecting both of them as long as she continued to gain strength, agility, and speed. She was going to *lose* that, though, if she grew heavy and awkward with a baby. She'd *seen* what pregnancy did to women even if she'd never had a baby herself. Their bellies ballooned out and before long they were waddling and holding their backs, unable to bend over. How could she run, dodge, and climb?

She couldn't.

They'd taken her damned IUD, though! Even if she was optimistic and considered the possibility that they hadn't managed it yet, they'd try again, and she didn't have any way to stop them.

She refused to think in terms of pregnancy and Kole. She wasn't sure how she felt about that little detail, but she was sure she didn't want to think about it.

Apparently he was no happier with the thought of fathering a child on her than she was at the thought that he might.

She hadn't considered how horribly embarrassing it was going to be to have to look him in the eye after what the slaver aliens had done to both of them. She did the moment she was allowed to leave the room again, but she'd been avoiding him a while already.

It was harder than before to ignore him, though, and after the second day, she had just glanced casually in his direction.

The look he gave her froze the blood in her veins. He wasn't embarrassed. He was furious--all six and a half feet and probably three hundred pounds of rock hard, muscle bound giant barbarian. Fear filled her at that look, but so, too, did dismay, and then anger.

He looked like he hated her and would cheerfully rip her head off of her shoulders if they would only grant him access to her for five seconds. That look made her knees go weak and the blood drain from her head so rapidly she felt faint. She couldn't seem to drag her gaze from him, though, could not look away once he'd pinned her with that furious glare.

Wildly, she searched her mind for a reason why he'd gone from friendly stranger to enemy in one leap. But it didn't take much of a search despite her fear and dismay. Her thoughts went almost at once to the reason for her own embarrassment.

He was angry that he'd been dragged into the slaver alien's breeding experiment--beyond anger actually to look at her that way. It hurt. It wasn't her fault they'd picked him. *She* hadn't picked him to be their lab rat.

It was his fault, she decided angrily, maybe even his fault that they'd thought of it at all! If he hadn't been looking at her that way it might not have occurred to the slavers to throw the two of them together.

Not that they actually had--what they'd done was almost worse. Well, it *was* worse in a lot of ways--turning something that should have been special into something cold, clinical, calculating. It would've been horrible to be thrown into a pen with him waiting to mount her, but at least if they'd been put together they could have had a pretense of it being their own idea. They might have managed to inject some semblance of higher thoughts and feelings into an act that lifted it above animalistic coupling.

She supposed she could understand some of what he was feeling--embarrassment, the horrible sense of helplessness, being used, having something that had been almost nice corrupted in such a way. She supposed she could even understand why a part of his anger was directed at her.

It was because he had tried to befriend her, because he had been interested in her.

But it still wasn't her fault!

Feeling hurt, angry, embarrassed, and ashamed herself, she finally looked away. The moment she broke eye contact, though, another thought sprang into her mind--that he was angry because, in her blind terror, she'd run to him for help. He'd been hurt, and there was no getting around the fact that *that* had been her fault.

It didn't matter, she told herself as she turned away abruptly and resumed her walk. She hadn't wanted to be friends with him anyway. If she'd had any sense of trust in him before the comment about Cory, she certainly hadn't since. Maybe he really thought the baby would be better off. Maybe he was even right, but she didn't agree. Her mother had suffered for years, and she'd still clung to life as long as she could. She had felt like whatever she had to endure was worth it. Maybe, if Cory could make the choice, that was what he'd chose? Life, no matter how difficult.

An image of the baby's face when she'd first found him rose in her mind.

He hadn't cared. He'd been completely apathetic.

Had *she* made the wrong choice for him, she wondered abruptly, feeling ill at the thought? Was it guilt that made her so fiercely protective of him? Because, deep down, she realized she really couldn't protect him. It had been selfishness as much as it had been pity that had driven her to take him and nurture him. Had she only been thinking of her own needs? Or even mostly of herself when she should have put his needs first?

She stopped when she reached the edge of her yard and settled near the line, watching Consuelo, who'd been frantically exercising ever since she'd warned her--poor thing! Would *she* have been better off in blissful ignorance?

Lifting Cory's carrier carefully off of her back, she brought him around to her lap and sat studying his little face. It didn't look like an ugly little alien face to her now. She loved him, and he was beautiful to her. When he smiled up at her and batted at her face with his fists, she felt like crying. Gathering him close to her chest, she rocked him unconsciously, taking in his scent and the feel of his warm little body and trying to convince herself nothing was going to happen to him, that she wouldn't let it.

Abruptly, it occurred to her to wonder if at least a little bit of Kole's anger was for the same reason, because he did like her and now wished he didn't. She'd been unconscious when he was hurt, but she didn't believe the bot would've attacked him if he hadn't attacked first. It was after her, not Kole.

She saw when she glanced toward him that he was watching her, but she couldn't tell anything about his expression--except that he wasn't looking at her like he hated her. As if he realized he might have given something of his thoughts away, he turned, stalking to the other side of his yard to talk to one of his tribesmen, she supposed. She watched them until Consuelo settled across from her, catching her attention.

* * * *

Kole had spent days battling his helpless rage and remorse, and he was no closer to containing it or dealing with it although he'd torn his habitat apart and pounded the walls until his fists were bloody. He couldn't get their faces out of his mind. He couldn't prevent horrific images from flooding his mind as to how the *Sheloni* had 'disposed' of them--their women.

He'd known most of them from birth, had trained with them in combat, had shared his body intimately with most of them. He had not been particularly attached to any one of them, not one more than another, at any rate--that was not encouraged because strong emotional attachments only led to doing something stupid at the wrong moment and endangering others. Rather, he had felt a closeness to all of them, just as he did the male tribe members.

There had been a time when that was not the case, so he had been told, but it was long ago--before even his parent's memory. Before the holocaust, when life on *Ach* had been good, the *Hirachi* had lived as families, in great cities, not banded together in tribes in barely adequate shelters. Most of the laws of their village had been designed to create a sort of group closeness that allowed them to trust in one another, know each other's strengths and weaknesses, and work as a team.

He could not imagine feeling worse about their deaths, though, and he wondered if they had really mastered the ability to stand their distance from others and protect themselves from the deep, emotional wounds such relationships caused. He would not have admitted it under torture, but he had felt crushed when the elders had died, hopeless.

And now the women were dead, too.

He wanted to kill something--the Sheloni--destroy everything they had tainted with their touch.

The fear that it was somehow his fault only made it worse. If he had shown no interest in Bri, would this have happened?

He thought it might not and the thought tormented him, made the rage boil out into physical violence against the only things near enough to vent his rage on. It exhausted him, bruised his body, but the pain that was inside didn't go away. The exertion didn't banish the images from his mind.

He had to tell the others. They had a right to know. And yet he was loath to tell them all that he knew of the *Sheloni's* plans. If they turned all of their pent up frustration and rage against the only thing available to them, the alien women....

He almost welcomed the likely consequences of that, except that it made him sick to his stomach to think of brutalizing such weak and helpless creatures. In any case, although he almost welcomed the thought of not having to deal with the grief and hate anymore, he didn't want to die without taking at least a few of them with him. As infuriating as it was that they could not defeat the Sheloni, it was many times worse that they could not even inflict appreciable damage in retaliation for all that his people had suffered at their hands.

The Sheloni were the enemy, he reminded himself. He couldn't help but resent the alien women who had replaced their women and were indirectly responsible for their deaths however unwilling they, themselves, had been, but he wasn't so irrational with grief and anger that he didn't know that. He would have to tell the others in such a way that it did not make them turn on the women.

He was still trying to decide how he would do that when he spied her. Instantly, images of the lab flooded his mind. The rush of desire that washed over him stunned him, seemed to knock the breath from his lungs.

He'd held out as long as he could, deliberately filling his mind with images that revolted him, but in the end it hadn't helped him at all. In spite of everything he could do he couldn't resist looking at her, and the moment he did other images crept insidiously into his mind, ousting the ones he'd used to protect himself. And he'd imagined thrusting into her, imagined that it was the feel of her body along his shaft, not the twice damned machine.

And they'd injected his seed into her.

A mixture of chaotic emotions went through him at the memory.

Fear for her was uppermost. It roused anger and disgust, mostly toward himself. And the fact that she refused to look at him only created more havoc inside of him. By the time she *did* look he was in such turmoil that he hardly knew what he was doing or where he was, but the *way* she looked at him penetrated his disordered thoughts and emotions with the piercing pain of a javelin to the chest.

Sucking in a harsh breath, he deliberately turned his back to her, trying to come to grips with the anger and resentment that boiled inside of him because she'd looked at him with both fear and reproach.

He had not touched her. He was fairly certain he would have if he could have, but he hadn't, and he had certainly not volunteered to have any part of that humiliating experiment.

Spying Yardof, he strode toward the man, trying to gather his thoughts together.

Yardof nudged a chin in Bri's direction. "Have you learned aught of the alien women?"

Kole shrugged. "Their world is called Earth. It's meaningless to me."

"Both females?" Yardof asked in surprise. "Did you not say they do not even speak the same tongue?"

Kole nodded absently. "Strange to be from the same world and not--particularly since neither seems to understand the other, but, yes, I think so."

"Primitives?"

Kole frowned. "No. Definitely not extremely primitive. They do not smell like animals." He was almost sorry he'd brought that up because the memory of her scent instantly filled his mind, and it was anything but repulsive. Shifting uncomfortably as his member stirred and firmly tamping the urge before it could betray his thoughts, he turned his mind to their women. "Have you seen our women of late?" he asked, wondering suddenly if the Sheloni had only told him that to fuck with his mind.

Yardof grimaced, shaking his head. "No one's seen them since the day they let them all out together and they discovered the alien women had two of the babes. If they've let them out since, it was when everyone else was confined … which worries me. Even if they rotate the times, someone should have seen them."

Bile climbed into Kole's throat. "I'd hoped the Sheloni had only said that to demoralize me," he muttered.

"Said what?"

Kole gave him a look.

Yardof stared at him for a split second and then his face hardened. "They're dead then?" he asked hoarsely.

"We knew that was a strong possibility if we defied them."

Yardof looked down at the ground, balling his hands into fists. "They didn't even get the chance to make their lives count, did they?"

They both knew they hadn't. The *Sheloni* were well aware of their physical inferiority to the *Hirachi*. He had no doubt that any one of the women had been capable of taking out three or four with their bare hands, but the *Sheloni* knew that, too. They rarely came near enough for any possibility of one of the *Hirachi* reaching them and only then when they were certain the droids were near enough to protect them.

There was rage in Yardof's eyes when he looked at Kole again. "They captured the alien females to replace them as breeders," he growled. "If we snap their necks, the Sheloni will see we will not breed more slaves for them."

Fury flooded Kole. "*We* do not prey upon those who are weaker," he growled.

"It would be a kindest to spare them the indignity and suffering of life as a slave. They will die like crushed flowers anyway. Do you not see how scrawny and weak they are? Our children are stronger! We have slain our own infants to protect them. How is this different? Do they deserve any less consideration only because they are not our kind?"

"*We* did not slay our young!" Kole snarled furiously. "The women decided upon that themselves. I would not have had the stomach for it!" If he'd known what they planned, he would have forbidden it … not that he thought they would have listened. If there was ever a time when they were not completely in control it was during the mating season. Their losses and grief, topped by the sharp spike in hormones had clouded their reason.

Yardof glared at him angrily and finally looked away. "Me either," he confessed finally. "But I am certain it was the right thing to do. We are fortunate our women had the strength."

Kole wasn't convinced it was strength, though he didn't want to say so. However much he wanted to honor the memory of the dead, though, and dismiss the doubts in his mind, he had known most of the women well, and he suspected spite had played a part in their decision--with some of them anyway. It was one thing to think of sparing the infants pain and suffering, and entirely another to consider they had died only to spite the *Sheloni*. He was willing to do almost anything to retaliate--but not that.

Surreptitiously, he glanced toward the alien women, wondering, not for the first time, if either of the babes were his.

"Likely they will die with the infants," Yardof said, dragging Kole's attention from Bri. "I can not see anything that fragile delivering a Hirachi into the world. You don't think it would be cruel to allow that to happen to them?"

He had seen their women deliver their infants, and he thought it would be unconscionably cruel, but even considering it hypothetically he wasn't at all certain he could bring himself to end Bri's suffering … supposing he had the opportunity, which most likely he would not. "Maybe they are stronger than they look," he responded, not believing it for a moment. "Or maybe they will only have small babies like themselves. Either way, there is nothing we can do about it. The Sheloni have decided to use them. If we refuse to breed them, the Sheloni will either force the issue or dispose of them as they did our women."

"The machine," Yardof agreed, looked as if he was considering asking Kole if that was where he'd been taken, and then apparently thought better of it. "Do you think we will have a chance of fighting once we reach the world they are taking us to?"

About as much chance as they'd had on *Ach*, Kole thought. He didn't need to point out that he thought they were less likely to, though. "We will find a way to avenge the deaths," he ground out instead.

"*Shentalgo*," Yardof muttered.

"Ritual suicide would only inconvenience them," Kole responded dryly, "and force them to return to *Ach* for others. If those captured before us had fought to the death instead of seeking *shentalgo* we might not be here."

Yardof nodded. "I will tell the others. Likely it will not stop Dansk, though. I did not want to say anything and shame him, but he allowed himself to grow … too attached to Lyaaia. He will very likely behave irrationally when he learns of her death."

Chapter Eight

Kole felt his throat close as he stared down at Bri. He had hoped/dreaded it would come to this. His seed had not taken, and, not to be thwarted in any way, the Sheloni had decided 'natural' might work where science had failed.

Or, more likely, they had decided natural impregnation might be achieved more quickly.

A wall of heat and desire had washed over him the instant it clicked in his mind that this time would be different. This time he had not been brought into the room first and bound to the machine. This time when they had brought him in, Bri had been strapped to the table already, her legs elevated, her thighs parted to receive--him. Fortunately, it was that same situation, and the frightened look in her eyes despite the glaze from the drugs, that had sent an equal blast of ice through his veins so closely upon the heels of desire that he'd thought for a moment he'd black out from the swiftness of the rush of blood to his cock and then away again.

"You will impregnate her," the Sheloni repeated.

Kole blinked, wiped the expression of befuddled lust from his face, dragged his gaze from Bri with an effort, and affected an expression of indifference. "As you see," he said, gesturing toward his flaccid member, "there is no interest. If you had cocks yourself, you'd know this is not something that responds to command." He did not, in point of fact, know whether they did or not--suspected they must--but it was impossible to resist the opportunity to insult their virility.

To his disappointment, the Sheloni didn't seem the least insulted. Instead, he looked surprised--not that they were capable of showing much by way of emotion, but Kole could see the face and eyes behind the shield go blank. "You have no interest in this female?"

"No," Kole lied.

The Sheloni studied him a moment more and turned to one of the bots. "Dispose of this one and bring another."

Kole's heart seemed to stop in his chest. Fury washed through him, but it was aimed as much at himself as the Sheloni. He should have known the creature would not hesitate to call his bluff and toss out a counter challenge. It flickered through his mind that the Sheloni was bluffing, as well, that Bri was of value to them in caring for the child even if she could not be used to breed, but he knew he couldn't trust that that was true. Swallowing against the bile in his throat, refusing to glance at Bri again, though he wondered if she could understand anything that was being said, if she realized her life was hanging in the balance, he maintained his look of indifference with an effort. "They all look the same. I would have no more interest."

The approximation of a smile settled on the Sheloni's face. "You must look at her face."

Kole felt his mask of indifference slip. Chagrinned that the Sheloni had obviously seen he was more than a little interested, he met Bri's gaze, wishing he could communicate to her that he had no more choice in this than she did, that he would not hurt her if he could help it.

He *did* desire her. That was part of the problem. He had thought of very little since he had first seen her besides possessing her, and yet it had been impossible to ignore the fact that nature had not made her for one such as him. He had never had to concern himself that he might inadvertently hurt one of his own tribeswomen. They were not as strong as their male counterparts. They were more delicate in form, but as long as he did not completely forget himself in the throes of passion, a woman of his own kind was perfectly capable of holding her own. He would have had to try *to* hurt one of them, or simply been completely careless.

Gods! Bri was just … small. He could tell without drawing any nearer her that he could snap any bone in her body with little effort … and some perhaps with no effort at all. He could crush her with his weight, suffocate her.

He wanted to bury himself deeply inside of her and think of nothing but the pleasure it gave him--and he was more than half afraid that was exactly what he would do once the heat was fully upon him, and then he would break … something.

He had always felt very confident in his strength and agility. Now he just felt big and clumsy and incredibly awkward.

Afraid that she would see his own doubts and become more anxious, he dragged his gaze from hers and moved closer to stare down at her body. The light pink of her arms and legs paled to nearly white on her body, and yet still retained a healthy pinkish glow. Her breasts, large and round in proportion to her body, would barely fill his palms. He stared at the blue tracery of veins beneath her fragile skin for a moment before he allowed his gaze to move to the dark pink tips. The flesh immediately surrounding the little button like tips, puckered beneath his gaze, tightening and extending the tips in a way that made his belly tighten in response, that sent more blood surging into his member and made him feel light headed.

Ignoring the Sheloni, he pressed himself between her pale thighs and leaned over her. Dropping one hand to the table beside her to support himself, he carefully placed one large hand lightly on the fragile bones of her shoulder and stroked it over her skin in the way he had seen her soothe the child, hoping it would calm her fears, show her that he meant her no harm.

The effect upon him was anything but calming, however. Her skin felt as soft as the petal of a flower, cool to his touch. She quivered faintly beneath his palm, tiny bumps erupting on her skin in reaction, almost as if it was lifting to feel him in return. Heat rushed through him in a tidal wave that nearly rocked him on his feet as he smoothed his hand up her body again, closed his palm over one breast, and lightly squeezed the rounded globe.

It was not just her skin that was soft, he realized, thoroughly bemused and enraptured. Her flesh, everywhere that he had touched her, was pliant.

He wasn't certain, at first, that he liked that. It felt strange and unfamiliar, but his body was in no doubt. His reaction was powerful, heady. Heat poured through him like acid. His heart rate shot into a gallop that had him struggling to regulate his breathing.

When he glanced at her face again, he saw that her eyes were closed.

To shut him out, he wondered, feeling some of the heated desire recede?

Because he was in no doubt at all that he was as strange to her as she was to him, or, unfortunately, in any doubt that she was inclined to find that 'strangeness' as unnerving as he found it intriguing.

He averted his gaze. He couldn't afford to think about that. He couldn't afford to think beyond the moment. Breed her now, or she was dead now, disposed of with no more thought than the garbage the Sheloni littered space with.

If she did not want his touch, though, would it be better to make short work of it? Or better to try to soothe her, coax her? Could he do either one if she was repulsed by him, or afraid of him?

Doubt shook him. He knew nothing about this alien woman. If she were one of his kind … he would never force his cock into her *tup* as small as she was unless she was ready for him, welcomed him. Her body would have to create moisture to lubricate his entry, otherwise he could not help but damage her fragile flesh.

That thought almost made him lose his erection entirely. As it was, it had gone from rock hard to only semi-erect.

Resolutely closing his mind to both her reaction and the Sheloni observing the proceedings, Kole focused on his own responses, knowing it was the only way he could do what was required. If he allowed himself to think she found it frightening, painful, or revolting, he could *not* enjoy it, and if he did not enjoy it he could not do it.

Shifting upright, he placed a palm on either of her thighs, studying the contrast in their skin tones, the pleasing softness of her skin beneath his palms. Her thighs were so small he could almost span them with one hand, but that aroused him even as it unnerved him.

He yielded to the impulse to examine her *tup* as he had wanted to before. Vaguely disappointed that he loomed over her in such a way that he still could not study it as he liked, he resisted the impulse to kneel and look his fill. Instead, he investigated the thin, deep pink petals of her sex with his fingers. Relief and heat filled him when he discovered that she was formed the same as the females he was familiar with. At least he would not have to search for *that,* would not be struggling to fit himself into a place not meant for male flesh.

With great care, he eased one finger inside of her to be certain. She was not cool there. The heat was almost scorching hot. Moisture coated his finger. Her flesh clung to him, closed around his finger. His surging heart made the blood begin to pound in his temples and in his cock as he slowly pressed into her as far as he could and withdrew, feeling her body respond.

Sucking in a harsh breath as he sensed the impatience of the Sheloni, he withdrew his finger and caught his cock, aligning it with her opening and pressing slowly against her. The moment he saw and felt her flesh closing around his, felt the almost painfully exquisite pleasure rocketing through him from the tight grip of her hot flesh, a dark haze of madness seemed to envelope him. Nothing registered in his mind any longer beyond the desperation to plunge fully inside of her and feel his sex engulfed by hers.

Catching her hips in his hands, he strained to push his way past her resistant muscles for several moments before he realized he couldn't without lubrication to ease his way. Letting out a pent up breath, he ceased to shove, allowed her muscles to push him almost completely out and then thrust again, over and over until her moisture coated his length, pressing a little more deeply each time. He found that he was shaking all over with the effort to fight the urge to ignore the resistance of her body and force his shaft inside of her. Sweat beaded his pores, collected, and then coated his skin as if he had been battling under Ach's sweltering sun.

He was so intent on the task, so caught up in the glorious sensation of her heat and soft, clinging flesh, his body reached its peak, began to shake with imminent release before he had managed to get his cock much more than halfway inside of her. Grunting as the first tremors squeezed the breath out of him, he released his frantic grip on her hips and leaned over her again, gripping the table on either side of her, gasping for breath, fighting the urge to give into his release with every ounce of concentration he could muster. The effort was in vain. Her scent teased at his nostrils, seemed to curl into his gut like claws, drawing him to her. And as he leaned nearer, felt the soft caress of her skin along his cheek, the urge to taste her clogged his throat with need.

The moment he drew the tight little bud that tipped one breast into his mouth, he lost the battle, groaned as the seizures caught him up and his body began to pump his seed into her in nearly painful convulsions.

Dimly, belatedly, he remembered that he'd meant to pull out and release his seed between her thighs.

He tried, gritting his teeth and jerking his hips back, but he knew it was too late. He'd spilled his seed inside of her. Uttering a curse under his breath, he pushed away from her, locked his arms to support himself as the strength fled his body, grinding his teeth as his muscles shook with the effort.

Finally, dizzy with the weakness, feeling as if his knees were going to give out, he shoved upright, wavering on his feet.

The *Sheloni* looked both of them over dispassionately, studied the semen dripping from her *tup* speculatively and finally seemed grudgingly satisfied.

"This is a revolting and, it seems to me, very inefficient method of breeding. It can not be disputed, though, that nature works best in these things. Now that you have shown that you can overcome your ... distaste for the creature, you will keep her with you until you have impregnated her," the *Sheloni* said decisively.

Still reeling from the magnitude of his climax, feeling the beginnings of chagrin creep over him as it dawned on him that he'd come before he'd even managed full penetration, Kole lifted his head to stare at the *Sheloni* uncomprehendingly. When he glanced back at Bri, he saw that the restraints on her wrists and legs had been removed and the bots were lowering her legs from the supports.

"Take her?" he repeated numbly and then in gathering anger, "This is not natural!" he growled. "She is not my kind, not of my world! She was never intended to breed with the *Hirachi*!"

"We have studied both species carefully," the *Sheloni* responded without concern. "The Earth women are compatible."

Compatible how? Kole wanted to demand. Not physically, except that her reproductive organs were the same, or seemed the same from his viewpoint, anyway.

He did not say it, though, because the thought was enough to arouse him again and he had to focus on taming his wayward body.

At the same time, he realized he not only had no choice but that his refusal was likely to cost her more than it did him.

Maybe, he amended, staring at her with equal parts lust and uneasiness.

He had no idea how she'd felt about the experience since she was drugged and bound, but he thought it was very likely she would have tried to fight him off if she hadn't been.

Still thoroughly rattled, he moved around the table to scoop her limp form into his arms. Even as weak as he still was it took little effort. She was so unexpectedly light, in fact, that he was completely unprepared for how easily he lifted her and nearly dropped her.

Gods help him! His wits had totally deserted him, and now he was going to be trapped with her until he managed to impregnate her!

* * * *

Confusion filled Bri when she realized that she wasn't simply moving. She was being carried. She was draped haphazardly between two supports, one beneath her shoulders and one beneath her thighs, not lying upon the platform that usually moved her. She could not seem to find the strength to lift her head, however, and when she opened her eyes, vertigo assailed her.

She closed them again, struggling against the remnants of the drug in her system, and discovered that her mind had begun to clear--enough that she realized she was naked.

She frowned at that. Generally, she wasn't undressed at all--not since the slavers had taken her clothing and replaced it with the gown which they only had to push out of the way when they wanted to examine her. There was also a stickiness between her thighs. That told her they'd been trying to impregnate her again. It told her the previous attempt had been unsuccessful. It also confirmed her fear that they wouldn't stop trying.

The disjointed memories typical of her experiences were nothing like before, though.

This time it had been Kole leaning over her, probing her.

That thought was enough to give her the strength to lift her head and open her eyes again.

Golden yellow skin, tattoos, nipple rings.

A jolt went through her when she recognized the chest she was staring at. Uttering a groan, she gave up the effort to hold her head up, tried to let go of consciousness.

The movements had drawn his attention. He shifted her closer to his body, cradling her head in the crook between his arm and his chest. A shiver went through her as his warmth penetrated her bare, chilled flesh. Instinctively, she wiggled closer to the warmth.

Why was he carrying her? Or was this a drug induced hallucination?

And why was it that her sex was throbbing when it was generally her belly cramping from the instruments they pushed inside of her?

Because she hadn't imagined Kole was leaning over her, probing her flesh. He had been.

But he hadn't been using a medical instrument.

That was why her body was pinging like a son-of-a-bitch all over.

She'd thought it was a wet dream. She'd been horrified that she could respond sexually to a clinical impregnation, but it was even more horrifying to realize she'd responded to Kole.

Had he noticed?

Could he *not* have noticed she was wet? Panting for breath with the rise of sensual heat?

Anger shot through her. They'd drugged her. She'd been helpless to prevent a natural response to the stimulus of his touch. If she'd been clear headed, she would have fought it.

They hadn't drugged her for that reason, though. They'd drugged her to make certain she didn't fight them.

Had they drugged him, too?

Probably, she decided.

Whatever interest he might have had in that direction before, he'd lost it when she'd nearly gotten him killed by the robot. He'd either pointedly ignored her since or glared at her in silent accusation.

Despite the fact that there was still enough of the drug in her system to make her feel dizzy and sluggish, the moment she felt Kole settle her on a hard surface and release her, she struggled to move even further away. A yelp escaped her as she tipped over the edge of the platform and landed with an abruptness that knocked the breath from her.

He was staring down at her, she discovered, when she opened her eyes.

"Are you hurt?"

After staring at him wide eyed for a moment, Bri turned her head to look around and discovered that they were in a small room unlike any she'd been in since she'd been taken--nothing like her own habitat.

It *was* a habitat, though.

It was Kole's, she realized.

It only took a moment for her mind to leap to the most logical conclusion for the change in her circumstances.

They'd given her to him for breeding.

Chapter Nine

Warily, Bri watched as Kole moved away from her after a moment. Snatching his breeches from the floor, he pulled them on in jerky, angry movements, then moved all the way across the room, settled on the floor, and drew his knees up. Dropping his forearms to his knees, he stared frowningly at his dangling hands as if wondering why they were attached to his arms.

When she saw he apparently had no intention of approaching her again, she shoved herself upright and looked for something to cover herself, trying to fight the panic that threatened to engulf her when it sank into her mind that not only had she not been returned to her own habitat, Cory had not been returned to her.

The room was a wreck, not just untidy. It looked as if he'd systematically pounded everything he could to pieces. That thought made her belly knot with uneasiness, especially when she glanced instinctively at his hands and saw that his hands and knuckles were bruised and scraped.

Discovering there was no sign of a coverlet like the one in her habitat, she got to her feet shakily, looked around again, and finally headed toward a door in the wall behind her. There was a fist print in it and streaks of blood, but she saw it opened to the facilities and went inside.

Surprised, at first, to see it looked basically the same as her own bathroom, it dawned on her after a moment that the reason it did was probably because it had been designed for beings that were much the same--only a hell of a lot bigger--and it had a tub that was not only twice as big as her own, but filled with water--by something that looked like a waterfall!

A constant flow of fresh water and she had to bathe in a fucking teacup?

What the hell?

Or maybe there wasn't any water in her bath because all of it was draining in here? Was it just … broken?

Dismissing her sense of misuse for the moment, she returned her attention to the need for something to cover herself.

There were no towels, not even anything that looked similar.

She didn't want to go out again naked, but she couldn't camp in the bathroom either. Covering herself the best she could with her hands and arms, refusing to look in Kole's direction, she scurried to a corner and wedged herself into a tight ball there.

What had happened here, she wondered? Had Kole fought the bot that had come for him? Or was this only from anger?

She decided she didn't want to know.

Not that she could ask him anyway.

It dawned on her then that he'd asked her if she was hurt when she'd fallen off the platform that served as a bed. She'd understood him clearly, and, try through she might, she couldn't recall that it had sounded the least bit stilted or choppy.

When, she wondered, had he learned to speak English so well?

He muttered something then, shoving to his feet. The sound drew Bri's attention, and she lifted her head again to watch him uneasily as he paced the room like a wounded animal. "Do not look at me like that!" he said harshly. "They would have killed you if I hadn't taken you."

Bri's heart seemed to stand still in her chest at that. She hadn't considered that they would kill her if they decided she was of no use to them. She'd thought they would take her home!

Why, she wondered, had she nursed such an idiotic thought? Just because it was what she wanted? Because it seemed reasonable to her? And yet she didn't doubt for a moment the truth of what Kole had said. If the aliens had had any sense of right or wrong their ship's hold wouldn't be full of beings from other worlds.

Shying away from the fear that knowledge engendered, her thoughts switched to Kole again. Was he angry and disgusted because of what he'd felt compelled to do to keep them from killing her? Because he hadn't wanted to do it at all? Or because, unlike the slavers, he knew it was wrong to do that to her without her consent?

Did it matter, she wondered?

She discovered it did. She discovered that it made her feel much worse to think that he hadn't wanted to because she didn't appeal to him.

Because she was focused on him, she also made another discovery.

Kole wasn't speaking English.

He was speaking in his own tongue.

Stunned by that realization, she listened more carefully, thinking maybe the drug was still affecting her mind. If it was, though, it was affecting it very strangely because she realized when she focused on the movement of his lips that she was translating his words. There was just a fractional hesitation each time he used a word and then she *knew* what that word meant in English.

How? She hadn't even tried to pick up his language--in fact, she had never heard him use more than a word or two in his own tongue. Mostly, he had listened to her and Consuelo, and when he'd spoken at all it had been using a combination of Spanish and English.

There was only one explanation that she could think of. The slavers, for reasons known only to themselves, and using technology that she couldn't even imagine, had somehow planted the knowledge in her mind. Subliminal teaching, she wondered? Maybe using the probes she dimly recalled that they had put on her head? Maybe, but she didn't remember them putting anything on her head but the once. Was it even possible to feed it directly into her mind like that and have her brain retain it?

It didn't seem possible, but it still seemed a lot more plausible than the possibility that she'd just learned it on her own. She'd tried hard to communicate with Consuelo, and she still didn't know more than a handful of Spanish, and she'd never even heard Kole speak his own language that she could recall.

Why, she wondered? Why would they care whether she could communicate with him or not? If she'd only been taken for breeding purposes, why would it matter what she thought?

Cory, she realized, would only learn English if that was all she could speak and understand. A thrill of hope went through her, but she tamped it with an effort, fearful that she'd only thought of that possibility because she wanted to believe they meant to give him back to her.

She hadn't panicked this time when they'd taken him from her because they had always given him back to her when they were done with her before. As confused as she'd been by all the things that had happened this time that were different, she'd still thought Kole was returning her to her own habitat, thought Cory would be returned to her then.

They'd said something to Kole, she remembered suddenly, something about impregnating her. She'd still been so out of it that she'd thought that was just her mind wandering, manufacturing things that weren't real.

They'd said something about him overcoming his distaste to impregnate her. He'd said it wasn't natural.

The memory sent a wave of hurt through her, but she thrust it away, focusing instead on trying to remember more of the conversation.

She couldn't remember that they'd said anything about Cory, though.

But the slavers had taken him from the yellow tribe--the Hirachi. She remembered that Kole had called them that--They had not given him back to her, she knew, because they didn't trust him not to hurt the baby anymore than she did.

As long as she was with him, she wouldn't see Cory.

And she was going to be stuck with him until he got her pregnant.

She didn't want to think about that. She didn't want to be pregnant at all! She certainly didn't want to be pregnant by him! She didn't give a shit if he didn't like her looks. She wasn't too taken with him, if it came to that.

She covered her face with her hands, wishing she was anywhere but where she was. As boring as her life had seemed before, and lonely, even if that was something she rarely admitted even to herself, it seemed like heaven compared to this nightmare.

Why the hell couldn't they at least have given her the damned gown again? She thought, abruptly angry.

She supposed she should be grateful the bastards hadn't chained her to the bed with the manacles they'd left on her wrists and ankles!

"No mean hurt," Kole said in halting English, interrupting her thoughts.

Bri lifted her head in surprise, staring at him while it slowly sank into her that he had no idea she could understand his native tongue. She was so stunned by that knowledge that it took several moments for what he'd said to sink into her mind.

He looked as if he sincerely regretted it, but she wasn't sure if that meant he really was sorry if he'd hurt her or if he was just sorry about the whole thing.

Maybe the truth was both. That did nothing to help the situation they were in, however--except that it made her feel a little less uneasy about being penned up with him. Which was the only bright spot she'd been able to detect, because she couldn't get Cory back until they were satisfied Kole had impregnated her and that could mean a *lot* of fucking with a man she not only barely knew, but who wasn't human. A man who disliked her--for good reason, she supposed, since it was her fault he'd taken the beating-

-and who she didn't seem to actually appeal to.

She supposed she could see that, too. Earth men hadn't exactly been falling over themselves to get her. She'd never really understood why. She had a good figure. She wasn't ugly. But then she'd never really had time to date. Maybe they didn't notice her because she didn't try to get them to notice, rarely noticed them?

And, even if that was true, she was on a whole new playing field. She hadn't seen their women well, but she'd seen enough to get the idea that she probably wasn't his concept of beauty anymore than he was hers. The skin color probably had a lot to do with it. She'd gotten used to it because of Cory and because it wasn't that radically different from some of the Earth races--more yellow than the people that tended to turn golden brown in the sun--but *they* all seemed the same, and she had a feeling he hadn't seen anything that looked quite like her.

And he could have other reasons for not wanting to, like strict taboos and customs she knew nothing about. Or he could just not want to because he hated being a slave to these slavers and didn't want to bring a child into a world of slavery. He'd seemed to indicate that when he'd told her Cory would be better off dead.

She didn't want to bring a child of her own into this, for that matter, but she found she couldn't identify with some hypothetical, as yet unconceived child when she was worried about Cory.

In any case, she doubted they had a choice.

He might think they did, but she didn't.

So what to do? Close their eyes and do it anyway?

She could do that, but could he?

She couldn't bring herself to simply assume the position, though, and she sure as hell had no clue of how to entice him to make the first move so she didn't have to.

Worn down from her anxieties, she finally drifted to sleep. She didn't sleep well, however. She dreamed alternately of being in the room, the slaver aliens probing and studying her, Kole touching her intimately and then driving into her until she felt hot and restless, and Cory, crying in the distance while she searched for him, growing more and more frantic. She woke finally with a jerk, her chest tight with fear and distress, struggling to call out to Cory.

A huge dark shadow loomed in front of her, eyes glowing an eerie silver in the darkness. When the specter touched her she nearly leapt out of her skin, uttering a frightened squeak.

Kole withdrew his hand abruptly. "No hurt Bri. No hurt Cory," he murmured in a low, soothing rumble.

Still groggy with sleep, Bri stared at him a long moment until it clicked in her mind that he was offering comfort. She did something then that she'd never done in her life--possibly because no one had offered her comfort since she was a child. She reached for it with both hands, launching herself at the warm, strong, broad chest offered.

The move rocked him on his heels, seemed to totally stun him for many moments. Finally, he shifted onto his knees, wrapped his arms around her tightly, and drew her closer, stroking a hand soothingly down her back and the back of her head as she had often soothed Cory when he was distressed. She wondered if he was merely mimicking what he had seen her do or if his people were more like Earth people than she'd thought. "The *Sheloni* will not hurt Cory. They want him to grow into a strong slave for them," he said bitterly in his own tongue. "They will give him back to you when they take you from me. They don't trust me not to hurt him because the women killed the others."

She wanted to ask him if they were right, but she wanted the comforting more. He was so big and strong it was impossible not to think of him as invincible, and she felt safe for the first time since she'd been taken. She knew it was just an illusion, that he couldn't protect her from the ones he called the *Sheloni*, but she wanted the illusion for just a little while.

It comforted her, too, that he seemed to believe what she'd already thought of, that they were only holding Cory until they sent her back to her habitat. It was thin comfort, but some reassurance--thin because even awake now, she felt like she could hear him crying for her. Closing her eyes, she burrowed closer to his warmth, wishing she could burrow inside of him and simply disappear.

"You are cold as ice," he muttered after a moment, and she sensed his head move as if he was looking around the room for something to cover her with. "And nothing to wrap you in to hold your warmth," he added after a moment on a sigh of irritation. "They are manipulative bastards. No doubt they thought it would be harder for me to control myself if they left you naked--no thought given to the fact that you might freeze without anything to keep you warm. Or are you aliens always this cold? Somehow I don't think so. You are hot...."

He broke off without finishing the thought, but Bri knew what he'd been about to say. Inside. Warmth filled her, but only part of it was embarrassment.

"Gods help me, I don't know what to do. The Sheloni are ruthless. They will have what they want and kill anyone that stands in their way. And no matter whether I do what they have demanded or not it seems to me that I will have your death on my hands. They will breed you--with or without me--unless the others are far better at controlling themselves than I am. And, if by chance, that is the case, then they will simply discard you as they did our women and find other females to breed somewhere else.

"I sense ... almost a sense of desperation in this latest plot of theirs, perhaps because they have killed the *Hirachi* off until they can not gather up enough to do what they need done. They have been raiding *Ach* for generations now to gather slaves, and we are scattered to the winds since their machinations that destroyed our world, and fewer of us all the time since most will no longer breed for fear of having their children snatched away by the *Sheloni*."

He fell silent for a time. He'd given Bri a good deal of food for thought, however, and she made no attempt to break it--mostly because she wasn't at all certain she wanted him to know she could understand him. He thought that he was merely voicing his thoughts aloud, which brought home to her that she'd missed the opportunity of telling him when she should have. He was bound to be angry when he discovered she'd understood everything.

Listening when he thought she didn't understand was like eavesdropping, she realized guiltily.

And then, too, regardless of what he'd said--which seemed to indicate he was a decent and honorable man, she couldn't bring herself to completely trust him. What if he knew she could understand and was using that to try to sway her opinion? What if the Hirachi were just as manipulative as they accused the Sheloni of being? What if none of what he'd said was true at all?

He uttered a ragged sigh and captured her face between his palms, tilting her face up as if he could see her in the dark--and quite possibly he could. She saw she hadn't imagined the eerie glowing eyes. His eyes caught the little light in the room and reflected it back at her--like the eyes of a night predator.

"The worst of this is that I want to believe that doing what I want to do is right," he murmured.

Startled when she felt his flesh brush hers, Bri flinched all over, but she'd been wrestling with her dilemma for hours, and she saw no alternative. More importantly, the sooner the deed was done, the sooner she would have Cory back.

She could do this. Truth be told, whatever she liked to think, she wasn't revolted or disgusted--not by Kole, by the idea, yes, and she had a wealth of reservations, but she didn't expect to merely 'endure' if anything she remembered from before hadn't been distorted by the drug in her system. Because the way she remembered it, it had felt pretty damned good.

She followed his lips even as he began to withdraw again, pressing her lips to his. It wasn't at all unpleasant to feel his lips against hers. They were firm, almost as hard as the rest of him, but smooth, and his scent and taste as she inhaled his breath into her lungs was like nothing she'd ever experienced. It invaded her body and bloodstream like a strong drug. Maybe it *was* a drug to her, she thought dimly, relishing the pleasure that swirled inside her mind and set her heart to hammering.

When he drew away, studying her, she thought, his arms loosening around her, she shifted and wiggled until she could get her knees on the floor on either side of his hips and rose up, blindly exploring his bare chest and arms and shoulders with her hands. A shudder went through him.

She hoped it was from pleasure.

He banished her doubts when his arms came around her again almost crushingly--definitely crushingly. He squeezed the breath out of her in an inelegant grunt and then released her as if he'd grabbed a hot coal. She didn't realize what he was about when his hands closed around her waist until he lifted her and plopped her on the floor beside him and then surged to his feet and left.

It took Bri several moments to grasp that she'd been abandoned. Disappointment and disbelief surged through her first, and then anger and embarrassment.

Well! That answered that! She thought, feeling the rejection soul deep, embarrassed that she'd practically thrown herself at him.

She was tempted to see if she could speak his tongue as easily as she could understand it, but she tamped the urge, glad now that she hadn't let on that she knew what he was saying, damn him!

As soon as the sting of rejection began to subside, anxiety took its place. It didn't look as if she was going to be able to coax him into trying again, and if that first time hadn't done the trick she might never get Cory back!

She was cold, too, damn it! She'd just begun to feel warm, and she could feel the cool air leaching the warmth out of her again. She shouldn't have pushed, she realized. She should have just enjoyed the warmth and let it go at that. Maybe if he got used to the way she looked, he'd be able to get it up for her.

Sighing irritably, she curled into as tight a ball as she could and struggled to go back to sleep. It seemed she'd barely achieved unconsciousness when she was roused again. He scooped her up and moved to the sleeping platform. Settling next to her, he tucked her against his chest and belly and then carefully looped one arm and leg over her. Grateful for the warmth, she snuggled as tightly against him as she could get, plastering her cheek against one hard pec and lifting her hand after a moment to slide it around his waist and pull herself closer still.

He caught her hand as it snaked around his chest. "No," he said firmly, placing her palm back on her own chest.

Miffed, Bri tried to wiggle away. He wasn't having that either, though. His arms tightened, caging her.

She stewed over it a while, but lying next to him was like curling up to a fireplace and the warmth seeping into her finally lulled her back to sleep. She was cold again when she woke to discover the room had lightened. Kole was pacing the room again like a caged beast she saw when she cracked an eyelid enough to survey the room.

Embarrassment immediately flooded her when he glanced at her and memories from the night before surged into her mind. She rolled over and put her back to him, refusing even to give him a look of reproach--as if she cared, damn it! She couldn't go back to sleep, though, and finally got off the sleeping platform and went into the bathroom. She'd already thoroughly doused herself with water before she thought about the fact that she didn't have a damned thing to dry off with. She glared at the ceiling, knowing the Sheloni was watching, but with no idea where the camera was that they used to spy. "I need a towel, damn it! And clothes, you stupid alien bastards," she snarled. "I'm going to freeze to death at this rate."

She'd barely gotten the complaint out when warm air began to rush into the room.

As grateful as she was to have it, it occurred to her fairly quickly that now there wasn't even any reason for Kole to cuddle her.

"Fuck!" she muttered under her breath, thoroughly enjoying expressing herself in the foulest language she could think of, feeling almost a sense of release.

Her mother would've slapped her into the middle of next week to hear her talk like that--if she'd been able to. Her mother was gone, though, and so was everybody she'd ever known--gone to her. What difference did any of the things matter that had meant something before? There was nobody to shock. There was nobody to condemn her for her language or her behavior--just aliens, and she doubted it meant anything to them.

"Fuck! Fuck! Fuck! Shit! Damn! Hell!"

She couldn't think of anything else, so she repeated what she'd already said as she stalked out of the bathroom. Kole, she saw, was staring at her, a surprised look on his face. She thought for a moment he might have understood, but she realized fairly quickly that the reaction was to the temper, not the words.

Food had appeared--some for her, some for him, she surmised, because it didn't look at all familiar. Feeling empty, she moved to the food. It tasted like saw dust, but it killed the churning emptiness in her stomach.

It was a damned shame she hadn't discovered this diet while she was on Earth. She could've been rich, because there was absolutely no incentive to eat more than it took to appease her hunger, and she could tell just from looking at her body that she'd lost that fifteen pounds she'd never been able to shake before. If she could've marketed it, she could've helped fat people everywhere achieve their weight goal and gotten rich in the process.

But she wasn't on Earth, and she was never going to see home again! She had to face that. As hard as she'd tried not to face it before, as hard as she'd worked to convince herself that, any day, the aliens were going to get done tormenting her and set her down on that country road, she knew that wasn't going to happen. If anything Kole had said the night before was true, the bastards had been stealing people all over the universe for years and years--like they were dogs or something, not people.

And now she'd been thrown in with a Great Dane who looked upon her with the distain of a pure breed for an undersized mongrel!

Except male dogs didn't seem to care what they stuck their dick into.

Tossing the food onto the tray abruptly, she looked at the ceiling again. "I want Cory! Please! He needs me. He's scared and crying for me! I know he is!"

She hadn't expected a response, but her chin wobbled with distress when she didn't get one. "I'm probably pregnant already! If it didn't take you can try again later and I can take care of Cory while you're waiting on the results. Give him back to me! Please, please, please! Just give him back!"

"No give Cory."

Bri jerked her attention from the ceiling to Kole, feeling fury surge through her. "You just stay out of this, damn it--you ... you ... yellow hulk! It's none of your damned business! He's mine! My baby now, fucking, alien, piece of shit asshole! *You* don't care! I care. I love him, and he loves me, too, and he's going to make himself sick crying for me if they don't give him back to me."

She could see from his face that he was growing angry, but she didn't care. She'd been trying to stay calm and beat back her fear ever since she'd woken on the alien ship. She could do it for herself, but she couldn't hold in the fear for Cory. It was eating away at her composure until she felt like she would just start screaming if they didn't let her at least see that he was alright.

"Stop!"

"No!" she screamed at him and grabbed up a piece of the hard bread that was supposed to be toast, hurling it at his head.

He ducked the missile, his jaw going slack with surprise.

The fact that she'd missed her mark only angered Bri more, though. Glancing down at the tray, she grabbed a block-looking something off his tray and threw that at him. It smacked him in the chest, crumbs flying in every direction as it shattered. He surged toward her. She bolted, bounding around the room like a startled deer.

He was surprisingly fast considering his size, but she was faster because she had to take two bounds to his one, and she still managed to outdistance him. His fingers grazed her shoulder, but before he could tighten his grip, she dropped, launching herself into a dive and roll she hadn't even tried since gym class forever ago.

As beautifully as she executed the maneuver, however, it cost her. Even as she tried to scramble away on her hands and knees, he dropped down and caught her ankle. Bri jerked to break his grip. When that didn't work, she rolled onto her back and aimed for his chin with her heel, catching him completely off guard.

Chapter Ten

Kole's head snapped back on his neck at the blow, his grip on her ankle loosened, and he sat back on his ass, hard. Pain flickered across his face, and then stunned surprise, and then anger.

Bri gaped at him, almost as stunned by what she'd done as he was. "Sor…."

She didn't get the rest of it out. He clamped two ham sized hands on her upper arms and snatched her toward him.

"Stop," he snarled, almost nose to nose with her.

Dangling from his grip, Bri uttered a snarl and compounded stupidity with idiocy, making a grab for his genitals. She missed, but his eyes widened when he realized she'd tried to go for his weak spot.

She set her chin belligerently.

"This will not help you get Cory back."

Her anger deserted her abruptly. She knew he was right. Her temper could well have cost her if it came to that. Why, oh why hadn't she thought about that before she'd acted like she was insane?

Because she was *going* to go insane wondering and worrying about him, imagining all sorts of horrible scenarios, from them dropping him on his head, to him crying until he choked, or refusing to eat and slowly starving to death or dehydrating.

She sniffed when he set her away from him, rubbing her bruised shoulders absently and studying him warily.

It was hard to read his expression, but he looked more puzzled than angry. Lifting a hand, he rubbed his chin thoughtfully and then, slowly, smiled. And then he chuckled.

Bri had just felt the beginnings of a smile welling in her in response when he spoke, and the words seemed to freeze her blood in her veins. "Sheloni think Bri like …," he paused, obviously searching for a word, "Cory."

Bri stared at him blankly while that slowly sank in. Gentle, weak, helpless--all the things Kole thought about her, she knew--probably why he despised her. It was impossible, given that insight, to ignore the likelihood that that was why the Sheloni had thought it would be a great idea to cross breed them--docile, small, weak mother plus big, ferocious father equaled tamer slaves that were still strong.

Oh god! She hadn't just got 'things' off her chest by blowing up and showing her ass! She'd worked hard to give the impression that she was no threat at all--which she wasn't, of course--but to convince the *Sheloni* that she didn't need pain to keep her in line like they used with the Hirachi.

She didn't want them to *expect* an attack from her, because if she had to fight them surprise was the only thing that was going to give her any sort of advantage.

Covering her face with her hands, she burst into tears--of anger for her stupidity, frustration, and fear for Cory. *Stupid!* She berated herself, wondering just how badly she'd fucked up.

Did they watch all the time? Was there any chance at all they hadn't caught her running around like a crazy person lobbing missiles at Kole? Hadn't seen her kick him in the head?

When she finally managed to choke down the tears and mopped her eyes and nose, she saw that Kole had retreated to the far side of the room. Irritation flickered through her. If that wasn't just like a man! All a woman had to do was burst into tears and they headed for the hills!

Sniffing, she got to her feet and went to wash her face. Towels had miraculously appeared in the bathroom, she discovered, feeling her heart sink. Maybe it was just--like computers that monitored the habitats though? When she'd finished drying her face, she wrapped the towel around her and tucked a corner in at the top to hold it in place.

Ignoring Kole, she settled in the corner furthest from him and stared at her hands in her lap, trying not to think about what might be happening to Cory. Since she also didn't want to think what the results of her screaming fit might be, she focused on trying to extract what she could remember about the *Sheloni* from her memory.

It wasn't much. She hadn't been near one when she wasn't already drugged so that she hardly knew where she was. A lot of probing finally produced the information that they had always been wearing suits when she'd been with them. Life support, as in space suit? Or hazmat type suit, because they were worried about germs?

The movie War of the Worlds came to mind, but it could *not* be that easy.

Besides, if her germs were harmful it was just as likely it would kill the *Hirachi* as the *Sheloni,* and she didn't want to kill them. As far as she could see they were victims just the same as she was. They might feel hostile toward her and Consuelo, in which case all bets were off, but she didn't see the *Hirachi* as enemies.

A jolt went through her as she realized the direction of her thoughts. *When* had she begun to think of the *Sheloni* in terms of killing them, she wondered?

The minute they became a threat to Cory.

Could *she* actually bring herself to kill, though, even supposing she got the chance? She'd never been able to bring herself to kill anything--not anything. She damned near wrecked her car every time something ran out in the road in front of her, and she *knew* she was risking her life to do it. She couldn't help it. It was pure instinct to break and swerve.

So where did that leave her?

In the position of making herself accept and come to terms with the possibility that she might have to kill to protect herself and Cory.

She could do it, she decided. She might puke afterwards. She might have nightmares for the rest of her life. She might lose her mind completely, but she *could* do it, and she would if it meant protecting Cory.

If those bastards thought they were going to enslave her baby, they had another think coming. She'd poison the sons-of-bitches!

That thought gave her pause. It actually wasn't a bad idea. Effective, not really messy unless the poison did something horrible.

How to poison them, though?

There was no getting to the bastards on the ship. Aside from the fact that she was caged and watched, somebody had to fly the thing, and she doubted any of the Hirachi would have any more idea how to do that than she did.

Poisoning them after they landed meant accepting that she was home, though, because she wasn't going to get back to Earth.

She'd worry about that later, she decided--she could *not* handle having to worry about that, too. Top priority was going to have to be getting rid of the *Sheloni.* Maybe, if she could figure out a way to kill all of them, she could figure out a way to run their ship--or somebody could.

There didn't seem to be that many of the *Sheloni*, now that she thought it over. They used robots for just about everything on the ship, but that might have been because they didn't want to expose themselves to danger.

It made her wonder why they needed slaves at all, though. They had robots. Why not just use robots if whatever they wanted the slaves for was dangerous? Maybe it was a money thing? Every society had some kind of economy. Maybe it was just cheaper to go capture the *Hirachi* and use them than to build enough robots to do the job?

She wasn't particularly interested in why, unless it had something to do with a weakness on the part of the *Sheloni*--as in there just weren't that many of them.

She didn't believe there were many on the ship. Would there be more once they landed where ever they were going? Or would it only be a small number to watch over the slaves?

She couldn't know that until they got there, but she didn't think she would be able to do anything on the ship even if she was willing to risk being stuck afterwards in a ship that had nobody to fly it.

The suits were a weakness. Whether it meant they had to worry about the germs she and the *Hirachi* were carrying, or if it was because the same atmosphere that supported them was poisonous to the *Sheloni,* it was still a weakness that could be exploited. She just had to figure out how.

She wrestled with her recalcitrant memory until she'd given herself a headache, but she felt like she was beginning to have an idea of how many *Sheloni* there were to deal with. There were never the same number in the room with her--the last time there had only been one--but they did not all look alike. One, the one who'd been in the room last time, was almost always in the room. His nose holes--there was no bridge to their noses--were larger than the others she'd seen, and his face seemed rounder, his forehead more pronounced. He had to be important, she felt certain, if she was right and he was always in the room. Either he was like their head doctor, or science officer, or he was high on the chain of command--maybe the captain.

She doubted that, but it wasn't impossible, and the more she thought it over the more certain she was that she'd not only recognized him as an individual but he was in a position of importance.

The most she could remember ever being in the room was the first time, and it seemed to her that there'd been five or six of them.

That couldn't be all that was on the ship! It just didn't seem possible. There were easily fifty or sixty male *Hirachi*. She didn't think there were that many females but probably close. To have captured upwards of a hundred or more....

On the other hand, they'd just knocked her out, beamed her up, and set the robots to taking her car apart. They could've done the same with the Hirachi, probably had, and one could have managed that all by himself.

It would've been helpful if she'd actually seen the ship. She might have some idea of just how big it was and how many people it could house. The habitat level seemed vast, but that didn't necessarily mean it made up a half or a third. For all she knew there could be a little pod sitting on top or beneath, and this, the habitat area, could be most of the ship--like an oil tanker, or some other ship that was designed mostly to carry goods and didn't have much of a crew at all.

It was all very interesting but nothing she could either prove or disprove, and she didn't know what use it actually might be to her beyond keeping her mind occupied with thoughts other than Cory.

Neither of them was allowed out, and, after three days of close proximity with nothing to do but stare at each other or the wall or the floor, Bri was pretty sure Kole was just about ready to blow. She was if it came to that. No matter how hard she tried to get her mind off of the baby, her mind just kept going right back to him and repeating the problem over and over.

She wasn't going to get pregnant by osmosis, damn it to hell! She was almost tempted to do a rendition of the exorcist and snatch the towel off, stick her pussy in his face, and scream 'fuck me!'.

It was humiliating! And infuriating!

Three days. She'd heard somewhere that that was as long as sperm could survive, human sperm anyway. If she'd ovulated sometime between now and then, she was good, and the next time they checked her she'd get to go back to Cory.

If she hadn't, she was screwed--unscrewed. She chuckled a little hysterically at that thought.

Kole, she saw when she glanced his way, was giving her a fulminating glare.

She glared back at him.

Maybe, instead of focusing on the big picture, what she really needed to do was focus on the more immediate problem--get pregnant, get Cory--kill the *Sheloni* later.

Kole was a hurtle--alright a mountain--she was going to have to go over. The question was how best to go about it? Maybe shaking it in his face and screaming 'fuck me' wasn't such a bad idea? She could lay down on the sleeping platform and spread her legs--and cover her face with the towel, because that was a horrifying idea, and she didn't think she could do it.

Besides, she was the next thing to naked, and he hadn't had any trouble resisting--because he didn't want it anyway, and he was just hardheaded enough that he would refuse to spite the *Sheloni*. And if he turned his back on her after she humiliated herself like that she might be tempted to try to choke him in his sleep.

She couldn't wrestle him to the floor and have her way with him. He was too fucking big!

She massaged her aching eye sockets, trying to summon some movie she'd seen that might help. Images of sexy, sultry femme fatales flitted through her mind, but she discarded them one by one. Those were useless. Aside from the fact that she was no beautiful starlet, all of them had to do with men just champing at the bit to be seduced in the first place.

Kole had seemed interested before, but the little run in with the big robot seemed to have dampened his interest. He hadn't given her any of *those* looks since. Mostly he just didn't look at her at all, which was still better than the mean looks he gave when he did.

She hadn't wanted to let him know the Sheloni had made it possible for her to understand him. She'd been at great pains to keep that to herself in case it turned out to be useful somehow. Maybe now was that time, though? Maybe she could ... barter with him or something?

Like what? Pussy? That might be fairly good currency in a lot of situations, but she wasn't in much of a position to barter with that since *that* was what she was trying to give away and he seemed indifferent.

Giving up on the idea for the moment, she shoved herself to her feet. She was cramped, she discovered, from sitting so long. Groaning at the pain, she hobbled to a clear area and began doing stretches. It helped ease some of the discomfort, and she decided she might as well do a workout. She was so tense she felt in imminent danger of throwing another screaming fit, and she wanted to avoid that at all costs. Besides, she hadn't been allowed out for exercise in days. She'd grown used to exercising. That was probably one of the reasons she felt so anxious and jittery.

Giving Kole her back, when she'd finished the stretching routine, she began doing strength exercises. There weren't many she remembered how to do properly since she had never really tried to work on that. Before, she'd concentrated on figure shaping exercises and cardiovascular. The cardiovascular workouts had certainly helped. Before she'd been taken she doubted very seriously that she would've been in good enough condition to give Kole a run for his money.

The towel she wore like a sarong sucked as workout clothes she quickly discovered. Every time she inhaled deeply it slipped, and she had to grab and tuck again. It came loose completely when she got down on the floor to do modified push ups, but gravity was working in her favor for a change, and she ignored it until she'd finished doing the reps.

When she couldn't endure the burn any longer or force her upper body off the floor even one more time, she flattened herself on the floor and rested until she caught her breath. She was so focused on getting up without losing the towel that she didn't notice Kole had crossed the room to stand over her until he suddenly appeared in her peripheral vision. Startled, she sucked in a sharp breath, flinging up her arms instinctively to ward him off as she fell back a step.

He caught her forearms, pulling her arms out to either side of her and using them to tug her toward him. Surprised by the move, she tipped off balance and fell against his chest before she could get her feet under her. Still breathing a little raggedly, she tipped her head back to look up at him with a mixture of wariness and confusion.

His expression was intent, but she couldn't guess what was going through his mind. "Why this?"

Bri frowned, trying to figure out what he was talking about, which might have been easier if she hadn't been plastered against his chest and keenly aware that the towel was loosing its grip--and he was holding her arms. She tugged, trying to free them so she could grab the towel before she lost it completely.

He ignored the tug--just long enough to make it clear he'd released her--and then slowly uncurled his fingers from around her arms. Irritation flickered through her.

As *if* she needed a reminder that he was so much stronger than her, there was no contest! "It's better than just sitting around with my thumb up my ass!" she said testily.

Confusion flickered over his face. He hadn't understood, but then she'd counted on that. Otherwise she wouldn't have spoken so crudely, because as liberating as it was to throw all her old habits and inhibitions out the window, as determined as she was to do it because she felt the need to nurture her inner beast, she still wasn't really comfortable with it.

She'd never thought she would find herself in a position where she was too civilized to have a fighting chance of survival, but she had. She wasn't going to cling to proper social etiquette if it meant she was going to feel compelled to behave like a lady when she needed to be a savage. When the time came, when her moment was upon her, she was going to be tough, wily, and strike like lightening, and they were never going to know what hit them!

He settled his hands heavily on her shoulders when she would've stepped away. "Not help. Get killed."

Her heart sank, but she refused to accept that she couldn't make a difference. Her lips tightened. "How would you know? You don't know anything about me!"

His grip on her shoulders loosened. She thought he meant to release her altogether. Instead, he traced light circles over her collar bone. Her belly spasmed. Her breath hitched in her throat. Slowly, holding her gaze, he slipped his hands along her arms and uncurled her fingers from the edge of the towel. It promptly fell to her feet.

Afraid to do or say anything for fear he'd change his mind, she held her breath as he carried her hands to his chest and pressed her palms over his pecs. The cold metal of his nipple rings dug into her palms, making her fingers itch to explore the taut flesh her hands cupped. Dragging her gaze from his after a moment, she stared at the swirling, intricate tattoo that covered most of his upper chest.

It said a lot for the changes in her that she was more intrigued than repelled by the tats and rings. She would've fainted dead away if she'd found herself this close to such a rough looking character on Earth. She would've been scrambling for a way to escape, not waiting in breathless anticipation to see what he would do next.

If she was honest, she would've been simply paralyzed, probably so loathe to create a sordid scene that she would simply have stood quivering like a lamb to the slaughter while he did any damned thing he wanted to her--up to and including cutting her throat.

Kole was no tattooed street thug with needle tracks on her arms, though.

He was the one the Sheloni had picked to breed her with, and she was desperate to get that done.

So desperate, she realized abruptly, that she hadn't spent any time at all considering the act itself, only the result.

It occurred to her that she had avoided thinking about the act because she hadn't been comfortable about her reaction to him before. She hadn't been comfortable reacting at all when she'd been staked down like a mare being serviced by a stallion--and watched. How could she have felt *anything* but repugnance in such a situation? How could she have felt any desire at all for this being who was so different from her?

It was unavoidable that she didn't know herself as well as she'd thought she did, because she didn't just feel relieved that it seemed he meant to have sex with her. She felt her body react with welcome, grow tense and expectant.

Reluctance moved over her as he caught her face in one hand, hooking her chin in the L between his thumb and forefinger and tipping her face up. She didn't want *this*! She wanted to be fucked, so she could put it from her mind as a disgusting incident that she'd endured for Cory's sake.

She tensed as he shifted, hunching his shoulders as he lowered his face closer to hers. She closed her eyes. *Just do it!* She screamed inside her mind as it exploded into chaos. *Don't make me feel things I don't want to feel!*

It was too late, though. He released a gusty sigh, as if he'd been holding his breath, and as she took his essence inside of her it decimated even chaotic thought, made her feel weak and heavy, eager, needful even before his lips brushed hers, opened over them.

The little resistance she still clung to crumbled as his tongue breached the barrier of her lips and raked along hers, filling her with the taste of him. Her fingers dug into the flesh beneath her palms reflexively. For several moments more, she remained completely passive, so enthralled by the heady effect of his taste and touch, she lost awareness of everything else. But as she felt him withdraw slightly, she closed her mouth around his tongue and sucked.

A shudder went through him. He slipped his palm from her cheek to the base of her skull, spearing his fingers almost painfully through her hair, caught one cheek of her buttocks with his other hand and drew her higher against his body, closer. Her breasts brushed his chest with the movement, and her nipples instantly stood erect, grew exquisitely sensitive with the blood that engorged them.

Her arms, crushed between their bodies, prevented her from feeling more than a teasing touch of skin against skin. With a determined effort, she managed to dislodge them and hooked her hands on his shoulders, drawing herself upward, closer, but focused almost entirely on the heat of his mouth and the stroke of his tongue as he explored her mouth thoroughly.

She wavered dizzily when he released her abruptly, lifting her heavy lids a slit to peer at him as the sound of tearing fabric reached her ears. She saw that he'd parted the closure of his trousers, shoved them from his hips. They clung for a moment, caught on his erection rather than his hips and fell away as he reached for her again before she managed more than a glimpse of his swollen member. Snatching her off her feet, he brought her tightly against his chest, turned, and strode toward the sleeping platform. In two strides, he reached it and almost dove onto it, somehow managing to settle both of them on top of the hard surface without completely breaking contact.

A moment of doubt arose as he pressed his body against hers and she felt the hot evidence of his arousal. He banished it when he slipped downward and opened his mouth over hers again. The hunger and urgency of his caress sent a shaft of need straight through her core. Her belly clenched, warmth flowing through it.

Dizzy and disoriented with the heat rising inside of her to fever pitch, Bri clung, then released her grip to explore any part of his body she could reach, unable to identify anything beyond smooth skin and taut muscles … until she felt the hard, almost spiny ridge of flesh along his arms. The unexpected discovery parted the veil of desire briefly, but before the alien feel of it had even fully registered in her mind, his exploring hand found her moist cleft. A jolt of keen sensation went through her as he parted the tender folds and zeroed in on her clit unerringly. The first stroke of his finger over the sensitive nub knocked the breath out of her.

He stilled at the sound she made in her throat, at the hard jerk that went through her. Breaking the kiss and withdrawing his hand at the same moment, he stared down at her with a mixture of confusion and uneasiness. Squeezing her eyes closed, she grabbed his wrist, pushing his hand between her thighs again, arching up to meet his touch.

She could feel his gaze on her face as he carefully searched again for the nub. She bit her lip against a groan as he found it and another hard jolt of pleasure shot through her. "There! Yes," she gasped, catching one of his fingers and guiding it in the motion that drove her toward mindlessness.

Releasing a harsh breath, he shifted to burrow his face against her throat, upper chest and breasts, stroking the smooth skin of his cheeks against her as if he wanted to coat his skin with her scent. She was hardly aware of anything beyond the feel of his finger until his lips closed over one engorged nipple. The stroke of his tongue across the almost painfully sensitive tip dragged a shaky cry from her, though, almost sent her over the edge when she hadn't realized how near she was to coming.

She fought it, reaching down to stroke his head, to urge him to continue even while she fought to stave off her climax just a few moments longer.

Disappointment flickered through her when he stopped abruptly and shifted over her, but it was replaced with eagerness to the point of desperation when she felt the probing of his cock head. This was better. She dug her fingers into his arms, lifting her hips to meet him as she felt him lock with her body, felt the skin stretch.

She skidded up the platform as he thrust.

Thoroughly confused by the lust raging inside of her, he'd already repositioned himself for another attempt before Bri even realized what had happened. The second thrust inched her upwards again. Her hair, trapped beneath her shoulders, jerked her head backwards at an uncomfortable angle. She bucked, lifted her head in an effort to free herself from the tether, but Kole was near mindless in pursuit by that time. Every time she almost managed to free her hair, he thrust again. And each time he thrust, instead of making headway at claiming her, he shoved her further up the bed.

They were both coated with the moisture of their efforts by the time they hit the wall, their skin clinging one moment, slipping the next.

Fortunately, since Kole was taller, his head hit first.

The loud ping of skull against metal distracted her momentarily, but Bri was too focused on freeing her head and engulfing his flesh within hers to register much besides the sound.

Uttering a frustrated growl, he caught her hips and dragged her down the bed again, freeing her hair, much to Bri's relief.

It didn't last. They waltzed their way up the bed again. Bri lost her frantic grip on his shoulders with the jolt as his head connected with wall and plowed eight furrows across his skin with her nails, eliciting a pained grunt from him. This time, though, Bri was so wet and frantic, he managed to penetrate her just enough to drive both of them beyond reason. Giving up on trying to dig her heels into the bed enough to gain leverage, Bri lifted her legs to wrap them around his waist at the same moment he seemed to realize the dilemma and wrapped an arm around her hips to hold her for his next thrust.

She gasped as he slipped deeper, panting at the sense of fullness as his flesh forced her muscles to part for him until she began to think she would pass out. He withdrew and pushed again, fighting his way inside of her like a salmon trying to swim upstream.

Bri caught her breath at the quiver of sensation that rocked through her as his cock touched her g-spot, tensed with the certainty that the next thrust would push her over the edge. It didn't. It came maddeningly close, but no closer. She needed him deeper.

She'd just begun to have the sinking feeling that he wasn't going to make it when he stiffened all over, sucked in his breath and held it for a fraction of a second. The jerk of his cock was a split second warning that things weren't going quite the way she'd hoped. Uttering a strangled groan, he began to shudder and quake, pumping his hips in jerky movements as his body yielded up his seed.

Disappointment and anger washed through Bri. Her belly clenched hopefully around his cock, she teetered on the brink, and then slid down the slope again as he went still, supporting himself above her on shaking arms.

Feeling perilously close to tears, Bri gave herself a mental kick. She hadn't wanted to enjoy it! She should've been relieved it had ended badly for her.

She wasn't, though. She'd been so close she'd *known* she was on the verge of having her first climax ever, damn it to hell!

Chapter Eleven

It took all Bri could do to refrain from boxing his pointed ears when Kole, instead of pulling out, heaved a heavy breath and eased deeper inside of her. "Get off," she growled through gritted teeth.

He lifted his head, studied her for a long moment and said, "No."

Narrowing her eyes at him, Bri planted her hands on his shoulders and shoved. She might as well have been pushing against a mountain. It didn't budge him one inch, but he grabbed her wrists, pinning them to the platform on either side of her head and hunched his shoulders, seeking her lips.

She turned her face away. He covered her ear instead, exploring the cavity with his tongue. Goose bumps erupted all over her as heat rushed through her. The muscles along her passage clenched around his flaccid member in reaction, thrusting it outward. He lifted his head to look at her in surprise, but the effect on his cock was almost instantaneous. It swelled, resisting her involuntary efforts to evict it.

She caught her breath as he curled his hips, pushing slowly until the head of his cock bumped her womb. It contracted, sending pain through her, and he eased off again, watching her face intently as he moved within her.

Her anger and disappointment evaporated as she felt her body stir to life, unfurl and tense with his stroking caress until she felt again the distinct, heady rise of passion. Closing her eyes, she lifted to counter his thrusts as pleasure moved over her, through her, winding more and more tightly.

He released his grip on her wrists, shifting his weight to one arm so that he could stroke her with his free hand. Cupping the nearest breast, he plucked at the taut tip with his fingers, and Bri found herself making little noises of pleasure as she gasped and held her breath and then sucked in another breath as darkness swarmed through her mind.

Lifting her now freed hands, she dragged her palms down his chest and then around him, stroking the small of his waist and digging her fingers into the top of his buttocks. God it felt good! It felt soooo good!

She tightened her arms around him, pulling herself more tightly against him, tightened her legs to meet each jarring thrust as he began to move faster. One moment she was clinging in desperation to the edge of release and the next her body began to spasm with the most unimaginable pleasure. She uttered a choked cry as the first wave hit her, gasped in a lungful of air and cried out again as another wave hit and then another.

She was the next thing to unconscious by the time her climax ceased to erupt within her, barely aware of the quaking and shuddering of Kole's body as he came in her wake and sagged limply against her.

Too weak to cling any longer, Bri's arms and legs slipped from him and landed with a thud on the platform when she made no attempt to break the fall. She didn't have the strength to do so even if she'd been mindful of it. Her heart was pounding so hard it was all she could do to continue to breathe.

Finally, becoming aware that Kole hovered above her still, she cracked an eyelid to look up at him. A chuckle escaped her at the look on his face. "Not dead," she muttered in a slurred voice.

He rolled away from her and onto his back, breathing as gustily as she was.

"Not hurt?"

Surprise flickered through her. Frowning slightly, she did a mental inventory. "Nope. I think you might have displaced my womb a little but not to worry," she added teasingly. "I'm sure it'll drop back into place if I jump up and down a few times. And if it doesn't … well, what the fuck? As long as you don't shove it under my rib cage I'm sure the baby can find his way out."

She thought for a moment that she'd been so enthralled with the aftermath of that glorious climax that she'd forgotten herself when Kole's hand settled heavily on her belly. Consternation went through her, but after mentally reviewing her dialogue, she decided she'd said it in English and supposed he'd recognized the word baby.

She used it often enough he should know it.

Guilt pricked her at deceiving him, though. She ought to just tell him she could understand, and probably speak, his language.

Doubts still niggled at her, however, and the reflection that it might just piss him off clinched the matter. Maybe after she went to 'the room' next time she'd tell him they'd *just* taught her? As long as he never found out she'd been able to listen and understand every word he said while he still had to struggle to understand her he couldn't be pissed off about the unfair advantage the *Sheloni* had given her.

She rolled onto her side with her back to him when he lifted his hand, teetering between the desire to sleep and the need to get up and wash off the stickiness. She'd never had sex vigorous enough to work up a sweat--Of course most of it was from trying to force that kong sized cock of his up her. God! The man was hung like a fucking horse! Not that she'd expected any different. She might not have a very clear memory of the first time, but she remembered that part.

Anyway, he was big all over. It stood to reason he would be there, too.

She supposed that was why he'd thought he might have hurt her. She rolled her eyes at that. Men!

Or maybe, she thought, biting her lip to keep from smiling, he didn't realize it was *his* head he'd been banging against the wall?

She was still more than a little wobbly kneed when she finally pushed herself up and headed for the bathroom to clean up.

"The feel of Hirachi on your skin is repugnant?"

Bri tensed and came within a hairsbreadth of giving herself away at the comment. Fortunately, she was so surprised that he'd followed her into the bath and that he'd interpreted her wish to bathe in that light that she merely gaped at him in blank faced dismay when she whirled around at the sound of his voice. He took that to mean she hadn't understood him, but he didn't leave it at that. He lifted his arm to his nose and sniffed. "Smell bad?"

Pursing her lips, Bri turned away, wondering what was up with him. He'd come twice, the jackass! He ought to be content if now downright happy! "Earth custom," she answered shortly, irritated that he'd come in to pick a fight just as she was going to wash her sex. Deciding to ignore him, she cleaned herself anyway.

"Think wash baby off?"

Oh he was spoiling for a fight! Bri turned the water off and came to her feet. Turning to face him, she plunked her hands on her hips and glared at him. "If you must know I don't like … dripping come! I'm lucky *baby* didn't shoot through my nose!" she snapped, making a motion with her hand.

She saw something then that was completely unexpected. His skin darkened. If she hadn't been looking straight at him she would never have noticed it … or the way the whites of his eyes pinkened with color.

Hirachi's *did* blush, she realized with dawning amusement. It just wasn't as noticeable when they did ... which meant he'd probably known all along that she was blushing and was just playing dumb to tease her.

He stared at her a long moment, but she thought she saw his lips twitch with the beginnings of a grin as he turned around and left.

After staring at the empty doorway for a moment, Bri looked around and made another discovery. She'd left the damned towel in the other room!

Letting out an irritated huff, she stalked back into the main room and looked around.

Kole was sitting on the edge of the sleeping platform dangling the towel. Noticing her scowl, he held it up in offering. When she stalked over to him and tried to snatch it from his hands, he gave the towel a sharp jerk that snatched her clean off her feet. She only had time for a look of stunned surprise and dawning dismay before he caught her as she flew toward him. Lifting her up, he settled her astride his thighs. Slipping one arm around her hips, he caught her hair with his other hand and tugged, tipping her head back so that he could inspect her face.

His expression was unreadable as he scanned her face, but his face tautened as he studied her, his eyes darkening. He swallowed thickly. "You are so ... strange to my eyes," he murmured. "I can't fathom why you are so beautiful to me."

Bri felt a heated blush of pleasure fill her cheeks even as he covered her mouth hungrily with his own, slipping his hand from her hair to her shoulder to draw her closer. Crushing her against him as if he wanted to feel every inch of her flesh against his own, he moved his hands restlessly over her back and buttocks and finally broke the kiss to suckle at the tender skin of her throat and neck.

Surprised at the intensity of his ardor, it took Bri's mind longer to catch up than it did her body, for the fierce hunger of his kisses and rough, demanding caresses was contagious. Within moments, Bri felt as needy as she had before she'd experienced the explosive climax only a little earlier, felt starved for the feel of him inside of her, fevered with the heat churning in her belly and breasts.

Dragging her upright after a moment, he hunkered down to capture the throbbing tip of one breast. With the first drag of his mouth on the keenly sensitive bud, Bri felt as if her lungs had collapsed. Struggling to catch her breath, she stared down at the play of his cheeks as he suckled her breast, her passage clenching almost painfully for his possession with each drag that sent a new wave of pleasure roiling though her. Looping her arms around his head as he switched his attention to her other nipple, she explored the intricate swirls of his ear, from the opening to the pointed tip and back.

He shuddered, moaned, and broke from her breast to recapture her lips in another heated kiss.

Blindly, Bri explored his chest with her hands and groped for his engorged member. Her fingers grazed the rounded head and then she curled her fingers around him. Guiding his cock to her cleft, she aligned their bodies and pressed downward, lifted slightly, and then pressed again until she felt the moisture of her passage begin to coat him, to ease the fit of their bodies.

Breaking from her lips, he pressed his forehead against hers, dragging in deep, harsh breaths, holding them and then releasing them in pained grunts as she struggled to mount his shaft. Crushing his arms around her abruptly as if he could no longer bear the tease, he bore down on her even as he lifted his hips to thrust upward. Bri groaned as he slipped deeper inside of her. He eased his grip at once, stroking his hands over her almost apologetically.

Lifting until he slipped almost completely out of her, Bri bore down again until he could go no deeper inside of her. She hesitated, feeling her body quivering perilously near release, wanting nothing more than to savor the thrill of having him inside of her for as long as she could.

His face was a mask of agony as she lifted her head to look at him. As if he sensed her gaze, he opened his eyes to stare at her before he pulled her close and began to nuzzle his face against hers, caressing her body with his hands. "By the gods, woman," he said on a ragged breath. "I want to pleasure you as you do me, but I can hold my seed no better than a Halfling when I feel your heat, feel your body fisting around mine."

His words sent a shaft of pleasurable response through her, making her belly clench around him harder. His touch, his scent, the feel of his hard flesh embedded so deeply inside of her, touched off an explosion of sensation. She began to move on him as she felt her body begin to convulse in imminent release, uttering a long, low groan as the first tremors of her climax hit her.

His arms tightened around her once more and then relaxed. Gripping her hips, he guided her in her shaky movements, held her tightly as he surged upward again and again until his own body peaked. Uttering a choked groan as his cock expelled his seed, he went still, clutching her tightly as the spasms of ecstasy shook him.

He lay back when the tremors had finally stopped. Carrying her with him, he held her against his chest, stroking her back. Bri wasn't certain if it was meant to soothe her, or because he seemed fascinated with the feel of her skin, but she found it didn't matter. It *felt* like the caress of a lover, and it gave her the illusion of being cared for and protected. It was nice to feel that even briefly.

"It is good," he murmured after a long while, taking one of her hands in his and studying it, "that you are not nearly as fragile as you look. I feared that if I did what I wanted to do that I would … hurt you.

"It is not nearly so good that I know now what I only imagined before. I will regret this. I know I will regret it. And I fear you will too … though not as I will.

"I only wish that you were as big and strong and fierce as you seem to believe you are."

The problem, Bri thought wryly, was that she had no illusions about how she stacked up next to the opposition. No reasoning person, suddenly discovering themselves in the land giants, could delude themselves into thinking they had a snowball's chance in hell of matching a Hirachi toe to toe. She supposed he thought she saw herself that way because she wasn't really afraid of him anymore, but that wasn't because she had this illusion that she was capable of taking him on. It was because she didn't believe *he* would hurt her, not intentionally.

She wasn't so sure about the others, particularly since he'd made it clear that she'd been right. They had never seen a race, or a representative of a race, that was, on average, so much slighter in stature. She supposed it was inevitable that some of them would look upon that difference with contempt.

Kole probably did for that matter.

Which made her wonder how they looked at their own women. Were they, poor things, just one of the guys? Expected to be as strong and fierce at fighting as the men?

Maybe she'd misjudged them? Maybe their way of life had snuffed the nurturing instincts the female of the species was supposed to be born with? Maybe they hadn't ignored the needs of their young so much as they hadn't been able to bond with them, had only been able to see them as a parasite that endangered them by limiting their ability to protect themselves?

That would certainly make all of them more fierce, wouldn't it, the males and the females? If they had no real nurturing, no one to 'coddle' them, they were less likely to develop the 'weakness' of gentleness.

Kole had some gentleness in him, though, or at least a recognition of the concept.

He hadn't thought he had it in him to be gentle, though, if she'd understood his thoughts. He'd realized that he couldn't grab her and toss her around as carelessly as he might one of his own women, and at the same time he'd doubted he could manage enough self control to keep from breaking something.

Why had he thought he would regret it, she wondered? What was to regret? It wasn't as if either one of them had a choice in this situation. For her part, she was delighted to discover it not only wasn't the chore she'd thought it might be, but it had a definite bright side.

She'd enjoyed it. With the exception of Cory, the sex had been the only nice thing that had happened since she'd been taken. She wasn't about to look a gift horse in the mouth. If one had no choice but to do something, discovering that it wasn't half bad, was actually enjoyable, was an unexpected windfall of good fortune. She sure as hell didn't regret that it hadn't been horrible.

More than that, it was actually a relief that he'd finally managed to work up the enthusiasm to do the dirty deed. She'd begun to fear the separation from Cory would be indefinite, but if he continued with this much enthusiasm surely to god he'd get her knocked up in no time and she'd get him back.

The doubts that had been teasing at the back of her mind, that she'd been at pains to ignore, surfaced.

She could only ovulate once a month--unless the *Sheloni* had done something about that, too. She didn't know whether to hope they had or hope they hadn't tampered with that. She knew what tampering with fertility could do to women--some of them had fucking litters, and she thought *one Hirachi* would be hard enough to deliver.

She didn't want to think about *that* at all, though. She hadn't, in point of fact, thought about that aspect of it before because it was not something she could do anything about and there was no point in borrowing trouble that hadn't come up yet. She had her hands full dealing with the troubles already upon her.

She pushed the worry about whether or not she was fertile at all to the back of her mind, too. The *Sheloni* wanted Cory to survive.

They had to know that he would've been dead by now if not for her, which meant that she would get him back.

She had to try to stop worrying about that or she was going to go crazy, and she wouldn't be any use to Cory if she was a blithering lunatic.

They were 'rewarded' for performing by being allowed out for exercise, 'allowed' being the operative word. Bri wasn't exactly anxious to leave the habitat and stroll around the exercise yard in nothing but a towel but, as before, there was no choice. This time they didn't have to give her more than a mild jolt to convince her that her modesty was misplaced.

When the door opened, they went out whether they wanted to or not.

Bri made a new discovery when she went out.

The Sheloni had been busy little bastards. Every Hirachi within her view had been handed a 'pet' to breed, and in the habitat that had housed the Hirachi women was at least a dozen 'unassigned' Earth women.

She wondered what had become of the Hirachi women but since she was far more interested in the Earth women, she didn't give it much thought at the time. Consuelo, poor little thing, had been handed over to an ugly looking brute that looked even bigger than Kole, but then maybe that was deceptive. Consuelo wasn't as big as a minute and the size difference was bound to be vast. The top of her dark head didn't reach much higher than the brute's waist.

Spying Bri, her face lit up with what looked like vast relief. She'd been standing in the giant's shadow, but the moment she saw Bri, she charged toward the line closest to the habitat where Bri stood. The Hirachi male stared at her as if dumbfounded for a moment and then strode after her, grabbing her hand and jerking her to a halt.

Consuelo didn't take it well. Bri couldn't hear what the male said, but Consuelo couldn't have understood him anyway, and she didn't seem to care. She cut loose with a stream of outraged Spanish, and, when that didn't work, she clobbered him.

He stared down at her in blank faced amazement for several moments and reached for her, and Bri's heart seemed to stop in her chest. Afraid that she was about to see total annihilation, she still couldn't close her eyes. Instead, to her relief, he merely thumped her on the forehead with one large forefinger.

Consuelo clapped a hand to her forehead, checked her palm for blood--obviously it stung--and then lit into him like she thought she could take him apart. He grabbed her shoulders, holding her at arm's length until she stopped swinging at him and began trying to kick him in the shins--succeeded in kicking him in the shins.

He let her go. She kicked him one more time for good measure and then turned and stalked to the edge of the exercise yard. The *Hirachi* male glared at her back and then stalked with what dignity he could muster to the opposite side, folded his arms over his massive chest, and sulked.

"*Hola*, Bri!" Consuelo called across the yard that separated them.

Relieved, fighting the urge to smile, Bri hurried toward the woman. "*Hola*, Consuelo! You ok?"

An expression of irritation clouded her features for a moment. "Machissmo, pah!" she said with a snort. "No have Manuel," she added, her expression changing to one of sadness. "Have big, hulking brute instead."

Bri bit her lip, keenly aware of Kole behind her, and wished she hadn't taught Consuelo that particular word group. "They took Cory, too."

Consuelo nodded. "Tink slaver give back baby?"

Bri swallowed against a knot of misery that had risen in her throat. "Yes. Soon."

Consuelo didn't look as if she believed that, but she summoned a smile.

"Hey! You American?"

The new voice drew Bri's gaze, and she saw that one of the women being held in the group habitat was moving toward them. "Don't cross the line!" she shouted quickly.

The woman kept walking until she'd reached the edge of the yard. "I already know about the dog leash," she said tightly. "Do you know what's going on? We've been taken, right?"

Bri stared at the woman for a long moment. "It isn't like the UFO stories," she said finally. "I've been here for months, and I don't think they're going to take us back. But, FYI, Big Brother."

The woman stared at her blankly for several moments as that slowly sank in. Despite the twenty feet or so that separated them, she could tell from the woman's expression that she was trying to figure out what she might have said that she shouldn't have. "Timely info," she finally said dryly. "Shit! Stupid of me not to think of that, damn it to hell! You sure BB grasps?"

"Unfortunately," Bri returned, feeling downright ridiculous trying to talk in code even though she knew it could be seriously dangerous to let the *Sheloni* get the idea they might pose a threat of any kind. From what she could tell, the *Sheloni* seemed to view them as much less of a threat than their other slaves and that could only be a good thing.

"I'm Becky, btw, from Texas."

"Bri--Georgia. What about the others?"

"Diana and Lisa are from Florida," she responded, pointing to the young women and then named the others and where they were from. "The four over there in a tight little click are from Russia or Germany or something. Nobody's sure because nobody understands what they're saying. Why are you there … with that … alien?"

Bri stared at the woman, feeling her face heat. "Breeding pens."

A look of stunned horror clouded the woman's face. "For real?" she asked, revolted. "Better you than me...." She broke off. "Sorry. I didn't mean that the way it sounded."

Anger surged through Bri, but she discovered it wasn't entirely because she didn't like the insult to the *Hirachi*. Part of it was because she realized it was just breeding to the *Sheloni* and they not only didn't care how any of them felt about it, very likely the plan was to rotate the 'stock'. "You should get used to the idea," she said tightly.

The comment elicited a wave of hysterical babble that made it impossible for anybody to be heard. She supposed she should have tried for a little more tact, but she didn't think they were going to have a lot of time to come to terms with the change in their circumstances, and the sooner they did the better off they would be and the more likely they were to survive.

Unfortunately, they were making so much noise it made it impossible to try to communicate with Consuelo at a distance. Waving, she turned away and focused on trying to get in a little exercise while she had the chance.

Whatever was bothering Kole, she discovered, it wasn't something easily swept aside and dismissed in favor of exploiting the moment. After displaying all that flattering interest, he went back to ignoring her. She tried not to take it to heart. She tried to convince herself that it didn't matter. She had gotten what she'd really wanted, what she'd needed to get Cory back, and that was all that mattered. And she thought he would 'perform' again if necessary.

It helped that she wasn't stuck inside with him all day of every day.

Three days later, the *Sheloni* came for her--to check her progress, she was certain--except this time they didn't gas her. This time, she supposed, she got the regular slave treatment. A small bot appeared through a concealed door in one wall, informed her she was to come, attached a 'lead' to one of the wrist restraints they'd put on her the time before, and led her from the habitat through yet another door that she hadn't known existed.

Chapter Twelve

There was a lot to be said for being drugged after all, Bri thought wryly as the bot led her down a long, dimly lit corridor that was more like a tunnel than a hallway. Fear was something she was barely even aware of in that state. Now, she had nothing to shield her from it, and she was afraid even though she was pretty sure she knew what to expect.

Struggling to ignore the knot of anxiety growing tighter and tighter in her belly, Bri tried to focus on the positive side of the situation. She would be lucid enough to maybe learn something valuable.

The bot leading her was small, not even quite as high as she was tall. She hadn't seen one like it before, which made her wonder at the number and variety of robots the *Sheloni* had.

It occurred to her to test the thing's strength, but she dismissed it. This was no child's toy. The thing looked solid, and she didn't doubt but what it could take her apart limb from limb if ordered to do so--and it was probably programmed to damage if attacked. She sincerely doubted the 'robot laws' applied to anything made by the *Sheloni*, except where the *Sheloni* were concerned.

The corridor seemed to go on forever. Even as much as she'd worked to increase her fitness level, she was tired long before they reached their destination. The corridor was also freezing cold and curved, which gave her the impression, correct or not, that it spanned the circumference of a very, very big, and probably disk shaped, or round, ship.

The corridor seemed too consistently curved to follow the line of a more stream lined vessel.

Despite the exercise, she was so cold she was shivering by the time she was led through a seamless opening that appeared in one side of the corridor. She glanced at the opening as she went through, wondering if it was even an actual door. Maybe it was something like a dimensional thing?

She managed to touch one of the walls as she was led inside. It felt solid, demolishing the brief theory that the whole thing was just an illusion and there wasn't a wall, or corridor, at all and therefore no need for an actual door.

There were three *Sheloni*, she saw at a glance as she entered the room. They stood back near the opposite wall, guarded by two more robots that stood like sentinels in front of them.

Either they no longer looked upon her as completely harmless, or they just weren't going to take any chances. Once she'd lain on the examination table and the bot had clamped her wrist and ankle restraints, the *Sheloni* approached, surrounding the table to stare down at her.

Bri's stomach cramped with fear. She'd had nothing but a dim recollection of the creatures before. Now that she could see them clearly, they looked even more horrible than she remembered.

Somehow, they reminded her of spiders. She wasn't certain why, because they had two arms and two legs, not eight legs, but there was a definite correlation between the two. Something in her subconscious grasped that even if she couldn't quite put her finger on what it was.

The examination was far worse with full use of her facilities, at times downright painful. They were as dispassionate and remote and 'professional' as any doctor, though, and that similarity, although no comfort, was at least familiar enough to keep sheer terror at bay even though she had to keep telling herself, over and over, that they wanted her alive. They weren't going to kill her … at least, she didn't think they would intentionally do anything that would lead to her death.

Unintentionally....

"Female."

Bri blinked, thinking at first that the thing was demanding her attention since it had spoken in a language she understood.

"This is no use to us. You must try again."

Confusion filled Bri. Obviously they *were* talking to her, but she still didn't completely grasp what was going on. "I'm not pregnant?" she asked doubtfully, wondering if they would even bother to answer.

"Female," said the one that she had recognized--the one she'd decided must be important.

"You will breed again."

Bri stared at the thing, feeling perfectly blank. "I don't...."

The pain caught her completely off guard and took her breath. It was so intense, she nearly passed out. She would've screamed if she'd been able to draw breath to scream. As it was, she struggled against the restraints, trying to pull in upon herself, until she lost the strength even to do that. When she finally managed to open her eyes again, she saw her thighs were bloodied. It sent a wave of mindless terror through her. "What did you do? What have you done?"

The thing ignored it. It was just as well. Bri was in no state to understand even if it had deigned to explain. The pain wracked her for a seemingly endless time before it seemed to reach its zenith and began to slowly dissipate.

"Cory," she gasped finally, a note of pleading in her voice even though she doubted very much that anything would move them except their own concerns. "The baby needs me. He won't … he won't thrive without me to take care of him."

A long silence greeted her plea, and she'd begun to think they wouldn't answer her at all, but finally the lead *Sheloni* did respond. "This will be considered."

Bri was barely aware of what was going on around her anymore, but she felt it when the restraints were disengaged, felt the tug on the 'leash'. "Come."

Opening her eyes, she struggled off the table, but blackness swam up to greet her before her feet had even touched the floor.

When she came to, Bri discovered that she was in her own habitat again. After staring at the familiar scene blankly for several moments, a jolt of excitement went through her. "Cory?"

She sat up too fast. Blackness dropped over her like a curtain coming down. Her head was throbbing like a son-of-a-bitch when she came to again. When she was able to lift her head, she discovered she was on the floor. She'd fallen off the sleeping platform when she fainted.

Disoriented, she finally managed to push herself up right. Darkness threatened again, but she drew her knees up and dropped her forehead to her knees and the heaviness finally went away. When her vision cleared, she saw she was still bleeding.

Her period, she thought blankly? She hardly ever had periods because of the birth control.

But she didn't have the birth control anymore, she remembered.

She didn't have any fucking pads either, she realized in sudden anger!

Dismissing her predicament for the moment, she struggled to get up to look for Cory, knowing it was useless. She would've heard him if he'd been in the habitat with her … unless he was asleep? When she'd assured herself he wasn't in the habitat, she flopped onto the edge of the sleeping platform and stared glumly at her feet, her mind perfectly blank.

After a while, she got up and went into the bathroom to bathe and find something to catch the blood. She was so weak and shaky it was all she could do to perform the simple task. Exhausted by the time she'd finished, she wobbled back to the sleeping platform, lay down, and finally drifted to sleep. The sting of the collar woke her.

The door, she saw, was open. That meant go out or get another jolt. It took an effort to drag herself up even so. She was feeling faint again by the time she got to the door, and it took every ounce of will power she possessed to make it through the door. She stood just outside for a few moments, trying to keep her knees locked and finally simply wilted to the ground and curled into a ball.

The Sheloni had done something to her, she knew, but she couldn't figure out what it was they'd done that would make her so weak and shaky that she hardly had the strength to drag herself around. Trying to figure it out seemed like too much effort.

When the next day cycle began, she woke to discover Cory lying next to her in the bed. Joy mingled with disbelief for several moments, but he wasn't an illusion. They'd given him back to her!

He screamed when she swooped down on him and gathered him to her. Startled, Bri settled him on her lap to see if she'd hurt him. She didn't see any signs of injury, though, nothing that would warrant the screaming. It seemed to take forever to calm him down and even when he'd cried until he'd exhausted himself, he stared at her as if he didn't know her.

Bri studied him in dismay, fighting the urge to burst into tears herself as it dawned on her that that was what the problem was … he didn't seem to know her. He was young, but surely he couldn't have simply forgotten her in such a short absence, could he?

They must have done something to him, she decided, feeling her grief abruptly boil into fury. No matter how carefully she checked him, though, she couldn't see anything to support that theory. She spent most of the time worrying over him, struggling with him because he seemed determined to fight every attempt to soothe or pacify him, even refused to take food from her until he obviously reached a point where he couldn't resist any longer.

She didn't go far from the habitat even when they made her go out. She was still weak anyway, and Cory howled when she tried to put him in the carrier. She was exhausted long before she managed to get him down for the night and still couldn't sleep herself for the anxiety churning inside of her. The second day wasn't as bad as the first, but it didn't miss it by much. He was still fussy, still looked at her as if he didn't know who she was, but sometime in the afternoon that seemed to change. Instead of looking at her as if he had no idea who she was, he looked downright distrustful, angry.

As hard as Bri tried not to interpret his expressions that way, she finally decided that he had finally remembered her, but he believed she'd abandoned him, and he was angry and distrustful because of that.

Inwardly, she raged at the Sheloni, for the first time feeling real, tangible hate for them--hating them so much she felt sick to her stomach. They'd destroyed something important that had developed between her and Cory, and she wasn't at all certain she could get back.

Trust was so hard to earn, and harder still to earn back once it had been broken, and it wasn't as if Cory could understand even if she tried to explain that she hadn't abandoned him. He'd barely gotten to the stage of making any kind of sound beyond crying.

Disinclined to attempt to socialize, still feeling weak and ill, and worried about Cory, Bri didn't even try to walk the baby when they went out for the first several days. Instead, she settled just outside the door and focused on Cory, struggling to get some response from him besides the blank stares, or accusing looks.

Long before her period finally stopped, though, she'd begun to feel desperate to seek advice from some of the other women. Some of them, she was sure, would know something about babies.

The bastards hadn't given her anything for 'the problem' though, and it took a while for her fears to outweigh the embarrassment of being seen in public in such a condition. She didn't even have any fucking panties to hold a pad in place, damn them to hell! It was just one more thing the bastards had done to reduce her to the level of lower animal!

If she hadn't needed answers about the baby, she would've just hid until the bleeding finally stopped, but unlike her normal periods, this didn't stop after a few days. Finally, hoping it just wouldn't show, Bri gathered Cory in her arms and moved far enough down her yard to see the women at the group habitat.

"Hey!" she called out to get their attention, only realizing after she had that she couldn't even remember the woman's name.

The woman she'd spoke to before approached the edge her yard, though.

"Do you know anything about babies?"

The woman looked at her and then stared at Cory. "Not that

kind," she finally said.

Bri stared at the woman in complete disbelief for several moments before fury washed through her. "Fucking cunt!" she yelled, whirled on her heel, and had already started back toward the habitat when Consuelo called to her.

She stopped, turning to look at Consuelo indecisively for a moment. She had the horrible sensation of drippage, but she couldn't get back into the habitat anyway. After a brief hesitation, she rushed to the edge of the yard and settled on the ground. Thankfully, the Sheloni had given her a gown to wear when they'd sent her back to her own habitat. She pulled it over her knees and settled Cory on her lap as Consuelo settled across from her with Manuel. "Cory doesn't act like he even knows me," she said agitatedly. "I don't know what to think. He just cries and looks at me like I … hurt him. And I'm afraid he really is hurt or sick. I'm at my wit's end!"

"Manuel cry, too," Consuelo said sorrowfully. "Miss. He miss."

Bri swallowed against the knot in her throat with an effort. "You think that's it? You think it's just the separation?" She made motions with her hands. "Take away?"

Consuelo nodded vigorously, but Bri could never be certain whether the Hispanic woman understood her or not.

It dawned on her abruptly to wonder if the Sheloni had given Consuelo the same knowledge they'd given her. After glancing around to be certain none of the Hirachi were near enough to overhear, she shifted closer and lowered her voice. "Do you understand the Hirachi tongue?"

Consuelo's brows shot up. She, too, glanced around. "They put this in your mind, too?"

Bri exhaled a sigh of relief. "Thank god!" This time, she told Consuelo from the beginning how Cory had been behaving.

Consuelo nodded. "Manuel, too. I think he'd forgotten me. They're young, maybe four months, maybe six, maybe older, though I don't think so. It's hard to say. They're so big, and then, too, they were neglected before. Babies don't seem to develop normally when they don't have a mother. This is what my mother told me, anyway. She had worked in an orphanage, and there were always more babies than women to take care of them, and she said they were slow to learn things.

"Anyway, they don't remember things very long when they are very young. So I think, maybe, they didn't remember us when they were taken away for weeks."

Bri thought that over, feeling angry all over again, even though she felt some relief, too, that Consuelo didn't seem to think anything had happened to either of them. "Sometimes Cory looks at me like he does remember, and ... like he's mad at me."

Consuelo looked surprised, but before Bri could take that as assurance that she must be wrong, she said, "It's possible. It's hard to say what they understand before they learn to talk, but if his expression seems to say that to you, you may be right." She shrugged. "If they were human babies, I would still not be an expert. I helped my mother with my younger brothers and sisters, but I've not had any of my own. And these babies are not human. It's just not possible to know how they should develop, what is normal for them."

Bri made a wry face. "You're a lot closer to an expert than I am. Until Cory, I'd never been around any babies at all."

"No?" Consuelo asked, obviously surprised. "You're a natural then, because you are very good."

Pleased with the compliment, Bri managed a smile. "I'm not sure Cory agrees, but thank you."

Consuelo nodded, smiling back, but then lifted her head to look around. "You did not tell the one called Kole that you had learned his language?"

Bri looked at her uncomfortably. "No." She frowned. "I don't know why. It's just ... I don't really trust any of the aliens."

"It would be easier to get to know them if you talked to them and perhaps learn trust," Consuelo pointed out.

"Maybe," Bri responded doubtfully and then gave Consuelo a speculative look. "But you didn't tell the one you were with either."

Consuelo made a face and then reddened. "Dansk. That one was not interested in talking."

"He looked ... really scary."

Something flickered across Consuelo's face. "They all look scary to me," she said non-committally.

Bri looked down at Cory. Taking his tiny hand in hers, she studied it a long moment and finally lifted it to her lips for a kiss. He closed his fingers over her puckered lips and pulled at them. "They're not complete barbarians, though."

"Just mostly. And at that, the more 'civilized', or at least more advanced, *Sheloni* are many times worse."

Bri glanced at her sharply.

"They killed their women."

A wave of shock rolled over Bri. "The *Hirachi*?"

"Dansk tended to mutter to himself a lot, probably because they have been kept separated since they were taken almost a year ago … his time. I don't know what that would be in our time. Or maybe only because he lost Lyaaia.

"He alternated between railing at the *Sheloni* and vowing to dismember them if he ever managed to get his hands on them, and cursing himself for his 'weakness' in growing attached to Lyaaia.

"She was one of the *Hirachi* women. They had all taken a sacred oath when they became warriors to fight to the death when the *Sheloni* came again, but they were denied the chance. The *Sheloni* merely rendered them unconscious and when they awoke they were here. They gave the *Hirachi* women to the men to breed, but the women vowed they would not give a child to the *Sheloni*. Some of them self-aborted and died. The *Sheloni* prevented the others from doing that, but when the infants were born, they strangled them.

"I got the impression that the men have no say about the children because they belong to their mothers. So they simply accepted what the women had decided."

Bri frowned. "So you think the men are as bad as the women because they didn't stop it?"

"Because they didn't try."

Bri didn't believe there was any way the men could have stopped it, but she didn't disagree with Consuelo. They could've at least tried to talk the women out of it even if they couldn't physically intervene. For that matter, how did either of them know whether the men had tried or not?

On the other hand, Consuelo had one very good point. They were reared to the same customs and beliefs … and those sounded pretty damned barbaric to her.

"He didn't … Did he hurt you?"

Again an indecipherable expression flickered across Consuelo's face. "Not … deliberately, I don't think. But he … you know … big."

"Oh," Bri said, turning as red as Consuelo and transferring her attention abruptly to the baby. She hadn't meant *that*! With relief, she heard the alarm ordering them back inside while she was struggling for something else to say.

Without a word, they both rose, gathered the babies, and headed back.

"Bri!"

Bri stopped abruptly at the call, trying to ignore the odd little leap her heart had executed at the sound of his voice. She had not seen Kole since they had taken her to the examining room, but that wasn't because she had been carefully avoiding looking toward his habitat. She hadn't been able to resist glancing that way, but he had not been out since she had been able to leave her habitat.

Pivoting, she turned to look at him. Instead, her gaze locked with that of the woman standing a short distance behind him.

Feeling very much as if she had been turned to stone, Bri didn't think she even blinked or breathed for several moments. It took an effort for her to drag her gaze from the tall þlond to look at Kole.

"Baby?" he asked when she looked at him at last, cupping one hand over his stomach and then pointing to her.

She stared at him uncomprehendingly, but when he pointed at her, she looked down. The spots on her gown sent another jolt of shock through her. This time, however, it galvanized. Without a word, she whirled, heading back toward her habitat at a fast walk, and then a run. She didn't stop running until she'd leapt through the door.

Chest heaving with the effort to drag in a decent breath, her legs shaking with the exertion, Bri finally wilted to the floor and settled Cory on his belly next to her.

For an endless time, she simply stared sightlessly, her mind perfectly blank. Slowly, the shock began to wear off, however, and as it did her mind degenerated into chaos.

A dry, painful sob erupted from her chest so abruptly that it startled Cory, but for once Bri was in no state to respond to his frightened cries.

Her baby. She hadn't been having a period. They'd aborted her baby because it was a girl.

Chapter Thirteen

Bri wept. She couldn't seem to stop crying. She cried until she couldn't see, until she couldn't breathe, couldn't seem to swallow, until Cory gave up crying and lay snuffling beside her.

Abruptly surfacing from her own misery, Bri picked him up and began rocking back and forth, holding him to her chest. He rubbed his wet face all over the shoulder and neck of her gown and then lifted his head to look at her. The moment she burst into tears again, he began wailing.

After a while, realizing that it was her distress that was upsetting Cory, Bri fought for self-control, drying her own face on the gown.

"Stupid!" she muttered under her breath as she struggled to rise with the baby and discovered she'd been sitting on the floor so long she could hardly creep. "I am so stupid!"

She hadn't even known she was pregnant. She hadn't wanted the baby. She'd just wanted to do whatever it took to get Cory back.

She didn't know why it hurt so badly to suddenly realize that that was what had happened to her. For that matter, she didn't know why it hadn't occurred to her before.

She'd been so ill, though, and then worried about Cory.

They'd given Kole another woman to breed. The thought alone was nearly enough to make her lose control all over again.

And she didn't know why that was either.

It took all she could do to pull herself together long enough to calm the baby down and get him to sleep. Once she'd settled him, though, she went into the bathroom and indulged her urge to fall apart until she was too exhausted to cry anymore, too exhausted to feel anything anymore.

She moved through the next several days like a robot, mechanically going about her life and tending to Cory. She wasn't certain when she would have awakened from her trancelike state if not for the baby, but one day as she sat just outside the habitat with him he pushed himself upright and smiled up at her. She stared at his hopeful little face for a long moment before she felt warmth begin to seep into the coldness inside of her and dispel it.

"Look at you!" she said, smiling back at him and grabbing for him when he began to lose his balance. "When did you learn how to do that, you smart boy!"

His tentative smile broadened into a grin when Bri lifted him up until they were face to face and smiled back at him. Her heart seemed to stammer.

Frowning, she studied his face more carefully. Did he really resemble Kole, she wondered? Or was it nothing but her imagination?

He frowned back at her, looking uncertain, and Bri dismissed the thought, kissing him until he began smiling again. "We should show Consuelo what you can do. I'll bet Manuel can't sit up yet!"

The moment she said it, she felt sick to her stomach. Going to see Consuelo meant going close to Kole's habitat, and she wasn't certain she could stroll by and act as if it didn't bother her that he had a new breeding partner.

Even if not for that, he'd asked about the baby, and she didn't want to talk about it. If he asked again, she'd start blubbering again.

She didn't know why she was so emotional over it. It was unreasonable given the circumstances, all the circumstances. She could've understood her behavior better, and the awful sense of loss, if she'd been far enough along to actually begin to think of it as a baby. Or if she'd been trying a long time to get pregnant-- there were any number of situations where her reaction would've been completely understandable even if hard to deal with.

It was because they'd taken it, she realized abruptly, discarded her baby girl as if she was completely unimportant without even asking if it was important to her! And it was to her!

She just didn't know why.

She heaved a sustaining breath. She had to deal with this. She'd dealt with everything after her mother's death. She could deal with this, too.

But she hated the Sheloni more with every breath she took, and if it was the last thing she did, she was going to annihilate the bastards!

Cory drew her back from her dark thoughts with a noisy complaint, and she forced herself to relax, to smile when she didn't feel like smiling because he needed to see that. He'd just begun to open up to her again. She wasn't going to let the Sheloni spoil that, too.

She felt like a prisoner on the way to the executioner as she crossed the yard, taking care not to look in Kole's direction at all, though she could see him in her peripheral vision well enough to know that he was watching her. Focusing on her breathing to try to stay calm, she smiled and waved at Consuelo. Consuelo smiled and waved back, hurrying to the area where they usually sat and talked.

"What happened?" Consuelo demanded in a low voice the moment she settled.

It was as if the question itself jerked a hard knot in her throat. Bri focused on situating Cory while she fought it, managed to swallow. "I just ... I wasn't feeling well," she managed. "Cory's doing better!" she added brightly.

Consuelo studied her searchingly for a moment. "Is he?" she asked finally.

Relief flooded through Bri, and she smiled at Consuelo gratefully. "He's stopped being so fussy and standoffish. And he's learned to sit up by himself! He's getting so big and strong. Just like his...." Bri stopped and cleared her throat. "Do you watch movies? American movies, I mean?"

Consuelo stared at her blankly for a moment. "Yes. I love movies. I haven't seen many American movies, though," she said slowly.

"Slaver movies?"

Something flickered in Consuelo's eyes. She frowned, but thoughtfully. "I don't like slavers."

"Me either. Actually, I really like *murder* stories the best, because there's always a puzzle to figure out--and suspense-- especially *spy* movies where they have something everyone's after and there's lots of guerrilla action and they use *codes*. Because they can't just say something outright, you know. The bad guys might figure out what's going on because they use all sorts of special devices to listen in and spy on people.

"I don't suppose you ever saw *five* little Indians?"

Consuelo frowned, thinking. "I think it was six."

It was Bri's turn to frown, but try though she might she couldn't recall ever having seen more than five Sheloni. She shrugged. "Maybe it was six. You'd think it would take more that six little Indians to man a row boat, wouldn't you?"

Consuelo considered that. "Maybe we're both wrong," she said finally. "You should talk to the others and see if any of them remember the story."

Bri didn't want to talk to them. She was still mad about that comment that woman had made about Cory. The two of them weren't near as likely to manage what she wanted, though, as all of them together.

Nodding, she got up and leaned down to pick Cory up. Settling him on one hip, she turned to look at Consuelo again. "Just think about, ok? Really hard, because it really bothers me when I can't remember *exactly* what something is."

She met Kole's gaze as she turned to head to the other side of the yard. Her heart seemed to stutter to a halt before it kicked in again in overdrive. He didn't attempt to speak to her, however. He merely watched her as she moved to the edge of her enclosure nearest the group habitat. Forcing a smile to her lips, Bri called out to them with false gaiety. "Hello fellow Earthlings!"

The women, who'd been gathered in a knot talking to one another, turned to look at her blank faced with surprise.

"Consuelo and I were just talking about movies, but she isn't a big movie buff like I am. I was wondering if any of you might remember this really old movie called, The Great Escape?" She paused for several moments, waiting to see if anyone seemed to grasp what she was trying to do. Most of the women continued to look at her blankly, as if they suspected she'd gone off the deep end, but several moved away from the others, focusing on her expectantly. "It was an 007 movie, I think, and he sent cryptograms to the other side because of the Nazis' surveillance."

"I remember that movie!" one the women called back, moving closer. "But it was...."

A second woman joined her, cutting the first off. "Yeah! I remember it, too. 007 was kick ass, but the Nazis gave me the creeps."

Bri nodded. "I thought that was the name of it. The Nazis were really good de-crypting, though, so they had to be careful."

The woman nodded. "I'm Angie. Com ... PC software specialist."

Bri blinked. Slowly a real smile curled her lips. "Nice to meet somebody from my home state! Any familiarity with Trojans, worms, or bugs?"

"Mostly from the extermination end. I'd try to grow one ... just for a pet ... if I had a proper habitat."

"Oh, that's too bad, but maybe we could improvise?" She paused when the buzzer sounded. "Maybe we can play movie trivia sometime?"

Angie curled her lips in a facsimile of a smile. "That would be fun! Relieve the boredom. It'd be nice, though, if we could figure out a way where everyone could play."

Bri couldn't resist glancing at Kole. "Everyone?"

The woman thought it over, turning to look at the Hirachi nearest her. Obviously, when she'd said everyone, she'd meant the women who couldn't speak English among them. Finally, she shrugged. "If you want them to play, I guess. You know more about them than I do, I imagine. Unless they've seen Earth movies, though, they wouldn't be any good at movie trivia, but we might be able to think up another game and include them. The more the merrier, right?"

"I'll give it some thought," Bri said and turned, hurrying back to her habitat with Cory. She tried to tamp the hope that had suffused her like a high energy drink, fearful that so drastic a change in her wouldn't go unnoticed, but it was impossible to hold all of it inside.

Settling on the floor to play with Cory, she divided her attention between him and the thoughts whirling in her mind. A software specialist! Of course, the likelihood seemed remote that they'd be able to use Angie's talent, but at least it was *something*. She had to wonder what talents and/or skills the other women had that could be useful.

They needed to know that so they could figure out what they had to work with and formulate a plan. They also needed to know everything they could about the Sheloni and that didn't seem like nearly as impossible a task with so many pairs of eyes and ears. They were closely monitored, and the *Sheloni* had obviously mastered the languages, which meant they would be very, very good at breaking down speech patterns and figuring them out-- which meant they'd be good at codes, too.

She still thought the movie trivia game could work well for them to pass information back and forth. It seemed doubtful the *Sheloni* would be familiar with their movies, and they could refer to plot lines without actually saying anything at all. The tricky part would be passing the info from one person to another, because they didn't all know the same language.

Maybe it would be better, though, if everyone didn't know everything?

Maybe it would also be a good idea to include the *Hirachi*? However they felt about Earth people, they had a common enemy. And the *Hirachi* had been with the *Sheloni* longer than anyone else. Whatever she thought about their customs, Bri knew the

Hirachi were neither primitive nor ignorant nor stupid. They might well have a plan of their own they had been working on since they'd been taken. Their war-like society, it seemed to her, meant that they would be well acquainted with battle strategies. Of course, given their brute strength they might not be familiar with guerrilla tactics--which they would have to use. She was pretty sure they outnumbered the *Sheloni*, but the *Sheloni* still had a tremendous advantage. They had an army of robots, which were more powerful even than the *Hirachi*. They knew the territory--the ship and the planet they were going to--better than any of their captives--who knew almost nothing about either one--and they had superior technology, whereas their captives had no technology they could use and no understanding of the *Sheloni* technology.

Those thoughts made her hopefulness take a nosedive, but she refused to allow defeatism to overwhelm her. There *had* to be a way.

Realistically, she knew the odds of ever getting home again were almost non-existent, because even if they could take over the ship and figure out how to fly it, they knew nothing about space travel. There hadn't been enough exploration from Earth for any of them to know how to navigate such vast distances.

It would still be better to be free of the *Sheloni*. They could find a way to survive, and they'd have an easier time of it without the *Sheloni* standing over them ready to exterminate them.

Or their children.

She *could* kill. She knew she could now, and without suffering a moment's qualm. Any doubts that had lingered before had been banished by the cold blooded way the bastards had snuffed the budding life inside of her only because it had been a girl.

The only thing she regretted about knowing she was going to find a way to kill them was that she knew she was going to have to strike with whatever means came to hand. She couldn't make them die slowly in horrible agony, unless she, or the group, was unable to devise any other method of wiping them out.

The one thing that worried her was that she was afraid she wouldn't be useful in the rebellion she was instigating. She wouldn't be satisfied with merely being a bystander or part of the cheering section.

It was almost a surprise when she realized that. The person she had been before wouldn't have wanted that either--she would've wanted to get as far from something that unpleasant and potentially dangerous as she could possibly get.

This was a personal battle, though. She wasn't a bystander here, watching and condemning cruel behavior toward others.

That was only part of it, though. She, like everyone else, had been brought up to believe in the 'system' set up to protect them. One called for help, or justice. Not only was a person discouraged from helping themselves, they were likely to find themselves on the receiving end of justice if they 'forgot' they were just supposed to hope somebody came, not do anything.

It was not an altogether happy thought. She'd liked the person she was. Maybe she'd been fairly colorless and commonplace, but she'd been comfortable with herself. Maybe she wouldn't like the new self as well.

She still meant to push herself, though. She knew it was the only way. She would deal with the ugly side of herself later. At the moment, she was only relieved that she had a vicious side she could call upon. To survive, she needed the strength it gave her. To ensure Cory survived, and any children she bore had a fighting chance of survival, she needed to cultivate her own inner barbarian. Soft would only get crushed.

Wrack her brain though she would, however, she couldn't think of anything she was capable of that was really useful. In her other life, she hadn't really been anything but a glorified housewife--a housewife for hundreds of working mothers who needed help in providing nutritious home-cooked meals for their family--but still just a housewife. As fulfilling as she'd found that at the time, as much pride as she'd taken in the thought that she was helping to support family life by giving families the chance to sit down to a dinner together, she couldn't see that it was anything that could be turned into warfare--not unless the *Sheloni* would let her bake them up a batch of poison brownies.

Shelving that anxiety for the moment, she considered the *Hirachi*, wondering if the *Sheloni* had implanted the knowledge of their language in all the women. If she was right about their motives, it seemed that they would. The *Sheloni* seemed to be counting on the Earth women to nurture their new crop of slaves and 'tame' their wilder side. A common language was necessary for a group to work together.

If she was right and they had, and the *Hirachi* hadn't figured that out yet, it was possible they could 'spy' on the *Hirachi* and discover if it was safe to take them as allies. Otherwise, if the *Hirachi* were a threat, too, they would have to deal with them after they'd dealt with the *Sheloni*--or at the same time. She was inclined to empathize with them, even though she despised some of their customs, but they would be in an unacceptable situation if they got rid of the *Sheloni* only to discover the *Hirachi* treated them as badly or worse.

There was only one way she could think of to discover whether she was right or not, though, and she was reluctant to do it.

She was going to have to strike up a friendship with that blond that was fucking Kole.

The thought made her feel vaguely ill. Grinding her teeth, acknowledging that it was jealousy, she struggled to accept the fact that it was an emotion none of them could afford. The breeding could be used as an advantage if they could set aside their natural tendency toward territorialism. The Hirachi didn't seem to suffer from that particular problem--probably something to do with their custom of eschewing close relationships, maybe even just a quirk of their nature that prevented it--so it shouldn't create problems. And the breeding was the only thing that allowed them close contact.

It still took all she could do to save her life to approach the woman. She spent the first half of her exercise time working out and working up her courage. Finally, mentally reciting a pep talk for herself, she hailed the woman when she reached the nearest point in the two adjoining enclosures. "American?"

The woman stared at her distrustfully for several moments and finally moved closer. "No, but I speak English."

Swedish, Bri decided. She should've guessed tall, beautiful, and blond equaled one of the Scandinavian countries. Trying not to feel resentful, Bri forced a friendly smile. "Seems the Sheloni spanned the globe for the best selection of fuck buddies they could find for the Hirachi."

The woman's eyes narrowed.

Stuck up bitch, Bri thought, holding her smile in place with an effort. "Don't take that the wrong way."

"Vat is right way?"

Ok, so maybe her diplomacy had slipped and a tiny bit of malicious jealousy had slipped in. She shrugged, resisting the urge to descend into childish name calling. "Actually, that just didn't come out the way I intended. My name's Bri--I'm sort of taking a survey."

"For vhat?"

Bri smiled thinly. "It can get pretty boring around here."

"Not here," the woman responded provocatively.

Allowing an image to settle in her mind of knocking the bitch to the ground and pounding her beautiful face to a pulp, Bri managed to hold on to her temper. "Oh. Guess you wouldn't be interested in playing allies and enemies, then? Musical chairs seems to be the only one anyone's playing now. We all get to play that one."

The woman studied her speculatively. "I thought the *game* was movie trivia?"

"We're going to play that one, too, but I've been trying to think up something that would include everybody since we don't all speak the same language. We'd have to have a common language to play the trivia game."

The woman tilted her head to one side thoughtfully. "Maybe you should check first and see if there is one that all know? I, myself, speak a bit of several languages, and understand two very well, my own and … a rare *Asian* tongue."

It took a moment for that cryptic message to sink in, but then Bri realized that *Hirachi* did sound a lot like an Asian word. She knew that *had* to be what the woman was hinting at. There was nothing *rare* about any of the Asian dialects. They were a prolific race and had more problems with over population than just about anybody else. "I'll do that," she said, smiling more easily. "I think it's a good thing to learn all we can about each other anyway since it looks like we're all going to be one happy family."

The woman nodded. Bri hoped that meant she had grasped the general idea, because generalizations were about all they could manage at the moment. She didn't dare chance anything at all that might tip the *Sheloni* off that they were trying to organize. That was the most crucial element to their success or failure, gathering and exchanging information.

She still didn't like the woman, but that hardly mattered. Common enemy, she reminded herself. They could go back to hating and distrusting each other for being different after they'd gotten rid of the *Sheloni*.

At the moment, it was much more important to focus on using what they had at their disposal. If the *Sheloni* had breached the language barrier for them, they'd given them a powerful weapon to use against them.

Chapter Fourteen

Bri was so caught up in her scheming, she almost overlooked a problem closer to home--protecting Cory from the machinations of the *Sheloni*. It wasn't altogether that, though, and it certainly wasn't because she was neglecting or ignoring Cory's needs.

Her memories of her last close encounter with the *Sheloni* were just so painful that she tried to block it from her mind.

Then again, she might not have remembered at all except for the fact that she was working so hard to make certain the women used their knowledge of the *Hirachi* language and the breeding to gather as much information as they could about the *Hirachi*.

It dawned on her abruptly, though, that she was one of the women. The *Sheloni* had told her that she would be bred again. She supposed the only reason they hadn't yet was because they realized she would need a little time to recover if she was to have a chance at being bred successfully and producing for them.

She had very mixed feelings about that prospect, aside from a revulsion of being passed around. She had wanted to play an active role and being bred would give her that chance. On the other hand, that also meant Cory would be subjected to the tender mercies of the *Sheloni* again, and he did not fare well under their care.

How could she circumvent that, though?

She was afraid she couldn't, but she had to try. God only knew what it would do to Cory to be traumatized by another abrupt separation.

The alternative wasn't any better. The *Sheloni* didn't trust the *Hirachi* not to hurt the baby. She didn't know if they could be trusted or not, but she sure as hell didn't want to test it. So trying to convince the *Sheloni* to let her keep him with her was definitely out. The only alternative that came to mind was Consuelo. If she'd already been bred, there would be no reason to separate her from Manuel, and she knew Consuelo would take good care of Cory, too. He might still be unsettled and upset. He might still forget her in the time she was gone and leave her struggling to regain his trust yet again, but it would be better for him with Consuelo, regardless. *She* would care whether he cried or not, and she would know what to do to soothe him.

The *Sheloni* might be cold blooded and unreasonable in her book, but they wanted Cory and Manuel to thrive. It didn't matter that their motives were different. It only mattered that their ultimate goal was the same in this case.

If they drugged her as they had before....

But they hadn't bothered with that the last few times, having decided, apparently, that she was docile enough they could manage her without the drug.

She hoped that was the case, because she didn't know how well she'd be able to plead her case under the influence.

Having decided on the best course, she resolved to speak to Consuelo about it the very next time she was allowed to go out.

She didn't get the chance. The bot came for her the following morning just as she was preparing Cory to go out.

"Leave the child. Come."

Bri stared at the chunk of metal that had appeared out of one of the 'rat holes' as she had begun to think of the invisible access doors to her habitat. Coldness washed over her, making her belly knot in anxiety. "Wait!" she exclaimed when the thing clamped a lead to her wristband. "I should give him to Consuelo to take care of while I'm … gone."

To her surprise, the bot seemed to hesitate.

Deciding it must be communicating with the *Sheloni*, she rushed to press her point. "She can take care of both babies, and he'll be better off," she added. "He isn't … he won't be any good to you if you keep screwing up his head! And, if I take him to her he won't be scared and confused."

"Take the child to the one called Consuelo."

This time the voice didn't come from the bot. It seemed to waft through the walls. Relief flooded her even though her anxiety didn't diminish appreciably. She didn't want to leave him at all. If she'd only had more time to adjust to the idea of having him torn from her again she thought it might have been easier.

Then again, maybe not. Nothing was actually going to make it easy.

Gathering him up hurriedly before they could change their mind, she followed the bot as it led her through the outer door. It wasn't until Consuelo emerged carrying Manuel that it dawned on her that everyone was out.

And everyone was watching.

Closing her mind to that for the moment, she focused on Cory.

"I have to … you know," she said uncomfortably when Consuelo stopped at the sight of the bot. "They're going to let you take care of Cory for me, though."

She could see Consuelo didn't really want to get anywhere near the bot, but she settled Manuel on the ground and sidled close enough to take him when Bri held him out. Cory began to fuss almost at once, but Consuelo bounced him and turned to distract him with 'the baby'. Cory instantly quieted, staring at the 'baby' in absolute fascination, as if stunned to discover there was another person his size around. Swallowing against the lump in her throat, both relieved and a little hurt that he could be so easily distracted, Bri didn't resist when the bot led her away.

As focused as she was on her misery, though, it didn't last. The moment she realized the damned bot had no intention of taking her back into the habitat embarrassment pierced her grief.

Talk about a walk of shame! It was bad enough to be thrown in with one of the Hirachi to be bred like she was nothing but a … dog, but to lead her to her stud in front of everybody and his brother!

She did her best to act unconcerned about it, but she could feel the blood pounding in her cheeks.

And, as acutely self-conscious as she was about being stared at by everyone, she was even more uncomfortable when she caught Kole's gaze as she was led past him.

It didn't matter, she told herself. Everyone was in the same boat as she was. They all knew it wasn't a matter of choice.

Besides, it meant she'd have the chance to discover another puzzle piece about the Hirachi, a little more information that would help them make the right decision about whether or not to accept them as allies.

The bot led her to the Hirachi called Dansk, the one who'd impregnated Consuelo.

Consuelo had said he talked a lot. It was a good opportunity.

She hoped like hell Consuelo wasn't thinking about cutting her throat right about now. Unable to resist the temptation to look to see how Consuelo was taking it, Bri glanced in her direction apologetically.

To her relief, Consuelo merely smiled and waved.

Kole, she saw as she swept her gaze back toward the mountain of man meat she'd been handed over to, was still watching. His face was not devoid of expression, however. He looked … pissed off.

She looked away quickly, unnerved by the anger, uncertain of whether it was directed at her or at Dansk.

Dansk, she saw when she finally nerved herself to look at his face, looked anything but delighted himself.

Her heart sank. What was it about *her* that made them so damned reluctant to fuck her? She couldn't see that they acted that way about the others, and she knew damned well he'd 'performed' for Consuelo, otherwise she'd still be in the breeding pen.

They were ordered inside. It was a relief in a way, because even though there could be no doubt that everyone knew what would be going on inside, and it was almost as bad as having to perform publicly, it wasn't quite as bad if she couldn't see them. Out of sight, out of mind, she told herself, knowing they had enough on their own plate that it really wasn't likely they would give it another thought.

It was still hard to convince herself of that. She felt horribly exposed.

Dansk slammed his balled fist against the door as it sealed behind them, making Bri nearly jump out of her skin. Sending him a frightened glance, she scurried to the far side of the room, wondering if Consuelo had lied to her about the Hirachi not being mean.

At the sound of her furtive retreat, he turned sharply away from the door. The tension seemed to go out of him. She could see his face darken and realized from his expression that it was embarrassment not anger that brought the blush. His skin was lighter than Kole's and his blush more noticeable.

She made an unexpected and not unpleasant discovery when she finally allowed herself to really look at him.

Contrary to what she'd thought before, Dansk was not ugly. Unlike Kole, whose face was more appealing because of the strength and virility evident in his harsh features than from any real claim to beauty, Dansk was handsome.

Maybe she just noticed because she'd grown accustomed to their skin tones and could see past it and maybe that wasn't it at all, but there was no denying she found his features came together to make a remarkably handsome face.

After staring at her uncomfortably for several moments, he crouched. Before Bri could get really worked up about that, he went to his knees, and she realized he'd hunkered down so that he wasn't looming over her threateningly. Lifting a hand toward her, he held it palm upward. "No hurt little ting."

Bri stared at him blankly for several moments, wondering with dawning indignation if he thought she was ... like a puppy dog. It occurred to her forcefully after a moment that it was not exactly a good thing that the Hirachi seemed to be learning English from two women talking baby talk to their infants. Correction, one talking baby talk in English and the other in broken English with a strong Spanish accent.

When the surprise passed, she did a mental double take. He'd spoken English! He hadn't learned that from Consuelo, she didn't think. It was possible, she supposed, but not likely because Consuelo didn't have much English herself, and she was way more comfortable using her own language. It hadn't been implanted either, otherwise he would've been able to speak more clearly, not merely piecing random words together.

Obviously, the *Hirachi* had been sharing information themselves. Kole must be the source, but he had no direct contact with Dansk. "Me or you?" Bri asked finally, staring pointedly at his barked knuckles.

This time the blush was more pronounced. He scrubbed a hand over his face, released a harsh breath. "Kole say no hurt little strange ones."

Indignation, not relief, swelled in Bri. Kole had called *her* strange? "Strange?"

He looked dismayed. "Cute?" he offered hesitantly, obviously having searched his mind for a word she might find less offensive.

Abruptly, amusement hit her. Bri bit her lip, trying to keep from smiling. "The word you're looking for is beautiful," she said, wondering where the urge to tease him had come from.

He smiled a little warily. "Beautiful?"

God! What was she doing playing with the monster alien? Five seconds in his company had shown her he was a little bit high strung--far more emotional than Kole. If he realized she was teasing and didn't take it well she could be in serious trouble.

She'd gotten a really skewed picture of the *Hirachi*, she realized, giving herself a mental boot in the ass for racial prejudice. She hadn't thought she was, and yet she'd formed a mental picture of all of them being just like Kole--as if they had no individuality!

Dansk might be a nightmare on the battlefield--in fact she would guess just that since it was patently obvious that he did not have Kole's iron willed self-control--off it he seemed more of a teddy bear. And, now that she thought back on it, she decided she wasn't giving him his due. He must have a good deal of self-control. Consuelo had cussed him up one side and down the other *and* lit into him and he hadn't done anything more than thump her on the head. Maybe she hadn't managed to do any real damage, but it *had* to have hurt.

Realizing Dansk was still holding his hand out and deciding the gesture actually was an 'olive branch' Bri pushed away from the wall and approached him. When she placed her hand in his, he curled his fingers around it and drew her down to face him. Caressing the hand he held lightly with his long fingers, he smiled faintly, bringing a dimple into play in one cheek. "No hurt, Kole no say no hurt," he said in a low voice.

It took Bri's brain several moments to interpret that statement, but she finally took it to mean that he was saying he wouldn't hurt her even if he hadn't been ordered not to.

She *was* reassured, as she was sure he'd meant her to be, but she was more interested in the fact that he seemed to be saying Kole was their leader. She'd wondered at that. Somehow, he'd *seemed* like a man accustomed to leading others, but it had been Kole who'd given her the impression that they didn't actually have a leader, that they simply worked as a team.

Dansk recaptured her attention by stroking his free hand lightly along her cheek. "No hurt beautiful...." He broke off. After a fairly significant pause, he added. "Baby."

Bri didn't manage to catch the smile that time, but the amusement wasn't just because he'd struggled so hard and then come up with baby. It was because it dawned on her that he was probably a real Casanova Hirachi where he was from. It was actually kind of sad that his vocabulary limitations made his romancing so difficult for him.

And it was cute.

"No word?" he asked, disconcerted.

Bri chuckled. "Lots of guys call their woman baby. I don't mind."

She could tell he didn't understand half what she'd said, but he seemed to grasp that she didn't mind. He tugged on her hand, drawing her slowly closer, and the amusement died.

Consuelo hadn't exaggerated, she thought wryly, trying not to be completely unnerved by the swiftness of his move from stranger to lover. Dansk wasn't conflicted at all about the breeding business if the bulge in his breeches and the gleam in his eyes were any indications, and she was pretty sure they were.

He was so gentle and careful of her as he gathered her against his broad chest, though, that an inexplicable tightness clutched at her heart. She'd more than half feared he had simply lulled her wariness, disarmed her with that shy smile, and meant to pounce upon her without restraint, without consideration for her fears once he had her within his power. The tightness eased as he stroked his hands over her body almost reverently stirring desire to life within her with so little effort she was almost appalled.

A twinge of guilt nipped at her as images of Kole clouded her mind, the uncomfortable sense that she was betraying both men by responding so readily to both. She pushed it to the back of her mind. This was no commitment anymore than the time with Kole had been. She had not agreed to any of this. If she could take pleasure from it, she had the right to do so, and it was far better to close her mind to the circumstances and take something good from it than to feel violated and abused. Enjoying it might make her feel guilty, but that was preferable to the alternative.

When he eased her away from him and gathered her gown in his hands to remove it, doubt niggled at her again, but she made no attempt to stop him or to try to delay the inevitable. She lifted her arms, allowing him to pull it off. When he'd tossed it aside, he simply sat staring at her. Lifting his hands finally, he explored her bare skin with his palms and fingertips. Faint tremors shook his hands as he molded them to her body and traced the contours of her breasts, her ribs, her waist, and hips.

Catching her hands where they had settled on her thighs, he lifted both, examined each in turn and placed a light kiss in each palm before he settled her hands one at the time on his shoulders. Circling her waist with his own hands, he rose, pulling her to her feet, and led her to the sleeping platform.

She climbed onto it, shivering slightly as she lay back and watched him remove his breeches. He had much the same fighter build as Kole, hard, well developed, and well defined muscle groups all over his body and, like Kole, he was virtually hairless with the exception of the long, dark hair on his head and the small patch of dark, nearly straight hair that surrounded his engorged manhood.

She thought there were as many subtle differences in his body as there were similarities, however. Thought, because she had learned Kole's body with her hands, not her eyes. When his restraint had finally broken, their coupling had been wild, tempestuous. There'd been no slow exploration of one another.

Dansk, she knew, was somewhat taller, and yet, even so, he seemed broader, had the more mature build of an older man. But perhaps that was merely imagination? She couldn't see that his face looked older.

He surprised her. Instead of falling upon her at once, he settled on his side beside her and continued the exploration he'd begun before, as if he was determined to savor each moment, each touch.

Or was it only that he was restraining himself to keep from frightening her? His hands shook noticeably as he stroked them over her body in caresses that were soothing and at the same time stirred warm currents through her, awakened every inch of skin to optimum sensation. She began to feel impatient for more as he cupped one breast, kneading it gently, then moving his thumb over the taut tip in a circular motion that sent stabbing quakes of pleasure through her.

As if he sensed the rising need in her, he shifted to gather her closer to his body. His face grazed hers lightly, cheek to cheek. He inhaled deeply as he turned his head slightly to brush the tip of his nose along her temple. "Sweet," he murmured in his own tongue. "Your scent …," he paused, swallowing, the sound loud in her ear, "drives me insane. I don't know what I want most … to claim your body at once and drive into you until I spill my seed or to savor the taste and feel of you until I lose my mind completely."

He opened his lips over her ear, sucking at her ear lobe for a moment before he explored the intricate swirls with his tongue. Heat washed through her as his heated breath and the moist heat of his mouth teased the sensitive flesh. He moved to the skin just below her ear, sucking at the patch of flesh and then teasing it with the tip of his tongue, then moved to another spot and repeated the action until he had covered the side of her neck with love bites and each time a headier wave of heat flooded her until she was a morass of molten sensation.

He lifted his head when he had reached her collar bone and traced a similar path up her throat to her chin. With an effort, she lifted her eyelids and tried to focus on his face above hers. "I think that I would rather go slowly insane," he murmured, smiling faintly, "to keep you only a little longer. The moment I give them what they want, they'll snatch you away from me."

His words had barely registered when he brushed his lips lightly along hers, nipping, sucking gently. The moment he opened his mouth over hers and breached the fragile barrier of her lips to possess her mouth, however, the tentative exploration vanished.

His mouth was demanding, possessive, his kiss filled with fierce, ravening hunger as he thrust his tongue into her mouth, explored it with a thoroughness that almost seemed to stop her heart and snatched her breath from her lungs. His hands, too, became more demanding than supplicating as they roamed her body in a restless quest for full possession of her senses.

Bri felt a sort of madness seize her, as well, felt a mindless fever overtake her. And when he ceased to explore her mouth and began a thrust and retreat of his tongue inside of her in imitation of sexual penetration, her belly clenched with desperate longing for the feel of his cock inside of her. Molten moisture flooded her passage, demanding, not merely welcoming, his full possession of her body.

She had to struggle to catch her breath. Without any awareness at all of lifting her hands, she felt the smoothness of his skin beneath her palms, the tautness of his muscles.

After stroking his hand along her back and side, as if learning the dips and curves of her body, he moved his hand to her belly, splayed his palm briefly over that quaking plane and then slipped his palm over her mound. She jumped when she felt his fingers carefully parting her nether lips. He traced her cleft, teased her clit briefly and then backtracked and slowly pushed one finger inside of her.

Bri caught her breath at the intrusion. Her fingers curled against him. Briefly, doubt warred with desire as she felt him exploring her passage with his finger. A fresh, harder wave of want blossomed inside of her as he stroked her with care, but with purpose. Her belly clenched at the waves of pleasure he evoked, the muscles of her passage closing tightly around his finger.

Breaking the kiss, he lifted his head to watch her face as he slowly withdrew his finger and began to tease her clit, alternating after a few moments between the maddening torture of her clit and delving his finger inside of her until she began to quake all over with imminent release. She was going to cum. Reluctance speared through her and a thread of embarrassment to find herself nearing climax when he hadn't even penetrated her with more than one finger, and both warred with a burning desperation to allow her body the release it craved.

"Dansk," she gasped on a shaky breath, arching her head back, squeezing her eyes tightly as she fought the leap, "no."

"Yes," he said, his voice hoarse with his own need, moving his hand to tease her clit again until jolt after jolt of exquisite pleasure was running through her almost continuously like an electric current and she couldn't catch her breath. She twisted her head back and forth, fighting it, feeling as if her entire body was on fire. Abruptly, she lost the battle, reached a point where her body simply couldn't handle any more pleasure without exploding. A low groan was forced from her as the first wave convulsed through her and then a sharper cry as the next hit her, harder than the first. He played her body, teasing the bud of flesh until she thought she would pass out from the powerful jolts convulsing her body, until she was gasping sharp little cries of ecstasy.

A sense of profound relief and complete and utter satisfaction wafted through her when her body finally ceased to seize in climax. She felt drained of every ounce of strength, felt as if her entire body had melted into a sizzling puddle of wax. Completely limp, barely even conscious, she was only dimly aware of the soothing stroke of his hands over her at first. She made a faint sound of complaint in her throat when he gathered her cooling body against his warm one, vaguely aware that she was the only one who'd come, that he was entitled to take his pleasure, and yet reluctant to be dragged back from her own sated bliss to perform.

Puzzled but relieved when he made no attempt to do more than hold her and stroke her soothingly, she relaxed, allowed her mind to drift aimlessly.

She was scarcely even aware of the point when his touch became more purposeful, when her body ceased to cool and began to grow warm with arousal once more.

Chapter Fifteen

One moment Bri was drifting between consciousness and unconsciousness, and the next she felt a stirring to life of the ashes of her desire as Dansk rolled her onto her back and moved over her. Supporting the bulk of his weight on his side and one arm, he cupped one breast and lowered his head to suckle the nipple he teased with his tongue until it was almost painfully taut. The burgeoning of her body from satiation to taut arousal was so swift, the dizzying rush left her reeling.

A protest died on her lips. She encircled his head with arms that felt so weak they felt almost atrophied, stroked her fingers through his long, silky hair in appreciation, kneaded his back like a contented cat. With slow deliberation at first, he savored the taste and feel of her flesh with his mouth and tongue, teasing first one taut peak and then the other, but his own arousal mounted faster and higher than hers, swiftly becoming a conflagration. Within moments, the faint tremors that began in his arms spread throughout his massive body and became a noticeable trembling and there was a hunger and desperation to his touch that ignited a fire of need in her.

No longer content to confine himself to teasing her to distraction by suckling at her breasts, he moved lower, sucking love bites along her flesh in a winding descent that left little uncharted territory until he reached her lower belly.

He stopped there, straightened to stare down at her with his heated gaze a long moment and then moved. Grasping one leg above her knee, he parted her thighs and settled on his knees between them. Leaning over her again, he supported himself with one arm and stoked her body from breasts to mound with his free hand.

Bri shivered in anticipation, parting her legs wider in invitation, arching her hips as his hand reached her mound.

Instead of entering her as she'd expected, however, wanted ... needed, he pushed himself backwards and settled on his belly, burrowing his face against her mound. Surprise froze her. The first stroke of his hot, faintly rough tongue across her clit as he delved her cleft sent a nearly painful jolt through her.

Before she could even think to protest, although she tensed with reluctance, he drove all thought from her mind by burrowing deeper and sucking her clit into his mouth. She cried out, bucked, struggled, but he merely caught her thighs, holding her for the feasting of his mouth on her until all thoughts of fighting or protest vanished. Threading her fingers through his hair, she kneaded his scalp, rising to meet his stroking caresses in a mindless fever of need as her body bounded at lightening speed toward release. The sharp edge of pleasure raked her. Before she'd entirely grasped the powerful intensity of the jolts of ecstasy rocking her, she came, so hard it seemed to stop her heart, squeeze the breath from lungs … and continued to convulse until she was almost screaming for surcease from the rapture racking her body, begging him to stop because she didn't think she could take anymore.

Relief flooded her when he lifted his head and she was finally able to draw breath. Barely conscious, her entire body still quaking and throbbing from the blood still pounding through her, she lifted her eyelids with an effort as he moved over her. It took far more effort to lift her arms to him in welcome as she felt him settle his hips against hers, felt the hardness of his cock sandwiched between the lips of her sex.

Dragging in a shuddering breath, she arched her hips, urging him to take the pleasure he'd denied himself.

The pain when he breeched her opening was so unexpected it forced a cry from her. She bit her lip, fought it as he went still, probing her with no more than the head of his cock. Catching her breath, she arched against him as he gently probed again, prepared, she thought. She wasn't. Her sex was raw. As careful and tentative as his efforts were to claim her, she felt as if he was thrusting sandpaper against her channel walls.

He withdrew after only a moment, settling beside her on his side. "No," Bri said, distressed. "It's alright. It doesn't hurt, really."

Pulling her snugly against his chest, he stroked her hair and then her back. "Hurt," he disputed.

Bri swallowed against an inexplicable tightness in her throat, casting wildly about in her mind to try to understand why she felt so raw there. It dawned on her finally that it must be from what they'd done to her--it was as if they'd scraped her inside--or maybe it was a natural side effect of a miscarriage? She didn't know which. She only knew she hadn't healed from it yet.

It seemed grossly unfair to deprive him of his pleasure after what he'd done to please her, but she couldn't bring herself to insist.

He caught one of her legs after a moment, lifted it slightly, and pushed his cock between her thighs. Understanding dawned as he thrust his pelvis against hers. She tightened her thighs around his erection, arching to meet him the next time. He made a pained sound. Slipping a hand down her back to her buttocks, he dug his fingers into the soft flesh and began to move faster.

Her heart fluttered, quickened. Meeting his thrusts, she burrowed her face against his chest, exploring him with her lips as he had her. He jerked, shuddering when she teased one of his male nipples and began to suck it. Uttering a groan that seemed to be filled with as much pain as pleasure, he thrust faster. The tremors in his body grew harder and harder. Suddenly, he stopped, uttered a choked sound. His cock jerked between her thighs. Warmth filled her as she felt his convulsions of pleasure, felt his body yield up his seed. It was more erotic than she would ever have imagined it would be to be so totally aware of his pleasure.

An inexplicable wave of tenderness caught at her as he sagged against her finally, breathing raggedly. On impulse, she shifted, pulling at him until his head rested against her breasts. Wrapping her arms around him, she caressed him with her hands. He snuggled closer, wrapping an arm around her waist. "I will crush my precious little flower," he muttered thickly after a few moments.

Bri came so near to responding to him in his own tongue that it sent a chill through her.

He felt her tense, but apparently he interpreted it as pain from his weight. He rolled onto his back, carrying her with him. She tensed to move off of him, but he wrapped his arms around her, holding her, and she subsided, content enough to lay draped over him, drowsy from the lingering aftereffects of two powerful climaxes and the satisfaction of knowing he'd found pleasure, too, even though she was more than a little dissatisfied with the manner of it. She couldn't help but wonder if he felt cheated. *She* felt as if he'd been cheated, certain that penetration would've given him more pleasure and a more satisfying release. After the heights of ecstasy he'd treated her to, it seemed especially unfair to do little more than jack him off.

She was still grateful for his thoughtfulness of her comfort.

To deny his own needs, to do so when he'd been driven to a fever of passion that should have left little room for awareness of anything else, he'd obviously meant it very sincerely when he'd promised he wouldn't hurt her--not merely meant that he would *try* not to hurt her in his pursuit of pleasure.

He almost seemed to read her thoughts. "It's as well I couldn't do what I wanted," he murmured after a few moments. "I'm not sure I would have been able to pull out, or remembered I'd intended to." He shifted, rolling until they lay side by side. Hooking a finger beneath her chin, he tilted her face up for his inspection. "I am greedy ... and probably the stupidest Hirachi ever born. The elders knew what they were doing when they denounced the old ways. Caring too much can make even a strong warrior weak, can divide his heart and mind so that he is careless in battle, more focused on the pleasure of being with his woman than on protecting the interests and well being of the tribe as a whole."

Releasing her, he rolled onto his back, staring up at the ceiling. "Gods! In all the time I lay awake wondering what it would feel like to be with you, I had not imagined it would be so...."

He didn't finish the sentence, much to Bri's chagrin. Disappointing?

He had every right to be, but he didn't *seem* disappointed. He seemed satisfied ... pleased with himself as if he'd enjoyed wringing cries of pleasure from her as much as he had enjoyed his own release ... and she still felt as if she'd cheated him. She couldn't help it. She hadn't realized she was so raw inside that she wouldn't be able to bear being touched there. If she had, she would have....

What? Denied him?

That would only have created a misunderstanding that she wouldn't have been able to explain, not without letting him know she understood his language. And, if he'd felt rejected, he might not have been willing to offer himself up for another dose of it.

He didn't seem inclined to dwell on his disappointment if that was what he'd felt. He seemed very disinclined, in fact, to allow her out of his sight. As unaccustomed as she was to having a man in her life, Bri was a little surprised to discover she didn't feel stifled by his attentiveness. Quite the contrary, in fact.

She felt ... worshipped, adored.

He would study her until she began to feel acutely self-conscious, until she began to wonder if he was searching for flaws--or had found them--and then he would simply pull her close and cuddle her against his body, as if the contact was a pleasure in itself and sex unnecessary.

Not that he eschewed *that* either, but, surprisingly, to her at least, he seemed to find equal pleasure in cuddling her when he was too exhausted from bouts of lovemaking to do anything else.

And it was hard to think of the things he did to her as anything *but* lovemaking when he was so tender of her and her needs.

Experience was obviously the best teacher, and just as obviously, Dansk had had plenty of it. Almost effortlessly, it seemed to her, he could drive her into a delirium of mindless need, bring her to completion, and then begin again until she was exhausted from the expenditure of so much pleasure.

She couldn't help but wonder what was running through his mind when he did lay for hours merely cuddling her, occasionally stroking his hands over her in a way that was almost possessive, though not really in a sexual sense … not as if his intent was to arouse her. Her own thoughts were disturbing. She enjoyed it far more than she was comfortable with, found herself wishing for things that were impossible given their situation.

But maybe it was only that he found it as calming and comforting as she did? After his outburst the first day that had unnerved her, he either managed to funnel his frustrations into the outlet of sex, or simply controlled them with grim determination to keep from alarming her again.

Bri lost all track of time. Dansk, whatever his feelings, either couldn't resist temptation, or he was determined to enjoy the situation to the fullest, or he was bent on convincing the Sheloni that he was cooperating. He didn't attempt full penetration again for nearly a week, but he didn't allow that to stop him from wringing every ounce of pleasure from her.

If she'd thought about it at all, she would've been certain she simply didn't have much of a sex drive. It hadn't really bothered her that there'd been years between the few relationships she'd had. She'd been willing to have sex, but that was more to please her partner than because she'd felt any great need, and she always ended up faking orgasm … also to please … maybe partly just to escape the bedroom without a fight.

She'd been thrilled to death when Kole had brought her to orgasm, not just because it made her feel fabulous, but because she felt as if it proved there was nothing wrong with her when she'd always secretly believed there was.

Dansk taught her she was not only capable of achieving orgasm, she was capable of multiple orgasms. The unnerving part about it was that it seemed the more she did, the more she wanted. It was like an addiction. She wasn't certain whether it was an addiction to

Dansk or just to sex, but either way it was not a good thing.

She was supposed to be focused on learning what she could about the Hirachi, and discovering what Dansk might know about the Sheloni and/or the ship.

Instead, he kept her so awash in sensations that she hardly knew one day from the next. They rested, they slept, they ate, they attended their personal needs, but primarily Dansk made love to her.

And the more he pleasured her, the more dissatisfied Bri was that she couldn't give him what she knew he wanted. She wanted his seed inside of her. She began to crave the feel of his flesh, hunger for it. It wasn't enough that he pleasured her. She wanted to *give, needed* to.

"I have often wondered if I am so different from everyone else, or if it is only that they hide it better, that they have more discipline that I," Dansk muttered one day as they lay curled together weakly after a bout of lovemaking.

Roused, Bri instantly noticed tension in him--strange that she'd become so attuned to him, she thought, when they'd only been together a little over a week, were still virtual strangers in every way except physically. In that sense, she knew him almost as well, she thought, as he did her, knew where and how to touch him to give him the most pleasure.

And yet she still didn't really know *him*, didn't know what his life had been like before, didn't know what he wanted out of life.

But even the thoughts went through her mind she realized, wryly, that maybe it wasn't so remarkable that she'd instantly noticed the tension in him. There'd been a feverish quality about the way he'd made love to her, a sense of desperation, as if some unnamed dread were riding him.

"There is merit to the new ways. No one is denied the simple pleasure of coupling with any woman who chooses them ... only the mating is forbidden. Even I enjoyed the freedom of dining at a different table whenever I was hungry ... at first. I've no idea when that ceased to ... satisfy me, when it was no longer enough. But the elders did not deny their own need to bear young, they only demanded it of us, as if they'd forgotten the ... madness that comes from denial."

He shifted uncomfortably. "I fared well enough the first few seasons, not so well the fourth or fifth. The sixth...." He grimaced. "Not at all well. If they had not forced me into the confinement lodge with the other males.... Most likely I would have been driven from the village for taking what was not offered.

"I understand, now, why the elders demanded the sacrifice, else I would be half mad now wondering what had become of my child when I was taken. And yet it availed us nothing! We have had the freedom to have *nothing* beyond momentary pleasure. We have had nothing to strive for beyond a good death in battle or an honorable death in ritual suicide. That is no life at all!

"I would almost be willing to embrace slavery if it meant we would be allowed to have what was denied before, but the Sheloni will not allow it either. I have hungered for you since I first saw you ... I was nearly a madman when they gave you to Kole, sick with rage that I had not even had the chance to court you for myself.

"And when I have done what they want, they will take you from me, and take my child from you. And I will still have nothing."

Heaving a harsh breath of anger, he rolled from the platform abruptly and began to pace. "Before the gods! I wish they had not given you to me at all! I do not want to give you up! I will do something unbelievably stupid when they come to take you!

"Gods! It is just retribution for the dark thoughts I held in my heart! In spite of the corruption of our ways ... in spite of the fact that I knew Laayia hadn't chosen me to sire her child, would have refused me if she had been able to deny the mating, I allowed myself to bind to her, allowed myself to believe I would have the family I had wanted.

"I wanted to kill her myself when I discovered what she'd done. But when *they* killed her.... " He stopped, scrubbing his hands over his face. "I do not know if I feel the weight of her death because I wished it, because I could not control my desire for a child, or because ... I did not want her."

Bri sat up and studied him uneasily, struggling with a confusion of emotions.

Most dominate was the urge to tell him the truth, to tell him she had understood everything he had said--to stop him from saying more that he would regret her having heard. She should, she knew. It was shameful to maintain the deception when he believed he had the privacy of the language barrier to prevent her from understanding his confession.

It was patently obvious he had needed to confess, that his sense of guilt, however misplaced she thought it was, was eating at him and needed some kind of outlet, but just as painfully obvious that she was intruding on his privacy.

He might have said it regardless, and yet, from what he'd told her, it was taboo to feel and think the way he did. It might shame him, and she couldn't bring herself to do that to him … and it was far too late to make her own confession without embarrassing him.

It was both sweet and flattering to think he'd gotten a crush on her, but she knew how painful they could be, and the first was always the hardest to deal with.

It occurred to her, briefly, to wonder if she was the one being deceived, to wonder if this was merely some sort of act designed to draw her out, but his distress and anger seemed too real to dismiss it as playacting.

And she found that she was far more interested in soothing him than risking upsetting him even more. He would have to deal with his own demons, though, she knew, whatever she did. Cuddling him like she wanted to might only make it harder for him. He seemed to think it would.

He was probably right, too, if all he'd said was true. He'd lost the ability to distance himself emotionally from others, despite the attempts of the elders to teach the young Hirachi to be completely detached and self-sufficient.

It didn't escape her that it could be risky to her, too. He'd already touched something inside of her, drawn feelings to the surface she should not consider nurturing.

There was no place for softer emotions here, no time for it. She had enough to deal with as it was. Cory was her first priority. She could not afford to be side tracked from the need to destroy the Sheloni by the desire to simply shut the world out and surrender to the urge to mate and nest.

It disturbed her that she identified that urge so easily, particularly when it wasn't something she'd ever experienced before, but then she realized that Kole had already brought that to the surface-- somehow. She'd been hurt and jealous when she'd seen him with the blond woman when she'd had no right to be at all, shouldn't have even had a reason to feel that way.

No matter how civilized people got, though, it didn't seem that they ever completely escaped their animal instincts. She suspected hers were urging her to seek shelter in the strongest available male.

If that was true, it explained her urge to attach herself to first Kole and then Dansk. It didn't make it any easier to deal with, but it explained behavior that seemed against her nature, or at least vastly different that she'd experienced before, and was definitely contrary to her upbringing.

Any old port in the storm!

She wasn't going that route, though. Her instincts were urging her in the wrong direction. She didn't really want to yield her destiny into the hands of anyone else.

Wryly, she wondered if that was the case with poor Dansk. Had his instincts to mate and produce off-spring become so pervasive that he was running purely on instinct? That he was struggling to attach himself to a female, any female?

That was an unhappy thought, making Bri worried that she was more at the mercy of her instincts than she liked to believe. It was absurd! She didn't even know Dansk--didn't know Kole.

On the other hand, she knew from personal experience that crushes defied logic. She hadn't known the boy she'd gotten her first crush on--had *never* gotten to know him. But that hadn't stopped her from pining over him, fantasizing about him, dreaming, yearning, suffering endlessly. That hadn't stopped her heart from breaking when he had moved away. She didn't think she could possibly have grieved any more if she had known him.

Maybe she would've grieved less. Maybe he hadn't been the 'prince' she'd imagined.

And maybe not. Sex was just sex until the heart was caught up in it. Then it became a force to be reckoned with. She should have realized something was up when she'd experienced such mind blowing sex.

Kole, she realized abruptly, must have sensed his vulnerability! That was why he'd worked so hard to keep his distance!

She gave herself a mental slap at that thought. She was *trying* to make herself believe that it had meant something!

She didn't need that to salve her conscience and make it alright. It *was* alright. There was nothing wrong with taking some enjoyment out of the situation if she could. It wasn't going to make her a bad person.

She wasn't cut out for this! At this rate she was going to be convinced every time the damned Sheloni switched partners on her that she was falling for the guy!

She was on the point of rolling off the sleeping platform and trying to put distance between herself and Dansk, mentally and physically, when he joined her again. She resisted, briefly, until she realized the futility of it. She could not avoid Dansk when she was trapped with him in the damned breeding pen, and she couldn't avoid sex, and she couldn't avoid becoming pregnant. Either Dansk did it, or someone else would.

Kole had been right. The quicker they took care of the task the better it would be for both of them … all of them. Forming attachments could be downright disastrous for them. It would certainly be an emotional disaster.

She could see why the Hirachi had elected to train their people the way they had, but it had to have damaged them, probably permanently, emotionally crippled them so that they could never accept a change now. Poor Dansk was having a hell of a time trying to deal with the conflict between his natural instincts and the unnatural ones his people had worked so hard to instill in him. It *was* debilitating.

Contrary to what she expected, however, Dansk made no attempt to initiate sex. He simply pulled her close against his body and held her in his arms until she finally dozed off.

It was she who finally convinced him to try full penetration again, not because she had enough sense to realize that she needed to get pregnant and that wasn't going to happen as long as there was no actual penetration, but because she desperately wanted him to.

He had already made her come twice, so hard that she'd screamed as if she was dying. She was the next thing to senseless, but when he pushed his cock between her thighs, instead of clamping them tightly around his engorge flesh, she reached for him, aligning his body with hers to show him what she wanted.

He swallowed thickly. His body was shaking with his need, and she could see he was torn. "No hurt, baby," he said harshly.

"You won't hurt me," Bri responded, arching to seat the head of his cock more fully inside the mouth of her sex.

He expelled a pained grunt and went perfectly still for several moments. Finally, he reached for her leg and dragged it over his hips. "Say if hurt, baby," he murmured huskily, arching his hips to thrust upward.

It did hurt, but not as much as it had the first time they'd tried. Biting her lip, she burrowed her face against his chest so that he couldn't see pain in her face. He wasn't fooled, and he wouldn't allow it. He pushed her onto her back and moved over her, watching her face intently as he slowly pushed and then retreated several times, penetrating her with little more than the head of his cock.

Seeing her discomfort, he stopped, began to withdraw, but Bri was beyond caring whether it hurt or not. She wanted him inside of her. Lifting her legs, she locked them around his hips, pulling at him insistently with her legs, arching her hips at the same time to bring him deeper. He lay passively, neither attempting to withdraw nor trying to thrust deeper. After a moment, he hunched his shoulders and leaned down to nuzzle her temple with his nose. "I want this, baby, so badly I can taste it," he murmured to her in his own tongue. "But I would not hurt you for all the treasure the universe holds. It would hurt me, not give me pleasure. You are … my heart and soul."

His words sent a current of warmth through her that was equal parts desire and affection. She tightened her arms and legs around him, clinging, determined to ignore the discomfort. "I want this," she said in her own language. "It feels … like heaven to have you inside me. I want it all." And she did. She felt desire rekindle at the thought of being possessed by him, felt moisture flood her channel, easing the discomfort. And when she arched against him again, she felt his flesh delve deeper, gliding through her body's lubricant without the uncomfortable resistance of before.

He felt it, too. Sucking in a harsh breath, he withdrew and thrust again, watching her face.

It was still uncomfortable, and it didn't help that he was huge, but the pleasure of feeling him inside of her far outweighed the minor discomfort. She relaxed her tense grip on him and began to caress him, planting her feet against the platform and countering each thrust until he sank to her depths, filling her so tightly she teetered for many moments between pain and pleasure. As he began to move rhythmically in and out of her, however, the scales tipped toward absolute pleasure.

She gasped, panting for breath as she felt the tension coil inside of her more and more tightly, encouraging him with soft moans of appreciation and the swift counterthrust of her hips until he seemed to lose the last vestiges of his control. He began to pound into her at a frantic pace that sent them both spiraling into bliss with unexpected swiftness. His chest heaving for breath, he held himself perfectly still above her as his body expelled his seed, uttering choked, almost pained grunts as the spasms rocked him.

His arms began to tremble with the effort to hold himself above her. She stroked him, drawing him down until his weight settled on her, nearly crushing the air from her lungs.

He chuckled shakily when he heard her grunt, rolling off instantly and gathering her against him. "It is a good thing for you, my heart, that I was not too far gone to support some of my weight else I'd have had a beautiful *flat* flower pressed against my chest."

Smiling lazily, feeling supremely satisfied, Bri snuggled against him.

They were both drifting toward sleep when the fucking door opened.

Chapter Sixteen

The sound of the door opening snatched Bri back from the verge of sleep. Still groggy and disoriented, she pushed herself upright and stared at the door blankly for a split second before reality crashed in.

Of all the fucking times for the fucking Sheloni to decide to send them out!

Bri rolled off the bed in such frantic haste that she sprawled on the floor. While Dansk scrambled to get his breeches and boots on, she ran around in frantic circles, dripping come, searching for her gown. She hadn't put it on since she'd been thrown in with Dansk, and she couldn't remember to save her life where she'd left it.

She'd just managed to grab it went a jolt went through from the collar. Gritting her teeth, she climbed into the thing as she hurried to catch up to Dansk, who'd paused in the door wait for her.

She'd only barely managed to get decently covered before she was shoved outside. The moment she glanced around and saw everyone else milling about, it dawned on her what she must look like. She and Dansk had just spent the last several hours mauling each other, and she knew everyone had only to look at her to know that was what had been interrupted by the 'exercise' buzzer. She could *feel* a trail of semen slowly winding its way down her leg!

Embarrassment didn't begin to cover her feelings!

Her hair, no doubt, was standing on end.

She looked up at Dansk, fighting a hysterical urge to giggle, or burst into tears, or both. His own gaze was amused, slightly embarrassed, but sympathetic. "All right, baby," he murmured reassuringly, trying to smooth the wild tangle of her hair with his hands.

It wasn't all right, though. She could see people glancing toward them. It was ridiculous to feel so embarrassed and awkward, she berated herself. Everyone else was in the same position she was. All of them had been put out to breed, but the humiliation of being on public display, knowing she looked liked she'd just been fucked silly, wasn't something she could calmly dismiss.

Catching her shoulders, Dansk walked her backwards until she was leaning against the wall of the habitat and then placed himself squarely between her and the vast majority of curious onlookers. Bri sent him a grateful smile. "I look bad!"

He shook his head, smiling back at her warmly. "Beautiful."

Bri covered her face with her hands. "God! This is soooo embarrassing!"

Dansk peeled her fingers away from her face and leaned down to kiss her. Chuckling good naturedly when she ducked her head in embarrassment, he kissed the top of her head instead of her lips, which he'd been aiming at. "I did not know you were so bashful," he murmured in his own tongue. "This is int...."

She had no idea how he'd meant to finish the sentence. They were both distracted mid-word by a sound of such fury that it made the hairs stand up on the back of Bri's neck. She and Dansk both whirled toward the sound.

Bri's jaw dropped to half mast, her eyes rounding. Kole was charging across the yard that separated them with death in his eyes.

Dansk stiffened, but apparently he was in no doubt of whom Kole's target was. Turning abruptly, he pushed Bri firmly behind him and braced himself as Kole launched himself at him. They collided like a pair of fullbacks on a football field. The blow as they slammed against one another made a sound like cannon fire. Bri screamed, too frozen to move until Dansk staggered back several steps and nearly slammed into her. Uttering another shriek, Bri scurried out of the way, her hands over her mouth as the two men struggled briefly, broke apart, and began hammering at one another with their fists. Tiring of that fairly quickly, they grabbed one another by the throat and began trying to choke the life out of each other.

Bri's mind had gone perfectly blank with shock, and brain activity was slow to return. "Stop!" she gasped finally. "Kole, Dansk, please don't do this! Stop it!"

It wasn't until both men froze and turned to stare at her that Bri realized she'd spoken to them in their own language.

In the dead silence, she heard the sizzle of burning flesh as a near blinding beam of light hit both men, knocking them from their feet. A jolt of shock went through her, but this time instead of rooting her to the spot, instinct kicked in. She rushed to the two fallen men. Falling on her knees beside them, she checked their pulses fearfully. She didn't realize she was crying until she discovered she couldn't focus on their faces, couldn't see how badly either man was hurt.

The mechanical claw that clamped around her wrist took her completely off guard, but she was in no state to assimilate what was happening around her, what had been happening. She fought the pull on her wrist, whirling and beating her free hand against the metal plate. It was futile. All she succeeded in doing was bruising her hand and nearly being jerked off her feet when the bot simply ignored her efforts to fight it and free herself and kept moving.

Dashing the tears from her eyes, she twisted around to see what was happening to Kole and Dansk and didn't know whether to be relieved of terrified when she saw that they'd been scooped from the ground by two other bots and were being carried away in the opposite direction. Were they alive? Dead? Were the bots taking them to attend their injuries? Taking them to dispose of them? She kept calling out to them, hoping both or either would respond, until the bot dragged her to a habitat and shoved her inside.

She stood where she'd stopped, staring blankly at the closed door, too numb for a while to think at all. After a while, when she realized she was alone, that she'd been standing like a stone for so long her feet and legs ached, she turned and looked around the room without recognition. It took her several moments to figure out she'd been returned to her own habitat, that she hadn't recognized it because she'd expected to find herself in Dansk's habitat.

Why had they returned her, she wondered fearfully? What was going on? Rubbing a shaky hand over her face, she finally wandered into the bathroom and sat down to stare at the shower for a while before she remembered she'd gone into the bathroom to bathe off.

She was shaking so badly by the time she'd bathed that her teeth had begun to chatter. After drying off, she went back into the main room, curled up on the sleeping platform, and wrapped the coverlet tightly around her. Warmth eluded her. The deep cold and shivering only seemed to get worse for a while, but in time it began to dissipate. Her teeth ceased to chatter, and the tremors wracking her slowed and finally stopped.

As she lay staring at nothing in particular, everything that had happened replayed itself in her mind over and over, and she still couldn't entirely grasp what had happened. In part, the images moved through her mind like a film on slow mo--except that she couldn't seem to grasp more than fractured images. The rest was a blur of speed.

She knew, though, that Kole had attacked Dansk. He'd charged right toward him. There was no way to deny that he had, or that he had intended to.

Why, she wondered blankly?

How?

He'd been wearing his collar. She distinctly remembered that because she'd thought when she had first heard the sizzle that it was the collar discharging. Maybe it was, but it hadn't brought him down--hadn't brought either man down, hadn't even seemed to slow either one of them down.

That was why the bots had been sent out, she realized, because both men had been in such a rage that they hadn't even noticed the jolts from the collars.

Was that even possible?

It didn't *seem* possible, but then she'd never seen any of the men brought down by the collars, she realized, only the women. It had certainly deterred the men from crossing the boundaries before, though.

She covered her burning eyes with her fingers, rubbing them, fighting the sting of fresh tears. Were they dead? Would she ever know? Or would they just disappear as the Hirachi women had?

And what would the Sheloni do in retaliation?

What she couldn't understand, and needed to understand, was what had caused the terrible incident to start with? She was afraid that one or both of them were dead. She needed to understand why. Why had Kole attacked Dansk at all? It was as if he'd suddenly gone mad!

She had no idea how long she lay staring into space while her mind whirled with questions she couldn't answer and might never know the answer to, but exhaustion finally overtook her.

When she woke, she discovered Cory had been returned to her.

Love and gratitude filled her heart as she looked down to find him staring up at her. "Hello my darlin'! Did you miss mama?"

He smiled suddenly, recognition filling his eyes, and tears filled Bri's. He hadn't forgotten her this time! He hadn't grown wary and fearful. Sniffing back the urge to cry, she gathered him against her and nuzzled his neck. He chuckled, nuzzling her back and soaking her with baby drool.

Rolling onto her side, she played with him for a while, talking to him to refamiliarize him with her voice and finally got up to bathe them both and feed him.

She didn't know whether to expect that her routine had been restored or not, but she hoped, and she was vastly relieved when the door opened at the usual time. Gathering Cory up, she hurried out, hoping Consuelo would know something about Kole and Dansk.

She was so anxious to see what she could find out, she didn't notice Consuelo's behavior at first, but she'd already begun to unconsciously draw in upon herself in anticipation of attack by the time Consuelo finally met her at the edge of the yard. Ignoring her instincts, she immediately launched into questions when the other woman reached her.

Consuelo didn't sit down to chat companionably as they always had before. Instead, she stood looking down at Bri, her expression guarded.

"Did you see what happened yesterday?"

Consuelo gave her a look. "Everyone saw."

Taken aback by the tone, the expression, and the body language, Bri again dismissed her misgivings. "Did you see if they were alright? Where they were taken? Did the Sheloni say what they would do to them?"

Consuelo shrugged. "I doubt I saw as much as you did. I was here."

Bri stared at the woman she'd come to think of as a friend, unable to continue to ignore the coldness in her behavior. "Why are you mad at me?" she asked, fighting the anger welling inside her to match that she felt emanating from Consuelo.

Consuelo pursed her lips. "Why don't you tell me?"

Bri's jaw sagged. In a split second, however, all of her repressed fears exploded into fury. "How the fuck would I know what's got your panties in a wad!" she snapped, surging to her feet.

Consuelo ceased trying to hide her own anger. "It was disgusting watching those two men fighting over you like a bitch in heat! Doesn't it bother you at all that they could've gotten themselves killed--and maybe everybody else--because you couldn't resist publicly wallowing all over Dansk?"

That time Bri's jaw dropped open in outrage. If a complete stranger had walked up and attacked her without provocation she couldn't have been more stunned. It was hard to decide which part of the completely vicious and false, allegations to respond to first.

None of it, she finally decided, warranted an answer. If Consuelo had interpreted everything that way, then it had been willful, skewed because of her own emotions, and nothing she could say was going to change that false perception. "We don't have to be friends," she said instead when she'd mastered the urge to explode into counter accusations and/or vicious observations to match Consuelo's. "We do have to try to unite, though, if we don't all want to die on this little picnic the Sheloni have taken us on.

"And, for the record, I didn't trot over there to screw Dansk. If I'd known you liked him I'd have tried not to enjoy it, but I sure as hell didn't have any choice in the matter ... no more than you did."

She left Consuelo standing at the perimeter and headed back, no wiser than she had been before. Not that she'd really expected to get information out of Consuelo, but she'd hoped. She didn't know why she glanced at the women in the group habitat--just to know for sure that the ostracism was wide-spread, she guessed-- but she did, and she caught several looks that seemed to confirm her suspicions.

It was unjust, and she returned to a spot near the habitat to settle with Cory, fuming over the unfairness of being condemned for something she had had no control over.

It was almost easier to deal with than her anxieties about Kole and Dansk.

Maybe it wasn't completely unjustified, she acknowledged after a while. She hadn't merely 'endured'. She'd opened herself to enjoy it, even flirted with them she supposed.

But why not? Why should she have suffered when she had been able to accept and even to enjoy? For *their* sake? Just because it would make them feel better if everyone was as miserable as they were?

Like she gave a shit what they thought about her!

For all intents and purposes, she'd always been a social leper. Her responsibilities growing up hadn't allowed her a lot of time for socializing, which had somehow led to her being lumped in with the 'different' kids--not because she was below or above average in any way, but because she didn't get the chance to join her peers, and she couldn't *be* as carefree and irresponsible as they were.

It wasn't that it didn't bother her at all, but little by little, she'd ceased to care. She'd grown comfortable with the existence of an 'outsider'.

She couldn't afford to be an outsider now, though. As determined as she was to make a change, to somehow defeat the

Sheloni and protect herself and Cory, she didn't think she could do it alone--maybe she could, but her odds were greatly improved if she was working with a group.

With an effort, she thrust the sense of injustice away and tried to figure out why she'd come under attack. She wasn't going to change anyone's mind. She could plead her case, but it would be a waste of time and energy.

She didn't think she'd been wrong when she'd assessed Conseulo's feelings about Dansk. She'd been almost contemptuous of him and, try though she might, Bri couldn't recall any telltale indications that Consuelo had been trying to hide an interest in him.

She'd felt the urge, though, herself to try to align herself with a strong male for protection. Was that it? The primal urge to seek protection from someone stronger? The territoriality that came with that urge?

How was she supposed to reason with that, if that was the case, and she sensed that that was probably what it was? Consuelo hadn't shown any indication at all that she'd actually cared about Dansk. Obviously, though, she'd hoped the interlude had insured a connection between them--particularly since she must be carrying his baby--and now she was angry with Bri for 'threatening' that.

They were all screwed if they couldn't get over that!

In the first place, none of them knew whether mating was going to create *any* kind of bond with the Hirachi, from the Hirachi standpoint, which, when all was said done, was all that counted in the quest for a mate willing and able to protect. They enjoyed sex, and any creature that enjoyed sex was completely willing to do it for recreation, not necessarily for procreation, not necessarily with the intent of mating. And, even if, in their own culture, that was the case, that didn't mean the Hirachi would consider the Earth women in the same light. It seemed far more likely that they would think all bets off because of the differences between them-- to say nothing about the fact that they'd been coerced into performing, however enthusiastically they'd accepted their fate.

In the second, the Sheloni weren't going to allow them to create a bond of the sort they, Earthlings, were instinctually inclined to, because they were treating them all like–barnyard animals, breeding according to *their* discrimination, or maybe lack of it. Consuelo didn't seem to fully grasp that correlation. She wasn't sure any of the others did, but it seemed very obvious to her now that the Sheloni would *also* slaughter them without provocation, without any more thought than they would barnyard animals because that was all they, any of them, were to the Sheloni.

In the third, it seemed doubtful the instinct would help even if it worked and the Hirachi males actually *did* feel bonded to the women they impregnated and protective of the children they'd spawned. The Hirachi were tremendously strong. From what she'd seen, pound for pound, that strength went considerably beyond the strength of the typical human male, and they were *still* slaves just like the Earth people. If she understood what she'd learned about them, they had been preyed upon by the Sheloni for generations now and they had not been able to free themselves or even to prevent more of their people being taken whenever the Sheloni felt the urge, or need.

Nothing could more surely insure that their fate would not be a happy one than to decide to sit back like 'the little women' and wait for the men to handle everything. The Hirachi had a history of failure with the Sheloni. Obviously, they were going to have to think of something different to do.

She was far more interested in her own personal problem at the moment, which just happened to be a problem all the Earth women on board shared, but it hadn't escaped her that success with the women they'd taken was only going to encourage the Sheloni to continue to target the people of Earth, just as they'd been targeting the Hirachi people.

Not that she thought it wouldn't be a good idea to have them as allies. She thought they needed them. The Hirachi knew the enemy far better than they did and that, and their superior physical strength was bound to be useful, but she wasn't about to put her entire future in the hands of a people who might, and probably did, have a different agenda than she had.

Some of the others had to see the situation just as she did, even if it wasn't something they were willing to openly acknowledge.

She should have considered that Consuelo's culture made her more inclined to lean on a man. Women might not, exactly, still be chattel in the South American cultures, but there was still enough of the 'old world' in their culture to discourage independence in women. Very likely her religious beliefs and culture together made it nigh impossible for her to behave contrary to the customs she was used to, to accept that, pregnant or not, there wasn't going to be a wedding to sanctify her situation as mother-to-be--not that there was anything she could've done about it, but at least she wouldn't have been broadsided.

It was still unjust to blame her for the situation, and she was still angry, and hurt if it came to that, but she would've realized that there was a possibility that she'd become 'the enemy'.

She supposed she should have anyway. Even knowing all she knew, understanding just how dire the situation was and how completely out of their control everything was, she'd been hurt and angry when she saw they'd given Kole another woman to breed. *She* had bristled at the woman, and the woman had bristled back--Reasoning hadn't eradicated useless, detrimental emotions. She'd *felt* territorial. Obviously the woman had, too.

If the fucking Sheloni had set out to use their instincts and emotions against them to drive a wedge between each individual and prevent any kind of unity, they couldn't have done a better job of it! Even worse, it seemed to her that she'd become the focus of all that was wrong with their 'world'. None of the others had said anything, but she'd seen the way they looked at her. Somehow she'd become the 'slut' after everybody else's man, because they believed, even if she didn't, that the fight between Kole and Dansk had been over her.

Flattering as it might me, she didn't believe it. It had to have been something else that had set them off. Kole hadn't even impregnated her.

Well, he had, but the Sheloni had nipped that in the bud, literally, and she was pretty sure he knew it.

Or maybe it was because he hadn't? Maybe it was his own instincts that were raging because, once begun, they staked a claim until they'd completed the cycle?

Her head felt as if it would explode with the pressure of all the thoughts whirling in her mind. She clasped her skull in both hands, applying counter pressure to try to relieve the pain.

It seemed to her that the budding promise that had buoyed her spirits was falling apart faster than it could be put together. If she was right, and she'd become the 'enemy', how was she going to pull everyone together?

Ignore the situation? Or face it head on?

Maybe it would be best to just ignore the situation as much as possible? Face it if she was confronted and try to reason with them, but otherwise not give it priority?

It was hard when they couldn't openly communicate. It only left more room for misunderstandings, distrust, mistakes.

Determination settled inside of her as she was finally allowed to return to her habitat. They could slug it out among themselves after they resolved the situation. They probably would, and it would probably get nasty without 'referees' like they were accustomed to having. She was going to have to convince everyone, though, somehow, that *now* was not the time.

Chapter Seventeen

Bri had braced herself to begin battering at the wall of thousands of years of human evolution that hadn't succeeded in producing humans capable of setting aside their natural animal instincts and hormones. Humans *were* creatures of reason and logic. It was just that they reverted far too easily to their roots and allowed the illogic of their emotions to cloud their judgment.

It came as a pleasant surprise to discover that not all of the women were determined to ignore reason.

Probably, she thought wryly, because they hadn't all experienced the wonder of the Sheloni 'dating' system yet.

"Bri!"

Bri paused at the call. She'd meant only to sit within full view of everyone for as long as it took to make them acknowledge her. She hadn't expected anyone to confront her directly.

She knew it was a confrontation from the look on the woman's face. "What?"

"I was just wondering about your pet. Do they have more of them? I'm kind of bored."

Rage surged through Bri. It was one thing for them to attack her. To attack Cory was another matter altogether. She merely stared at the woman--she had no idea what the woman's name was--for several moments, her lips tight, struggling against the impulse to let her inner savage out and curse the woman. "The Sheloni killed his mother," she finally said, her voice trembling with suppressed rage. "I expect you could talk to them about it--because they'll almost certainly kill some of the other breeders--that's what we are, you know. Not Americans with rights, not individuals of significance or importance. We're breeding animals."

She could see the remark had terrorized some of the women. She had their full attention.

She didn't regret frightening them. If that was what it took to shake them out of their stupid complacency and make them wake up and smell the roses, then that was what they needed, and she was willing to be as brutal as it took.

"They need us to breed--and take care of the--things."

It was another woman that made that remark. Racial prejudice, even here, even when their lives depended on each other. God! She had to wonder sometimes if the human race even deserved to survive! She supposed she *could* understand some of it. Humans were unlike any other creature in creation--segregated by races and cultures, and all of them far more comfortable with 'their own'--she was if it came to that--but humans were the only ones that did that, or at least the worst.

"I guess it escaped your attention that they don't actually consider us pets, or irreplaceable? It might inconvenience them to flush you into space and get another Earth woman, but they wouldn't blink at doing it."

When no one else seemed inclined to challenge her, Bri looked for a good spot to settle Cory and began her stretches. It was getting harder and harder to exercise with the baby. He'd gone beyond sitting up to begin creeping, and, although he wasn't really good at it yet, he was progressing rapidly now that he'd begun to get the idea.

As bad as she hated to, especially after the nasty remark about Cory being a pet, it looked as if she was going to have to figure out a way to tether him to keep him from getting into trouble while she exercised. She couldn't afford to stop exercising, that was for certain. She was stronger, and she'd tremendously improved her stamina, but she felt like she could get stronger still. At the very least, it was imperative that she maintain what she'd gained.

Angie, the software specialist, stopped her when the exercise period ended. "I'd still like to play movie trivia sometime."

Bri wasn't about to play hard to get. "You should gather all the information you can from the others in your group so it'll be a good challenge when we start. Even if they don't want to play with us, I'm sure they've seen something that would be useful."

As hard as Bri tried to focus on the big picture, she couldn't completely divert her mind from Dansk and Kole. She didn't want to believe, couldn't accept, that the Sheloni had killed them. Emotions she refused to openly acknowledge boiled just beneath the façade of surface calm she managed, grief she wouldn't face, let alone try to release or deal with.

After days with no sign of either man, she finally had to accept that she cared about both of them. She wanted to weep and scream and threaten the Sheloni with dire consequences, but she was totally helpless to do anything for them, or even about their deaths if the Sheloni had killed them.

It was useless to try to lie to herself that she hadn't become emotionally attached to both of them though she did her best to consider it as no more than she would've felt for any stranger that had been kind to her. They *had* been kind, and careful of her.

Dansk had been sweeter, more romantic, more loving when he'd taken her than any man, human man, she'd ever known, and she'd been no more immune to that than she'd been to the excitement and passion Kole had stirred in her. Struggle though she might to view her interludes with them as 'just a good time' or think of them as 'good lays', she couldn't be that detached about it.

Maybe it was because it just wasn't in her nature to fuck indiscriminately? Or maybe it was her hormones and natural animal instincts that had her struggling to attach significance beyond mere animal lust? It didn't seem to matter. She couldn't distance herself emotionally no matter how hard she tried.

The Sheloni had no idea of the powerful emotions they were stirring up, no clue of just how vicious they were making the Earth women by heaping emotional dependence on top of the instinct for survival. That instinct was powerful enough in its own right to turn humans into savages.

She didn't think even her own instinct to survive, whatever it took, would have been strong enough to overcome her fear. Her love for Cory had done that, though. Her feelings for Kole and Dansk just strengthened her resolve and pushed fear further into the background.

The fact gathering expedition strengthened her hope, and her belief that they had a fighting chance. One of the women had been in the Navy. She had put together a projection of the Sheloni 'strength' by taking the knowledge she had of sailing vessels and the accumulated observations of all the women of the Sheloni and their machines and extrapolating an educated guess of their numbers. No one knew how accurate the guess was, but it was based on all the knowledge available to them, and they had to trust that it was reasonably accurate--give or take.

It was a formidable force. Even if they could trust that they wouldn't have to deal with any more of the Sheloni than was on the ship, and they couldn't, she realized with dismay and a sense of defeat that threatened to swamp her; even if they could put together weapons to fight with; even if they could ally with the Hirachi and the men would attack, it would probably take a dozen to bring down even one of the huge, many legged bots. And by Judy's calculations, there were at least a dozen of the things--and those were fully equipped to fight, or attack. The bots of the type that had fetched her on more than one occasion were also equipped to attack. It had been one of those that had shot Kole and Dansk.

As far as they knew, those two bot types were the only ones that seemed to present a threat. There were others, but they were more task oriented and seemed very limited in their abilities.

Without the bots, the Sheloni would be fairly easy to overcome. No doubt they had weapons besides the bots, but, together, the Hirachi and Earthlings far out numbered them.

They were going to have to figure out a way to disable or destroy the bots.

They needed to know just how closely they were watched and, in fact, how they were being watched. She'd gone over and over her habitat. There was nothing in it that even closely resembled a camera, or cameras. The policewoman, who was somewhat familiar with surveillance equipment, had come to the conclusion that the Sheloni used something like infrared to detect heat signals. That might mean they were constantly under surveillance and might not. It could mean random surveys like bed check in a prison. It also might mean the Sheloni could only see them moving around or sleeping and might not be able to detect or interpret more furtive movements.

Did that mean it was possible, assuming they could find a way out, to slip out of the habitats to reconnoiter? Gather materials they could put together to make weapons? Plant traps?

Could they afford to wait to arrive at their destination and see if conditions were better? Or would they find when they arrived that the Sheloni outnumbered them even more?

She wasn't prepared to kill herself just to make sure she killed the Sheloni. That was a fairly universal sentiment among the women. She didn't know how the Hirachi felt about it, but she decided it wasn't an option she was willing to consider.

Fighting them on the ship still meant that, if successful, they would be stuck in space in a ship none of them knew how to operate.

It became a moot point long before they'd managed to gather enough information to try anything.

Ten days after the fight between Kole and Dansk the ship reached its destination.

Chapter Eighteen

Bri panicked when the Sheloni sent the bots to round up everyone, certain that the Sheloni had figured out they were plotting rebellion. It took all she could do to contain the stark terror and try to reason through what was going on. It was only the fact that she could not *do* anything, though, and that there was no place to run to or to hide that kept her from trying.

That didn't subdue everyone. There were those among the Hirachi and the Earth people who struggled and tried to break free and run, for all the good it did them. Those who struggled or ran were struck down and hauled off, unconscious or dead.

Some of Bri's panic receded when she finally reached a point where she could see that they were all being herded toward something that was obviously a transport. It wasn't big enough to transport all of them at once, however, and everyone who wasn't herded into the gaping maw of the ship had to stand and wait.

It wasn't until then that Bri discovered that there was undoubtedly at least one other level of habitats because there were far more people, both Hirachi and Earth people, than had been housed on the level she'd grown so familiar with.

Did that mean that their guesstimate of the enemy had been totally off the mark, too?

She feared it probably did, but then she realized that the more times the number was multiplied, the greater the odds in their favor ... possibly.

Briefly, as they all converged in the docking bay, she encountered Consuelo, the first time since they'd fallen out. After looking at her uncomfortably several times, Consuelo finally broke the cold silence between them. "I'm sorry for what I said to you, Bri. It was just that ... it frightened me ... the fight ... the bots coming out. I was afraid they would turn and begin to shoot all of us."

It was an apology, she supposed. It didn't make Bri feel any better, but she swallowed the dregs of her own anger and nodded. "It scared the hell out of me, too--not that I realized what was happening with the bots."

Consuelo's face crumpled. "I'm disgraced!" she gasped.

"Everyone will say I am a whore when I go home. My mother will disown me. My brothers ... I don't know what I will do!"

She'd suspected as much, and a jolt still went through Bri at the distressed confession. What could she say? Don't worry, you'll never go home again so you *can't* be in disgrace? It wasn't something that would comfort *her*. Before she could think of anything at all to say, though, they were separated as the lines began to move forward again.

The ride down to the surface of the planet was absolutely the most terrifying thing Bri had ever had to endure in her life. Like cattle, they were packed into the transport until they could do nothing but stand shoulder to shoulder and back to breast--and the much shorter Earth women could hardly even breathe. Cory began to wail long before the thing took off, and there was nothing about the ride to reassure him at all. He alternated between screaming and crying almost non-stop.

Bri struggled to protect him from the powerful battering they took the best she could as the ship entered the atmosphere, but if not for the fact that they'd been packed too tightly to actually fall down she thought all of them would've. When the ship impacted with the ground, however, she discovered they *could* fall. The jar of the impact made her knees give way, everyone's. They crumpled into a screaming, clawing, tangled mass as the transport slammed into the ground.

The trip down didn't take nearly as long as she'd thought it must--not surprising since it was practically a freefall. The time element of the round trip seemed to be mostly taken up with disentangling the cargo once they arrived. Battering and bruising was the least of the injuries. Cory's forehead had slammed into her face at one point, busting her lip and lifting a hen egg on his forehead. She was pretty sure she'd gotten several broken toes from being stepped on. Her ribs ached because someone's elbow had caught her, and she was afraid that one or more ribs were cracked.

Some of the women had to be carried out, however. Some to be treated, and a half dozen to be disposed of because by the time the Hirachi managed to get off of them, they'd been crushed to death.

Needless to say, the Hirachi fared better. Some were limping as they moved off the transport, but she didn't see any of them in the growing pile of bodies being tossed to one side of the off ramp the Sheloni used to unload them.

She didn't want to look, but she couldn't seem to keep her eyes from straying to the horror of piled human bodies. Angie, the software specialist she'd placed the most hope on, was in the 'discard' pile, and recognition of the woman's face not only sent a jolt of shock through her but crushed the hope she'd clung to like a lifeline since she'd been forced to accept the fact that she was never going to be free of the Sheloni unless she freed herself.

She looked away at once, fighting the sting of tears of hopelessness, struggling even harder for breath with the choke of tears added to the pain in her ribs. It was the realization that she had to know the worst that directed her gaze toward the human refuse pile again, the realization that she had to know how many of the women they'd pinned their hopes on that had died.

Pain like a knife blade stabbed through her chest when she saw Consuelo and Manuel among the dead. Bile rose in throat. Between battling the urge to throw up, the tears that blinded her, and the painful tightness of her chest, Bri gave up on trying to see what she hadn't wanted to see to start with.

She hadn't had the chance to patch things up with Consuelo. It had seemed that Consuelo was trying. She'd finally put aside her anger and resentment and offered a truce, but the friendliness they'd had before was gone, and now there would be no chance to try to regain what they'd lost.

Anger finally sparked to life, quelling the urge to cry or be sick. If the bastards had spared any thought at all to the welfare of their slaves they would have had enough sense to at least separate the females from the males and give the women a little better odds of surviving! Consuelo had been too little to protect herself in that mass of giants, let alone poor little Manuel!

She fought down the anger when it had suppressed the sense of hopelessness and grief. She was still alive and Cory was still alive, and he depended upon her to save him. She wasn't going to let him down! She had to be strong, physically and mentally. She couldn't allow herself to wallow in useless emotions.

A bot waited at the end of the ramp, threading lengths of chain into the ankle restraints everyone wore, allowing only enough room between them to take a step, which forced them to march in sync. The world, what she could see of it, as everyone was allowed to spread out a little and she could see more than broad backs, sent her spiraling off into a profound shock of the senses. Feeling as if she'd been caught up in a dream/nightmare, she gaped at her surroundings, unable to really assimilate what her eyes recorded around her.

It was more than her banged up ribs, she realized finally, that made it so hard to breathe. The world--or at least the part where they'd set down--was like a primal, equatorial jungle--hot, unbelievably humid. The ground beneath her feet was as hard and unyielding as rock. Patches of red and yellow and black soil alternated with crushed vegetation. Sprouting from the ground to either side of the line of bodies were plants so bizarre it was almost impossible to think of them as plants--except that they were predominantly green like plants.

Their movements were halting and awkward. Chained together, they followed a narrow trail like ants threading their way through tall grass. Behind and before her were Hirachi men tall enough to see over a good bit of the plants, she was sure, and plants crowding close on either side. She caught a glimpse of a red sun, huge in the sky--which was pinkish and studded with what appeared to be a mixture of storm laden clouds, smoke, and dust.

Mars' sky had a pinkish look to it because of all the Martian dust in the air. Was that why the sky looked more pink than anything else? Or was it the color of this world's sun? Or maybe a combination of many factors? It wasn't lack of oxygen. She was sure she would've felt the effects of that very quickly. In any case, she was familiar enough with high humidity.

No blue skies. No golden sun. She couldn't even pretend the plants looked familiar or were just exotic--like the unfamiliar plants of a tropical region.

Homesickness assailed her.

She hadn't realized that somewhere in the back of her mind she'd nursed the hope/belief that the world would look like home, that she'd be able to draw comfort from that and try to pretend she *was* home. She'd tried to convince herself she had no real expectations, but she'd figured since they were all oxygen breathing beings that the planet must be similar to Earth. To have to provide breathing equipment and/or protective suits for so many would surely defeat the purpose of stealing biological entities for labor rather than using robots.

One of the Hirachi muttered a comment to another. She didn't catch all of it, but she caught enough to realize that he was remarking on how similar the world was to *their* home world.

Bully for them, she thought angrily!

She had suspected the habitat had been designed for them--red sun, warm, and humid, and she still felt persecuted, an irrational sense of injustice that the world was like theirs rather than Earth, even though, reluctantly, she had to admit that it was at least similar to what she was used to in temperature.

Except it was far worse than anything she'd ever experienced before, despite the fact that she'd grown up in a semi-tropical, very humid area.

She realized it must be nearly unbearable for the women who were from cooler climates. As hard a time as she was having, it was going to be harder on them, and she wondered how many more would die before they could adjust.

She'd walked until it had begun to be a race to see which part of her body was going to give out first--her arms and back from carrying Cory, or her lungs from struggling with the thick air, or her legs. Pain dogged her from the first because of her injured toes and ribs, but it became more and more unbearable as time went on. She shifted the baby from one hip to the other and back again, but when the Hirachi male behind her offered to take the baby, she shook her head, clutching him tighter.

She was ready to drop where she stood when they came at last to a knoll overlooking a vast, yellow sea. Walls rose up at the edge of the jungle almost like a part of it. Like embracing arms, the walls wrapped around a wide, virtually bare area of land and sea--more sea than land from what she could see from where she stood.

The ground was bare of anything. There were no habitats, no limits that she could see at all beyond the walls.

Disbelief, and then fear settled in her belly in a knot.

They were turning all of them in together!

She saw the same dawning of fear in all the other women's eyes as they reached the bot that was removing the tethers from their ankle restraints at the yawing gate in the side of the wall. The women who'd already been freed moved into a growing cluster just inside the compound. The Hirachi men seemed content to ignore them in favor of investigating their surroundings.

It lessened her anxiety, but not as much as she would've liked.

"God! What are we going to do now?" a woman near Bri asked in a suffocated voice as Bri instinctively moved toward 'her own kind'.

Bri glanced around until she'd identified the woman who'd spoken. She didn't recognize the woman, but she didn't know if that was only because she hadn't seen her up close before, or if she was from one of the other areas of the alien ship.

It was really a rhetorical question, she supposed, and, weighed down with pain, grief, and depression, she was tempted to simply ignore it. She realized, though, that everyone, including her, needed something to bolster their spirits. "We assess the situation and formulate a plan," she responded finally, infusing as much confidence into the statement as she could muster.

She didn't feel any. She felt as hopeless and scared as the rest of the women looked.

The comment evoked a cacophony of responses from the other women, mostly questions she didn't have an answer for. And most of the questions only added to her own fear and depression. The defeatism in everything they said, their postures, and their faces sparked a thread of irritation in her, though. She stepped away from them and turned to face them, waiting until they'd gotten quieter. "Did anybody *not* see the women who died on the trip down and were tossed aside like yesterday's garbage?"

The question silenced the few who'd continued to exchange worried, unanswerable questions.

"We're slaves. I've got no more idea what the Sheloni are expecting of us than you do, but I do know I'm not going to simply accept this fate. Maybe we'd be better off under their thumb, but I don't think so."

"They want us alive. They'll take care of us, feed us," someone deep in the group pointed out. "It isn't like we wouldn't be working to live if we were still on Earth."

Damn the woman for unerringly pinpointing the root of all their fears. "I can't argue with that," Bri responded. "I can't even argue with the fact that we've always had someone to tell us what to do-bosses, maybe husbands, or boyfriends, or fathers, or mothers. We've had 'big brother' watching over us, too, our governments, police, military. This is different, though. We can't quit. We can't move out. We have no protection or recourse if they decide we've done something wrong. There's no one to stop them from punishing us anyway they feel like punishing us, whether we're guilty or not, whether the punishment fits the crime or not. There's no one to stop them if they decide to kill any one of us because they've decided they have no use for us.

"The trip from Earth was enough to convince me that the Sheloni are by far the worst thing we could face. If the rest of you aren't convinced yet … let me know when you change your mind."

"You're talking … you aren't seriously considering living out there? My god! Did you see this place? It's … like prehistoric! I half expected to run into a dinosaur! There's no place to escape *to*!

The wildest woods at home are like a walk in the park compared to this place--and at home there'd be civilization somewhere. There would be hope of reaching it. Here, there's nothing."

As bad as Bri hated to admit it, the woman had a point. In all the time she'd considered how impossible and dangerous it would be to try to take over the ship, she hadn't imagined they'd be dumped on anything like this. How could she? When she thought of woods, she thought of the woods she passed by on the highway. "Well! Far be it from me to suggest you give up the luxurious accommodations here!" she responded angrily, gesturing around at the empty pen where they all stood looking around hopefully as if their miserable habitats were going to suddenly appear. "I'm going to look around and find a comfy spot for me and Cory."

"We should stick together."

When she halted and turned, Bri discovered it was Becky of Texas who'd spoken, the woman she'd called a fucking cunt because of her hateful remarks about Cory. She still didn't like the woman.

"The … aliens," she said when Bri merely stared at her.

Bri shook her head, almost feeling sorry for the woman. "In case you haven't noticed there are no lines here, nothing to keep them back if they were inclined to do anything to us. We could all pile together--safety in numbers and all that--but they outnumber us and they're a hell of a lot bigger. Anyway, I can't see that they look all that interested."

Someone snickered maliciously as she turned away. "Obviously, she likes the Hirachi horizontal tango."

Bri stiffened but decided to ignore the remark.

Then she decided not to. Turning her head, she smiled vaguely, uncertain of which one had made the remark. "Actually, you're right. I did enjoy it. Faced with the choice of resisting the inevitable and feeling persecuted, or relaxing and going with the flow, I chose to be open minded and positive, and the reward was well worth it!"

And they could lie all they wanted to, to themselves and everyone else, but unless Dansk and Kole were *really* remarkable, she'd be willing to bet she wasn't the only one.

Actually, she thought they *were* remarkable.

A lump welled in her throat at the thought. She hadn't seen either of them since they'd been carted away, and she'd finally locked her fear for them, and her guilt, and her grief on the dark side of her mind with all of the other horrible things she'd seen since she'd been taken. It didn't bear thinking on, none of it, because if she allowed it to, all of it would crash over her and she'd be useless to herself and to Cory.

She didn't know what was hardest to bear--all of it, all of them, Kole, Dansk, Consuelo, Manuel, Angie.... She was afraid that without Angie there was no hope, and truth be told, she was no longer certain what she hoped for, but the loss of everyone she'd grown close to, attached to, since she'd been taken except for Cory made her wonder if it was even worth trying to do anything.

Maybe the women were right. Maybe they would be better off to simply accept their fate? It had taken no more than one look at the planet to assure her that life was going to be hellish no matter which road she took, dangerous, a constant battle for survival. At least if they stayed they'd be fed. The fortified walls weren't shelter, but it would keep things out the same as it kept them in, and there was no telling what was out there.

Nothing intelligent, she supposed, no help. If there'd been natives surely the Sheloni would have just used them.

What did she know about surviving in any kind of wilderness? Nothing! And even if she had that knowledge, and experience-- which she didn't--it would probably be useless in this environment.

Dragging in a shaky breath, fighting the urge to simply give up, flop on the ground, and wail 'woe is me', she stopped when she'd put some distance between her and the women whose attitudes were dragging her down and looked around at the walls, trying to force herself to assess the situation with reason rather than emotion. There was a knot of Sheloni standing on an observation platform at the top of the wall holding the jungle back studying their captives like someone might study an ant farm. Though she supposed they had not been brought all this way merely for entertainment.

The thought had occurred to her before, especially when they'd pitched everyone in to breed, but although that possibility would almost be welcome now, she had had to dismiss it long ago.

Dragging her gaze from them after no more than a glimpse, she looked around the enclosure. There was a rawness about it that seemed to indicate it had not been here long. The ground was perfectly bare. Surely, considering how dense the jungle, it wouldn't have been if there'd been time for plants to reclaim it?

What of the Hirachi who'd been brought here before, though? Were there more camps like this one? Had this been created just for them?

After a few moments, since it didn't seem that the Sheloni meant to do anything right away, she moved down toward the beach where waves crashed ashore. The water had a sulfurous smell to it that drew stronger the closer she came to it. She wondered abruptly if it actually was an ocean, or merely a large body of fresh water.

Not that anything stinking of sulfur could really be called 'fresh'!

She stood near the water's edge for a few moments, trying to ignore the throbbing pain in her face, and lip, toes, and ribs. Finally, giving in to her weariness, she settled on the dry, coarse black sand at her feet and, with relief, settled Cory's weight on her lap. Staring at the walls that rose up far out to sea, she wondered why the Sheloni had found it necessary to wall off such a huge area of water.

Either restless from being held or fascinated with the water pounding against the shore not far away, Cory commenced to struggling to get down. Her arms hurt from holding him so long. Finally, she sat him on the ground next to her. He promptly rolled onto all fours and tried to scurry toward the water. Smiling faintly, she dragged him back. Apparently incensed at being denied the opportunity to explore, Cory pitched a fit.

She picked him up, meeting his indignant gaze. "NO! Behave yourself and I'll let you play in the sand."

He understood no, and it wasn't a word he liked very well. He continued to fuss and fight to get down until she settled him on the sand again and distracted him by scooping up a handful of the coarse stuff and letting it drift through her palm. That caught his attention. Instead of heading for the water again the moment she let him go, he began digging in the sand and trying to stuff it into his mouth.

A shadow fell across them.

Bri's heart was already in her throat when she whipped her head upward to stare at the Hirachi man towering over her. Blinded by the sun, she lifted a hand to shield her eyes.

Her heart executed a little somersault and began to pound with a strange mixture of fear, disbelief, and happiness. "Kole!" she exclaimed on a breathless gasp.

After studying her for several heart stopping moments, he shifted so that the sun wasn't directly behind him and dropped to his knees in the sand beside her. She swallowed with an effort when she'd examined him, assured herself it really was him. "I thought

… I thought...." She swallowed again, unable to complete the sentence. His expression was almost unwelcoming, accusing. The desire to express her joy at seeing him alive and hale died in her throat.

She looked away, dragging Cory back when she saw that he was preparing to make another break for the water and redirecting his attention to the sand again. "I'm glad you're all right," she said finally.

He said nothing, and finally Bri couldn't stand the suspense anymore. She glanced at him warily.

"How long have you known my tongue?"

She'd known he would be pissed off if he realized she did. She'd known she'd given away at least some knowledge when he and Dansk had fought, but that hardly seemed to matter given that she'd believed they were both dead. It occurred to her that she could pretend she still only knew a little, but what was the point other than keeping him from being mad at her? Obviously he already was and just as obviously it seemed unlikely he'd believe her if she tried to lie and say she only knew a little. "I don't remember," she hedged.

"Before they brought you to me, though."

Bri reddened, struggled with the urge to lie, and decided against it. "Yes."

He looked angrier for a moment, and then thoughtful. "Did you learn what you hoped to learn?"

The blush, that had only begun to abate, returned full force. She shrugged. "I had no reason to trust you," she pointed out, abruptly feeling indignant. "You've no room to accuse me. You were trying to learn my language for the same reason."

He didn't deny it. "Partly," he responded finally, his lips twisting in a wry smile.

Intrigued by that, Bri sent him a questioningly glance. He didn't elaborate, and an uncomfortable silence settled between them.

"Do you carry his babe?"

Shocked by his demand to know, Bri sent him a startled glance. It was on the tip of her tongue to demand to know what business it was of his anyway. She squelched the urge, realizing it would sound like she was trying to discover if she meant anything at all to him. The question seemed to imply he did, but that was only if she attributed human traits and motives to him, and she still wasn't sure how closely their thoughts and behavior mirrored typical human behavior. They seemed to feel the same emotional range as humans, shared a lot of similar personality traits, and yet she knew there was a vast difference in their cultures, that there were as many differences between the races of man and the Hirachi as there were similarities, and that was bound to have an effect on the way they looked at things, felt about things.

She averted her gaze from his penetrating stare with an effort, realizing she was reluctant to share her intimacy with Dansk with him. Because of loyalty and affection for Dansk, she wondered? Or because of her feelings for Kole, from a reluctance to say anything that would drive a bigger wedge between them?

Damn it! It was unfair! She'd lost Consuelo's friendship because the damned Sheloni had decided to toss her in with the same man who'd impregnated her friend. Everyone behaved as if she was the anti-Christ or something because of the fight between Dansk and Kole, and her falling out with Consuelo! Why target *her* for their anger and frustrations? It was the damned Sheloni's fault!

Because it was easier to target somebody they could actually punish?

"No," she said finally. "I was...." Embarrassment flooded her cheeks with color again, and the pain of the memory clouded her eyes. She thought he knew about the baby she'd lost, but she couldn't bring herself to tell him if he didn't, or explain that she had not been 'well' enough to resume relations when they had put her with Dansk. In any case, she didn't think he wanted or needed the details. In truth, she could have been, she supposed. Once was enough. But she hadn't even considered the possibility before it became evident that there was no possibility, because she hadn't been able to think of much beyond worrying over what had become of him and Dansk after they were taken away. "I'm sorry about ... about...."

His lips tightened. "I'm not," he said harshly.

Chapter Nineteen

Stung both by the comment and his tone, Bri stared at him. Was he saying he wasn't sorry she'd lost his baby? Or that he didn't care that she was worried sick about him and Dansk? Or was he only saying he wasn't sorry he'd fought with Dansk and it had nothing to do with her so she needn't apologize as if it had? She was glad for the distraction as Cory managed to evade her. She looked away from Kole. Startled to discover how rapidly Cory was moving, she made a lunge for him and missed, rolling onto her stomach when she threw herself off balance. "Cory, no!"

He ignored her, naturally, crawling toward the waves for all he was worth. Alarm ran through her veins like ice water when she saw that he'd put more distance between himself and her than there was between him and the water. Bri scrambled up and gave chase, swooping down to make a grab for him again when she came even with him. Her fingers brushed him, but he was wearing nothing but the cloth she used to diaper him, and she didn't manage to grab a hold. Water washed over her ankles as she made another grab for him, but the moment the water crashed over him it lifted him from the ground, and as the wave receded it took him with it into the murky water.

"Cory!" she screamed in panic, falling to her knees and feeling blindly for him. "Cory!" Water filled her nose and mouth as she fought the waves to find him.

Kole splashed into the water beside her.

"I can't swim! I can't swim!" she babbled. "I can't find him! Oh god! Cory!"

The water was waist high when she struggled to her feet and looked around frantically. Giving her a strange look, Kole dove into the next wave. The wave caught her chest high, knocking her backwards. She strangled as she went under, adding to her fear and the mindless panic that gripped her as she struggled to claw her way above the surface to catch her breath. A hand caught her waist, dragging her clear of the water at last. Coughing, sputtering, still gripped by panic, it took Bri many moments to register the sound of Cory's indignant wails.

Relief flooded her. Sloughing the water from her eyes so that she could see, still wracked with coughing spasms, she looked for Cory and discovered Kole had him caught against his chest with his other arm. He didn't release her until she'd managed to get her feet under her, firmly planted on the ground beneath the water. She wavered, weak from the adrenaline rush, from breathlessness, and from fighting the current, and disoriented by the movement of the water. Slipping a hand along her waist again and pulling her close against his side, he walked her up onto the beach.

It took all she could do to remain on her feet when he let her go again, but she locked her trembling knees. She needed to feel Cory securely in her arms, to know absolutely that he was going to be all right.

Kole, she saw when she looked up at him, reaching for the baby, had lifted the child away to study him. A jolt of anxiety shot through her. His expression was stern, his gaze assessing. "You are too young to brave the sea, little warrior," he said gruffly.

The sound of the man's voice penetrated Cory's anger--and his cries *were* angry Bri realized with surprise. He stopped wailing, opened the eyes he'd squeezed shut, and stared rounded eyed at the man that held him. After examining the face for several moments, he reached out and caught Kole's lip and tried to remove it.

Kole made no attempt to disentangle his lip, although Bri knew from experience that the baby's grip was strong and painful if he managed to grab hold of anything sensitive. He let go of his own accord once he'd figured out he couldn't tear it loose and patted Kole's cheeks with both hands.

After staring back at the baby for several moments, Kole seemed to come to himself. He lowered the baby into her outstretched arms. Giving up the effort to stand on her shaky legs, Bri clutched him against her chest as she wilted to the ground and promptly burst into tears of relief.

Kole dropped to his knees beside her, although she could see from his expression he was fighting the urge to decamp. Controlling herself with an effort, Bri mopped her eyes with one hand and sniffed. "Thank you! I was so afraid I'd lost him!"

Kole frowned, allowing his gaze to drift over her speculatively. "How can you not swim?"

The tone was tentative, curious not accusing, and yet Bri felt her own inadequacies keenly. She'd allowed herself to be distracted, and Cory had almost drowned because of it! She sniffed again, resentfully this time. "Because I can't!" she snapped.

"*He* can swim."

Drowning wasn't swimming! *She* could drown! Instead of pointing that out, though, she said, "He isn't old enough to be afraid."

Kole sat back on his heels. "Afraid of what?"

"The water!"

Impatience flickered in his eyes at her tone. "How can you be afraid of the water? You bathe all the time."

"I can't...." Bri broke off, realizing she couldn't think of the Hirachi word for drown. "I can't smother in a bath!"

He digested that for some moments. "You can not breathe in the water," he said flatly.

Bri's lips tightened. "Of course I can't breathe in the water!" she said testily. "No one can--not unless they're wearing ... under water gear," she finished the sentence in her own language, realizing that was the second time she hadn't been able to think of the Hirachi words she needed.

It struck her as odd. She hadn't had to even think about speaking or translating before. Was it wearing off? Or was it just that she was still so upset?

"Your people can not live in the sea."

There was something about the way he said it that fully caught her attention for the first time. She dismissed the thought that leapt into her mind, but it wouldn't obey her determination to ignore all the little hints that had been building in her mind.

She'd thought the thin, almost silky growth of flesh along the Hirachi's lower arms and legs looked strange until she'd grown accustomed to it, but it hadn't occurred to her that there might be a reason for it, or that there was a strong resemblance to fins.

Kole must have thought it odd that she didn't have them, but she supposed he'd dismissed it just as she had.

Maybe for the same reason? She'd been looking for kinship to the Hirachi, maybe out of self-preservation.

How close was the kinship, though, if his people came from the sea?

She could almost see the same thoughts in his eyes.

Scientists had claimed that everything on Earth had originally come from the sea, but no one had ever figured out why some mammals had chosen to leave the sea completely and evolve as land creatures while others had stayed and become exclusively inhabitants of the oceans.

"This is why the Sheloni prey on the Hirachi," she said with sudden insight. "Whatever it is they want so badly is under the sea."

And no matter how technologically advanced *they* were, the sea was still a huge mystery on Earth because they had a hard time dealing with the unfamiliar environment, the temperature and pressure extremes, the limited amount of light that filtered down into the water.

The Sheloni were undoubtedly land creatures, too, or surely they would've been able to come up with robots that could handle the task of a large scale underwater operation.

She refused to believe she had more in common with those creatures, though, than with the Hirachi. Reptiles lived on land, too, and there was a hell of a difference between them and mammals.

The new knowledge explained so many things--their strength, the fact that they were practically all muscle with scarcely any body fat--maybe even their size and the color of their skin. They must spend almost as much time on land, though, as they did in the sea. Otherwise, why would they have arms and legs? And, if they weren't used to spending long periods out of the water, being out of the water as long as it had taken for the crossing would surely have damaged their skin?

There'd been the pools, of course, in their habitats, but neither Dansk nor Kole had spent much time in them--not when she was with them.

And she'd been pissed because they had 'better baths'!

Kole withdrew, both physically and emotionally, as if he'd suddenly discovered he'd been fraternizing with some loathsome thing that had been masquerading as something familiar.

Her chest tightened as she recognized the withdrawal for what it was. "Well! It's nice to know humans aren't the only ones afflicted with bigotry," she muttered. "It must suck to know you've been breeding with land dwellers. I suppose that's why you're glad I'm not having your baby! Only thing is, I didn't notice you having any trouble getting it up, or fucking me! I guess it's just a universal male thing! Anything with a hole, right?"

His expression hardened. Obviously, he'd caught the meaning of the unfamiliar word, or at least realized it was intended as an insult. "We depend upon the sea for protection … food … everything. A Hirachi unable to live in the sea can not survive long."

Bri swallowed against a lump of hurt that lodged in her throat.

"And it's protected you so well!" she snapped angrily.

He ignored that. "And I did not want to breed a child on you for your sake! You are too … you are not.... It is likely it would be too big for you to safely bear."

If he hadn't been so careful to avoid pointing out her size, his contempt wouldn't have been nearly as obvious. But what had she expected, really? Just because a lot of Earth men seemed to like dainty women, it didn't follow that the Hirachi would--particularly when it was obviously not something they had ever seen before.

Especially, she supposed, when ensuring that they had big, strong warriors to fight for them was of vital importance. Earth men might want big, strong sons, but it wasn't crucial to their way of life.

Not that she could see that being big and strong had helped the Hirachi any more than their ability to live below the sea!

"It didn't seem to bother Dansk," she said angrily, more hurt than angry and wanting to take a stab at him in retaliation. She wasn't prepared, however, for just how angry he got.

"Because he was too enamored of you, and too caught up in the mating cycle, to consider what it might mean for you!" he growled.

"I hadn't realized how lucky I was that you're so cold blooded it wasn't a problem for you to think with your head instead of your cock!" Bri growled back at him, instantly dismissing her uneasiness about his anger the moment he insulted Dansk.

A jolt went through her when he seized her upper arms and dragged her against him, pinning Cory between them. Before she could do more than open her mouth to object, he ground his mouth down over hers and kissed her with a ruthlessness and heat that knocked the breath and the fight out of her.

Her eyes felt as if they were rolling around independently in their sockets when he released her. Fire had erupted within her and baked her brain. She was still trying to gather her wits when he shot to his feet and left her.

Feeling rather as if a steam roller had just leveled her, Bri sat where he'd left her, disoriented, too weak even to consider getting up. What had he meant about mating cycle, she wondered a little vaguely?

Cycle? The *men* had cycles? Or they all cycled together?

What else didn't she understand about the Hirachi?

She looked down at Cory, who was wiggling impatiently in her arms. "It's a damned good thing I learned the language!" she said, irritated all over again. "We couldn't fight nearly as well when we were hampered by *not* being able to understand each other!"

She'd already gotten up and headed toward the Earth conclave when she saw a wave of excitement run through the women. Turning to see what it was that had unsettled them--again--she saw Hirachi men emerging from the sea--what looked like nearly a hundred but might have been a lot less. It was hard to say when one was looking upon a wall of yellow skinned giants emerging from the sea like a herd of Poseidons.

Unnerved herself to see so many, Bri put a little more speed to her step. As she glanced back to judge the distance, though, her gaze collided with one who was very familiar to her, and she stopped. Dansk smiled when he saw that he'd snagged her attention, his gaze roving her as if hungry to refamiliarize himself with her. He shook his head slightly as she stilled indecisively. Glancing significantly toward the bots waiting at the front of the line the men had formed, he warned her away.

She'd been too caught up in her argument with Kole to notice the bin that had been brought out--from somewhere--which said a lot for her focus on Kole. The thing was huge, almost as big as a freight car, she imagined. The men, who'd come from the sea were all carrying large net bags filled with something colorful and porous that reminded her of coral. As they reached the bots, the bags were taken and emptied into the bin.

Was it coral, or something similar, she wondered?

It looked … innocuous considering the people who'd died getting here, those who still stood to lose their lives. What was so important about it that made the Sheloni so willing to enslave other species in order to get it?

Was it just … like gold, or diamonds, or pearls? Of value to them because it was pretty and something rare or hard to get?

Or was there far more to it than she could see?

The sense of outrage boiling up inside of her deflated when she reflected on Earth's history. Men had been willing to commit wholesale slaughter of their own kind for 'riches'. Maybe it said something for the Sheloni that they weren't willing to kill their own for it?

And maybe not. If they were as frail as they appeared to be, it wouldn't have done them any good to try to use their own people.

Her eyes narrowed as it occurred to her the value of the mineral, or whatever, to the Sheloni might make it a weapon to use against them--could, if they could only figure out how to use it against the

Sheloni.

Abruptly feeling the sensation of being watched, she glanced away from the bin.

Kole had begun to move toward the sea with other men, but there was something about the tension in him that told her it was his gaze that she'd felt and not Dansk's, although she saw Dansk flick several glances in her direction as he shuffled along the line waiting to empty their haul.

She was sorry she couldn't talk to Dansk, tell him how glad she was to see that he was alive and seemed none the worse for the attack ... attacks if she counted Kole's assault. But then it had been more than a week. He'd had time to heal from anything but a serious injury, and Kole had said the beam had merely knocked them out.

'Mere' was an understatement, of course. She'd been knocked for a loop by the Sheloni's weapons. There was nothing 'mere' about it.

She didn't particularly want to rejoin the other women, especially since she suspected they'd observed her byplay with Kole and probably seen the exchange between her and Dansk, as well. But as she turned, she saw the robots were herding the women across the compound. Hurrying to catch up even as she felt the sting of her collar, Bri struggled against the hitch she quickly developed in her side.

It said a lot for her increased tolerance for pain that she'd managed to put it from her mind until she'd had to push herself again. Her toes had gone numb, though, and only hurt now when she walked because she couldn't help bending them. The pain in her ribs had eased, too, which meant bruising not breakage.

It was a relief to know she wouldn't have to worry about healing properly, or having to endure the Sheloni examining her. Not that she could avoid that, unless the Sheloni had decided they didn't need to force them to mate anymore, either because they had enough women impregnated they were satisfied, or they thought 'nature' would take its course now that they'd thrown them all in together.

It probably would, too. Whatever the women said, even if it was true and all of the others were still revolted at the thought of accepting men of the Hirachi race, the Hirachi were the *only* men available to them now.

And she had not seen any Hirachi females, which could either mean the men had managed, primarily, to 'protect' their females and keep them from being caught, or the Sheloni had decided just to do away with the strong, aggressive Hirachi females and replace them with females that were easier to control. Maybe it was a little of both, or something else entirely, but the fact was there weren't any Hirachi females in *this* prison that she'd seen.

It was almost comical to see the expressions on the faces of the 'easily controlled' females once they had gathered as ordered and learned the purpose of the gathering.

They were to be issued the wherewithal to prepare food for themselves and the workers and to erect sleeping shelters.

There was no real escape from destiny, Bri thought wryly. Women were the breeders and hearth tenders. It didn't matter where they landed.

* * * *

It took time and a great deal of effort to tamp the fury and desire raging inside of Kole. He had been fighting a losing battle with both from the moment he'd spied Bri in the encampment--almost from the first moment he'd seen her if it came to that--mostly because his reason and his instincts had been at war almost from the start where she was concerned.

It was unfortunate for everyone that the Sheloni had struck at the time they had, because the timing, whether intentional or not--and he thought not--had been at peak crisis for the Hirachi--peak mating cycle. It would have been bad enough if that was all, just an unfortunate coincidence of timing, but the fact that he and the others had already endured seven fruitless cycles made it all the more difficult for them to ignore the call of nature. It was harder *each* time, and it had built into a raging storm that could not be ignored any longer when the Sheloni had dropped the women in their laps, torturing them with the exotically delicate and beautiful creatures who called themselves humans of Earth by giving them no chance even to escape them for a moment to regain their self-control.

He thought he had a good deal of self-control, but giving him Bri when his body had already been raging for mating--with any available female that was even close to satisfactory--had been like waving water under the nose of someone perishing for it.

Mating with their own women should have appeased the urges. It hadn't, though, because their women had aborted their young. They knew it, and it had stirred the instincts again to fever pitch--because they *had* to produce once they were in cycle. And having already caved in to the need once, none of them, even him, had been able to overcome or ignore the urge. Discipline, willpower, and the logical thinking mind had gotten him through the previous cycles, but it had been hellish. He prided himself on the fact that he had had enough strength of will to do what had to be done without having to be physically restrained as some had. But he had been miserable long after the urges had passed, unappeased by casual intercourse with the women, and each successive cycle had taken its toll, weakened his resolve a little more.

He wondered if he was only making excuses for himself, trying to justify his weakness. He didn't know. The plain truth was he was still in cycle and less than his usual rational self.

Rage surged inside of him all over again at the thought. He had feared that it would be a bad thing to get a child on Bri as dainty as she was, and he still hadn't been able to resist.

And then they had taken it.

In one sense he was relieved. He didn't want to chance that she could not birth his child without help--and the gods knew the Sheloni were butchers. They were far more interested in the offspring than the mother. They would not care if she lived or died so long as they managed to remove the child from her body.

Irrational or not, he had still been fiercely glad when he thought that he had gotten his child on her and half mad when he discovered they'd aborted it.

And then they had given her to Dansk.

By their customs, she was *his* for the mating cycle! She might not have chosen him, but she had accepted him! And she had lost his child! He had the right to a second chance at breeding her with his seed!

He shook the thought off. It had been beyond insane to attack Dansk. Quite aside from the fact that he knew Dansk was in cycle, too, and driven just as he was, he had so lost his reason when he had seen the two of them together that he had breeched the Sheloni security, *shown* them how completely inadequate it was. And they had been at great pains to convince the Sheloni that they were completely at their mercy!

The only saving grace of the entire fiasco was that the Sheloni had apparently decided that both of them were mad and that explained why the collars had failed to bring them down. Apparently their chemical levels had still been spiked when they'd been examined. The Sheloni had kept them isolated until the levels had returned, more or less, to normal and returned them to general population--with their collar settings a good bit higher than before, but they hadn't changed the settings of the others' collars.

Actually, there were two positive things that had come out of the incident.

He realized that the Sheloni had never actually dealt with Hirachi in mating cycle--meaning those they'd captured before had resisted the seventh year call of the wild--and therefore the Sheloni did not know that when their hormones spiked, so too did their strength.

And he had prevented Dansk from breeding on his woman--for the time being.

He was going to have to confront Dansk. He didn't know how they were going to resolve the issue without alerting the Sheloni, but they would have to. He could see Bri was inclined to accept Dansk. He didn't like it, but he knew she had the right to choose another male, any male, any time it pleased her, and he could live with that. She had already accepted him for this cycle, however. If she bore a child, it would be his. Dansk could father the child of the next cycle if that was what Bri wanted. He would try not to interfere. The urge to reproduce was rarely as strong after a male had managed a successful mating anyway. He should be able to control the urge to dispose of rivals.

As he at last reached the point where the land dropped away and dove into the chasm beyond the shelf that lined the beach, a sense of peace washed over him as it always did when he returned to the sea. This time, though, the joy of feeling the sea engulf him was fleeting. Even as he followed the others deeper and deeper into the peaceful silence and darkness of the ocean deaths, fresh anxieties arose to plague him.

He still could not completely accept that the Earth women were not able to live in the sea. He had wanted to dismiss it as beyond believable, but when he had prodded her Bri had left him in no doubt. She could *not* live in the sea, couldn't even swim! How could the Earth people look so similar and be so different?

And what would than mean to their offspring?

He shook that thought off. As maddening as his urges were at the moment, the child was not the problem--they would be long gone before the children were born--and he couldn't afford to allow himself no room to think beyond that.

Bri was the problem. *All* the Earth human females were a problem.

They could escape, but the sea was their best hope if not their only hope. It had not occurred to him when he'd begun to formulate the plan that they would not be able to escape *with* the women that way.

They had bred their children on these women. They could not leave them, even if they wanted to--and no one wanted to.

Chapter Twenty

"It's like … sushi," Caroline muttered in surprise.

Bri glanced at the woman she'd been working beside for hours. They'd seemed to hit if off instantly, but she rather thought that was just because of who Caroline was. Caroline from South Carolina was friendly, cheerful, and uncomplicated. She was pretty, but she had the look of someone who'd been more than a little plump and had suddenly, drastically plummeted in weight--probably because of the tasteless Sheloni diet--which made it all the more surprising that she managed to remain cheerful.

"You like sushi?"

"God no! Uh, I've never actually tried any. It's gross even to think of eating anything raw. At least we don't have to cook, though. I hate cooking. I suck big time at cooking."

Bri glanced at her in surprise.

Caroline chuckled, but this time it was a little forced. "I know what you're thinking. How did I get fat if I don't even cook? Right?"

"Actually, I was thinking you would've made the perfect customer--if I still had my business. In my old life, I used to prepare home cooking for women who didn't have time to do it from scratch themselves, or didn't know how to cook, or just didn't want to. Everything was carefully prepared--meat, veggies, and seasoning--and ready to go into the oven or the frying pan."

"That must have been interesting."

Bri laughed. "You're just too sweet to say boring, but I didn't mind it. I started it to help support myself and my mother. It was something I could do and still stay home to take care of her, and it was actually a pretty successful business. Just before I was taken I'd landed a chain supermarket deal to sell in their delis."

"Wow! You might have been rich! That sucks a big hairy one."

Bri laughed even though it occurred to her that in her 'old life' she would have been shocked, probably disgusted by the comment. Maybe she would even have turned her nose up at Caroline for her 'gutter talk'.

Now it was just so nice to hear someone chattering back at her in her own language she didn't much care how they expressed themselves. Sometimes she didn't even feel like the same person at all. It was almost like remembering a past life where she'd been someone else.

"So...," Caroline said, changing the subject. "You think maybe these Hirachi people are like ... Asians from another world?"

Bri stared at her blankly.

"I mean ... sushi, and Hirachi sounds a little Asian, doesn't it? And they have dark hair and the Asians are supposed to be the 'yellow race', though I never really figured that one out because they're not. Well, maybe a little yellow toned--guess we're not exactly white, either. Himini calls us pink."

Suppressing the urge to laugh, Bri considered it. "You're talking about the alien seeding theory sci-fi buffs like?"

"Yeah. Except I never heard anything about it being Asians, but there seems to be a lot of similarities to me, so it's possible. Don't you think?"

"You're just saying that because you like Himini," Lisa, one of the women from Florida, said teasingly.

Blushing, Caroline glanced at the woman on her other side suspiciously and finally smiled. "So? I do like him. What's wrong with that? He's really sweet to me."

"He ain't human," Becky 'the fucking cunt' said. "Asian!" She snorted. "It's like ... fucking a dolphin."

Caroline reddened with anger.

Bri felt her own anger surge to the forefront. "I've never tried that," Bri responded agreeably. "But I'll take your word for it. I did hear somewhere that they've got really big cocks. What was it like for you?"

Caroline let out a snorting laugh. Several of the women gaped at her and then began to snicker.

Becky, she saw when she met the woman's eye, was glaring at her, her face red with both anger and embarrassment.

Bri gave her a saccharin smile.

Becky's hand tightened on the knife she was using to skin the fish.

"You don't want to do that," Bri said coldly. "If you can't take it, don't dish it out. Caroline likes Himini. I like ... Kole and Dansk. And I love Cory. And we don't like people talking nasty about them."

After glancing around the group of women and discovering their expressions were anything but encouraging, Becky focused on her task.

The job they'd been given was revolting. Food preparation might have been something they were all familiar with, but not *this* kind! Slabs of protein wrapped in plastic was something Bri could handle. *This* was disgusting. The Hirachi had begun bringing up both the coral looking stuff and ... things that only vaguely resembled any kind of fish any of them were familiar with. It was easiest just to call them fish because they came out of the water, though.

Thankfully, Bri had landed near the middle of the assembly line the robots had formed because the women at the beginning had to behead and gut the smelly things. Most of them, she was sure, had never done anything like that. There'd been a lot of screaming and cursing going on at first when they'd had to struggle with the wiggling, flopping, and occasional attempts to bite, but that had been hours ago.

She glanced over to where some of the other women were struggling to figure out how to erect the shelters. They were supposed to be watching Cory, but aside from forming a barrier all the way around him, none of them were paying him much attention. Still, he seemed content enough to watch them-- fascinated, in fact. Every once in a while, he'd make a sound--his version of exercising his voice--and one of the women would glance at him. He always smiled sweetly at anyone that paid him any attention, but he rarely got a smile in return.

Poor baby!

Trying not to be angry about the snubs, Bri rolled her aching shoulders and flicked a few glances around the compound. The Sheloni had disappeared some time ago after moving around the wall to stare down at the harvesting bins that were slowly being filled. None of them had ventured any closer, and she wondered if that meant anything. It seemed possible that whatever the stuff was it had properties that didn't set well with them. That would be yet another reason the Sheloni couldn't handle harvesting it themselves.

She wasn't certain why she'd gotten that impression. It might have been no more than laziness about climbing down the walls to look it over--or wariness about venturing into the slave den--but it seemed to her than she noted both excitement over the harvest and uneasiness in them.

That ruled out the possibility that it was something they ate, she decided, which also ruled out the possibility of poisoning it.

But if it was poison to them in its natural state ...?

The walls looked like stone. She hadn't gotten close enough to examine them very well, and she wasn't certain that would've made a lot of difference, but despite the fact that they looked to be as smooth as glass, she didn't think they were made of any kind of metal.

She wondered why. Too expensive to haul metal across the galaxy? That seemed plausible, and yet it was almost strange to think of the Sheloni using natural materials. There hadn't been any on the ship that she had noticed. In fact everything, including the ship itself, seemed to be made out of the same stuff--a sort of plastic/metal material.

The walls were thick. She'd noticed when she came through the gate that the walls were at least five feet thick, bottom to top, too narrow, though, she thought to be hollow--as in rooms or cells-- but awfully thick just to be a retaining wall for prisoners. She doubted much shy of a truck load of dynamite would blast through them.

The gates had been made out of the same material as the ship and about eight inches thick. If she was a betting person, she would've bet they were equal in strength to the stone walls, but it still seemed the only way out. No way could a climber, even an experienced one, go over the slick walls with no hand or foot holds, nothing even for traction.

She had to wonder if the place was like Fort Knox just to keep them in, or if there was something on the other side the Sheloni was worried about keeping out. That was a creepy thought, but she couldn't recall seeing anything at all that would support that theory. True, she'd been in pain, struggling with Cory, and upset over the deaths of Consuelo and the others, but as thick as the jungle was with plant life, there should have been furtive scurrying of creatures somewhere along the way. She should have seen some sort of flying things, tracks, or maybe broken down vegetation from something passing.

It was certainly not a dead world by any means. She'd seen a few fairly horrible looking insects--not many thankfully, but a few--beetle looking things and crawly things with way too many legs. The woman who'd described the place as looking prehistoric was right. There was something about this world that seemed fresh and just born, even though, if she remembered her science correctly, the sun was probably an old one.

On the other hand, it might not be a red sun at all. The atmosphere might alter the perception of it.

If plant life had emerged, other life had, too. There had to be land creatures--the sea seemed to be teaming with life if these monstrosities the Hirachi had brought up were any indication, but did it necessarily follow that some alien version of dinosaurs were roaming the land? Was there a blue-print for developing worlds? A 'this must happen, and then this' sort of absolute? Even if there was, who was to say dinosaurs, or their equivalent would have to evolve here and, even if there was a 'must', then it still didn't necessarily follow that they had landed in that time frame.

She dismissed the speculation after a bit. After they'd been here a little while, they would all have a better idea of what was outside the walls. They would hear them, she felt certain, even if they couldn't see. Those flimsy shelters weren't going to prevent them from hearing the noises animals made when they challenged one another, fought, and died.

It didn't matter anyway except that it would be nice to have some idea of what they'd be facing outside, because this world was what they had to work with. The Sheloni ship remained in orbit. They weren't going to get the chance to take over it and figure out how to fly it home.

They might just as well try to summon some enthusiasm for being new colonists on a fresh new world.

It was a shame she'd never *wanted* to be a fucking colonist conquering a new world! She'd liked the boring, mostly uneventful, life she'd had, with all the creature comforts she could afford--to buy, not make herself. She didn't mind homemaking as long as she had plenty of the tools that made that easy.

The men began to line up to get the food long before they'd finished 'preparing' it. Bri couldn't resist glancing at the men to see what they thought about it. A few merely grabbed handfuls and popped the rolled fish 'cakes' in their mouths, but most of them looked at least a little doubtful, their expressions cautious as they tasted.

She was relieved that the food seemed to please them--either that or they were just starving from the heavy labor.

She hoped *they* weren't going to have to eat the raw stuff! Sushi might be a great delicacy to some. It might even be a wonderful flavor, but she still didn't want raw food. She'd spent way too much time studying the proper preparation to prevent food poisoning to have any interest in trying anything uncooked.

And the worst of it was that none of them had any idea if any of these creatures they were so busy cutting up might be poisonous if eaten.

God, she missed the FDA!

Nobody keeled over. That was a good sign. Unfortunately, it still didn't necessarily follow that Earthlings could ingest the stuff without keeling over.

Caroline, she discovered, was covertly popping fish cakes into her mouth from time to time. Nice of her to volunteer to be food taster, Bri thought wryly. She didn't say anything. Caroline had already swallowed one before she could get a warning out.

She was nearly ready to drop with exhaustion by the time the men had all had their fill and the robot guarding them allowed them to leave the food line. A handful of the women who'd been fortunate enough to be far enough away from the butchering end of the table not to be completely revolted, and who apparently also managed to see Caroline eating the fish, decided to try it themselves.

Bri thought she'd rather starve. She was too tired to be hungry anyway. Ignoring Cory's demand when he saw her pass by on her way to the water, she moved down to wash the stench of fish off. Washing her hands didn't do the trick, though. She had icky all over. After a moment, she cautiously moved a little further into the water and scrubbed at the gown she was wearing, wishing she was uninhibited enough to just take the thing off.

The threat of almost certain death might have greatly liberated her, but it hadn't changed her into an exhibitionist. If there'd been nothing but women in the compound, she still wouldn't have been comfortable wandering around stark naked.

Unfortunately, she was the next thing to naked by the time she'd finished. The plastic-like properties of the material didn't keep it from clinging when wet or from becoming embarrassingly transparent. Looking down at herself when she waded out, it hit her that she'd been neck deep in the water when she'd gone in after Cory--way too upset to realize how indecent she looked.

Belated discomfort settled in her. No wonder Kole had looked at her like that!

Cory set up a wailing demand for attention when he saw her come out of the water. Bri glanced toward him, holding the wet gown out from her skin, debating whether she had the moxy to stroll through the encampment looking like she did. She saw when she looked around, though, that she wasn't the only one who'd gone down to bathe. Half naked women in clinging gowns abounded.

The hell with it, she decided. Trying not to draw more attention to herself by flapping the gown self-consciously, she headed purposefully toward Cory. Dansk reached him first. The boy let out a Comanche yell as the strange man caught him beneath the arms and lifted him into the air. Spurred by the note of alarm in Cory's voice more than any real fear that Dansk would hurt him, Bri broke into a jog.

She had a stitch in her side by the time she reached the pair, but the sense of alarm faded when she saw Dansk nuzzling the baby affectionately. Surprised, she stopped a few feet away and watched the two of them. When Dansk lifted the baby slightly away and studied him keenly, Cory simply stared back at him wide eyed.

A broad grin finally lit Dansk's features. He turned to look at Bri. "Mine," he said, obvious pride in his voice.

Bri blinked, all at sea. "Yours?" she said, dawning possessiveness in her voice.

He didn't seem to notice. Instead, he settled in the sand and propped Cory on one knee, still studying him--now with a definite look of pride and possessiveness, and Bri didn't like either emotion directed at *her* baby. "Kole said he looked like Laayia. I didn't believe him. I thought he was only saying so because...." He sent her a look she found hard to interpret. Slowly, his gaze warmed with desire that heated her insides. It died after a few moments, or rather was firmly tamped. A look of regret crossed his features. "I would still have liked ... but that isn't possible, not now."

Bri still wasn't certain what he was talking about, but she had the uncomfortable suspicion that Dansk had just 'broken up' with her. "We're ... still friends?" she asked hesitantly, but realized that although she'd thought 'friends', the Hirachi word that had come to her meant companions. She supposed that was close enough. Mostly she was just anxious to know he didn't mean he wouldn't, or couldn't, have anything else to do with her.

His face brightened. "I was not certain. The Sheloni didn't allow you to choose ... but if you choose me, yes. I would be honored. *Am* honored. Pleased. Very happy."

Bri couldn't help but be amused that he seemed to be stumbling for words. Somehow, she'd thought he would be--smoother, a player sort of Hirachi, not shy and awkward. Intrigued though she was, however, there was something about his reaction and what he'd said that made her feel as if they weren't actually communicating.

Or maybe they were. She wanted to be his friend, but she wanted to be more than just a friend.

But there was Kole. She didn't want to be just Kole's friend either.

God she was a slut!

She would never have believed that about herself before, but the plain truth was that both of them had rocked her world, and that wasn't something she could take lightly or dismiss--not when no man had ever even almost had that effect on her before. She was greedy. She couldn't bear to think of giving up one for the other or, god forbid, both because she couldn't make up her mind which man she cared most for.

She wanted more time to decide if she had to decide between them.

She glanced at Cory, who'd become comfortable enough with the man holding him to begin exploring the chest he'd been staring at for several moments as if hypnotized. Bri reddened when he grabbed one of Dansk's nipples and began trying to pull the 'button' off. She cleared her throat. "You think he's yours?" she asked hesitantly.

He chuckled. "Know. Laayia was my mate this cycle. I thought he had died with the others. He has a strong likeness to his mother. I can not doubt that he is mine. "

Bri frowned. Kole had said something about cycles. She studied Dansk speculatively for a moment, but how was she ever going to understand the Hirachi if she didn't ask? "I don't ... we're different, maybe a lot different. I'm not sure I understand the cycle."

He looked surprised and then thoughtful. "Kole said that the Earth human females could not live in the water, but no one believed he was serious."

Bri stared at him, wondering just how damning it was to them that the 'Earth human females' were so different. She knew they had already fallen short, literally, because they were so diminutive and weak beside the larger race. Instead of confessing that, no, Kole had not been making a funny, they really, really couldn't live underwater, she directed him back to her question. "The cycles?" she prompted.

He seemed to shrug. "For us it is seven cycles (years)--supposed to be. After the Sheloni, we discovered the mating cycle made us more vulnerable and easier to capture, because we must leave the sea, of course, and mate on land. And stay until the children are born and old enough and strong enough to return to the sea--four cycles, at the very least. The elders forbade it because of that and the women began to ignore the call when the Sheloni continued to raid us for more slaves, so none of us had actually gotten the opportunity to breed. I've passed six cycles myself--everyone here at least that many--Kole seven--since we reached the maturity to begin cycling."

Bri's jaw dropped--mostly in dismay. "You only have sex every seven years?"

Dansk burst out laughing, but warm promise filled his eyes. "We only *produce* every seven years. The women choose companions as they like, of course, but for the breeding there can only be one chosen and until he has produced she doesn't allow her other companions to touch her. In that way, we know our lines." He studied her expression speculatively. "This is not your way," he said with conviction.

It boggled the mind, or hers, at least. She still wasn't certain she had fully grasped his explanation. "The women--they're only fertile every seven years?"

He looked surprised. "Yes."

Uh oh. Problems. She supposed the Hirachi must be laboring under the belief that the Earth women were in cycle, too, and continued until they produced.

The other Earth human females weren't going to be happy about this. No birth control and men who thought it was ok to screw any time--Wait! That was like their human counterparts.

Realistically, it changed nothing. The damned Sheloni had taken everyone's birth control. That was a down the road problem, though. It looked like they were going to have to go to plain old abstinence if they wanted to have any kind of control over their reproduction. It sucked a big hairy one, as Caroline would've said, that they hadn't gotten the same kind of natural birth control the Hirachi women apparently had!

She discovered Dansk was frowning at her. "You said, only every seven?"

Bri plastered a fake smile on her lips. "It's a little different with us," she hedged. "How long does it usually take the women to bear their children?"

He frowned thoughtfully. "Almost a full cycle."

Which could mean the same gestation period as humans or possibly somewhat longer, maybe even shorter. It could be a good thing or a bad thing. It was going to be a disaster for everyone if they gestated their usual nine to ten months and the babies weren't mature enough to survive. Their cycle could be shorter for that matter, she realized. A Hirachi year could be anything, she supposed, but it was unlikely that it would be the same time frame as an Earth year. God only knew how long the year was on their world. For that matter, she thought uneasily, she wasn't entirely certain that he *meant* a year when he said cycle. It had translated as year, but then something seemed off on the references, and she began to wonder if cycle was a generic sort of term for them--day cycle, week, month, year--all shortened just to 'cycle' and the meaning clear to them only because of the way they used it. It wasn't impossible. In fact, given the way so many Earth people shortened up the language in just that way, it seemed probable.

They had no control over their own body cycles, though. None. Whatever happened, happened. She just hoped the Sheloni had thoroughly researched before they'd decided breeding the two species would work. Otherwise, life was going to be really rough.

"You'll accept me as one of your companions after ...?" Dansk asked, somewhat hesitantly.

Dragged back from her thoughts, Bri stared at him blankly. "After what?"

"Once you've bred with Kole."

Blood gushed into Bri's face. Her jaw dropped. Heat that wasn't embarrassment flooded every other part of her body. She went catatonic while her shocked brain wrestled with unfamiliar information. Apparently, it had somehow been settled that she was Kole's for breeding purposes and afterwards she could screw either or both to her heart's content. She didn't know whether she was comfortable with this new set of rules or not. Wicked creature that she was, though, her heart leapt at the thought.

She could have both, she thought with a mixture of delight and doubt?

It was just as well the robots signaled the end of the rest period. She had way too much food for thought.

Dansk looked upset that she hadn't given him a firm commitment. She smiled apologetically.

He seemed to take that as a yes. Handing Cory back to her, he caressed her cheek and finally leaned down to kiss her briefly on the lips. "I have missed you," he murmured.

Kissing, then, Bri thought, thoroughly bemused, was acceptable even though it seemed to have been settled between Kole and

Dansk that she was to 'save herself' for Kole for the time being? Irritation filtered through her shock. Dansk had implied that women made these decisions. How had it come about that *they* were doing all of the damned negotiating over which of them got to fuck her and in what order? She'd been Kole's breeding partner first--and their baby had been taken. Dansk was apparently convinced he'd produced. So, it was Kole's turn because of both of those circumstances?

How civilized of them!

Actually, now that he mentioned it, Dansk looked as if he was sporting some of the 'negotiations'. She'd noticed his lip and one eye looked slightly swollen, but she hadn't associated the marks of a fist fight with the settling of a dispute until he suggested that he and Kole had ironed out the situation and come to an understanding.

Consuelo had been right, she realized. The fight *had* been over her--sort of. She supposed it was more a pecking order sort of thing. No one got to mess with Kole's pussy until he'd plugged the old womb with his seed, because he'd been first at the trough.

So what the hell had happened to the 'I'm worried about you having a baby elephant, baby'? Apparently hormones and the instinct for procreation were outweighing reason right now-- because the Hirachi males were in season.

The Earth human females were going to be delighted to hear that! Here they'd been preening themselves at suddenly becoming the focus of so much desire, as if they'd awakened to discover they were all great beauties and sex goddesses, and it was nothing more than the fact that the great lugs were caught up in a mindless need to propagate their species! That was a dampening thought, to say the very least!

It was somewhat mollifying, she supposed, that they didn't limit themselves strictly to procreation. Dansk had definitely been hinting at recreational sports.

She wasn't sure she liked the idea that they were willing to share her. They wouldn't be willing to if they actually cared about her, would they? Or was she still trying to fit a round peg in a square hole? They weren't human. Everything she'd learned about them emphasized that there were as many differences between the two as there were similarities. Maybe they just weren't as territorial-- excluding breeding time--as the human male--and female if it came to that?

Come to think of it, why would they need to be? Territorial

behavior was directly linked to spawning--a way to insure one's line. Nobody thought of it that way anymore, but that was the origin of it anyway. It had worked out differently for the Hirachi species, and they seemed very comfortable with it.

Could her species accustom themselves to it, though? Or was it something else that was going to make life hard?

Pushing the thoughts aside, she settled Cory in his pen again, did her best to pacify him over being abandoned, and went back to work.

Chapter Twenty One

Bri had missed the opportunity to eat at the first meal, but as empty as she was, she still didn't want the raw fish. She discovered she was going to get plenty of opportunity to accustom herself to the possibility, though.

The Sheloni obviously didn't subscribe to the U.S. labor laws. When the women had lugged water up the beach and cleaned the preparation tables, they were ordered to start all over again. This time, somehow, she was shuffled to the end beheading and gutting the creatures. She had to fight nausea the first hour or so, but after a while her stomach seemed to settle. Then it was just revolting to hold the things down and lob off their heads.

She hadn't realized how squeamish she was. It was mighty thoughtful of the fucking Sheloni to cure her--all of them--of that reluctance to butcher live things. It was going to make it so much easier for her to stomach murder--not that she felt like disposing of the Sheloni actually qualified as murder, intelligent species or not.

She pictured them as being something like intelligent spiders. It was just going to be messier and more disgusting to splatter them.

She didn't know what it was about that idle, random thought of violence that triggered a deep memory. But as she stood quietly working like a good little slave, thinking about retribution, staring at nothing in particular, she remembered something she'd learned so long ago she hadn't realized until that instant that she still remembered it.

Lying at their feet, if she wasn't completely mistaken, was one of the first and most powerful of the weapons man had invented-- the raw ingredients for gun powder. Disbelief followed in the wake of that epiphany, but as she jogged the errant memory and stirred it with the sights and smells she'd been unconsciously cataloguing since her arrival she realized she *was* on to something.

Struggling to tamp the rise of euphoria inside her with a good dose of caution, she glanced at the woman next to her. "Any science teachers in the group?"

The woman lifted a grimy hand, used the back of it to push her hair out of her eyes and studied Bri for a split second before turning to the woman on her other side. "Science teacher?"

The question traveled almost the length of the line and a 'yes' came back. Bri leaned over the table a little and looked down, trying to figure out which woman it was. Several of the women glanced at her. Shrugging inwardly, she focused on her task again. "Ask the teacher if she likes fireworks," she murmured about an hour later.

That time, she leaned out and glanced down the table several times until the question stopped. The woman, who looked to be in her late twenties, looked completely puzzled for a moment. Finally, her frown cleared. She exchanged a brief look with Bri and then looked around them.

Bri held her breath, waiting, trying to pretend she was as tired and bored as before, but it was hard to ignore the excitement that had begun to thrum through her blood. After several moments, she glanced down the line again.

The woman nodded.

It took an effort to contain the jubilation that went through her. Gun powder!

Now all they had to do was figure out how they were going to gather the ingredients under the Sheloni's watchful nose and refine them, and how to use it once they'd gathered enough to blow the bastards to hell!

It was as well she had excitement to sustain her for a time. She wasn't certain she could have made it through the remainder of the day without something to buoy her, but even that waned after a while, drained away by the weariness of standing so long.

There was no privacy for anything, even relieving themselves, but the women set to erecting the shelters had duly noted the lack early on and had set up one shelter as far from everything else as possible. Crude as it was, they were glad to have it, but Bri was inclined to think this lack of consideration was going to be the straw that broke the camel's back. Nothing could more surely enrage a group of women to the point of considering violence more than the lack of privacy and a decent toilet!

When she was finally released for her rest period, she lined up with everyone else for the little bit of privacy the shelter afforded and then moved to the opposite end of the beach to clean up the best she could. She was sunburned from standing out in the sun all day. Every muscle in her body was sheer torment, and she'd passed beyond hunger, but she didn't think she could sleep to save her soul with the stench of dead fish in her nostrils.

Cory had behaved remarkably well considering he was

accustomed to having her undivided attention. Mostly, it was because the Hirachi males had made it a point to pass as close to his pen as possible whenever they could and entertain him for a moment or two, and the women, apparently feeling it was a reflection on them, had begun to do the same so that he was never completely alone more than a few minutes at the time. But he had done well even when he had been left to merely watch what was going on around him.

She was proud of him and at the same time sad that she hadn't been able to spend any time with him. It made *her* feel deprived.

He was asleep when she finally made her way to the pen to collect him.

She had missed his whole day, hadn't had the chance to change him or feed him or play with him, and now she was just glad he was asleep because she was so tired she didn't have the energy to rock him to sleep. Guilt filled at her at the thought. She felt like a terrible mother wanting to put her own needs before his.

She'd already carefully gathered him up before she realized she had no idea where she would sleep. She'd been wandering aimlessly for several minutes when Kole found her. Too tired even to summon a spark of resentment for the fact that he seemed to expect her to accept him as a sleeping partner, she nevertheless eyed him a little doubtfully. Without a word, he dropped a hand to her shoulder and directed her to a shelter near one end.

It looked barely big enough for one Hirachi, but she was too tired to argue. Ignoring her half hearted objection, he took the baby from her so that she could climb inside. When she'd settled, he handed Cory to her and then climbed in himself while she carefully settled Cory, praying she could do it without waking him. Relieved when he merely burrowed into the loose sand beneath the thin sheet that covered the bottom, she fell back, closed her eyes, and lost consciousness.

She roused over and over during the night because the unfamiliarity of her sleeping arrangements, dimly aware of Kole's warmth on one side and Cory on the other. A cool, almost constant wind blew off the water, chilling her as it brushed her sunburned skin, but she merely burrowed closer to Kole's warmth, dragged the baby close to her chest, and drifted off again.

It seemed to her that she'd barely closed her eyes when she was wakened by the annoying mechanical buzz that summoned them. Groaning, she opened her eyes and found herself staring up at Kole.

It was odd that that seemed right somehow.

He brushed his hand lightly over her cheek. "Your skin is red."

She sighed, closing her eyes, trying to summon the strength to move. "Sunburn," she said dully. "I'll be fried after a few days of this."

"You did not eat either."

Dragging in a deep breath, Bri sat up reluctantly. "I can't eat cold, raw fish."

He frowned, a look more irritated than thoughtful. "You'll grow weak if you don't eat. You have no ... flesh. You have lost too much already."

Bri gave him a look. "I have plenty of damned flesh, and it's too damned early in the morning for insults!"

He caught her arm before she could wiggle out of the shelter with Cory. "You need to eat to live."

Bri glared him. At this point she wasn't even sure there was a lot of reason to worry about *not* living.

"For Cory."

Her shoulders slumped. She dropped her gaze. Unfair! That was so damned unfair!

He tipped her face up again with an index finger, forcing her to look at him. "For me."

Because he cared? Or because she was supposed to care what he wanted?

And yet, despite the irritation, as simple as those two little words were, they brought a lump to her throat. Defeated, she nodded, scooting out of the shelter before the guard bots could decide she'd dawdled long enough to deserve a jolt from the collar. He steadied her when she got to her feet and wavered. "Work at the end where they cut the fish. I will bring something for your skin."

Bri stared after him as he strode quickly to where the men were assembling for work. She was supposed to *volunteer* for the head chopping? That was worse than the skinning!

Sighing, trying to decide whether she wanted something for the sunburns badly enough to be stuck hacking the heads off the fish, she hurried to feed Cory and get him situated before joining the women to set up the food line. The bots seemed to have been programmed to allow her some time for attending Cory's needs, but she didn't dare push it. As soon as she'd finished feeding him, she settled him in the 'playpen' that had been erected for him. Someone, one of the women, she thought, had erected a shelter above it the day before to protect him from the sun, but she saw that his skin looked a little pinkish, too. That clinched it. If Kole knew something that would protect the skin from the sun she had to have it.

The sun was already half way to its zenith before the first men returned with fish. As hungry as she knew the Hirachi must be, having to work so hard when they'd had nothing to eat before they left, Bri enjoyed a guilty pleasure in it, because they were allowed to rest once they'd readied the tables for the food preparation. She settled near Cory, her head propped on the edge of the stones used to form his pen, half drowsing while she watched him pull himself up and shuffle unsteadily around the small area, using his grip on the sides to help him to balance.

He was going to be running before long, trying to climb over the thing. She hoped they could get out from under the Sheloni before keeping up with him became a real problem.

Sighing tiredly when she saw the first of the Hirachi emerging from the sea, she got up and went to take her place. Kole was right, as irritated as she had been at him for pointing it out. She needed to keep up her strength. She was going to be useless if she could do nothing but drag herself to work and then into the pallet to sleep at night.

The other women didn't look to be in any better shape than she was. As much as it relieved her to know she wasn't alone in being totally wiped out after the first day, that wasn't a good thing.

True to his word, Kole was among the first to arrive, and he was carrying a dead thing that looked even creepier than the fish. He dropped it on the table before her. She stared down at it with revulsion.

"There is a bladder inside. Milk the fluids from it and rub it on your skin. It will block the rays from the sun."

Struggling to uncurl her lip, Bri looked up at him. It wasn't bad enough she had fish guts and blood all over her? She had to smear the disgusting stuff on herself?

His lips curled faintly, but he looked irritated, as well. "It is better than burning."

To him, maybe. She wasn't sure she agreed.

Wondering if it was his idea of a sick joke but uncomfortable about being impolite about the gift when he'd been so thoughtful, Bri reluctantly took the thing and hacked it open. The bladder he'd described was black--no missing it--the substance inside looked like cold cream. Something fatty to help her fry better? Shrugging inwardly, she decided to try it. She doubted she would burn worse and maybe it *would* help.

Squeezing the bladder, she quickly dabbed the disgusting mess on the areas that had already burned. To her surprise, the stuff felt like lotion, soothing and cool. A few moments after she'd applied it, she noticed an almost menthol like burning and then--nothing. Pleased when she realized that it at least had the property of numbing the burned areas, she looked around for Kole, but discovered he'd already vanished again.

"It helps?" the woman beside her asked doubtfully.

Bri glanced at her in surprise. "It really does. You want some?"

She hadn't actually intended to share it with everyone if sharing meant she wouldn't get anymore, but she saw it was too late to object. The women passed the thing along the table so quickly that it was gone before she could say more.

Mildly irritated, she dismissed it and focused on her work. She could ask Kole to bring her another and hope he could catch one.

The task was fairly mindless once one got over the revulsion of it, and her mind wandered to the gun powder for a time while she considered first one thing and then another that it might be used for and possibilities for collecting it and refining it. The more pure it was, the more bang they'd get, she knew.

She hoped the teacher knew the correct ratios of the components. She hadn't learned, or just couldn't remember, how to actually make it. All she remembered were the ingredients used to make it--which was still invaluable even if they ended up having to experiment a little.

That thought brought her mind back to the sea creatures. The Hirachi would be as familiar with the terrain and animals below the sea as Earth people were with land animals and plants--which might or might not do them any good. But Kole had recognized the thing he'd brought her. This world and its inhabitants must be more similar to his world than hers. She wondered if there was anything, plant, animal, or otherwise, in the sea that would have other useful properties--like acid. Methane deposits like had been found on Earth's sea floors? That would give the Sheloni a hell of a bang!

Lifting her head, she studied the robots stationed about the compound speculatively. She'd thought they were in a pretty hopeless situation after Angie had died, because they couldn't hope to overcome the robots that guarded them. Acid, though, the right kind, could disable them--could burn up whatever kind of electronics the aliens used. They wouldn't *have* to figure out the alien technology.

And without the robots, the Sheloni would be virtually helpless.

The Sheloni might still escape them, though. They were never in the compound. They observed from a safe distance--the walls above them--and if the Sheloni escaped to the ship orbiting the planet that might mean the end of all of them. They could be blasted from space without ever knowing what had hit them.

So they would have to figure out a way to hit everything at once, or almost at once. That was going to take everyone working almost in concert.

She was so deep in thought, she didn't notice when Kole returned until he shoved a fish cake under her nose. She jumped back instinctively, her gaze flying upward to connect the hand under her nose to the face that went with it.

His expression was stern. "Eat."

Bri's lips tightened. She looked down at the cake again, feeling her stomach execute a flip flop. Feeling like a difficult child balking at medicine, she sucked in a breath and held it and then took the thing from his hand and took a tiny bite, swallowing it before she could taste it. Her stomach revolted anyway. The thought alone was enough to make her feel like throwing up.

"Eat!"

"I will!" she snapped testily, her teeth clenched as she fought to keep the morsel down. "It's not going to help if I throw it back up!"

A look of sympathy flickered in his eyes, but he squelched it. "Promise?"

Bri nodded. Have to, she kept telling herself as she struggled to take the thing down one minute bite at the time until she'd finally eaten the whole thing. She didn't feel a lot of triumph when she managed it, because her stomach was still threatening to revolt, but it settled after a while.

She still couldn't say that she felt any better, or any stronger, but she knew she was being childish about it. She hadn't eaten enough to help that much. Her stomach still felt as if it was caving in upon itself--which was a bad thing, she realized. Kole was right. If she didn't eat, she would quickly reach the point where she couldn't. She hadn't realized it, but he was right about her lack of stored fat, too. The food had been so tasteless on the ship that she'd had no interest in eating it, and she'd grown too thin to have much in the way of reserves. She supposed that was why poor Caroline looked deflated. She'd lost too much, too fast, and her skin wasn't shrinking as quickly as the fat reserves.

It was a damned good thing, she thought with wry amusement, that most of the women captured had had some reserve fat or they would all have been looking like starved third world citizens by now.

The amusement left her as it dawned on her that they *were* seriously third world citizens now--having a little reserve fat for hard times wasn't a luxury or a matter of beauty, or lack thereof. It could mean the difference between surviving, or not.

It was hard, but she gritted her teeth and did what she knew she had to do to survive. She ate as many of the fish cakes as she could make herself eat without bringing it back up. She despaired of growing accustomed to the diet, though. It did not have a strong or even repulsive taste. It was the texture that revolted her and the knowledge that it was raw. Sight, smell, taste, and texture all played a part in the appeal, or lack, of food and the fish cakes were lacking in all areas as far as she was concerned.

She was still exhausted when they were finally allowed to rest that night, but she didn't feel as if she would drop at any moment. Either the food helped, or she was starting to adjust, and since she doubted she could adjust to the labor that quickly, then it had to be the food.

It also helped that she wasn't burned worse. In fact, as disgusting as the stuff was she'd had to smear all over herself, it seemed to have helped heal the burn she'd already gotten.

Kole met her as he had the night before. She felt more capable of fighting him, and she was still irritated that he seemed to take it as a foregone conclusion that she was somehow his. On the other hand--who was she kidding? She hadn't merely accepted him and endured when the Sheloni had tossed her to him like a prize. She'd reciprocated his passion. He had every reason to believe she wanted him.

Not that she felt energetic enough for *that*! He made a hell of a substitute for a blanket/heater, though. And he'd been thoughtful enough of her welfare to make sure she had protection from burning and that she'd eaten.

She couldn't remember the last time anyone had shown concern for her welfare, let alone her comfort.

When they'd settled beside one another in the shelter, she not only didn't make any attempt to place any distance between them, she snuggled closer in the shelter of his body. She felt his cock harden against her backside as she wiggled her butt against his pelvis, though, and a mixture of warmth and irritation warred inside her. She *was* tempted, but she was too tired to have that much interest. She began to feel put upon, to mentally berate him for his lack of consideration for her exhaustion.

To her surprise, he didn't make any attempt to push the issue, however, and, contrary creature that she was, she began to feel insulted that he didn't. Did she look that bad, she wondered? She *must* look awful!

She hadn't realized that the fucking Sheloni had pampered them on the trip over until they were dumped in this godforsaken place with nothing. She had no way to groom herself beyond the most primitive methods--finger combing her hair to try to keep it from being a complete rat's nest, using her finger to clean her teeth. She was sunburned. Kole himself had remarked about how thin she'd gotten.

He probably found her completely unappealing now!

She lay perfectly still for a while, hardly breathing, stirring her resentment.

Kole stroked her arm lightly. "Go to sleep, dear one."

A knot about the size of a baseball swelled in her throat. Tears stung the backs of her eyes. She was *such* a bitch! She'd been thinking all sorts of nasty things about him, and he'd called dear!

She cleared her throat as the tightness eased. "I'm not pregnant," she offered tentatively, since it had occurred to her that he might not want to touch her until he was certain she wasn't carrying Dansk's baby.

His arm tightened around her. He dragged in a halting breath. "Don't tempt me, dear one. It is best if you're not."

Bri frowned. From what Dansk had said she'd thought Kole must be desperate to breed his child on her. She'd thought that was why he'd taken her into the shelter with him. "Why?" she asked finally.

She heard him swallow.

"I will take you from this place. But I don't know how long it will take to find a way and make arrangements. I don't want to risk that you could be heavy with child and in danger because of that."

A stillness settled over Bri. Was he saying he loved her? Or was it just that he was that sort of man, careful and protective? Was there any real distinction between the two when it was her welfare that seemed of utmost importance to him?

She tried to turn in his arms. He held her, gently but firmly.

There was wry amusement in his voice when he spoke again. "You can not know how hard it is to deny myself or you wouldn't be tempting me."

"But … won't your fertile cycle pass?"

He stiffened, and she thought the question had disconcerted him. "The gods willing, there will be another and a safer time. If you chose me next time, I will be honored. I would … not sever the companionship if you chose Dansk instead."

The last comment sent a jolt through her. Stunned, Bri wrestled with the comment. Dansk had mentioned companionship, too, but she'd thought he was talking about friendship--friends with benefits, actually. The way Kole spoke, it sounded like something more … permanent. The Hirachi version of marriage, she wondered?

She realized there were no words for love or marriage in the language. Obviously, they didn't actually form family units, at least not permanent ones. Maybe seven year cycles? They'd come together to produce a child, rear it together until the next cycle and then change partners?

Bizarre as it seemed to her, she supposed it wasn't that farfetched. Humans tried, with varying degrees of success, to mate for life. Very few animals in nature did. Mostly, they mated, reared their young to maturity together, and then parted, searching for a new mate when the season came for it again.

She didn't especially dislike the notion, but then again, she realized she wasn't too keen about Kole deciding to change partners for the next dance.

Except that he said, now, that he wouldn't. That didn't mean he wouldn't, though.

It occurred to her that now would probably be a good time to explain that Earth human females weren't like Hirachi women, but she decided he didn't need that to worry about. In any case, the Hirachi seemed to cycle together from what she understood. It wouldn't matter whether she was fertile or not if he wasn't.

Seven cycles was a long time to ask him to wait, though, when he'd been deprived of the children he wanted so many times before.

He was right about a pregnancy making it harder on her, though.

The other women didn't have the option of saying no. Most of them were probably already pregnant considering the breeding program the Sheloni had instigated, at least half of them certainly were.

They couldn't wait long or they ran the risk of a real disaster with the pregnant women slowing everyone down.

She sighed. "Thank you for bringing me the icky, disgusting stuff. It helped."

She felt him shift and thought he was looking down at her. Amusement threaded his voice when he spoke. "I will bring you more icky, disgusting stuff tomorrow since you shared with the others."

Bri thought she detected a note of censure. "They were burning, too."

He settled again. "*You* are the one who is dear to my heart. Their men can look after them."

A smile curled Bri's lips and warmth filled her. She hadn't exactly been fishing for that, but it pleased her no end. He *did* care for her!

As much as she wanted to explore that, she let it go. "I was wondering if there was anything down there that had other … interesting properties?"

He tensed. "Like what?"

She rolled onto her back, but she discovered she still couldn't make out his features in the darkness. His eyes glowed eerily, though, and she doubted he was similarly challenged. "Something that would corrode the stuff the Sheloni use to make everything."

Even though she couldn't see his expression, she felt the tension in his form that told her she had his full attention. "We need to disable the robots. They're too strong even for you Hirachi. We lost our programmer on the trip down--otherwise I'd hoped she could reprogram the things. We wouldn't need to, though, if we could find something that would eat up their circuits--or whatever the Sheloni have used to animate them. It would mean getting up close and personal, but those bladders would work to direct a stream of acid...."

He placed his fingertips over her lips, halting her mid sentence.

Bri's heart skipped several beats. She'd been so excited about her idea, she'd been careless. Had she given everything away, she thought, dismayed? Ruined all the plans she'd worked so hard on?

He lifted his fingers after a moment. "It's passed."

Surprised, Bri was silent for a moment. "What passed?"

Her question surprised him. "The beams they use to see and hear us."

"You can *see* them?"

Obviously, he realized it was a rhetorical question. "What would this *acid* be like?"

"It would burn your skin. Everything the Sheloni make is made out of the same stuff, though, I'm almost positive. We could test it on the materials in the shelters until we find something that seems strong enough. Then someone would have to try it on one of the bots, I'm afraid. Otherwise, we wouldn't know for sure that it would work. We have to work out a plan that would take down the bots quickly so we could attack the Sheloni. Otherwise the Sheloni could escape, and we wouldn't be able to stop them from using the ship to attack us."

Kole settled behind her again, stroking her almost idly. Bri's excitement waned, and irritation took its place as it occurred to her that he'd dismissed her ideas. What had she expected anyway, she thought angrily? Men never took women seriously. They were too damned macho to consider women might be just as good at some things as they were. She was just surprised he hadn't patted her on the head when he dismissed her.

"Even if we could kill them before they communicated with the main ship," Kole said after a few moments, "the others would realize something was wrong, and they would attack. We might escape anyway, but I don't care for the thought of being hunted. This is one of the things that I have not been able to work out." He seemed to shrug. "The other is that Earth human females can not swim. I'd thought we could breach the sea wall and escape into the sea. It would not be easy. The walls are strong, proving others escaped before, and the Sheloni know about the *way*, but we could still burst them. Now, we are stronger than we are when not in cycle. And they send many of us down together, enough that we could work in concert and focus the *way* on the stone to make it crumble and collapse, and if the base collapses, the wall will come down.

"Which does us no good if we can not take our companions with us," he finished wryly. "I would take freedom even with the threat of being hunted otherwise, because there are places beneath the sea where even the Sheloni can not reach us. But I will not take freedom if I must leave you."

Chapter Twenty Two

Bri didn't know what pleased her more, the fact that Kole seemed to see her as an equal, considered her input as important as his own, or the fact that he was willing to give up his own freedom if he couldn't free her, as well.

It thrilled her to her toes to know she meant enough to him that he would willingly sacrifice his freedom to be with her. It humbled her, warmed her, filled her with a sense of awe to think that he could care so much.

She swallowed the bubble of emotion that swelled in her chest with an effort. "Then we'll have to think of a way to bring the Sheloni up in their ship down to us," she said finally, "and have a trap waiting for them. What is the 'way'?" she added curiously.

He was silent for several moments. "Hard to explain," he said finally. "It is … force … that we can throw … like sound, I suppose, but we can focus it as if it is something solid. Ordinarily, it is something we can use when we are in the sea to protect ourselves from predators and rarely used for anything else. But it is stronger now because of the hormone spike of breeding season. And I know, when we link our minds, we would be able to crush the stone."

Sound waves, she wondered? Like the sound waves used in medicine on Earth, to break up the stones that formed inside of people--gall stones and the like? Possibly, but then even though it wasn't something unknown to humans, it certainly wasn't something they could do without a machine.

"The *way*--this is something you can only use underwater?"

"The water carries it. The air--dissipates its strength."

Disappointed, but not terribly surprised, Bri settled and was already drifting toward sleep when a thought occurred to her. "The coral!"

Kole was silent for several moments, and she thought he might have gone to sleep. "Coral?" he finally asked.

"Whatever that is that you're harvesting for them! That's important to them, very important! If they think they can't blow us up without blowing it up, too, they'll try to save it. We might be replaceable, but that stuff isn't or they wouldn't have gone to so much trouble to get it."

Kole said nothing for many moments, obviously considering the possibilities. "You must have been a great commander on your world," he said finally.

The comment was flattering, but it surprised a chuckle out of her. "No ... I was...." She broke off as a novel thought occurred to her. Marketing required a firm grasp of strategy. It had never occurred to her that, in a real sense, it was battle ... and a fight to the 'death'. If you weren't good at it, your company 'died'. She *had* been good. She'd started with nothing and built her little company into something. "You know? I think I might just love you, Kole!" she said teasingly.

He caught the tone, seemed to grasp the gist of what she'd said, but the word didn't translate. "Love? ---Think? Don't know?"

She pulled his arm tighter, tucking his hand against her cheek when she felt him stiffen as if he would pull away. "You don't even know the word," she murmured.

"It doesn't mean care?"

"It's more complicated ... more everything," she said, sorry that she'd teased him. She hadn't expected him to feel hurt about it. She wasn't even sure of why she'd said it or, having done so, why she was reluctant to commit herself to a definite yes or no.

Because she really wasn't sure, she decided, wasn't certain she felt that depth of commitment, trust, devotion. She still felt divided by her feelings for Dansk. Whenever she was around him, she felt much the same as when she was with Kole. Did that mean she loved both? Or neither? And if it did mean that she loved both, then it must be a different kind of love, mustn't it?

The idea confused her more. She certainly didn't feel sisterly, or motherly toward them. And love seemed a strong word for friends, though she supposed there were plenty of people who felt strongly enough toward friends that it was love.

She'd never really analyzed love, she realized. It *was* a complicated emotion. Was it just degrees that separated the love for a parent, sibling, child, friend, lover, and/or spouse? Or was it the same emotion and just ... tinted according to the person one loved? And why was it acceptable to love so many people, unless it happened to be two men?

She didn't think it *wasn't* possible to love two men at the same time. It was just unacceptable in her society.

She didn't think it was unacceptable in the Hirachi society, though. Everything Kole and Dansk had told her seemed to point to the fact that they not only didn't find it unacceptable, they embraced it, or at least accepted it as a fact of life.

Maybe it would be all right to love them both and she wouldn't be hurting either one?

She fell asleep while she was still struggling with her disturbing thoughts.

The following day was much the same as the first two, and the day after, and the day after that. Bri gave up the effort of even trying to keep count when it occurred to her that it was not only hopeless. It was pointless. The only thing that mattered was trying to come up with a battle strategy that would break the Sheloni hold on them before the pregnant women began to balloon with baby and were too heavy and awkward to run for their lives.

By the end of the week, the women, even the die hard 'I don't want to rock the boat' type and the 'I am woman, hear me whine, I need somebody big and strong' type had lost all interest in just 'going with the flow'. One by one, they came to the same conclusion she had--whatever was 'out there' they were ready to face it. The 'known' was not nearly as desirable as they'd thought it would be once they realized that the Sheloni could, and would, work them into the grave if necessary to get what they wanted.

It was a relief when they also concluded they needed the Hirachi as allies, because she'd already allied with them--and just as well the Hirachi didn't realize that many of the women they were trying so hard to protect, had willingly given up their best chance of escape for, didn't trust them and weren't particularly enthusiastic about being 'their women'. Not all of them felt that way, but for many of the women it was more a matter of accepting what they couldn't change.

It was a shame. It angered Bri, because she thought the Hirachi were worthy of a lot more than mere acceptance. They had their share of faults--Thank god! She didn't think she could've stood perfection!--but overall they were good people, and it sure as hell wasn't as if the women didn't have plenty of faults of their own! They were damned lucky that, regardless of how fierce the Hirachi looked, and even possibly were, they were also capable of gentleness! No one seemed to realize that they were as strange to the Hirachi as vice versa--or at least *had* seemed.

It almost seemed more strange to her to realize that the Hirachi *were* alien now, enough that she was surprised whenever she discovered radical differences between them. She thought Kole was that way, too, that he'd stopped thinking of her as one of the 'odd little people' from Earth--even though he claimed he had always thought she was pretty.

He'd said he cared about her. He wouldn't think of her as different in any way that mattered to him, surely?

A jolt went through her when she looked up from her work and discovered the object of her thoughts standing in front of her--both objects. Dansk, she saw, was directly behind Kole. Her heart executed a little hop and skip that was part thrill and part uneasiness as she looked from one man to the other warily. Dansk smiled, displaying his dimple. Kole's lips curled faintly, she saw when she looked at him again, amusement dancing in his eyes.

She hadn't realized until she'd seen them side by side what absolutely magnificent specimens of the male animal they were-- tall, broad shouldered, muscular as young gods. And their faces were equally pleasing to her. Kole was just plain sexy in that harsh, totally manly featured way. Dansk was almost pretty boy handsome but had just enough maturity about his strong features to look all man.

An electrifying warmth sizzled through her. She found herself smiling back, even though it had dawned on her that there was more amusement in both men's gazes than desire. "I look like hell, right?"

Kole chuckled.

Dansk's grin broadened. "It's only that the little general looks as if she has done battle." He pointed to the tip of his nose and then his chin and one cheek. "Spattered with gross stuff," he added, borrowing from her vocabulary.

Bri let out a huff. Using the back of her hand, she tried to mop the fish spatter off. Apparently, she only succeeded in smearing it around, however. Dansk chuckled, and Kole's grin widened.

Rolling her eyes, she handed each of them a fish cake she'd finished rolling.

Kole leaned a little closer than necessary when he took the offering. Almost shyly, he placed an object in her hand. She stared down at it blankly for several moments until it dawned upon her that he'd fashioned a comb for her from the shell of a –something like an oyster, she supposed. It looked like mother of pearl. A mixture of pleasure and irritation filled her--pleasure to have something besides her fingers to comb her hair--irritation to have confirmation that she'd begun to look like a wild woman. Tamping her embarrassment over her appearance, she smiled up at him gratefully. "Thank you! This is such a thoughtful gift!"

He reddened faintly, but merely nodded. "We've found what you wanted."

Bri's eyes widened with excitement when she'd interpreted the cryptic remark. She nodded breathlessly. "Tonight."

Dansk handed her a smaller pair of combs similar to the one Kole had fashioned. "To hold here like a proper Hirachi woman," he said with a gesture toward the pony tail at his crown and a teasing look.

Moved by their thoughtfulness, Bri beamed at him in thanks. The combs were better than chocolates and flowers.

The suggestion that they might have found the means they'd been looking for was rather more like having been given the keys to a Rolls Royce, though.

Tamping her excitement when Dansk and Kole had wandered off, she glanced at the woman beside her. "Did you get the list?"

"No mechanics or engineers. The closest thing we have is Linda."

Bri frowned. "What does ... did Linda do?"

"Housewife ... but she says she's repaired everything in her house at least once. She knows electronics better than any of the rest of us."

Bri felt her belly clench in empathy. She hadn't asked any of the women about their families. She wondered how many had left loved ones behind--probably most of them--but it wasn't something she wanted to dwell on, and she certainly didn't want to dredge it up for any of the women. They were having a hard enough time coping as it was. She cleared her throat. "Hopefully that's close enough."

She fell silent, waiting for the men across from her to signal that it was alright to speak again. "Doctors or nurses? Any kind of medical knowledge?"

"Stacy was training as a midwife. Linda D. was studying to be an EMT. She knows some basic first aid, but ... there's nothing to work with, really. Stacy was almost ready to get her certificate."

It was a struggle to feel optimistic about the report when she'd hoped for a doctor, or a nurse, at least. It was still more than she'd really expected. A doctor would have been a miracle, or a chemist, or a pharmacology specialist. Having a trained midwife, even partially trained, was a miracle for that matter.

With at least half the women pregnant, they couldn't afford to let anything happen to the midwife. They'd probably be relieved that they were going to get to sit this dance out. They might as well be, because she doubted she was alone in the determination to hang onto whatever medical help they had. There were a couple of Hirachi medics, but they were trained to treat battle wounds, not help pregnant women deliver babies.

When she got the ok signal, she said, "Tell Linda she needs to give us her best guess on where it'll be most effective to deliver the bombs. This place will be crawling with bots at the first sign of trouble. We need to know we can take them down. We won't get a lot of second chances. I don't want to waste the acid bombs on a spot that won't do anything, or will just slow them down."

It wasn't just that she didn't want to risk something like that when they needed to know before they tried anything that they had a chance of pulling it off--though it was bad enough to think of racing around the compound ineffectually. The worst was that the harvest area was limited. The seawalls the Sheloni had erected allowed some water flow, but it was limited to holes small enough the Hirachi couldn't get through them, which meant not a lot besides the water flowed from the ocean into the 'pit'.

Despite physical exhaustion, Bri was wired by the time they were finally released to rest. After rushing through her bath, she hurried to the shelter she shared with Kole, barely able to contain her excitement. They had to sacrifice the sheet that covered the floor of their shelter for the first experiment. When Bri had folded it as tightly as she could, they waited until the scans had moved away and set the pad outside the shelter so that Bri could watch. Even with the light from the night sky, she had difficulty, but she needed to see it for herself not just listen to Kole describe it to her.

The creature was a squid like thing in that it had long, thin tentacles. When Kole had torn one off, he carefully squeezed the thing so that the fluids inside the thing dripped on the waiting material. Holding her breath, Bri peered at it in focused concentration of every sense, counting in her head until she noticed the first reaction, then counting from there to see how long it took to burn through the layers.

It was so fast it was almost scary to think of touching the thing, and excitement boiled inside her. "It works!" she whispered to Kole, fighting the urge to jump up and down and scream for joy. "It really works!" She frowned. "This is thin layers, though. We need to try it on something more solid--closer to what the bots are made out of. How long do you think it stays active? Does the thing have to be alive, I mean? Or will we be able to store it up?"

Kole shook his head. "These things are like the *choi* on my world--but a nuisance to us. Sometimes they attack and kill young Hirachi. We've no use for them, but I do know that if they are found on the beach or floating in the water many days after death they can still burn--the *choi*. This, I couldn't say for sure."

Bri nodded, her enthusiasm properly subdued. She glanced back at Cory, who was crawling over her legs instead of sleeping like he was supposed to. "We'll have to keep this one for testing ... someone will have to. I don't want it around Cory."

Kole frowned. "The boy could sleep with his father ... for a few days only. You should know this yourself, not have to rely on someone to tell you."

Bri studied Kole doubtfully. "You think Dansk can manage him?"

She sensed more than saw his reaction to that. "He is Cory's father."

Which meant nothing as far as she was concerned. She was the one who'd tended to Cory. He was used to her. He wasn't used to Dansk. On the other hand, Cory had grown used to being around a lot of people since they'd arrived at the camp. It was worth a try. Kole was right. This was something she didn't want to rely on anyone else to report to her about.

Still feeling uncomfortable with the suggestion, she finally nodded. It was probably just as well anyway since they'd donated their sheet to the cause. Cory would be trying to eat the sand.

She hadn't expected immediate action, but Kole shifted around and picked the baby up, hesitated for a moment, and then called out to the occupants of the shelter next to theirs. "Dansk," Kole said when the Hirachi next to them looked out, handing the baby off.

Bri bit her lip as Cory made the trip down the line of shelters, hand to hand, until, five down, Dansk emerged to take the baby. When she finally dragged her gaze back, she saw that Kole was studying her face. Unable to interpret the look, but feeling warm for no reason in particular, Bri returned her attention to the *choi*-- or squid thing. "Bury it in the sand?"

Kole nodded. Scooping out a trough with his hands, he put the beast in the bottom and carefully covered it. When he'd finished, he scrubbed sand over his hands, and they ducked back inside the shelter.

Tired as she was, Bri discovered once they'd settled that she couldn't sleep. Between her acute consciousness of the fact that she and Kole were alone together without a baby that might or might not wake up; her excitement that they'd found one more tool to use--she hoped--to destroy the Sheloni; and the reek of the squid, she couldn't seem to get comfortable or stay still.

Her wiggling got a rise out of Kole. He shifted away, and then shifted closer again, as if he couldn't decide whether it was more uncomfortable to be pressed against her, or to try to keep his distance, maintain his balance on his side, and still share his warmth. Keenly aware of his discomfort, Bri went still, but as his hand drifted up to hover near one breast, she found she couldn't contain herself any more. Something between a snort and giggle escaped her.

Kole lifted his head to look down at her questioningly.

"Oh god, Kole! That thing *really* stinks!"

She heard the amusement in his voice as he agreed. "Bad, very bad!"

She shifted onto her back, grinning up at him. "I think I should have passed you down to Dansk and kept Cory," she said teasingly. "You have ick all over you."

Shaking his head, he sat up and tried using more sand to remove the stench. When he settled back, he lifted a hand to her cheek.

"Oh god, no!" she exclaimed with a snicker, twisting her face away and burrowing against his chest. "Not the face. I'll smell it all night."

He went perfectly still when she brushed her face along his chest, more at first in search of a smell less repellent, but once she'd caught his scent into her simply for the pleasure it gave her. She lifted her head slowly when she felt him tense all over, heard him swallow. "Would you rather sleep with Dansk?" he asked finally.

She stared at him for a long moment, trying to interpret the emotion behind the question. She couldn't. She didn't know if he'd suggested it out of consideration for her comfort, or because he thought she was looking for an excuse to go to Dansk, or if it was for his own comfort since he'd vowed not to touch her. "No," she said finally, allowing the hand she'd placed along his ribs to steady herself to glide upward along his chest to his neck. Curling her fingers around the back of his neck, she tugged, urging him to meet her. "And I don't especially want to *sleep* with you at the moment," she added, lifting upward until she found his face with her own. It felt wonderful, just the touch of his rough cheek against her forehead. She drifted upward, rubbing cheek to cheek and then the tip of her nose along his cheek, dragging in deep breaths of him, relishing the feel of his skin against her own.

He settled one large hand along her waist, clenching and unclenching as if he was of half a mind to pull her closer, and half to push her away. "This is not what I want for you," he managed to say finally, his voice ragged and harsh, almost a growl.

She could see no more than a dim outline of his face in the darkness and the gleam of his eyes when she tipped her head back to look at him, but she saw him clearly in her mind's eye. She swallowed with an effort as she felt emotion clog her throat, felt an unfurling of passion inside of her. "It's what I want for me," she said huskily. "Doesn't that count?"

He closed his eyes, fighting a battle, no doubt, she thought affectionately, a losing one, she hoped. Lifting slightly, she found his mouth with her lips, brushed her lips teasingly along his and then plucked at them. His breath hitched in his chest and then sawed through his parted lips in a harsh exhalation. She licked her lips, tasted him on the fragile surfaces, and then ran the tip of her tongue along his lips teasingly.

When he refused to take the bait, she leaned away from him, releasing her hold on him. He let out a shaky breath, then sucked it in and held it as she pulled her shift off over her head and tossed it aside. Turning to face him, she rubbed her body slowly along his. Her nipples hardened at the first contact, grew more and more achingly sensitive as she lightly brushed back and forth.

He caught her wrist almost bruisingly as she settled her hand on his belly and inched beneath the waist of his breeches in search of the hard ridge of flesh she'd felt brushing the cleft of her ass earlier. Balked of her goal, she nuzzled her face along his chest instead until she found one nipple ring. He made a sound deep in his throat as she sucked his nipple, ring and all, into her mouth and teased the bud with her tongue.

His hand slipped from her wrist to catch her arm just above the elbow. She seized the opportunity to delve deeper, brushing her fingers over the head of his cock. It jerked at her touch. Kole jerked all over, uttered a sound between a growl and a groan, and shoved her onto her back, breaking her hold on both nipple and cock.

Stunned at being shoved away, Bri was still gaping up at him in dismay when he swooped down to capture her lips in a kiss that seared her to the bone. Her body reached dew point almost instantaneously as fiery sensation erupted within her.

She'd forgotten how wonderful his mouth felt, how delirious

with need his kiss made her. Making a sound that was part want, part undiluted pleasure, she sucked his tongue as he thrust into her mouth with rough possessiveness. Curling her fingers into his flesh, she tugged at him, trying to pull him closer and when that failed she wriggled closer to him instead, lifting a thigh across his hips and arching her mound against his engorged member.

He dragged his mouth from hers, scooped an arm beneath her shoulders, and dipped his head to nuzzle and nibble at her throat and neck, the upper slope of her breasts, and finally captured one turgid nipple in his mouth.

She gasped as if she was dying, felt as if she was falling into a heated pit where fire and darkness and madness swirled together, thoughts were as insubstantial as mist, and her entire body had become a receptor of glorious, breathtaking sensation. For many moments it seemed her entire being was focused on the tug of his mouth on her breast as he teased the almost painfully sensitive nub, and then the focus shifted to a tautening within her belly, and then back again as he switched his attentions to her other nipple.

Something like an electric current jarred through her as she felt his hand cover her mound, his index finger delving between her nether lips and finding her clit with unerring accuracy. She began sucking in harsh breaths like a drowning victim as he strummed her clit. She *felt* as if she was drowning, overwhelmed by the intensity of pleasure that jolted through her so constantly that she couldn't catch her breath between the electrifying shocks.

She was babbling, she realized after a time, feeling a flicker of surprise when it registered in her mind, "Yes, baby … There … It feels so good," and kneading his flesh like a contented cat, claws bared. The taste of him was on her tongue as she nipped and sucked and licked at his skin, his neck, his ear, drove her wild with wanting.

She was going to come. She felt it like an unbearable hunger, driving her, felt her body trembling, clenching rhythmically around his finger as he delved inside of her. For a few moments she wallowed in it, gave herself up to the escalating tension and then she began struggling against it, trying to hold off the avalanche she could feel pending as she drew closer and closer to the point of no return.

She reached between their undulating bodies, searching for his cock, gripping it frantically when she managed to separate the closure of his breeches. He uttered a pained grunt as her fingers closed around his engorged flesh, shifted as if to draw away.

Kaitlyn O'Connor

"No!" she said fiercely. "I want you inside me. Kole, please."

He murmured soothing sounds against her breasts and then her throat as he lifted his head to suck a love bite along the side of her neck, but he continued to thrust inside of her with his finger, continued to tease her clit with the heel of his hand, driving her toward completion. She released her grip on his cock and began to push at his hand a little frantically, struggling to seize control of her body when she'd already yielded control to him. She pleaded and then demanded, almost weeping with the conflicting needs screaming inside of her.

Abruptly, his control broke. Pushing her onto her back, he shoved his breeches down his hips jerkily as he wedged his hips between her thighs. She caught her breath as she felt the blunt head of his cock bumping along her damp cleft, nudging against that sensitive area in a brief, blind search before his flesh connected with hers. She wrapped her arms tightly around his chest, dug her heels into the soft sand, and arched into his shallow, frantic thrusts to gain entry. Moisture flooded her channel in greedy anticipation, easing his way despite his girth, despite the desperate clinging of her flesh around his. Groaning, muttering his own litany of curses and praise and pleasure, he gripped her tightly in his arms, pumping his hips and driving into her.

She'd held on as long as she could. She let go, though, as his engorged flesh caressed her channel, coming with the first brush of his cock along her g-spot. Unable to hold back the storm, she twisted her head and clamped her mouth along his arm to muffle the cries of ecstasy wrenched from her with each hard convulsion of release. The clenching of muscles around him as she came drove him into a desperate frenzy of lurching, pumping need, a wild, fierce ride that caught her up even as the quakes of release subsided into a mellowing heat.

She clung, absorbing the shocks of each pounding thrust with a sense of completion unlike anything she'd ever felt, relishing the feel of his thick flesh inside of her, the strength of his arms and breadth of his chest, the pounding of his heart against her ear. His harsh breaths and the choked sounds of pleasure he struggled to contain sent a thrill through her, coiled the tension of building release again until she was uttering choked moans in concert with his. And when she felt his body jerk and begin to shudder as he convulsed with pleasure and began to expel his hot seed into her, it touched off a climax that was more intense than the first. Despite her best efforts, she couldn't completely stifle the cries of ecstasy it wrenched from her.

Wilting together in a weak tangle of body parts in the aftermath, they lay panting for breath for some time before Kole finally shifted, pulling his flaccid member from her body and inching downward to rest his cheek against her breasts. She wrapped her arms around his head, holding him to her as she stroked his shoulders lovingly, smoothing his long hair.

"I've scooped a stone's worth of sand into my breeches," he muttered after a few moments, dragging a chuckle from her. "And made friction burns on my knees."

"I've got sand in the crack of ass and friction burns on the cheeks," she retorted with amused tolerance.

He dragged in a deep, sustaining breath and let it out shakily. "I'm sorry, dearest. I could have given you pleasure without the risks to you."

Her hand stilled for a moment as that reminder washed over her, but she dismissed it as the realization swept through her that she wasn't sorry at all. "I'm not. I wanted you inside of me. I want your baby."

Chapter Twenty Three

Kole, Bri reflected, not for the first time, had amazing self control, and it wasn't something she was inclined to see in a good light when it came to intimacy between them. Under most circumstances, she considered it as one of his most admirable qualities, a strength of character that undoubtedly accounted for the blind loyalty most of his men showed him. There were times, though, when she looked upon it as pure pig-headedness ... like his determination to protect her from himself. But whatever thoughts she'd nursed that she'd eliminated his objections were banished when she joined him in their shelter the following night.

He'd woke that morning in a foul mood and gave her a cold shoulder most of the day--when she saw him, which was only twice and both times at a distance, but although it had bothered her, Bri dismissed it with the thought that it was only because he was tired and anxious about their plans. She'd told him she would not count the cost, that she was prepared to take the risks--that she wanted his baby. She had meant it. It hadn't been an impulse of the moment. She'd considered it, and she'd realized that, even if he did impregnate her, it wasn't going to interfere with their plans--because those plans would have to be implemented before it could possibly be a problem. Her pregnancy was the least of their worries. With so many other women pregnant, it was going to be impossible to execute the plan at all if they couldn't do so before everyone was in their second trimester ... and everyone else that was pregnant was well ahead of her.

She knew he was worried about her. It was sweet--more than sweet. It assured her as nothing else that Kole was not merely interested in her because his hormones were raging at the moment and he couldn't help himself. He cared about *her*.

As tired as she was when they were finally released to rest, she'd looked forward to making love to him all day, allowed her mind to dwell on the night before throughout most of the day until she was already aroused and ready when they settled together in the shelter.

Instead of pulling her to him at once, though, Kole dragged out the sheet they'd used to test the acid and settled down to wait until they'd been scanned by the Sheloni security beams. Mildly irritated, Bri brushed it off. He was right. Business first, and then they could make love.

Settling beside him at the opening, she waited until he'd unearthed the beast, which stunk a good deal worse since it had been ripening in the sun all day. Again they tested the properties of the creature's acid and, to relief of both of them, discovered that it was as potent as the night before. Bri timed it carefully, despite the overwhelming urge to move as far away from the thing as possible and hold her nose and allow Kole the honors.

Relieved and happy as she was at the discovery, Bri was more than ready for him to bury it again and wondered if the smell alone was going to give them away. It almost certainly would if the thing stank worse every time they dug it up again to test it. At this rate, it was going to smell up the entire compound.

Their shelter reeked. Kole reeked from handling the thing, because no amount of sand was sufficient to cleanse it from his hands.

And Bri discovered she'd lost her 'hard on'. It was all she could do to breathe. She covered her nose and mouth with her gown, breathing shallowly as they settled down at last to sleep, hoping the breeze off the ocean would carry the smell away before she hyperventilated from trying to catch a breath of air not laced with the smell of rotting beast. She would never have thought the sulfuric smell of the water would be preferable to anything else, she thought wryly.

Eventually, the smell seemed to dissipate--either that or she just became accustomed to it.

Which was when she discovered Kole was asleep.

Piqued, she had to resist the temptation to wake him up, but finally she dismissed the idea. He was tired, she told herself. He needed his rest. Dansk had Cory, and would be keeping the baby with him for the next few nights, until they were satisfied with testing the sea creature. They would have more nights alone.

And maybe she could figure out some way to get rid of the repulsive smell, which wasn't doing a thing for her libido.

The second night Kole fell asleep before her, Bri was not only not nearly as understanding, she was peeved … and deeply suspicious that he wasn't asleep at all. She was too irritated with him, though, even to consider trying to initiate sex herself.

Besides, the stench was worse than it had been before and showed every sign that it was going to get progressively worse.

By the third night, Bri was ready for battle. As much as she appreciated his grim determination to protect her from herself, she didn't by damn need protecting! She was an adult! She was capable of making her own decisions.

When Kole joined her inside the shelter she'd already shucked her gown and hidden the test cloth. Kole eyed her warily. "We must test this each night in order to be certain the properties remain the same."

"Yes, we must," Bri agreed, trying to sound reasonable. "But we needn't test it *first*."

He stared at her for a long moment. Almost against his will, it seemed, his gaze strayed down her body. He swallowed audibly. "You will … regret this. We both will."

Bri shook her head slowly and moved closer to him. Steadying herself by placing her hands on his chest, she leaned to brush her lips along his hard pecs. "The only thing I could possibly regret is *not* having your baby," she murmured. Maybe she wasn't being completely rational about it, but she was afraid she wouldn't get the chance if she accepted his terms. She was nearly thirty. Seven years, if what he said was true, was too long for her to wait, might mean she never got the chance at all.

If she was wrong, if she'd somehow misunderstood, or if it turned out that Kole was wrong, and he *could* father a child as long as he was with a woman whose fertility periods were monthly instead of only every seven years, so much the better. They could have a family … a half a dozen children if that was what he wanted. But she couldn't bear to take this chance of not having his child at all. "You want this as much as I do," she said, kissing her way up his chest to his throat. "And I want to give you the baby you want."

He speared his fingers through her hair. "I want *you*," he said raggedly. "I want you safe. I don't want anything that would add to your risks. It's bad enough...." He broke off. "You are strong, spirited, intelligent. I know you are capable. I trust your judgment in these plans we're making. But … I am not easy in my mind that you will be in the midst of the battle as it is."

A mixture of emotions washed through her at that. Amusement was dominant. He was afraid he'd insult her if he mentioned doubts about her prowess as a warrior!

It was just as well, she thought wryly, that he apparently had no clue she wasn't one. If he was worried now, he'd be frantic to discover she had no training and no knowledge, nothing but grim determination to see her through it. She supposed, if the Hirachi women hadn't been warriors, it might have occurred to him that there was no way she could be, but he was guilty of the same prejudice most people were. He saw what he expected to see, made conclusions based on his own perception of things.

No doubt he'd concluded that her people had developed sneaky methods of warfare because they were so undersized they couldn't use brute strength.

In a sense, she supposed they had ... women, because the only way they could achieve their goals in a society dominated by aggressive men was to use guerilla tactics.

Hooking her hands behind his neck, she tugged, demanding he lean down to her. "You know I have to be here," she murmured against his cheek as she caressed him. "I have every intention of being around to do this for a very long time. I'm not going to take unnecessary risks ... but I don't want to throw away the time we have now."

Maybe it was unfair to point out that they were both at risk and might not have time later to be together, but she realized the moment she said it that that was part of her need for him. She hadn't been willing to consciously acknowledge the possibility that one or both of them would die, but she knew there was the possibility.

It broke the last of his restraint. He carried her down to the ground, kissing her with a fierce possessiveness that drove the uncertainties from their minds, but there was a desperation in his caresses that hadn't been there before. They both felt it, a hunger for one another that couldn't be appeased.

He didn't object again, didn't voice any of his doubts. Each night when they came together in the shelter, no matter how weary they were, no matter how tense with worry, with setbacks, they made love until they'd pushed the world away, if only for a little while.
* * * *

Bri had not once dared to allow thoughts of failure to enter her mind, though they'd skated the periphery of her thoughts from the first moment she began to prod everyone to join her insurrection. Time had little meaning, but weeks and maybe even months went into the plotting and planning and execution. She was more than a little surprised that the Sheloni couldn't *feel* the adrenaline rush that went through them as they drove nails into the Sheloni coffin one by one.

The Hirachi had no real understanding of the black powder

beyond the assurance from Bri and the science teacher that it was going to cause a hell of an explosion. If it was something they'd invented themselves, it had been so long ago none of the Hirachi working with them remembered it.

It took patience to purify it, and nerves of steel to plant it. They took turns so that none of them were ever seen in exactly the same place twice. They used the rest periods they had each morning to perfect their throwing arms the best they could, playing a ball game with bladders stuffed with sand. Bri was a little surprised the Sheloni allowed it, but they didn't seem to see it as any sort of threat and didn't appear to care what the women did so long as they worked quickly and efficiently at preparing food to feed the workers.

Range and accuracy was the goal. Few of the women had the strength to manage much range, unfortunately, and some were down right uncoordinated--including Bri. She was going to have to practically hand place the fucking acid bombs, she realized with disgust, because she couldn't hit the same mark twice no matter how much she practiced.

She was better at placing the gun powder bombs. Each time Bri placed a 'biological' bomb--with no access to any other materials to use, they'd dried the internal organs of the fish and packed them with the powder and shrapnel of broken rocks--a mixture of fear and excitement filled her so completely that it was hard to preserve a façade of nonchalance as she strolled idly by the drop point, dropped it into place, and casually brushed sand over it with her foot.

None of them, including the science teacher, were certain of what kind of explosion they were going to get. They hoped it was going to be big enough to serve its purpose, but not big enough to blow them all to kingdom come--but they didn't know.

Bri wasn't certain if it would have dissuaded anyone. None of them were soldiers, although the Hirachi didn't seem to grasp that, but hatred of the Sheloni built until they became rabid on the subject of them, too consumed with hate and determination to waste much thought on fear.

They'd been torn from their homes, separated forever from people they loved, starved, worked half to death, tormented with the collars that inflicted excruciating pain if they even appeared reluctant, and used as breeding cattle. Hate was barely strong enough to describe how they felt after the months on the ship and within the prison.

The air fairly vibrated with tension and excitement when the day of reckoning finally arrived.

They'd carefully noted and marked each hole the robots crawled out of along the perimeter of the wall and planted explosives in front them. The hope was that the explosions would stop some, delay others. Bri wasn't completely certain of the weapon the Hirachi intended to use to bring down the seawall, but none of them seemed in any doubt they were capable of it--She hoped they were right. She hoped everything went as planned. There wasn't much she could do but hope for the best. They couldn't test everything. Though they'd tested what they could, and Bri had considered the desirability of actually using some of the acid on one of the bots to see how effective it was, she was afraid even if they managed to make it look accidental that disabling one of the bots might set off alarms.

The biggest threat was the plot they'd hatched to bring the Sheloni ship down to attack. Try though she would to come up with an alternative, the only thing that Bri could think of was blowing up the shipment. That might make the Sheloni on the ground call for help, and it might not. If, instead, they simply began blasting everything that moved....

The Sheloni had provided them with the detonation devices they needed to set off their gunpowder bombs. They'd used the acid to remove the collars the night before--everyone was wearing an acid burn to prove it--and planted the collars with the bombs.

Bri's heart was in her throat when she gave the signal they'd agree upon to alert everyone to take their positions.

Closing her eyes as she waited, she prayed to any deity that might be out there that they were about to see something a lot more dramatic than a Fourth of July fireworks bonanza and a great deal less than Hiroshima. When she opened her eyes again, she glanced toward the bomb shelter they'd dug out in the middle of Cory's 'playpen' to make certain that Stacy and Linda, their medics, had taken up their positions inside with him, and then nodded at Kole.

He'd said it would take them a count of twenty to reach their position in the sea. She started counting as the Hirachi men dove beneath the waves. "One, Mississippi, Two, Mississippi, Three....Twenty!" she yelled the last word. "Hit the dirt!"

It almost seemed for a handful of seconds that everything and everyone around her froze. She turned in a slow circle to make certain the Sheloni who, predictably, had gone out to peer down into the water at the progress of their excavation, to make certain they hadn't realized the threat and begun to race back along the wall toward shore.

They were mere insects at this distance, but she could almost feel the tension that went through them as her voice echoed out across the water, imagined she could see the frozen looks of shock on their faces. A rumbling growl like a bear awakened from slumber began, grew louder and louder until it was a deafening roar of sound. The ground beneath her feet began to tremble.

Time shifted, began to race until everything seemed to be moving at blinding speed. A deafening roar filled her ears. Smoke, fire--the earth itself rose into the air as if trying to shake them off. She threw herself toward the ground, but it seemed to take forever to reach it. A concussion rolled over her, rattling every bone in her body even as she clamped her arms over her head to protect it.

Dirt coated her, stinging every inch of exposed skin, scouring her until she wasn't certain if it was the abrasion of the sand or actual fire burning her. "Attack!" she screamed the moment she could find her voice, command her shaking body to push free of the blanket of sand that covered her. Pushing herself up, she staggered drunkenly toward the shelter where they'd concealed the bladders filled with acid. Her ears felt as if they were as filled with sand as her eyes and mouth. Screaming, dulled by the aftereffects of the blast against her eardrums, further confused her.

Around her, it looked like total chaos, but even as she gathered her own wits, she saw the women dashing about the compound, dodging the robots that were still mobile, pelting the bots with acid filled bladders. Sparing a few moments for assessment, Bri whipped her head around in a dizzying glance.

They'd underestimated the power of the blasts or overestimated the strength of the walls. Huge segments of the walls had crumbled. The gates hung ajar, twisted and curling. Robots lay in pieces. The entire seawall had vanished.

Bri's heart seemed to lodge in her throat when she saw that, and the fear assailed her that the men who'd gone down to blast the support from under it could be trapped beneath the rubble they'd created.

She couldn't afford to think about that now, though. Switching her focus to the robots clambering over the debris in search of victims, she grabbed up a bladder in each hand and raced toward the nearest spider bot, zigzagging in and out of its legs until she'd managed to hurl both at its vulnerable underbelly. The bladders stuck when they splattered, acid oozing out, dripping down and taking liquefied robot skin with it. It spattered her, as well. Screaming and cursing at the fire, she raced away again, pausing when she dove into the shelter to grab more bombs to scrub sand over her skin to remove the burning drops of acid.

"Oh my god!" a woman screamed nearby as Bri struggled to her feet again.

"There's two! There's two!"

She looked up instinctively, not because she was able to fully grasp what the woman was screaming about. She went still with disbelief when she saw the crafts barreling down upon them from the sky--a huge disk shaped craft led the way, plummeting toward them as if it was falling out of the sky. Behind it was a second craft shaped like a triangle.

A sense of defeat welled up inside of her. Gritting her teeth, she shook it off. It was the moment of truth. They were going to take out the Sheloni or die trying. "Go! Go! Go! Now!"

As loud as she'd screamed the order, she wasn't certain she could be heard above the screams of the other women, but they either heard or were simply caught up in a mindless instinct to escape. Everyone broke off their private battles and darted away in different directions, the women toward whatever breach in the wall was closest, the Hirachi who'd been battling beside them toward the sea.

Bri raced toward Cory, but when she'd snatched him up, she realized she didn't have time to reach anything but the sea. She didn't hesitate, didn't think beyond his safety. She ran for all she worth. She had to get beneath the water before the Hirachi brought up the bubble of methane or she and Cory both would be burned to death.

A hail of fire pinged into the water around her as she fought the waves. She gasped in painful gulps of air, trying to oxygenate her blood as much as she could before she dove under, but a sense of defeat began to pull her even as she reached the moment of truth. Terror caught hold of her.

She gulped. "Cory, I love you. Please remember that," she gasped, closing her eyes, clutching him tightly in her arms and stepping off the shelf into the black abyss. Something slammed into her even as she went under, like a huge hand driving her toward the bottom. As if she'd been shot from a cannon, she torpedoed into blackness. Her lungs had already begun to burn with the need to breathe when she was snagged around the waist hard enough it forced the air she was trying to hold onto from her lungs.

She fought, feeling something tug at the baby. All she could think of was holding onto him, but he was wrenched away from her. Resisting the urge to scream, she clawed and pounded ineffectually at the thing that wrapped around her, becoming weaker by the moment.

A hand clamped around the back of her head, stilling her. A mouth clamped over hers, forcing her lips apart, and air filled her lungs as he forced it inside of her. Kole's taste and scent swept into her lungs. She stopped struggling, opened eyes as he removed his mouth from hers.

Something tickled at her. Words formed. *Come. This way.*

Cory, she thought with renewed panic.

With Dansk.

She twisted her head to see as Kole pulled her snugly against his chest and began to swim with her. Relief flooded her when she saw that Dansk swam beside them, Cory clutched closely to his chest with one arm.

Her fingers tightened on Kole as her lungs began to burn with need again. He paused, gave her breath and pushed onward, cleaving through the water at a dizzying speed. It was torture, a nightmare of torment. Fear clawed at her mind every time she felt the burning need for air, but each time Kole breathed for her, filled her lungs until it drove the fear and need away.

When they broke the surface at last, Bri was weak and shaking from her ordeal. Grateful to breathe on her own, she gulped the air, choked and coughed, and sucked in more air until the desperation began to subside. "Did we get them?" she managed finally.

Kole's voice was grim. "No. *They* got them."

Twisting around in his arms, Bri searched the ocean briefly. Smoke marked the spot where their prison had marred the landscape. On the water's surface, chunks of the material that had once been the Sheloni ship floated. Just above the surface of the water, the black triangular ship hovered.

Bri simply stared at the thing while fear gathered inside of her. It merely hovered, however, and the sense of threat began to ease. "*They* destroyed the Sheloni craft? It wasn't the methane?"

"We aborted when I saw you and Cory."

Consternation filled Bri. *She* had ruined the plan? "You shouldn't have done that!"

He caught her face between his palms. "I would far rather be a slave with you, Bri, than a free man without you. I couldn't do any else."

Something painful gripped her chest. "I wanted this for you and Cory and Dansk … for everybody. I was willing to risk it!"

Kole glanced at Dansk. "We weren't."

There seemed no arguing with that, and it was too late anyway. She felt like crying. Everyone had tried so hard, risked so much! "We should go back," she finally said, her voice dull with fatigue and defeat. "I'm not Hirachi. My skin's pruning."

The black craft moved ashore as they turned and began to swim back, settling just above the ruins of their prison. Bri was too weak to walk without support by the time they reached land again. Holding her close to his side, Kole walked with her, Dansk and Cory on her other side. Around them, the Hirachi emerged from the sea. Those who'd taken to the jungle to avoid the blast, returned, as well, until the compound was filled with the Hirachi and Earth women still standing.

There were many who couldn't. Many who'd died in the effort, and Bri had to struggle with tears of anger and grief as she stood waiting to see what the inhabitants of the craft would do.

A ramp appeared beneath it, lowering slowly to the ground. Moments passed and still they waited. Finally, when everyone had begun to shift restlessly, alien legs appeared at the top of the ramp, many legs. Bri's heart leapt into her throat and lodged there as she watched, expecting to see dozens of soldiers carrying weapons. Instead, three creatures emerged. They had the look of giant, armored insects, but she couldn't see that any of them were carrying anything that looked like weapons. The three halted at the foot of the ramp and surveyed their audience. Finally, the one in the lead dipped its head almost regally, as if bowing to its subjects. "We come in peace," a mechanical voice pronounced in tones that reverberated against the ears of those listening to hear their fate.

Chapter Twenty Four

Bri, Dansk, and Kole exchanged doubtful glances. It had seemed to Bri that the creature had spoken in English, but she could tell from their expressions that Dansk and Kole had both heard and understood, they simply hadn't believed any more than she had.

The creature that had spoken lifted one of its arms and gestured toward the debris still floating on the water. "We have destroyed your enemy. We wish to negotiate a mutually beneficial alliance for the *jasumi* which grows in such abundance on your world."

This time, although she felt Kole and Dansk glance at her again, Bri kept her focus on the aliens as enlightenment dawned. These were the creatures the Hirachi had been enslaved for. Whatever agreement they had had with the Sheloni, they had 'revoked' it when they saw the *jasumi* that was so desirable to them was threatened.

The wonder was that they seemed perfectly willing to work out a peaceful trade agreement.

'Seemed' being the key word. That was yet to be established. "What are you offering?" she asked bluntly.

The creature fastened its multi-faceted gaze on her face. She wasn't certain whether it was translating her question, or ruminating over it--or wondering if she was the one they needed to speak to.

"You are the leader?"

The question threw Bri completely off guard. She tried her best to hide it, but she felt the gazes of everyone gathered around her. No one said anything, either to dispute or agree. No one seemed inclined to talk either. "Yes," she responded firmly. "What are you offering?"

He--she guessed it was a he--seemed to mull that over. "This world lies within those claimed by the Sheloni. We have broken treaty to protect … you."

Even without the significant pause Bri knew it hadn't been any interest in *them* that had inspired the 'protection'. She lifted her brows doubtfully. "The *jasumi*, you mean."

The creature almost seemed to shrug. "We will protect the source, which benefits you."

"To benefit yourselves," Bri pointed out. "You're not actually offering us anything."

She could tell her bluntness was making everyone uneasy, and yet she wasn't going to simply bow and scrape to these damned things and pretend stupidity. They were only willing to negotiate because they wanted the *jasumi*. If they wanted it, they were going to damned well have to offer some sort of real incentive.

"If we withdraw, the Sheloni will send more ships to attack and reclaim this world for their own."

"And then you could negotiate a new treaty with them, but they might be pissed off about you blowing their ship to hell, and they might not give you as good a deal as they did before ... and they can't harvest it themselves or they wouldn't have stolen us from our home worlds."

The silence lasted longer this time. "We are willing to barter for what we need," the creature said finally. It gestured around the ruined compound. "You have nothing by way of technology here, or shelter, or even small comforts."

Bri nodded. "We need time to discuss this among ourselves and decide what we feel like would be a fair trade."

The creature didn't look particularly happy about that, but Bri was just guessing. Like the Sheloni, their faces didn't appear suited much for facial expression. In fact, she was inclined to think there might be some sort of connection between the two species. She'd thought from the first that the Sheloni reminded her of spiders.

Again, it signaled agreement with the nod of its head. "We will withdraw then and allow the discussion."

"We'll meet with you when the sun rises again," Bri offered.

Nodding again, the creatures turned and made their way up the ramp again. When the ramp had closed, the craft began to hum and then lifted almost silently into the air, drifting seaward, it paused when it was perhaps a mile from shore, turned and hovered.

Feeling weak kneed, Bri sank to the ground.

As if a spell had been lifted, everyone rushed together, babbling all at once. Bri let the voices flow over and around her as Dansk knelt beside her and handed Cory to her. Cory smiled, patting her cheeks with both hands. "Mama!"

A choked half sob, half laugh escaped her. His first word! And it was English, not Hirachi. She was suddenly so glad that Kole had saved her. She'd known Cory's chances of surviving were good--

hers not so good. She still felt that it was worth the risk she'd taken to save him, but she was so glad she was going to be with him to watch him grow up!

It wasn't until she finally realized that Kole and Dansk were watching her with almost identical expressions of anxiety that she realized what the focus of the conversations were around them.

"Home! We can go home! You have to tell them we want to go home!"

It was like a chant ... all in English. But the Hirachi understood. She saw they did.

She had to wonder what thoughts were running through their minds. Were they as desperate to return home? Did they just not want to voice their own wishes because they didn't want the women to feel as if they cared more about getting back to the lives they'd left than being with them?

The aliens weren't likely to grant that request, she realized, not for all of them anyway. The negotiations were for the *jasumi*. They couldn't harvest it for themselves. Hugging Cory to her, she called for quiet until they finally settled down. She saw that most of the women were looking at her resentfully, though.

"These aliens are working out a trade agreement," she pointed out. "They might be willing to take some of us home, but they're not going to be willing to take everyone. Whether you like it or not, some will have to stay to harvest. Otherwise, there will be no deal with any of us."

Dansk and Kole exchanged a long look. Finally, Dansk nodded. "Dansk and I will stay," Kole said. He hesitated for a moment more. "So that you can go home."

Tears welled in Bri's eyes. She stared at his face until she couldn't even focus for the stinging tears. Home! Her heart soared momentarily at the wonderful word and all it meant to her mind.

It meant comfortable surroundings, being clean--going to the grocery store for food, driving in her car, hearing English every where she went--seeing everything that was familiar and nothing that was unfamiliar.

It meant leaving Cory.

It meant leaving Dansk and Kole.

It meant risking the life of the child she and Kole had made together.

Sniffing, she wiped her eyes with her hand. "We have a saying on Earth--Home is where the heart is." She reached for Kole's hand and settled it on her belly. "I love you, and the baby we made together. I love Cory … And I love Dansk. My heart's here. My home is with you."

Chapter Twenty Five

Bri sighed blissfully and relaxed limply against the mattress--a real, honest to god, almost like home mattress--drifting lazily in the aftermath of release. She'd already begun to glide toward sleep when she felt something hot and moist close over her toes, felt the tickle of a tongue. Uttering a giggle, she snatched at her leg but Dansk held it in an iron grip, sucking at her toes until her belly began to flutter and clench with anticipation.

A moan replaced the chuckles.

Beside her, Kole shifted, bending his head to nuzzle her breasts lazily and finally sucked a sensitive tip into his mouth, nipping it lightly with the edge of his teeth and then sucking the sting away.

She moved restlessly beneath the two, feeling wonderfully decadent to have both of them in bed with her. They'd long since given up whatever reservations they'd had at the idea, though, yielding finally to her determination to have both of them in her bed … at least occasionally.

She'd lied outrageously. Insisting it was an Earth custom.

What did they know?

Maybe they suspected she made up the rules as she went along, but she hadn't heard any objections.

And, despite the fact that the Hirachi were generally very nomadic about lovers, the men and the women changing partners as often as they liked except during mating season, they hadn't shown any inclination to wander.

Of course, some of that was due to the fact that the women had all the power on the world they'd decided to name Earth--so imaginative!--because the Hirachi outnumbered the Earth women almost five to one--and they weren't 'in' to same sex relationships.

A demanding cry interrupted, just when things were starting to get really interesting. Bri, Kole, and Dansk all froze. Lifting their heads, the three of them listened for a second demand. It came--in chorus!

Damn it, Bri thought irritably! Kyle had woken Cory!

"Your turn," Dansk said, daring Kole to dispute it.

Kole glared back at him for a moment and finally, uttering a long suffering huff of irritation, rolled out of the bed and padded across the stone floor to her bedroom door. When he opened it, the chorus sounded louder, the baby's mewling newborn cries almost drowned out by Cory's more hearty wails.

The door closed again and a few moments later the cries ceased abruptly.

Bri relaxed and looked down at Dansk questioningly.

He was still poised over her right knee. He returned her look with one of slumberous intent. Grabbing her legs just above the knees and hooking them over his shoulders, he dove at her. She flinched, but as he buried his face against her mound and dragged his tongue along her cleft, a shaky gasp was torn from her.

"I can't!" she gasped, grabbing two handfuls of his hair. "I swear it, Dansk!"

He lifted his head enough to peer up at her, teasing her clit with his tongue. "Yes, you can!"

"I came twice already!" she complained almost petulantly.

"For Kole," he reminded her.

The statement distracted her. *Was* it Kole both times?

His tongue totally drove the ability to think from her mind after a handful of moments, however. She ceased to tug at his hair and dug her fingers into the sheets instead, writhing and groaning beneath him as she felt her body, contrary to her expectations, or her wishes, climbing toward climax again.

He stopped just as the tremors began, shifting upwards.

She caught a glimpse of a dimple as she pried her eyelids up, but before she could fully grasp what that implied, he drove into her. She groaned, lifting to meet him, clinging to him as she felt his shaft inch deeper inside of her with each thrust until he'd claimed her fully and she could feel his hard flesh gliding along the length of her channel with each stroke, teasing her g-spot until rapture exploded inside of her, touching off Dansk's climax.

Spent, they curled lazily together as their pulses evened out again. "I saw that smile," Bri said finally.

"What smile?"

Dansk was grinning unrepentantly when she glanced at him out of the corner of her eye. "Liar," she muttered without heat.

He stroked her cheek. When she opened her eyes to look at him questioningly, he smiled. "I love you, Earth woman."

Bri's throat closed with emotion. She didn't doubt it for one moment. It still made her feel like crying that he and Kole had been willing to give up the chance to go home to give it to her. She was glad things had happened the way they had, because she might have wondered if not for that--They might have doubted that she cared for them as much as she did if she hadn't had that moment in time to give the gift of knowing it didn't matter to her as much as staying with them.

As it turned out, no one could go home. The Vernamin, the aliens who'd rescued them from the Sheloni, had no idea, so they claimed, of the whereabouts of the home world of either the Hirachi or the Earthlings. She wasn't certain she believed that, and it was for damned sure none of the other Earth women did, but they'd had no choice about staying.

She couldn't say she blamed them for being angry about it. Beyond the trials of establishing civilization on a world that had none, some of them had families they loved and wanted to go back to. She loved Kole and Dansk, or she might not have been able to understand that. She'd still felt ashamed of her own people. The Hirachi, noble creatures that they were, had offered to stay if that was what it took to free the Earth women--and a lot of them had very willingly taken them up on the offer.

Not all. Nearly a third of the women, although they'd clearly hated the idea of staying on New Earth, had cared enough for the men they were with to agree to stay.

Everyone's outlook had improved immensely, though, when they discovered just how valuable the *jasumi* was to the Vernamin. They hadn't had to wait weeks, months, or years for the reward. To show good faith, the Vernamin had delivered comfortable, if temporary, shelters for them and the tools they needed to build.

New Earth was still a raw frontier, but the hard times they'd endured had made them humble. Every little advance they made in convenience and comfort was a cause for rejoicing, the simplest things--like outhouses and later real plumbing--appreciated and enjoyed as much as it would've been if they'd won the lottery back home--maybe more.

And both the Hirachi and the Earth women were as proud as they could possibly be of the new race they'd created together.

Bri rolled onto her side and studied Dansk's face with love. "I love you more, you gorgeous hunk of Hirachi male, you!"

Kole entered the room on the heels of that declaration. He studied the two of them for a long moment and finally crossed the room and slipped into bed behind her. Hooking an arm around her waist, he dragged her back until his cock was nestled between the cheeks of her ass.

"They're asleep," he murmured, nibbling a trail along her shoulder.

"All of them?" Bri asked in surprise.

"Zoe didn't wake up. She sleeps like you do," he murmured, amusement threading his voice.

"Not for the same reason, though," Bri pointed out. "She doesn't have two men fucking her into oblivion."

"Give her time," Kole responded with a chuckle. "She's only three. But if she's as beautiful as her mother, she's bound to have her pick when her time comes."

Bri twisted her head to look back at Kole. "Maybe it wasn't such a good idea to have both of you in here at once."

Kole's eyes gleamed with amusement. "You said it was an Earth custom."

Bri couldn't help but look a little conscience stricken. "About that...."

Kole laughed, rolling her over so that she was beneath him, staring up at his face. "You love him more?" he demanded, nudging his chin in Dansk's direction.

"No! Of course not! But...."

"I'm not a gorgeous hunk of Hirachi male?"

"Kole!"

He lifted his brows, but finally relented. Dipping his head, he kissed her lightly on the lips. "Go to sleep," he ordered, settling on his side and tucking her against his chest. She snuggled, stifling a yawn, but finally glanced back at Dansk and wiggled her butt at him provocatively. He grinned, slapping one ass cheek. "Stop it! I'm tired."

Chuckling, she returned her attention to Kole, tipping her head to kiss the underside of his jaw. "I love you!"

"You gorgeous hunk of Hirachi male," Kole prompted.

Bri sighed blissfully. "Yes, you are."

The End

Printed in the United States
74484LV00001B/53